Praise for Ke

The Phryne Fisher Mysteries

"Miss Fisher is quicker, kinder, racier, and more democratic than any character from Dame Agatha... If you haven't fallen for her yet, prepare to be seduced."

—*Australian Women's Weekly*

"Kerry Greenwood captures the 1920s style perfectly as she weaves crime and intrigue in the dark streets of Melbourne Town, together with the glamorous high life of the one and only Phryne Fisher... Step aside, Miss Marple. Kerry Greenwood has given us the most elegant and irrepressible sleuth ever."

—*The Chronicle* (Toowoomba)

"It's *Underbelly* meets Miss Marple."

—*Emporium*

"Always elegant, always sophisticated, always clever, and damn it, always right, Phryne is the finest detective to be found in the 1920s."

—*Ballarat Courier*

"Miss Fisher, as usual, powers through this newest case with grace, poise, and unerring confidence, the sense of underlying tension is palpable."

—*The Age*

"Kerry Greenwood's writing is always a joy."

—*Stiletto*

"Together with Greenwood's witty and fluid, elegant prose, Phryne Fisher is a sheer delight."

"Greenwood's strength lies in her ability to create characters that are wholly satisfying: the bad guys are bad, and the good guys are great."

Also by Kerry Greenwood

The Phryne Fisher Mysteries
Cocaine Blues
Flying Too High
Murder on the Ballarat Train
Death at Victoria Dock
The Green Mill Murder
Blood and Circuses
Ruddy Gore
Urn Burial
Raisins and Almonds
Death before Wicket
Away with the Fairies
Murder in Montparnasse
The Castlemaine Murders
Queen of the Flowers
Death by Water
Murder in the Dark
Murder on a Midsummer Night
Dead Man's Chest
Unnatural Habits
Murder and Mendelssohn

The Corinna Chapman Mysteries
Earthly Delights
Heavenly Pleasures
Devil's Food
Trick or Treat
Forbidden Fruit
Cooking the Books
The Spotted Dog

DEATH in
DAYLESFORD

DEATH in DAYLESFORD

The NEW
Phryne Fisher
Mystery

KERRY
GREENWOOD

Poisoned Pen
PRESS

Copyright © 2020, 2021 by Kerry Greenwood
Cover and internal design © 2021 by Sourcebooks
Cover design by Christabella Designs
Cover illustration by Beth Norling

Sourcebooks, Poisoned Pen Press, and the colophon
are registered trademarks of Sourcebooks.

Published by Poisoned Pen Press, an imprint of Sourcebooks
P.O. Box 4410, Naperville, Illinois 60567-4410
(630) 961-3900
sourcebooks.com

Originally published in 2020 in Australia by Allen & Unwin.

Library of Congress Cataloging-in-Publication Data

Names: Greenwood, Kerry, author.
Title: Death in Daylesford / Kerry Greenwood.
Description: Naperville, Illinois : Poisoned Pen Press, [2021] | Series:
  Phryne Fisher mysteries ; 21
Identifiers: LCCN 2020031806 (print) | LCCN 2020031807
(ebook) | (trade paperback) | (hardcover) | (epub)
Subjects: LCSH: Fisher, Phryne (Fictitious character)--Fiction. | Women
  detectives--Fiction. | GSAFD: Mystery fiction. | Historical fiction.
Classification: LCC PR9619.3.G725 D435 2021 (print) | LCC PR9619.3.G725
  (ebook) | DDC 823/.914--dc23
LC record available at https://lccn.loc.gov/2020031806
LC ebook record available at https://lccn.loc.gov/2020031807

Printed and bound in the United States of America.
SB 10 9 8 7 6 5 4 3 2

*This book is dedicated to the glorious
memory of Dougal, prince of cats;
my sisters, Amanda and Janet;
and also my parents, Jean and Al, whom
I still miss more than I can say.*

Chapter One

The Sons of Mary seldom bother, for they have
*   inherited that good part;*
But the Sons of Martha favour their Mother of the
*   careful soul and the troubled heart.*
And because she lost her temper once, and because
*   she was rude to the Lord her Guest,*
Her Sons must wait upon Mary's Sons, world
*   without end, reprieve, or rest.*

—Rudyard Kipling, *The Sons of Martha*

It was a lazy, late summer's morning in St Kilda. The early sun was no longer the copper-coloured furnace of January, and instead of beating at the window with bronze gongs and hammers was knocking respectfully at the shutters, asking leave for admittance. Without, the tide was gently turning, lapping over the mid-ochre sands of the beach and promising light refreshment for anyone wanting a matitudinal paddle. Last night's windstorm had blown itself out, and through the open window drifted a cool, damp sensation of overnight rain.

Phryne Fisher rose from her bed, wrapped a turquoise satin dressing-gown around her impossibly elegant person, tied the cord, and tiptoed towards the bathroom, where a malachite bathtub and unlimited hot water awaited her. Pausing at the door, she turned and raked her boudoir with a long, ever so slightly greedy and thoroughly complacent look. She admired the wickedly crimson satin bedsheets. The hand-painted silk bedspread (the Book of Hours of Marie de France, now wantonly disordered, with its scenes of medieval life carelessly strewn over the aquamarine Chinese carpet). The half-empty crystal decanter (with matching balloon glasses, both empty) whose contents had been imported at absurd expense from the sunny vineyards of Armagnac. The outstretched paws and arched back of the sleeping cat Ember, jet-black and sleek with good living. And the jet-black eyebrows and perfect features of Lin Chung, who arched his golden back and burrowed further down between the sheets. She admired his bare, muscular shoulder, smiled with a thrill of retrospective delight, and entered the bathroom.

From her extensive collection of bath salts, Phryne chose the china pot labelled *Gardenia* and emptied a goodly pile into the shaped malachite tub. She opened both brass taps and watched as the twin torrents of water swirled and effervesced. A warm, fragrant aroma of English Country Garden caressed her nostrils. Phryne slipped out of her gown and lowered herself into the water. She surveyed her slender body with a certain level of satisfaction, her imagination still ravished by the previous night's passion. A woman on the brink of thirty always nurtured secret suspicions of fading charms—even someone with Phryne's armour-plated self-esteem. Yet, judging by her lover's awed reactions and responses, it would seem that this was far from being the case. Lin himself was utterly unchanged by marriage. So many businessmen let themselves go; their waistlines expanded along with their incomes.

Lin's copper-coloured body was as smooth and strong as a teenage boy's. The only sign of change she had observed was a small knot of ebony hair in the centre of his delectable chest, with the merest suggestion of a line of down heading due southwards. Her tongue had given this matter some considerable exploration the previous evening.

Phryne grinned, and began to soap her person. *I'm well and truly on the shelf now, and the world can watch me not care,* she told herself. How fortunate that her idiotic father had shown the foresight to dismiss her from his baronial presence some years ago, otherwise she would have been visited with a plague of suitors of varying degrees of loathsomeness. For the English nobility, an unmarried daughter of twenty-nine was a matter of some uneasiness, somewhere on the continuum between Unsuitable Entanglements and Failure to Ride to Hounds. Her father's threat to cut her off with a shilling for gross disobedience had been rendered toothless when, upon obtaining her majority, Phryne had calmly removed her assets from her father's rapacious fingers. To compound his sense of disgrace, his other daughter Eliza had combined the twin horrors of Socialism and Unnatural Vice.

Phryne's opinion of her father had not been improved by this attitude. Socialism was frequently affected in noble families, and lesbianism could easily be forgiven in polite society given that Eliza's Chosen had been of impeccably noble birth. Once you were in Debrett's, unnatural vice was magically transmuted into Passionate Friendship, which had been socially acceptable ever since Lady Eleanor Butler and the Hon. Sarah Ponsonby had set up house together as the Ladies of Llangollen. Even the Duke of Wellington had visited them. Although that said less than it might, since the Iron Duke was renowned for not giving even one hoot for popular prejudice. Nevertheless, Father had broken off all contact with both daughters, and all his attention, such as it was, had been lavished on his son and heir Thos. Of whom the best that could be said was that the future Baron of Richmond-upon-Thames would be a worthy heir to the present one. Neither the present nor future lords would ever visit either Phryne or Eliza. Phryne felt she could moderate her grief.

She sank down deeper into the smooth embrace of the steaming waters. It was so much easier dealing with the Chinese. Lin's wife Camellia was a typical exemplar of Chinese womanhood: small of body and voice, discreet, self-assured, and possessing a will of pure adamant. The greeting she gave Phryne whenever they chanced to meet was gracious, polite, and filled with iron Confucian certainty. *You are my husband's honoured concubine and I trust you implicitly. You may walk through Chinatown in perfect security. Anyone who offers you offence may expect consequences of considerable severity, up to and including a small battleaxe to the back of the head. I, on the other hand, am Lin's First Lady. I have my position, and you have yours. We understand each other perfectly.*

Phryne sat up in the bath and listened. Noises Off appeared to be happening. Since Dot was unlikely to outrage her maidenly modesty by attempting to bring her employer breakfast in bed when Phryne was Entertaining, this must mean that Lin himself was doing the honours, with the assistance of Mr and Mrs Butler. She climbed out of the bath, dried herself off with two towels of spotless white cotton, and wrapped herself anew in her turquoise silk robe. 'Do I smell eggs and bacon, Lin?' she enquired, opening the bedroom door.

Lin Chung pushed a prodigiously laden tea trolley into the centre of the boudoir and gestured to the two cushioned seats. 'Eggs, bacon, and all the accoutrements of an English breakfast,' he announced. 'I believe there are roast tomatoes, sautéed mushrooms, and sausages made from absurdly pampered pigs. There is also toast, Earl Grey tea, marmalade, and strawberry jam. Will the Silver Lady join me at breakfast?'

Phryne lifted the lids of the chafing dishes one by one and inhaled deeply. 'I was scarcely expecting such luxury. How did you manage to get the trolley upstairs? Was Cantonese magic involved at all?'

Lin folded his hands in an imitation of a stage Chinaman. 'Ah! The East is filled with mysteries.'

Phryne gently pushed him down into one of the chairs. 'Well, yes, Lin, otherwise why would it be called the Mysterious East? But how—oh, of course, I forgot: the dumb waiter.'

Mr Butler had of late come down with a serious outburst of Home Handyman and had installed a dumb waiter where one of Phryne's wardrobes had been. Phryne had been about to object in the strongest terms when she recollected that Mr Butler was, it must be admitted, getting on in years and that, moreover, the day would inevitably come when Dot would finally achieve holy matrimony with Hugh Collins and might not be available to attend upon Phryne. Yet refreshments must be conveyed to the lady of the House in her first-floor bedroom. So, the dumb waiter had been installed, skilfully concealed behind a Chinese silk screen when not in use.

For some time, conversation gave place to unbridled gluttony. It was not Phryne's habit to eat breakfast at all, beyond a French roll and a morning coffee, but erotic adventures awoke her hunger for other forms of bodily delights. As Phryne closed the lids on the devastated remains of the hot dishes and looked with devotion at her beautiful lover, he reached out his right hand and closed it around her left. 'Phryne? May I ask you something?'

'Ask me anything, and I shall answer.'

'Yesterday I saw Bert and Cec driving their cab, and as their fare debouched right in front of me, I enquired after their health.'

'As one does.' Phryne buttered herself another piece of toast and smeared it with marmalade. 'And how did they respond?'

'Cec looked inscrutable and muttered something, and Bert gave it as his opinion that he was a menace to shipping. What does this mean?'

Phryne clasped his hand tighter and raised it to her lips. 'It means he is in robust spirits. Your English is perfect Oxford, but I presume Australian argot did not feature in the curriculum at Balliol College.'

'No, it didn't. Is this like a bald man must always be called Curly?'

'And a red-haired man is always Bluey. It's similar, but...not quite the same.' Phryne pondered for a long moment how Lin Chung had got along with the rowdy undergraduates, deciding there were several reasons why he would have flourished there. Balliol was one of the more intellectual seats of learning at Oxford. His imperturbable calm would have unnerved most of the bullies. And the whiff of serious money would have inspired automatic respect.

As she nodded to herself, Phryne became aware that Lin was studying her closely.

'You are perhaps wondering how I fared at Balliol, being so blatantly Oriental?'

'I was,' Phryne confessed.

'It was largely trouble-free. Don't forget I had Li Pen with me. Having one's own servant in college lent a certain cachet. And...' He paused and allowed himself a complacent smile of recollection.

'And Li Pen was also available to chastise the rowdier elements under the influence of excessive alcohol?' Phryne suggested.

'He was. It is his duty and pleasure to serve.'

'I trust no one was seriously injured?'

'He inserted three of them into an ornamental fountain. They suffered nothing worse than bruises, both to the person and personality.'

'Youthful high spirits?'

'That was indeed the official verdict.'

'I see. Lin?' Phryne leaned back seductively. 'How soon must you depart?'

He gazed with appreciation at a glimpse of perfect ivory breast beginning to escape from her robe. 'I have a meeting at noon.'

Phryne glanced at her bedroom clock: a modest walnut arrangement standing on the mantelpiece. 'It's only nine thirty. Plenty of time.' She leaned closer to Lin. 'Tomorrow I am departing for the countryside.'

'And which district will be favoured by your august presence?'

'Daylesford. I have received an unusual request, and I am minded to investigate. Do you know of the place?'

'A little. They are building a new lake there. And, unfortunately, the market gardens of the local Chinese will be submerged by it. There has been a great deal of talk about it in the *Daylesford Advocate*. Everybody wants the lake, but nobody wants a rather expensive road diversion. But no one has spared a thought for the market gardeners.'

'That is very careless of them. Perhaps I should intervene on their behalf. Or perhaps the Lin family...?' She allowed the sentence to hang delicately in the air. Lin leaned back in his chair and retied his crimson dressing gown around his delectable body.

'There is no need, Phryne. Measures have already been taken. The gardeners are being moved to Maldon and elsewhere. The land did not actually belong to our people; it was theirs by grace and favour, and now it is being resumed by the local community. I will send someone around with copies of the newspaper from my files, if you like?'

'That would be most helpful. Lin, do you happen to have files on every town in Victoria?'

He laughed aloud. 'Only those where my people are involved, directly or indirectly—which is perhaps more than you would think. Only thus can we maintain our honoured position here.'

Honoured position! But at least there had been no massacres of the Chinese in Victoria, thanks to Constable Thomas Cooke of the Castlemaine police station, representing in his lonely self the awesome majesty of Queen Victoria and her laws. But fear, loathing, ill-will, and general xenophobia there had most certainly been, and it had not yet abated. Still, divining that Lin would like the subject changed, and quickly, she returned to the subject of her own forthcoming visit to the region.

She stood up, reached into her purse, and unfolded a letter, handing it to him. Lin perused the following with raised eyebrows.

The Spa
Hepburn Springs
23 February 1929

Dear Miss Fisher,

I write to you at the recommendation of Dr Elizabeth MacMillan, who has visited here on occasion. I know that you served with distinction in the war, and you will be aware that all too many of our brave survivors suffer from shell shock. The Army and the Ministry offer them little sympathy, and even less help. They are not shirkers or cowards, but men who have endured more than flesh and blood can manage. At my spa, I am attempting to provide my patients with the rest, recuperation, and care they so badly need. I would like to invite you to see my establishment for yourself, after which I hope you may see your way clear to supporting

my endeavours. Would you care to join me for dinner this
coming Friday?

Yours sincerely,
Herbert Spencer (Capt., ret'd)

'What do you make of that?'

Lin slipped one hand inside his dressing-gown and ran his hand over his chest. Phryne suppressed the erotic thrill that surged through her body. Any information this admirably well-informed man could supply beforehand might be vital. 'The first thing I should mention is that Hepburn Springs is not Daylesford. While the two communities are contiguous, they have quite different characters. Hepburn Springs is further into the mountain forest.'

'How far away from Daylesford?'

'They are about three miles apart, town centre to town centre. Though there are houses all along the road connecting them.'

'And the spa?'

'It was once a place of secret women's rituals among the local Aboriginal tribes, who were, naturally, comprehensively dispossessed last century. The spa is said to have extraordinary healing properties. And now this Captain Spencer is using it for shell-shock victims? Intriguing. Your Captain sounds like a kind and generous man.'

'Indeed. And how is Daylesford so different?'

'Hepburn Springs is a place of quiet refinement. Daylesford, which is far larger and more spacious, is rather more boisterous. And it possesses a remarkable curiosity.' Phryne raised an eyebrow. Lin matched her by raising both of his own, with matching grin. 'There is a licensed premises called the Temperance Hotel.'

'That does appear to be one of the less successful advertising decisions in history,' Phryne remarked.

'So one would think, at first glance. However, the pub does serve wine, beer, and cider; only spirits are forbidden. This appears to be a compromise widely acceptable in the local community.'

How very Australian! Vociferous arguments in favour of temperance would be made so long as drunken husbands staggered home from the local pub ready to take out their incoherent frustration with the world on their long-suffering wives and children. But while it was possible to get rolling drunk on beer alone, it required a good deal more focus to attain the condition of violent drunkenness; thus, while many Australians had agitated for total prohibition (which had worked so well in America), a substantial body of opinion held that such a compromise was both achievable and prudent.

Phryne smiled at her lover. 'I would be intrigued to visit this place. Perhaps, when I have seen Captain Spencer, I should pay a visit to Daylesford as well. Do any of the other pubs serve spirits?'

Lin chuckled. 'They do. But married patrons are severely discouraged—by their wives—from visiting such places, whereas a few drinks at the Temperance Hotel is something the women of Daylesford can accommodate for their hard-working husbands. Also—' Lin paused, and smiled the smile of a fallen angel '—apparently one of the barmaids is a famous beauty. Her hand in marriage is comprehensively sought.'

'But not yet attained?'

'Not thus far. And I imagine that the rivalry between her suitors sells many a drink on the premises.'

'No doubt. You mentioned wine and cider as well as beer. The wine is because of the Swiss Italians, I expect. Do they make it locally?'

Lin nodded.

'But cider? It is hardly a common drink.'

'This would be the local Cornish influence.'

'Lin, you are a minefield of information.' She squeezed his hand. 'It is now almost ten. You said that you have a meeting at noon?'

'I do, Silver Lady, and I must depart a half hour before.'

'But until then?' She leaned forward, allowing the front of her gown to fall open.

Lin's almond eyes flickered over Phryne's breasts for a moment. 'Until then, I would be pleased to accompany you once more among the chrysanthemums. If it be your will?'

Phryne reached out and took his face between her hands. Her mouth opened, and she traced the tip of her tongue around his lips. 'It is indeed my will.'

Lin's hand closed around her left breast, and Phryne stood up, reaching for the cord of his dressing-gown. She began to chant a poem she had recently discovered. It was called 'Butterflies in Love with Flowers,' and she hoped that Lin might know it, even though it was originally written in Mandarin, and his family spoke Cantonese.

> *'I would rather drink to intoxication.*
> *One should sing when one has wine in hand,*
> *But drinking to escape offers no reprieve.*
> *I do not mind that my clothes are getting looser.*
> *My lover is worthy of desire.'*

Lin's strong arms pulled her body close as their garments fell unregarded onto the carpet. 'Come, little flower, the butterfly is impatient,' he whispered, and he carried her, without effort, back to bed.

Chapter Two

Awake! For Morning in the Bowl of Night
Has flung the Stone that puts the Stars to Flight:
And Lo! The Hunter of the East has caught
The Sultan's Turret in a Noose of Light.

—Edward Fitzgerald, *Rubáiyát of*
Omar Khayyám of Naishápúr

The next day dawned hotter, with a north wind which blew rasping, unpleasant odours from the Unwashed Suburbs of the inner east. Phryne awoke fashionably late to receive Dot, already clothed in a light summer dress (beige), a thin woollen jumper (cocoa), sensible walking shoes (henna) with lisle stockings (cinnamon), and a light silk shawl (fawn). Phryne had never realised quite how many flavours of brown one wardrobe could accommodate, but Dot was, it appeared, determined to encompass them all. One day, Phryne considered, she would attempt to discover, as discreetly as possible, if her devoted companion were subject to a particular form of colour-blindness. She desperately wanted to introduce Dot to the possibilities of blues and reds. Perhaps she could begin with the milder shades of maroon.

Since Phryne was unaccompanied this morning, Dot had brought up her employer's more customary morning repast: a pot of fragrant Italian coffee and a French roll.

'This is very kind of you, Dot. Are we packed?'

Dot stood with her hands clasped together, rather as if waiting for her first communion. 'Yes, Miss. I've packed enough for a week's stay. Will that be enough, do you think?'

Phryne poured herself a cup of steaming Arabica and sipped it gratefully. 'I think so, Dot. I hope this will be a pleasant holiday, but a week away from civilisation will be quite long enough. I don't want to leave the girls and Tinker for any longer than that.'

'It was very kind of you to invite Hugh to come and stay here while his bachelor quarters are being rebuilt.'

'The timing was propitious. Hugh can keep half an eye on the girls and Tinker.'

'Yes, Miss Phryne. Oh, and Mr Lin sent some newspapers around this morning.' Dot's normally pale features coloured somewhat, as they generally did whenever Lin Chung was under discussion. 'The *Daylesford Advocate*. I've been reading a recent issue this morning. It says there'll be a Highland Gathering tomorrow. Should I have packed something Scotch?'

'Unless you mean whisky, Dot, no. I would love to attend a Highland Gathering, but I am not dressing up in a MacSporran tartan. I think Sir Walter Scott has a good deal to answer for. The Highlanders of my acquaintance are not over-fond of tartan culture, such as it is.' Phryne thought for a moment. 'Dot, I know it's still summer, but did you pack any warm clothes?'

'Yes, Miss. I looked up Daylesford and Hepburn Springs before I packed. It is two thousand feet above sea level and it's in the middle of something called the Wombat Forest. Do you think we'll meet any wombats?'

'I hope so, Dot; there is something gloriously single-minded about wombats. All right, I'll meet you downstairs in an hour. Ask Mr B to get the car ready.'

Dot hovered for a moment. 'We could go by train, Miss?' she suggested hopefully.

'Yes, we could, Dot—but I don't want to. We'd have to go via Ballarat, and I've had quite enough of that train line. In any case, Hepburn Springs is three miles from the nearest train station, and the hills are a little too vertiginous for comfort. The car it is, Dot.'

'Yes, Miss.'

With that, Dot withdrew, and Phryne began upon her breakfast in earnest.

———

An hour later, Phryne emerged from the house dressed in a long leather coat, leather boots, a flying helmet, goggles, and a white silk scarf. Mr Butler had left the motor purring to itself, and stood to attention at the front door, waving a handkerchief and smiling. Phryne was perfectly able to crank the six-cylinder monster into action herself, but it was Mr Butler's pleasure to do the honours himself. She opened the boot and observed her own enormous valises, which occupied most of the available room. Dot's own valise was nestling under a wicker picnic basket. She closed the boot and climbed into the driver's seat. 'Dot?' she called. 'Time to go!'

A moment later the front door opened and Dot emerged, dressed as she had been earlier but with the addition of a cable-stitch cream cricket jumper, a chocolate brown overcoat and an extraordinary contraption covering her head which suggested that she expected imminent attack by squadrons of bees. Dot hurried past Mr B and slipped into the passenger seat, her gaze fixed straight ahead.

'Whatever are you wearing, Dot?' Phryne enquired.

Dot shot her mistress a quick, fiercely embarrassed look. 'It's a Freda Storm Veil, Miss. For when you're driving fast.'

Phryne nodded, and forbore to question any further. She had heard of Freda Storm Veils for Frightened Passengers and accepted the implied reproach on her reckless driving. She engaged the clutch, selected first gear, and chugged out into The Esplanade. Here along the beach, the air smelled of old seaweed and salty sand—a considerable improvement on the odours of Richmond and Collingwood, which Phryne remembered only too well from her impoverished childhood. Once into second gear, the car began to purr. 'Not long now, my tigress,' she murmured under her breath, 'and you shall have your chance to fly.' The four hundred and three cubic inches of her motor could achieve speeds greatly in excess of either speed limits or Dot's comfort. Marc Birkigt, who had designed the motor, was better known as a maker of engines for aeroplanes, and the Hispano-Suiza's block was exactly half of one of his aviation V12s.

———

As Phryne surged through the inner north-western suburbs, Dot considered her headgear. It was grey, like Dot's mood, with double elastic, and further anchored by two vicious-looking hatpins stuck into her brown plaits, one from each side. It did obscure her vision if she chanced to open her eyes, and that was all to the good, but it was not helping as much as she had hoped.

As a result, her eyes remained resolutely shut for the most part, and Phryne was able to pursue her imperious path through

Melbourne's traffic unobserved by her prayerful companion. (Dot was now invoking the succour of St Christopher, patron and guardian of travellers; a small silver medallion hung from her neck, and both her neat hands were clasped around it.) While her eyes were closed, however, her ears were receiving a good deal. Curses, shouts, car horns, police whistles, and the rebuking clangour of a passing tram. Better not to know, she decided, and continued her novena.

When she had finished, Dot inhaled deeply. The passing air was astringent, but clean, and there was no sound but the roar of the six-cylinder engine and the wind. She opened her eyes to find Phryne slowing down. They were approaching the top of a substantial hill, and beside the road another car had paused on the gravel verge. A red-faced man was standing beside the open bonnet of a two-seater sports car. Occupying the passenger seat was a young woman in a tight bonnet. Her eyes appeared to be rolled upwards in resignation. The man's gloved hand was fiddling with the radiator cap, which was steaming ominously. As they drew to a stop, the radiator erupted, drenching the man's coat in grubby brown water.

'Need some help?' Phryne called out.

The man flourished a tin jerry-can. 'No worries, Miss, I've got a refill. But thanks anyway!'

Phryne waved her gloved hand and accelerated away. Cars and steep ascents did not play well together as a rule, but apparently the Hispano-Suiza laughed at mere hillocks such as these.

After a few more undulations, they careered down a steep hill into what appeared to be a valley of apple orchards.

'Where are we, Miss?' Dot ventured in a timid voice.

'Heading into the Avenue of Honour in Bacchus Marsh, Dot,' Phryne informed her. 'Where the speed limit is thirty miles per hour, a restriction which I intend to obey.' She eased the motor back to a gentle purr, and Dot looked at the road with interest. Flourishing elm saplings lined both sides.

'There are plaques there, Miss,' Dot observed. 'Were these trees planted in memory of those fallen in battle?'

'Yes, Dot. Most of them brutally murdered by incompetent generals.'

Dot, who knew well that Miss Phryne had played a considerable role herself in the Great War, decided to let this pass. 'You don't mean Sir John Monash, surely, Miss?'

'Indeed not. He and Allenby were the only generals commanding who seemed to have any idea how to win a war without getting half their own men killed.'

So many dead, from one small town. Dot crossed herself. 'Miss, I hope you can help Captain Spencer,' she ventured. 'From his letter he seems to be a good man.'

'So he does, Dot,' said Phryne, as they passed by a most impressive town hall and began to climb out of the snug valley again. 'The Captain intrigues me. I feared the war had killed off every Herbert, Albert, and Clarence in the nation; I am delighted to discover that one Herbert at least remains alive and helpful. And with any luck he may prove to be a most attractive young man. The girls and Tinker are back at school, Mr and Mrs B can mind the house and the domestic animals, and I can feel a small adventure coming on. Besides, I have never been to Hepburn and Doctor MacMillan recommends it highly. The roses should be out, and I hear that it is a most beautiful village.'

Since they were travelling at a modest, refined speed up the long hill, Dot took out the Victorian Government Tourist Bureau guidebook and perused the page on Hepburn Springs. The curative properties of the mineral springs were extolled at length, although sinusoidal electric baths sounded a trifle extreme, even for her headstrong and fearless employer. Dot made a firm vow to herself that having electricity applied to her bath would happen over her lifeless body. And a shilling a time? A mere sixpence would purchase a hot or cold mineral bath without high-voltage shocks being applied to her person. A hot bath sounded like a splendid idea.

'Miss, it says here that one of the springs is sulphur—that can't be right, surely?'

'Indeed it can, Dot. The idea of a brimstone bath is appealing, in a strange way. And the others sound wonderful.'

They reached the top of the hill. Away in the distance a line of hills loomed. Phryne pointed. 'That is where we are going, Dot: into the hills and the Wombat Forest.' She pressed her foot on the accelerator; the Hispano-Suiza emitted an excitable roar, and the car leaped forward once more. Dot closed her eyes and resumed praying.

When she opened her eyes again, they were turning right into a broad stretch of nondescript farmland. 'Here we leave the highway.' Phryne reached over and patted Dot's arm in sympathy. 'Only about twenty miles to go, Dot. Bear up. We'll be there in half an hour.'

'Yes, Miss. I'm sure we will.'

As they entered the forest, Phryne slowed down. 'Smell the eucalypts, Dot!'

'Yes, Miss.' Even through her veil, Dot found the scent overwhelming, but it was undeniably refreshing. 'I can also smell water, Miss.'

'Yes. We're now entering spa country, and even in summer it's wet.' As they motored through the canopy of trees, Dot saw many farms, with houses of wood and stone. Occasional horses nibbled the verdant grass. Contented cows grazed, and sheep munched in asinine oblivion. Occasional villages lined the roadside. One was called Sailors Falls, which seemed extremely odd. Was this a place where maritime workers fell off furniture? Or was it the place of a waterfall, discovered by a sailor, or a man called Sailor? What would it be like to live on one of these isolated farms? Dot wondered. In the city, there were lawless pockets in the slums where terrible things could happen, but at least there were neighbours to whom you could turn for help. In the countryside, anything could happen and who would even know?

She was distracted from her morose reflections by a flash of colour. 'Miss, what's that?' Dot pointed to a post on the edge of an ill-kept paddock by the roadside.

Phryne stopped the car and looked hard at it. It was a brightly coloured woollen scarf, knotted loosely around the top of the post and held in place with twine about ten feet above the ground. It flapped occasionally as a stray breeze caught it.

'Well spotted, Dot. Perhaps it's what they use for a scarecrow here. Maybe the original scarecrow ran away from home because it was all too depressing.' Phryne indicated a dilapidated farmhouse set back from the road. A door hung drunkenly by one hinge. Two of the windows were broken. There were no humans in sight anywhere, but a depressed horse stared at its paddock in a brown study, and scrawny chickens pecked aimlessly at nothing in particular. A generalised sense of doom hung in the atmosphere, summarised by a single washing line strung forlornly between two worm-eaten wooden posts. Sadly pegged together were a pair of overalls, a shabby print dress, two indescribably awful towels, a stained woollen jumper, and an assortment of grey underwear that looked like it had died without mourners. Beneath the laundry, a shaggy black-and-white cat glared at them as if it held a personal grudge, then stalked off in medium-to-low dudgeon.

'I don't know how this farm strikes you, Dot, but it's a little bit too Thomas Hardy for my liking.'

'It gives me the shivers, Miss.'

'Quite. Let's get out of here.'

Phryne engaged the clutch and they sped off around the corner. Suddenly the sun came out from behind a cloud and bathed the open road in radiant sunshine. The forest gave way to more farms. Phryne wound around a corner and cruised over a bridge. On the other side, a solid-looking red-brick pub announced its availability for luncheon and refreshments. Three horny-handed sons of toil raised glasses of beer, and Phryne waved happily to them.

The road wound still further and began a long climb to the top of a hill, crowned by some imposing architecture. At the summit was a crossroads. This, it appeared, was the centre of Daylesford, and quietly impressive it was. Deep bluestone guttering lined both sides of the road, which widened into the sort of thoroughfare in which a coach and four could easily be turned about. Shoppers shopped in prosperous-looking establishments, children chased each other along the footpaths, and the entire scene was charming to the eye.

Phryne was about to advance down the hill when a raucous whistle sounded. She observed a very large, uniformed police-man standing in the middle of the road. His puffy right hand was held palm outwards, right in their path. Phryne stopped in the middle of the road and leaned over to address the obstacle. 'Good afternoon, officer,' she said brightly. 'How may I be of assistance?'

An unfortunate conglomeration of flabby, porcine features frowned horribly at her. 'Hold it there! May I see your driver's licence, ma'am?'

The Irish brogue was unmistakable. So was the exasperating air of self-righteous stupidity which accompanied his shiny ser-geant's stripes. He sweated profusely. He had shaved inexpertly, and jet-black stubble mingled with cuts and abrasions, as if he had just gone three rounds with a cheese-grater and been defeated on a technical knock-out.

Phryne handed over her licence, wondering if he would need any help with the longer words.

He frowned again. 'Miss Frinny Fisher, is it?'

'Something like that, yes.'

'And where would you be off to, then, Miss Fisher?'

'Hepburn Springs. And if you would be so kind as to give me my licence back, I would like some afternoon tea. I am staying at the Mooltan, if you think that is any of your business.'

The sergeant started as if he had been bitten by a snake. 'You don't want to do that, Miss! Some very dubious characters there.'

Phryne held out her gloved hand, and with reluctance the sergeant returned her licence and stood aside.

'Thank you, Sergeant. And I hope you have a really annoying day.'

Chapter Three

Dreaming when Dawn's Left Hand was in the sky
I heard a Voice within the Tavern cry,
'Awake, my Little ones, and fill the Cup
Before Life's Liquor in its cup be dry.'

—Edward Fitzgerald, *The Rubáiyát of*
Omar Khayyám of Naishápúr

Detective Inspector Jack Robinson made his thoughtful way back to City South police station. The commissioner was not happy, and had said so at length. He had concluded his remarks by suggesting that perhaps Detective Inspector Robinson should Consider His Position. Detective Inspector Robinson made it clear that he had already considered his position. The commissioner went on to suggest that, in view of his considerable services to the Victoria Police, it was even possible that another promotion might be in order, provided always that there was a satisfactory conclusion to his next assignment.

Detective Inspector Robinson had silently called upon his Maker to give him strength and opened his mouth to tell the commissioner to go and take a long walk off a short pier. He had closed his mouth again while the ancient grandfather clock in the corner of the room ticked its erratic journey around the roman numerals. The assignment was about as welcome as the delivery of a consignment of dead rats onto the front verandah. Nobody else had made any headway on this case, for the very simple reason that the offender in question had most of the senior management of the Victoria Police (and a fair portion of the government) in his capacious and unsavoury raincoat pocket. But—and it was a highly significant but—the current incumbent was rumoured to be entirely honest.

Robinson had stared long and thoughtfully at James Gordon, His Majesty's Commissioner of Police in the Sovereign State of Victoria. It was not a pleasing face. The pallid, sweat-beaded complexion looked like uncooked damper. The watery eyes resembled those of a goldfish who has forgotten the where-abouts of the treasure chest. The overweight torso bulged in unsavoury places. And yet the magic words 'chief inspector' had been uttered. In consequence, Detective Inspector Robinson had agreed that the posting would receive his assent. And so the meeting broke up, with a remarkable absence of cordiality on either side.

Jack reached the station in no good temper and summoned his faithful offsider with a peremptory wave of his right hand. Detective Sergeant Collins was only too glad to be diverted from his morning's dusty paperwork—which contained little of interest—and followed his superior officer into his private office.

'Close the door, will you, Collins?'

Hugh Collins did so, making as little noise as possible, and looked at Robinson with the air of a favourite dog being invited for a walk.

'How did your meeting with the commissioner go, sir?'

Jack Robinson shook his head in sorrow. 'Collins, I have good news and bad news. I am being seconded to a special project.'

'Is that the good news or the bad news?'

Jack laughed. 'I don't really know. The good bit is the opportunity to put behind bars one of our most prominent citizens. The bad news is that three blokes I know have already tried. One's dead and the other two were dismissed from the force.'

'So who are you going after?' Hugh wanted to know.

Robinson gave him a Look. 'The business conglomerate controlled by a certain Barry Mortimore.'

Collins yelped. 'Not Barry the Shark!'

'The same. However, I have grounds for optimism.'

'But, sir—' Collins began to march up and down the shabby carpet, registering alarm '—the Shark has all the government bigwigs in his pocket. You can't go after him!'

'Nevertheless, I am going to try. And that's as much as I am going to tell you, Collins, because you won't be part of this particular operation. The squad has been hand-picked by the commissioner, and whatever we may think of him, I have reason to believe that he at least is straight and not in anybody's pocket—except possibly that of the General Assembly of the Presbyterian Church.' Jack waved a hand. 'Sit down, Collins, you're giving me a headache.'

Hugh Collins subsided, steaming with equal parts concern and relief. Serving officers who found themselves on the wrong side of the Shark tended to have the life expectancy of a tulip in a blast furnace. If you were lucky, you were accused of police corruption and dismissed. If you were unlucky, you might well find yourself investigating the Yarra River, or the clammy depths of Victoria Dock, in concrete overshoes. But he had faith in his boss. If anyone could pull this off, then surely Robinson could. Since his engagement to Dot, though, Hugh had become a little more careful of his own person.

'Good luck, sir.'

'Thank you. Unfortunately, Collins, this means that you will be working for Acting Detective Inspector Fraser. You will call him "sir"; you will obey his instructions; and you will only investigate behind his back if it becomes clear that a miscarriage of justice is imminent. In that event, you will present him with the results of your own investigations. And when he takes all the credit for your work, you will keep your mouth shut, salute enthusiastically, and reflect that in the Victoria Police credit is eventually given where it is merited. I hope to be back in due course. Good luck.'

Jack stood up, as did Hugh. They shook hands with the solemnity normally afforded to the laying of foundation stones or the opening of bridges. Then Jack clapped his hat on his head and took his leave.

———

The wrought-iron front gate of Lonsdale Technical School was invitingly open, and Tinker strolled through it into the street. He was happy—as he always was, even in the temporary absence of his rescuer and patron Miss Fisher. 'I'm happy!' he said aloud, careless of whoever might overhear him. *I've got a house,* he went on in an interior monologue. *I've got no screaming babies and hungry young kids to look after and be tormented by.* Instead, he had Jane and Ruth, who were quiet and easy to get on with. He had Mr Hugh, who openly encouraged Tinker in his career aspirations. Hugh was already a policeman and worked for Detective Inspector Robinson; Tinker hoped to one day do the same. And there was Dot. Tinker was puzzled by Dot; he had never met anyone who had Religion before, and he found it a bit strange. But Dot was so kind and loving you soon forgot about it. There were Mr and Mrs Butler, who were always ready to feed him from their seemingly inexhaustible pantry. *I really am happy*, he concluded. *I reckon I'm walking on easy street.*

Today had been a good day. He had put up with his mathematics classes and had managed to get most of his sums right. Fractions made more sense when you could see them in front of you. Obviously seven and three eighths of an inch was smaller than seven and a half inches. It was right there in front of you, on your ruler. He had received a mark of approval from Mr Bradbury for his technical drawing of a workshop. 'Is that something you'd like to make, Tinker?' Mr Bradbury had enquired. Tinker had explained that it was where he lived. He had borrowed the household tape measure (a proper spring-loaded tin one) and taken all the measurements. His shed was nine feet four and a half inches by six feet two inches, and seven feet six and three eighths of an inch high. Everything in it was his, and it felt good.

He walked quickly to Swanston Street, arriving just in time to catch a southbound tram. He was in no hurry to return home, and he felt the need for some adult male company. As the tram sauntered down the hill towards Bourke Street, Tinker stared out the window in open admiration of the huge buildings. In one he counted no fewer than eight storeys. There had been nothing like this in Queenscliff, where he had grown up. The click-click of the conductor marking tickets mingled with excitable conversation and the whine of the tram's wheels on the shining metal tracks. Passengers alighted, others climbed on board, mostly women with brown paper parcels under their arms or stowed inside bulging string bags. One heavily laden woman was struggling with a screaming child.

Tinker leaned forward and looked the tow-haired toddler straight in the eye. 'No need for that, mate. Mum's doin' her best.'

The child stared at him and opened its mouth wide.

'Yair, mate, that's the way. Take it easy.'

This was rewarded with a dazzling smile. Mum shot Tinker a grateful look then drew a lolly out of her coat pocket with her black-gloved hand and shoved it into the child's gaping mouth. Tinker looked her over without particular interest, but noted that she was very pretty. Remembering his life's ambition to become a detective, he composed a detailed description of the woman, in the event she had been a material witness to a crime. He closed his eyes and ran through his list. Age: early twenties. Height: five feet one. Weight: seven stone. Complexion: fair, with faint lines beneath her brown eyes. Hair: auburn, curly, just above the collar. Coat: summer, light brown with a fur trim. Hat: expensive, cloche, deep brown. He opened his eyes again, nodded briefly to her and smiled.

Tinker got off the tram at Flinders Street. A rich peal of bells rang out from St Paul's Cathedral as he stood and admired the great arches of Flinders Street station, with its row of clocks proclaiming the next departure time for each line. Some of the boys at school spoke in whispers about Meeting a Girl Under the Clocks; Tinker wasn't interested in girls, but the information had been filed away as General Background Detail. The St Kilda line, he noted, had a train leaving in four minutes, but that was not what he wanted. Instead, he set off west down Flinders Street, heading towards the docks.

Bert and Cec would probably be there, fishing. They had explained the intricacies of the Great Strike of 1923 to Tinker, who was, to tell the truth, less surprised and outraged than they had expected. Of course the bosses would oppress the workers if they could! And they had got away with it. The strike had collapsed, and now the wharfies had to beg for work, resulting in the local version of what Sydney's harbourside workers called the Hungry Mile. If you wanted work in the morning, you had to present yourself at two different docks, with a long trek between them. Because Bert and Cec had their own taxi, which they drove in the evenings, they no longer bothered to turn up at seven a.m., but they still presented themselves at both docks for the three p.m. shift. They were rarely picked, however, as the shipping companies' representatives invariably recognised the two notorious communists and would only hire them if there was no alternative. As a result, they had plenty of time to fish.

Tinker's eyes were fixed on the river as he walked. It was a bright, sunny day with little wind, and the seagulls gathered by the oily waters of the Yarra, picking through piles of weeds and discarded rubbish. Tinker recognised the gulls as fellows, having grown up very like them, gleaning a precarious living on the waterfront from whatever was unattended or unwanted. The elegant grey stone of the Seamen's Mission loomed up amid the grubby sheds and wharfside clutter. This was Bert and Cec's favourite spot.

And there they were. Cec: tall and Viking-like, with clipped flaxen hair; and Bert: short, rotund, and dark-haired. They had been mates all through the war, and they were still mates now. Having a mate was important. But Tinker was in no hurry to acquire one. His ideal mate would be a fellow cop. An honest cop, naturally. Bert had already told him about Crook Cops and how to identify them. Crook Cops could not be trusted. To begin with, they would be your best friend. Then they'd start showing you easy ways of picking up extra cash on the side. Until one day your so-called mate had dropped you right in it.

Tinker approached slowly, waiting for his cue. He looked at the wickerwork fishing creel, their rough-hewn dark trousers and checked shirts, their elderly hats.

Eventually Bert turned to face him and nodded. 'G'day, Tink.' Tinker paused for the requisite dragging second and responded. 'G'day, Bert, Cec.'

Bert made a small, almost indiscernible gesture with his jaw, indicating that Tinker's company was acceptable, and he joined them, watching as Cec dangled a single line down into the fetid waters. No rods today. He looked questioningly at Bert but did not speak. Bert gave another infinitesimal nod of approval and deigned to expound. 'This is niggling, Tink. River's too dirty right now for anything but eels.' Bert indicated a galvo bucket of water next to the creel. 'When we catch 'em, we put 'em in fresh water and carry them home like that.'

Tinker was impressed. Bert and Cec did not need to go fishing any more than they needed to walk the Hungry Mile. But they were wharfies by preference and fished because it was part of being a Man Among Men. Tinker really wanted to be like them, even though he was going to be a copper, and hence technically a class enemy to the comrades. But they respected his ambition nevertheless. As Cec had explained, it was better to have decent blokes in the police force than crooks and outright criminals.

Cec niggled the line some more, but drew it out again in silent disgust.

'Bastard get away?' Bert enquired out of the corner of his mouth. Cec nodded.

'Let me 'ave a go.'

Bert took the fishing line, rebaited the now bare hook with a small piece of unidentifiable fish-like substance and cast the line back into the turbid water.

Cec regarded Tinker with a friendly eye. 'School all right, mate?' 'Yair.' Tinker paused, wondering if he should elaborate. The silence seemed inviting enough. 'Fractions, English and technical drawing.' Bert drew a wriggling eel from the river and cast it into the bucket. 'English?' he repeated. 'What do they teach yer in that, Tink? Poetry?'

'I have to write essays. I'm not very good at it.'

'Worth doin' though, I reckon. Stands to reason you should be able to write.'

'And read,' Cec put in. 'Otherwise the bastards'll rob yer blind out there.'

'I suppose I'll need to be able to write reports when I become a detective,' Tink mused.

This produced, if not enthusiasm, at least silent assent. At length Bert extracted another eel from the river and sent it to join its fellows. 'Youse want a go, Tink?'

'No thanks.'

Cec resumed command of the niggling and Bert rolled himself a smoke from his rusty tobacco tin. 'Youse are in Leaving, yair?'

Tinker admitted that he was, which meant that the police academy beckoned.

Bert nodded. 'Mate, the cops'll want to see a young bloke who works hard, so get your certificate with as good marks as yer can. Anyone who wants to give you a job, they'll want to see a nice shiny report.'

Tinker digested this. The unspoken message was clear. *Forget being wharfies like us. It's a mug's game now.* Without the taxi, and Miss Fisher, he knew, Bert and Cec would be seriously up against it. 'I will,' he said. 'And I'll join the union.'

Bert gave him a baleful glare. 'Too bloody right you'll join the union. And when the comrades go out, you go out too. One in, all in.'

'It's all right, Bert. I'll never be a scab.' Tinker shut his eyes for a moment, trying to remember something he'd heard once. *'You scabbed, old son, in ninety-one. And then once more in ninety-four.'*

'Yair.' Bert stubbed out the butt of his cigarette and rolled another one. 'Blokes wouldn't work with scabs twenty years afterwards. Blokes remember. Once a scab, always a scab.'

At that moment, Cec drew another eel out of the river and

deposited it in the bucket. It complained vigorously, at first, but subsided eventually into acquiescence with its comrades.

'Right, Cec, let's get this down to Port,' said Bert. 'You coming, Tink?'

'Where to?'

'We're just gonna drop this lot off at Comrade London's place for his missus, and then we can take yer home.'

'Oh. Yair, sure. Thanks.' Tinker pondered for a moment. 'London? That's an unusual name.'

Cec grinned. 'London fog—never lifts. Actually, he's not that bad, but he was bludgin' one long night shift and the name stuck.'

'Yair, and one night he met the Hook comin' the other way and didn't make it home at all.' Bert held Tinker's eyes. 'Yair, I know what yer thinkin': we could just give her money. But she wouldn't take it. When the union had money, we'd distribute to everyone accordin' to their needs, but the union's bust these days. And while London's missus would take money from the union, she won't accept it from us. Instead, we give her whatever we can catch. She can make a decent eel pie out of this.' He gestured to the bucket.

'All right.' That sounded sensible. Tinker looked around. 'Where's the cab?'

'Over near the dock.'

Cec picked up the bucket in one hand and slung the creel over his shoulder. Bert led the way along the wooden jetty. A great iron ship was standing by the pier.

'The comrades look after us, Tink,' Bert confided. 'We do the odd favour for them, and they keep an eye on our taxi. No bludger comes near our cab. And there she is.' He stopped to admire his battered black taxi then turned to his mate, who had stopped a few paces back and was frowning at the river in consternation. 'Cec, what's wrong, mate?'

'Nothin' good. Have a look.'

Tinker followed Cec's gaze. A girl's body was bobbing gently on the water's surface. She was face down, and she was not moving.

'Jeez.' Bert had a short think and came to a decision. 'Cec, you drop off the eels then take Tinker home. I'll stay here for now. You can come pick me up later.'

'What're we gonna do?' Tinker wanted to know.

Bert looked at Tinker with a stricken face. 'Call the cops, mate. Just get the taxi out of here, all right?'

Cec nodded, loaded the bucket into the cab, and drove off with Tinker.

'It's bad when it happens, mate,' said Cec, driving around the bay. 'Bodies floatin' by the wharf. Sometimes blokes have a disagreement and one of them finishes up in the water. We don't get involved, 'cos it's none of our business. But girls is different.' Cec changed gears and slowed the car to a stop. 'Won't be a mo'. Stay put, mate.'

Tinker did so, his mind still filled with the horrific image of the bobbing corpse. The details were burned into his mind. The blouse that must once have been white was grey, and a long black skirt enveloped her pale, stockinged legs like an obscene jellyfish. His skin crawled at the memory. Her single plait drifted about her head helplessly, already gathering weed and refuse. Abruptly, he flung open the car door and got out. Crumpling to his knees, he was sick in the gutter.

When he was done, he wiped his mouth and slowly stood up. One day, when he was a detective, he would have to face dead bodies, he reminded himself. And they wouldn't all be blokes who'd had it coming; it might even be girls like this one, who looked to be no older than Jane or Ruth. But how could a girl like this have ended up in the river? He clenched his teeth and stood up straighter. A sudden flame burned inside him. He, Tinker, was going to solve this case. By himself, if needs be.

Chapter Four

And, as the cock crew, those who stood before
The Tavern shouted—'Open then the Door!
You know how little while we have to stay,
And, once departed, may return no more.'

—Edward Fitzgerald, *The Rubáiyát of*
Omar Khayyám of Naishápúr

First it was the hats. Through long practice, they sailed in curving trajectories across the bedroom and landed on the brown, furry heads of Henry and Pootel, a matched pair of teddy bears whose quiet, impassive sympathy had been of great assistance during the last year. Next came the gloves, which sailed into a wicker basket on the floor, from which emerged Ember the black kitten. She glared at the humans who had dared intrude upon her royal slumbers and tiptoed out of the room.

'It is offended!' cried Jane.

'See! It stalks away,' finished Ruth, who had been reading *Hamlet* and was greatly impressed by the opening ghost scene upon the ramparts of Elsinore.

Phryne's adoptive daughters had arrived home together and continued their diurnal post-school ritual. Ruth hung up their jackets on coathangers in the tall blackwood wardrobe while Jane tossed their softened leather satchels, which spun across the room in epicyclic parabolas and landed on the floor next to their matching desks. Next came their pleated school tunics—heavy with perspiration and the worse for wear— which sailed majestically into the washing basket. The two girls hastily donned their straight, sleeveless linen housecoats (slate blue for Jane; pink for Ruth). They kicked off their shoes, which landed on the carpet directly outside for Tinker to take them away and apply boot polish thereto. (This part of Tinker's going-to-sleep ritual gave him a deep and utterly improbable satisfaction.)

'I cannot believe we don't have summer uniforms, Jane.'

'I can. It's ridiculous, of course. But everyone wants their children to look like English scholars, and that includes school uniforms more suitable for the retreat from Moscow.'

'I will never feel comfortable in these,' Ruth commented as she sat on the edge of her bed and extricated her toes from her silk stockings. 'Oh, dash it! I've laddered them!'

'We've got plenty.'

They exchanged a look. Both girls had grown up (if that was the term) in direst poverty in a boarding house run by a villainous woman who could have been Wackford Squeers' grandmother. Stockings, silk or otherwise, were utterly unknown in the slums of Seddon. Thanks to Miss Phryne, they now had more pairs of stockings than they would ever need. Ruth blushed. Here she was complaining about being forced to wear expensive clothes on a hot day. By tacit consent, they dropped the subject and wandered into the kitchen.

There, the impressively starched and aproned Mrs Butler

looked at them with the air of a mother duck regarding her two most adventurous ducklings and handed them two long glasses filled with chilled lemonade. The girls sat on chairs in the kitchen and sipped, savouring the homemade refreshment. The plate of biscuits on the kitchen table was lessened by two, and quiet crunching sounds indicated entire satisfaction.

'Well, girls, how was school today?'

Ruth put down her glass. 'We've got a mystery, Mrs B!' The exclamation mark was perfectly audible.

'What are you talking about?'

Jane sipped again then set down her glass. 'It's Claire, who's in my class. She's gone missing.'

'It's true, Mrs B,' Ruth added excitedly. 'She wasn't at school yesterday, and we thought that was a bit strange, because Claire studies really hard and never misses school. Then she missed today as well, and we saw her mum drive into the school grounds; we noticed the car because it was so big and expensive. She had a long talk with the headmistress.'

Mrs Butler sighed and shook her head. 'And from that you've decided that she's missing? You're jumping to conclusions, both of you. How do you know she isn't just changing schools?'

The girls exchanged glances in which both guilt and mischief featured prominently.

'Unless one of you was listening?' Mrs B suggested.

Jane blushed. 'Well, yes, I was. It was lunchtime, and I know that Miss Barclay keeps her front window open all the time.'

'So you eavesdropped?'

Jane squirmed uncomfortably. 'Yes.'

'And that's where you found out that the girl's mother doesn't know where she is and neither does the school?'

Jane nodded. 'But Ruth and I thought *we* might be able to find her.'

'You are not going to risk your necks poking your noses where they aren't wanted. I forbid it! What would Miss Phryne say?'

Jane looked downcast, but Ruth unexpectedly protested. 'Why shouldn't we, Mrs B? I like Claire. She's a good girl. No one takes much notice of her, but just because she's quiet and not pretty doesn't mean we shouldn't look out for her.'

Mrs Butler thought about this. Jane was very intelligent, and probably street aware enough to take care of herself, but Ruth, bless her, was liable to get in over her head. Still, if they were determined, they might make plans between themselves. Better they did it openly, and in her presence, so she could intervene if necessary. 'All right,' she said. 'Tell me about her.'

Jane shot Ruth a quick look of gratitude and began. 'She lives in Kew, in a really big house. We've never seen it, but girls who have say the family must be seriously rich. She's an only child. Her dad is a doctor, and her mum paints watercolours. Claire is in all my classes; she wants to be a doctor too. So we do science and maths together and she's quiet. And nice.' She paused, remembering the chastisement of Miss Brown, who had handed her back an essay with a big cross on it and the written comment in red fountain pen: *Nice is NOT a descriptive word, Jane!* 'She's pleasant, I mean. She doesn't talk much, but she's friendly.'

'Are we looking at boyfriend troubles?' Mrs B wanted to know.

'I really don't think so. She's never talked about boys, not once. I think that's why I like her so much.'

'All right. Not boys. Does she have any enemies?'

Jane shook her head, but Ruth nodded. 'Oh yes. Some of the fashionable girls are very cruel to her. She wears glasses, and they call her Four-Eyes. One of them—Isobel—pretended to be her friend and she was really happy about that, until the day when in front of all the other smart set Isobel called her an ugly, four-eyed frump.'

Jane looked at Ruth in surprise. 'I didn't know that. When was this?'

'About three months ago. And she never told you?'

'No. You're sure?'

Ruth folded her hands in her lap and nodded with emphasis. 'Yes. But Claire didn't cry; Isobel was very disappointed by that. She just shut her mouth in a tight line, walked away, and never spoke to them again. I've been watching her.'

Of course you have, Mrs Butler ruminated. Ruth the kind-hearted, keeping a watchful eye on the unpopular girls. Was Ruth unpopular at school? Probably not. And if they tried to bully Jane she wouldn't even notice. 'All right. Investigate by all means, but be careful!'

'It's what Miss Phryne would want us to do,' said Jane. Ruth nodded in silence.

———

By the time Tinker arrived home, Jane had adjourned to her room to study and Ruth was in the kitchen helping Mrs Butler with dinner.

Not long after, Ruth rang the dinner gong—an extravagance purchased last year—and the family (minus Hugh Collins, who was working late) assembled around the dining table. When Dot was present, a proper Catholic grace was spoken before meals, but what would happen now Dot was away?

Mrs Butler looked at the girls and smiled.

'You can say grace any way you like, girls.'

'Grace!' Jane announced, trying to keep a straight face.

'Grace,' echoed Ruth, and giggled.

Mrs Butler's mouth opened and shut again. 'Very well,' she said finally. 'While Miss Dorothy is away, we'll say no more about it.' With that Mrs Butler retired to her kitchen.

Since the prayers, such as they had been, were now concluded, Tinker carved the pies with a large knife supplied by the beaming Mr Butler. With Hugh absent, Mr Butler had anointed Tinker man of the house. To Tinker, this meant carving. Carving pies was probably overkill, Mr Butler considered as he hovered beside the boy's left arm, but he didn't want to discourage him.

Mr Butler carried the pies around the table and the company helped themselves to generous portions. 'What's in these pies, Mr B?' asked Jane.

'Fish, beef, and chicken, Miss,' he answered with an indulgent smile.

'And the vegetables smell wonderful,' Jane continued. 'I don't recognise these sauces.'

Mr Butler turned to Ruth, who was beaming, and nodded.

'I'm trying new ways to cook vegetables,' Ruth said. 'Mrs B let me try. So the mashed potato has cream cheese and chives in it, with black pepper, salt, and butter.'

Jane shovelled some onto her plate then lifted her fork to her lips. 'Oh my! That's wonderful, Ruth.' She spooned some carrots and broccoli onto her plate. 'And what's in these?'

'The broccoli has a sauce made of lemon juice, garlic, and butter, and the carrots have fresh ginger, sesame seeds, and honey. Oh, and butter.'

Tinker tried some of everything and found them all delicious. The pies were superb, too, with crumbly crusts that melted in your mouth and dissolved into liquid ecstasy. While Mrs B had managed the other two, Ruth had made the fish pie. She wasn't entirely happy with how it had come out. She had overdone the lemon and lime, she realised. It seemed that a little lime went a very long way.

When at last the trio had put down their knives and forks, arranged decorously together to signify repletion, Mr Butler reappeared with Mrs Butler in his wake. 'I shall leave main course dishes on the table for Mr Hugh, I think.'

Mrs Butler nodded. 'That would be best. He'll be here soon. And dessert can wait for a while, after a splendid main course like that.'

She turned to Tinker, who had thus far contributed only monosyllables to the feast of reason. 'Well, Tinker, I've heard about the girls' day. How was yours?'

'It was all right, Mrs B, except...' Tinker paused. Nothing would induce him to let on about the dead girl, nor the presence of Bert and Cec at the crime scene. Aware that everyone was looking at him, he improvised. 'We did a lot of maths. I think I'm gettin' the hang of it.'

And that seemed to be that for the moment. Soon dessert was laid on the table: more pies, but this time with tinned fruit. And (of course) apples. With cream. The company picked up their silver spoons, but at that moment came the sound of the front door opening and shutting, and an inrush of size twelve police-issue beetle-crushers, followed by the sound of Hugh's helmet being thrown onto the sofa, missing, and rolling onto the floor with a dismal clang. And presently Hugh was with them, breathing heavily, with his face flushed like a bad-tempered beetroot.

'Hello, Mr Hugh,' Ruth called out. 'As you can see, we left dinner on the table for you.'

'Thanks.' Hugh wiped his brow and sat down opposite Tinker. Normally he would have changed out of his dark blue police uniform before dinner, but tonight he disdained such niceties. He loaded up his plate with pie and vegetables and began to eat with more enthusiasm than decorum. Mrs Butler watched him, suspicion beginning to steal over her. It would never have done to cross-examine Miss Phryne or her guests, but since Hugh was now temporarily on the premises, he was for the time being Family. And as such...

'Mr Collins, are you quite well? You seem somewhat disturbed.'

Hugh put down his fork and looked embarrassed. 'I'm sorry, Mrs B. It was a really quiet day until about four, and I was looking forward to knocking off on time. But then...well, we got called out to something bad. I don't want to talk about it at the dinner table, though, if that's all right.'

He motored through both courses like a famished labrador, then finally laid down his spoon and grinned. 'That was amazing!'

Ruth gathered the dessert bowls and began to carry them out to the kitchen. As soon as she had left the room, Hugh gave Mrs Butler a stricken look. 'I'm sorry, Mrs B. But yair, disturbed is putting it mildly. We've just fished a dead girl out of the bay.'

From the kitchen came a deafening crash. Ruth appeared at the open door, her eyes wide and her face stricken with grief.

Chapter Five

And look—a thousand Blossoms with the Day
Woke—and a thousand scatter' d into Clay
And this first Summer Month that brings the Rose
Shall take Jamshýd and Kaikobád away.

—Edward Fitzgerald, *The Rubáiyát of*
Omar Khayyám of Naishápúr

Dot gasped as the car roared off down the main street, considerably in excess of the speed limit. The road presently bent to the left, and Phryne slowed down. Rows of cottages lined both sides of the road. To the left was a narrow river valley, with dense forest beyond it. The scent of lavender filled the air. Dot was no admirer of the countryside as a rule, but she had to admit that this appeared to be tolerable. Her fears of Discomfort in Foreign Parts were abating considerably.

The Hispano-Suiza purred gently down a hill into a village which announced itself as Hepburn Springs. Suddenly, Phryne turned off the road and puttered around a curving gravel pathway flanked by rose bushes (partly in flower) and lavender bushes. As they drew near the house, Dot looked at what was evidently the Mooltan guesthouse. It was a snug two-storey bluestone house with an iron-laced slate roof and two windows each side of the front door, and five on the second storey. Balconies with pot plants lined the upper storey.

Phryne engaged the handbrake and stepped out of the car. 'Smell that country air, Dot!' she urged.

Dot did so, and unobtrusively kissed her St Christopher medallion, giving devout thanks that she would not have to be driven anywhere far for many days.

A square, youthful figure emerged from the house and walked towards them.

Phryne smiled and greeted the young man. 'Hello, you must be Dulcie. I'm Phryne Fisher, and this is Dot. Dr MacMillan sends you her best.'

Dot realised that she had been deceived by the woman's male attire and close-cropped hair.

Dulcie grinned. 'Yes, we were expecting you,' she said, adding, 'This is Alice,' as another young woman appeared (easily identifiable as such in a long, grey skirt, and light woollen jumper).

'Afternoon tea's ready,' said Alice. 'I hope you like scones, cream, and jam?'

'Yes, we really do,' Phryne assured her. 'And we could do with some tea to wash away the grime of roads—and policemen.'

Alice coloured. 'You've met our sergeant then? He's...abrupt.'

Dulcie patted Alice's hand. 'Stupid and offensive is what you mean. His name is Sergeant Offaly.'

'Never mind him,' said Alice dismissively. 'Come inside and have tea. Dulcie will get your luggage. Tea is in the parlour.'

As they sat down to feather-light scones, mulberry jam, and thick, fresh cream, Alice poured the tea and Dulcie hustled their bags up the wooden staircase.

'This is wonderful,' Phryne approved. 'Who made the scones?'
Dulcie reappeared and leaned on the back of a chair. 'Alice did.
And the jam. We're not usually open this late in summer, but any
friend of Dr MacMillan is welcome. She stays here a fair bit. It's
comfy.' Dulcie's light blue eyes flickered. 'Business or pleasure,
Phryne? And will you be dining in?'

'Just pleasure, I hope. I'm here to see Captain Spencer, and I'll
dine with him. Dot will be delighted to have dinner here, though.'

'So what did our cop want with you?'

'He stopped me in the middle of the road in Daylesford, and
when he found out I was staying here, he warned me off.'

'He wouldn't know if a tram was up his backside till the conductor rang the bell. You'll want a rest, I'm sure.' Dulcie sniffed
then disappeared again. Phryne made small talk with Alice, while
Dot had a second cup of strong tea. When she'd drained the cup,
she stood up. 'Miss? I'll put away our things in our rooms, shall I?'

Phryne nodded, and Dot hurried off to unpack.

———

'So, tell me about Daylesford, Alice,' Phryne suggested.

Alice put down her teacup. 'To be honest, we don't have that
much to do with them over there.'

'But you must hear things?'

Alice shrugged. 'Yes, we do hear a few things. It's just—it's
hard to explain, really. I've lived in other country towns, and
everybody knows everybody. But here? Daylesford is like—well, a
big, brawling, elder brother. Hepburn is the quiet little sister who
just wants to get on with her sewing. Don't get me wrong: I'm
sure they're good people. But once you get over that hill—' Alice
waved her small, olive hand in a southerly direction '—the place
has a completely different feel. We keep mostly to ourselves here.'

'Yes, I did notice a change in the atmosphere,' Phryne observed, looking carefully at Alice. The girl was clearly Dulcie's lover: quiet, refined, and gentle in contrast with Dulcie's good-humoured brusqueness. Alice's eyes were startlingly blue, yet her face was oval and tanned. Or possibly not tanned, for there was no sign of the ravages of the harsh Australian sun. Phryne diagnosed a touch of Mediterranean in her ancestry, even though her accent was pure Australian of the more genteel variety. She radiated comfort and contentment. Not for the first time, Phryne made a mental note to the effect that medical opinions stating that women who were same-sex attracted must be neurotic were so much ill-informed drivel. 'To what would you attribute the difference?'

'Oh, the water. Definitely. We have the springs.'

'And Daylesford doesn't? I see. What about this lake they're going to make?'

Alice sat up a little straighter. 'I think it will do them the world of good.'

'Interesting,' Phryne murmured, noting that—as Lin had remarked—the locals seemed to be hardly aware of the effect of the development on the Chinese market gardeners. 'Now, I'm still trying to orient myself. Have you heard of the Temperance Hotel?'

Alice laughed. 'Who has not? Even we've heard of Gentle Annie.'

'I thought that was a song by Stephen Foster. You have a local version?'

'Annie Tremain—she's the barmaid there. Every boy for miles around wants to marry her.'

'So what is this paragon of womanhood like? And does she favour any of her suitors above others? I would have thought this might create unrest.'

Alice smiled. 'Miss Fisher, she's beautiful. Really she is. And you can't help liking her. Trouble seems to melt away whenever she looks at the boys. They can be on the brink of throwing punches at each other, but one word from her and all the aggression leaks out through their boots.'

'So you've been to the Temperance yourself?'

Alice blushed, and her long, dark eyelashes blinked and covered her eyes. 'Once or twice, yes. But she's very young. I don't think she's in any hurry to marry anyone.' Alice fell silent, and Phryne was just making up her mind to change the subject when Alice spoke again. 'The thing with Annie is, the boys' attention doesn't go to her head. She's not vain and silly, like so many pretty girls. She makes everyone relax. It's a gift. I think…' Alice paused again, as if searching for the right words. 'I think her special talent might be that she makes everyone believe they are better than they are.'

Phryne patted Alice's slender arm. 'I must see this paragon for myself, then.' Phryne leaned back in her chair, aware that Alice was looking at her with what seemed to be frank admiration. Phryne raised an eyebrow in query.

'I've heard so much about you.' Again the glorious eyelashes fluttered.

'Nothing good, I hope?'

'Oh yes, Miss Fisher!'

The girl was looking at her in an odd way. Phryne wondered for a moment if she was to be the subject of Alice's unwanted affections, but she suspected not. What she read in those sapphire eyes was hero-worship.

'You chastise the wicked and assist the good. So many people with your advantages in life think only of themselves and their own comforts.'

'Phryne?' Dulcie called from the doorway. 'Your rooms are ready. Dot's already having a nap. Do you want a rest before you go out?'

Phryne rose. 'Yes, that would be lovely.' She turned to Alice and smiled. 'Thanks for keeping me company.'

Ten minutes later, Phryne sat on the balcony, smoking a cigarette and admiring the quiet, elegant village below her. Her room was tasteful, well-furnished, and unobtrusive in the right way, and the whole house smelled deliciously of lemon floor wax and lavender. She could hear the small river in the distance. She stubbed out her cigarette, rose, and went inside. The bed was magnificent, and she was asleep in a moment.

———

Dot and Phryne came downstairs shortly before dinner. Dot was dressed as before, but Phryne had attired herself in cream-coloured trousers, a white Russian *blouson* with pearl buttons on the left, and a French biretta stuck at a rakish angle. She considered that she looked not only beautiful, but also visible. Noting the dearth of street lighting when they had driven through the village, she thought this might be advisable in Hepburn Springs by night.

In the parlour she found a distrait young man talking quietly to Dulcie. His face was pale, and his dark eyes darted back and forth without rest. Dulcie urged him to sit down, then addressed her guests. 'A drink, Phryne? Dot?'

'A gin and tonic, please.' Phryne looked at Dot, who shook her head.

'This is my brother Aubrey, Phryne,' announced Dulcie, shaking gin, ice, and tonic into a glass. 'He's one of Captain Spencer's patients.'

Aubrey nodded. 'He's such a good man. I have shell shock, you know. I managed Gallipoli, but the Western Front... We're not cowards, no matter what they say. It's just—'

'It's all right, Aubrey,' Phryne broke in. 'You don't have to explain. I was there, driving an ambulance. I remember. It was the guns pounding for days on end. And one day you can't bear it any longer.'

Dulcie was at Aubrey's side in an instant. 'Take your valerian drops, Aubrey. Come on.'

Aubrey rummaged in his pocket and brought out a small bottle. Dulcie put a glass of water on the wooden table in front of him, and he shook several drops into it. He sipped carefully at it, and when it was finished he replaced the glass on the table. Then he leaned back in his chair and sighed.

At that moment, a silver tabby cat entered the room, sniffing. 'Hello, Tamsin,' said Dulcie. 'Come for your fix?'

Tamsin flowed upwards and landed on the table without a sound. Her red-brick nose sniffed at the glass. Soon she was rubbing her head around the rim of the glass, purring in ecstasy. Finally the little cat put her head right inside the glass and began to roll around the table on her side. The glass rolled off the table, but Dulcie caught it dextrously in mid-air. Dot giggled, and Dulcie placed the glass on the floor. 'Come on down, Tamsin.'

The cat thought about this, then leaped down, resuming her love affair with the empty glass.

'Not all cats like valerian,' Phryne observed. 'But she certainly does.'

Aubrey's hunched shoulders began to relax, and he managed a smile.

Phryne began to sing: '*Take a sniff, take a sniff, take a sniff on me; I've got the valerian Blues.*'

Aubrey laughed, and Phryne stood up. 'I'm off to see Captain Spencer,' she announced.

'You know the way?' Dulcie asked. 'You can't miss it. Straight down the road to the bend. It's on your right.'

'Take care, Miss Phryne,' Dot called after her.

'I will.'

It was a cool twilight, but the walk to the spa was barely two hundred yards. Yellow lights shone from several houses, and there were small, cosy movements in the trees; nocturnal possums were probably foraging already. She knocked at the freshly painted door and waited.

Almost immediately the door opened, and soft light welled out into the valley. Phryne drew in her breath. Captain Spencer (for she assumed it was he) stood before her and offered his hand. 'So good of you to come.'

———

Captain Herbert Spencer was everything Phryne could have wished for in a dining companion: taller than some but slender-hipped, with firm shoulders, impeccable evening dress, hazel eyes, a clear, slightly tanned complexion, and a friendly smile. Taking her hand, he led her inside and conducted her into a small, carpeted alcove at the edge of a larger dining room. A silver candelabra with three beeswax candles stood in the centre of a spotless tablecloth. The table was set for two, with three wineglasses on each side.

'Please, sit down,' he said.

Phryne was anticipating a most enjoyable meal—until Herbert fixed her with a steady eye. 'I am afraid I have a confession to make: we are vegetarians here. We have all seen too much blood, and we cannot abide it. Besides, humans do not require it; legumes are a perfectly adequate source of sustenance. And, of course, Australia has magnificent vegetables and fruit.'

Phryne smiled brightly, but her heart sank. This promised to be a dreary repast, with everything boiled to extinction. Every ounce of taste and nourishment would be expelled from the sad remnants of whimpering vegetation, and the cadavers would be reanimated with bicarbonate of soda.

As soon as they were both seated, a youngish woman in a plain black dress with a white apron appeared with a bottle. She filled two of the glasses, nodded to Phryne, and disappeared back into the kitchen.

Herbert grinned shyly. 'I hope you like this. It is herbal wine, such as I give my patients.' He must have seen her eyes flicker with momentary dismay, as he added hastily: 'I have a Barossa Valley red and a dessert wine to follow.'

Mollified, Phryne drank. The wine was unexpectedly sweet, and strongly flavoured with mint, thyme, sage, marjoram, basil, and other herbs that she could not identify.

'There is a romantic story attached to this wine,' Herbert explained. 'A monastery was in desperate straits, and a monk dreamed that a stranger would come and save them. Next day, a shipwrecked sailor was cast ashore and the monks took him in. They shared what little they had with him and told him of their direst poverty. When they showed him their herb garden, the mariner laughed and showed them how to make this wine. They kept his secret and sold most of what they made at a high enough price to pay off their debts and prosper ever afterwards.'

Phryne drank a little more. 'It is more subtle than I expected. Well done! I take it the recipe is a secret no more?'

He smiled. 'I found it in *The Gentle Art of Cookery*. So I did not break any confidences. But my poor guests find it most restorative.'

'Tell me about them,' said Phryne, as the silent woman reappeared with two bowls of potage Lorraine. It smelled delicious, and was.

'*Merci*, Violette,' said Herbert.

As she disappeared again, Phryne lifted one eyebrow.

'I found her in France and brought her here. Her fiancé and all her family were killed in the war, and she wanted nothing more to do with Europe—or men,' he added.

'But she likes you.'

'Oh yes. But not in that way.' He dropped his eyes for a moment before resuming. 'You know that shell shock is a disease, and not malingering?'

'Indeed I do. I have seen brave men lying in their beds inert and unable to respond.'

'The term is dissociation. They see without seeing and hear without hearing. Sometimes they even lose the power of speech. It took a long while for anyone to understand. They are beaten down by blood, gunfire, and accumulating horror, and the condition can only be cured by prolonged rest and recuperation.'

'Which you provide.'

'Indeed yes. I am also learning…' The Captain looked embarrassed for a moment.

Phryne inclined her chin encouragingly.

'Miss Fisher, have you heard of chiropractic?'

'I am given to understand that it is a controversial topic among the medical profession.'

'It is.' Colour rose in the man's cheeks. He looked at her defiantly, as if daring her to proclaim him a charlatan. 'At least in part, the medical profession is right to be cautious: all manner of quacks claim mystical powers for it, and doubtless there will always be those who do great harm. And yet…'

'And yet you have seen it work?'

'I have!' He leaned back in his chair in relief. 'Miss Fisher—'

'Phryne, please.'

'Phryne, I have seen a man—one of my own patients—all but crippled. Yet within a month of chiropractic treatment he was cured.'

'I am very suspicious of miracle cures.'

To her delight, the man laughed heartily. 'Oh, so am I! The war taught me not to believe in them. Seeing really is believing, however. We had a visit from a chiropractor, an accredited physician who had become disenchanted with conventional medicine. He expounded to me the mysteries of the spine. Have you ever wondered about the human spine, Phryne? It is a miraculous thing in itself: filled with nerves and blood vessels entwined around the vertebrae.'

Phryne raised her glass and stared at the herbal wine. The candlelight illuminated the sweet drink with highlights of emerald and amethyst.

'I believe that the spine is a most delicate piece of machinery,' she suggested. 'And I think healers should be very careful with it.'

'Indeed yes.' The Captain drained his glass and set it down on the damask tablecloth. 'I offered Dr Hansen a permanent position here, but he prefers to be itinerant. But he gave me his textbook on physiology and told me to study it carefully. He also left me three examination papers, with the correct answers in a sealed envelope, and bade me refrain from adjusting spines until I had passed them all. And I shall.'

'Very wise. I understand you also use baths, massage, and quiet? Have you tried music?'

Captain Spencer looked pleased. 'Yes. We encourage our patients to sing, both individually and together. You are staying at the Mooltan, I hear? Then perhaps you have met Aubrey. He has a fine tenor voice. Violette accompanies him on the piano.'

At that point the woman in question appeared to clear away the soup plates, and brought out a bottle of rich, red wine. Herbert drew the cork, poured a little into his glass and sniffed it, nodded, then filled two glasses. As he did this, the main course was brought out.

'And what do we have here?' Phryne enquired.

'Vegetarian loaf, *pommes* Lyonnaise, glazed onions, *épinards au sucre*, and *navets glacés*,' Herbert announced.

'It looks wonderful,' Phryne enthused. If Violette could make spinach and turnips fit for a civilised dinner table, then she really was a cook in a thousand.

Soon Phryne was staring at her miraculously empty platter. As she laid down her fork a slow smile crossed Herbert's manly features. 'You are surprised?'

'I am,' Phryne confessed.

Violette appeared again as if by sorcery. Phryne smiled at her. '*Mille remerciements, Madame. C'etait magnifique.*' Violette smiled briefly and exited.

Phryne turned to the Captain. 'What was in that vegetable loaf? It was delicious.'

'Eggplant, celery, cottage cheese, breadcrumbs, and…sundry other things.' He gestured vaguely in the direction of the kitchen.

In due course, Violette brought out the dessert wine, *crème chocolat* and surprisingly excellent coffee. Phryne and the Captain chatted easily of the sights of Paris. It seemed that he had met Violette there. The sweet, fruity wine was excellent. Herbert's eyes began to shine, and Phryne noticed his eyes constantly upon her. This did not displease her at all. As Violette came to clear away the plates, Phryne addressed her in a low voice, certain that, as the conversation was in the *patois* of Montparnasse, Captain Spencer would not catch a word.

When their exchange was concluded, Herbert rose to his feet. 'Phryne, that was wonderful. Thank you for your charming company.'

Phryne nodded, embraced Violette, and kissed her in the French fashion. To Herbert she extended her gloveless hand for him to kiss, which he did with enthusiasm. At the same time Phryne leaned forward and kissed him on the cheek.

'Thank you, Herbert. I would love to see more of the spa soon.' Phryne considered for a moment. The Daylesford Highland Gathering was tomorrow, and she wanted a good look at the town. On Sunday morning, she would drive Dot to mass at the local church. Phryne had no intention of accompanying her. 'Herbert, are you open on Sundays?'

The Captain raised an eyebrow. 'Observance of the Sabbath is a little more relaxed in these parts,' he commented with a slow smile, 'so yes, we are open on Sunday morning. We find that organised religion does not sit well with our patients. I think perhaps they are surfeited with metaphysical comforts which, alas…'

'Have failed to comfort sufficiently,' Phryne suggested. 'I would be delighted to see you on Sunday morning then, if that is convenient. Shall we say nine o'clock?'

'Perfect. Shall I walk you home?' he asked.

Phryne shook her head. 'It's not far, but I'd like to listen to the forest for a little.' *By myself*, she added silently. *Not that you aren't extremely pleasant company.*

She walked back to the Mooltan, carefully placing one foot in front of the other. The road was rutted and uncertain, and darkness had fallen. There were no streetlights, but the stars were bright enough to cast a faerie shimmer over the forest. She heard night-birds fluttering, and the grunt of a koala. She smiled, thinking how very much at odds with the creature's cuddly body was its throaty voice. Phryne had been offered a koala to hold once, and the creature had dug in all its claws and widdled down her dress. Never again. Beneath all the other sounds was the whisper of the creek. Even in late summer there was water here. In Australia, this was almost unheard of. She now understood why people who moved here could not be shifted. If she ever got tired of city life, she might well consider it. But that would be in a far distant future.

Phryne wondered about her host. If he truly were what he seemed, he was a very good man—one whose enterprise she was inclined to support. And Violette? She smiled. There was a good deal going on at Hepburn Springs of which Captain Spencer was blissfully unaware.

Chapter Six

It is their care in all the ages to take the buffet and
    cushion the shock.
It is their care that the gear engages; it is their care
    that the switches lock.
It is their care that the wheels run truly; it is their
    care to embark and entrain,
Tally, transport, and deliver duly the Sons of Mary
    by land and main.

—Rudyard Kipling, *The Sons of Martha*

'Ruthie? What's happened?' Hugh Collins was on his feet in a moment. His chair clattered to the floor, where it lay unregarded until Mrs Butler quietly restored it to a sense of decorum. Ruth ran straight to Jane and hugged her tightly. Jane, somewhat at a loss, rummaged in her memory for appropriate responses. She decided upon a main course of There There It's All Right, with added sweet nothings.

This did not go as well as she had hoped. Ruth turned a teary face to Hugh. 'What sort of girl?' she demanded.

Hugh Collins stared at her, somewhat horror-stricken, put down his fork, and looked towards Mrs Butler for elucidation.

'It's all right, Mr Hugh. One of their school friends has gone missing, that's all. What is it, Tinker?' she added.

Tinker had dropped his dessert spoon on the floor and was looking suddenly unwell.

'Nothing, Mrs B. Just—well, I can see why Ruth was so upset.'

Hugh Collins gave Tinker a searching look. Having signally failed to provide comfort by word, Jane put her right arm around Ruth's shoulders and hugged her. Ruth sobbed into Jane's neck, now weeping uncontrollably. Jane looked over Ruth's head. 'Please describe the deceased, Detective Sergeant,' she requested.

Hugh blinked. 'Really, Jane, I'm sure you don't need to hear the details.'

'I'm perfectly sure I do,' Jane retorted. 'It's ten to one your corpse looks nothing like Claire, and so we can rest easy about her. Please, tell us what the dead girl looked like.'

'Well, if you insist. She was, let's see, about five feet two, broad-ish shoulders for a girl, pale skin, with a few spots on her face and nose, dark hair in a long plait, and there was a pair of horn-rimmed glasses around her neck. They'd fallen off, but were attached by a cord—' But Hugh Collins got no further, for a renewed wail arose from Ruth, and he desisted.

Thereafter, events moved quickly. Claire's parents were contacted, and agreed to meet Hugh at the city morgue at eight o'clock. Ruth and Jane went to bed, and Tinker disappeared to his shed out the back. It was nearly ten o'clock when Hugh returned, grumpy, tired, and in the lowest of spirits.

Jane met him in the kitchen. 'Well?' she demanded. 'What news?'

Hugh Collins looked at her sadly. 'I'm so sorry. I wish there was something I could say to make it better, but there isn't anything in the world I can think of.'

'No, there really isn't. I'm sorry you had to tell us about it, but we needed to know.'

In Hugh's eyes, Jane suddenly looked terribly grown-up. 'Will you deliver the news to Ruth?' he asked.

'I have to. She's pretending to be asleep, but I know she isn't. I can't keep her waiting.' And with a curt nod, Jane departed.

The back door opened silently, and Hugh nodded to himself. He was reluctant to knock on the door of Tinker's shed, but they needed to talk. That Tinker was perfectly well aware of this and had volunteered his presence was, Hugh thought, a positive sign. He beckoned Tinker into a chair and sat down opposite him.

'Tinker, what was all that about?'

Tinker, feeling that this would be a good career move, decided to give Hugh the honest, manly stare of the born liar.

Hugh, who had seen it before, raised him with a lifted eyebrow. 'Maybe I'm imagining things,' he continued, 'but you had an awfully guilty look when I told the girls about the body. And you dropped your spoon. You're not clumsy, Tinker. Not ever, so far as I know. What's going on?'

Tinker moved smoothly into avoidance of eye contact, which also failed to impress. Seeing this, he decided on a partial confession. 'I was down on the docks, and I saw the body.'

There was a thunderous silence, broken only by the arrival of Molly the dog looking for uneaten fragments of dinner on the floor. Presently there was the sound of satisfied crunching beneath the table.

'I see. And what did you do then, Tinker?'

'There were men there and they told me to go home. They said they'd call the cops.'

'So you went home?'

'Yair.'

Hugh rolled his eyes and thumped the table. A teacup clattered in its saucer. Hugh reached out to stop it from falling but it tumbled off the table and smashed on the floor. Molly retreated, carrying her unofficial supper with her.

'Never mind, I'll clean it up later. Tinker, when you give anyone in authority that look straight in the eye, it only means one thing: you're about to let rip with a total whopper. Now, nobody thinks you drowned the girl—not that we know how she came to be dead yet. That comes after the autopsy. I want to know what you were doing down on the bloody wharves, Tinker. Don't mess me around. Out with it!'

Tinker stared at the table in front of him for a moment. 'I was there with some men,' he ventured. 'We were talking about the waterfront strike.'

'I see. And would these men have names?'

'I expect so.'

'Jesus bloody Christ, Tinker. I've had a really rotten day and you're not helping. If you were on the wharves with Bert and Cec, you don't have to deny it. I don't mind what they were doing. They could be smuggling in diamond tiaras for distressed orphans for all I care. This is a murder investigation; I don't care about dodgy wristwatches, I am completely indifferent to sly grog and have a total lack of interest in stuff which fell off the back of a ship. Now for the last time, were you there on the wharf with Bert and Cec when the body was discovered?'

There was an infinitesimal pause while Tinker thought about this. 'Yes.'

Collins breathed an animated sigh of relief. 'Finally! And were the three of you together, in company, all the time leading up to this moment?'

Tinker agreed that this was indeed the case.

For approximately how long?

About an hour.

And they had only gone to that particular wharf because, as it might be, a certain vehicular conveyance which might possibly belong to them was parked there? And had Bert and Cec done a runner because they were reluctant to have their taxi inspected by inquisitive police officers?

These were not inconceivable theories as to what might have occurred. With increasing confidence, Tinker gave an affirmative to each of these, and Hugh leaned back in his chair and smiled.

'Because you see, Tinker, not that any of you actually need alibis, but in case you did…' Hugh Collins hesitated, thinking over his first day on the job with Acting Detective Inspector Fraser. 'Just in case you did, all three of you are your own alibis. Unless someone got it into their heads that you were all in it together, of course, but I don't think that's going to be anybody's theory. So you met them straight after school?'

Tinker nodded. 'We were all together from about three forty.'

'And you found the body floating in the water at four thirty-five quite unexpectedly, because whatever you were doing on the wharf, it wasn't looking for deceased girls. All right, Tinker, you can go to bed, and so will I. This has not been one of the better days of my life, but with any luck tomorrow will be a brand-new, shiny, upstanding sort of a day which we may salute with enthusiasm and eagerness for the fray.'

Tinker nodded his head and rose. 'Goodnight, sir.'

'Night, Tinker.'

Hugh Collins bent down to the floor and fossicked around on the American oilcloth for all the pieces of broken china. The smaller shards cut his fingers twice, but he was past caring. The tin dustpan he ceremonially emptied into the rubbish bin, thinking all the while of spending another bright new day in the company of Acting Detective Inspector Fraser, to whom tonight's inquisition of Tinker would not be broached, save in the unlikely event that it would be necessary. He hoped Dot had enjoyed a better day than he.

———

Having to go to work on Saturday was not something to which Hugh Collins wished to become accustomed. Having to accompany Acting Detective Inspector Fraser was not improving his day. Fraser was a tall, lanky, lantern-jawed individual who wore an expensive brown tailored suit with a thin, navy blue silk necktie. His shoes were of expensive black leather, for he eschewed the commonplace police issue boots. He had been to Scotch College and never allowed anyone to forget it. He had Opinions, which he aired liberally. And he drove a sports car—a 1920 Kissel Gold Bug in tasteful chrome yellow—which was on permanent loan from Daddy. In short, Hugh came reluctantly to the conclusion that even the hints vouchsafed him by Jack Robinson fell altogether short of the direful reality. His new boss was a lathe-turned moron without enough sense to come in out of the rain.

Fraser drove with pedantry, ostentatiously obeying all traffic laws and proceeding at a steady twenty miles an hour up the long hill of Barkers Road. Hugh sat miserably in the passenger seat and stared out the window. The foul aroma of North Richmond gradually faded, to be replaced by the fragrant breezes of the Privileged Classes. They passed the wrought-iron gates of Methodist Ladies' College, and Hugh listened while his superior officer vented his opinion that this vast arena of prime real estate was utterly wasted on educating girls and ought to be given over to property developers who could make some serious money out of it. Hugh had yesterday realised that his best strategy was to make encouraging noises at fifteen-second intervals and allow the dreary rodomontade to wash over his head. In one ear, and out the other.

'Collins? Wake up, you dozy beggar! We're here!'

The car jerked to a halt. Collins adjusted his police helmet, opened the passenger side door, closed it carefully, and looked at his superior officer. 'Ready when you are, sir.'

The house was indeed a mansion. It had bay windows, picture windows, conical turrets, and everything short of battlements. The front verandah could have housed a boutique garden party, and the lush and well-manicured lawn a full-sized one with marquee and bandstand. Exotic blooms teemed in tropical splendour. Both men removed their hats. As Fraser rapped sharply on the knocker, Hugh Collins expected to be received by a butler in full evening dress. However, the massive door was opened by the bereaved mother in person.

'Mrs Knight?' Fraser enquired. 'I'm very sorry to bother you again, but I'd like to interview everybody here.'

Mrs Knight went pale. She was an attractive woman in a plain black dress. Signs of prolonged weeping were evident. She would be around forty, but looked younger save for a few touches of grey in her bobbed black hair.

'Please, do come in,' she murmured, turning back into the house.

Hugh Collins considered the brief frontal view he'd had of the bereaved mother. For a moment there had been a wild burst of irrational hope, immediately replaced by a curtain of self-control. The poor woman!

She led the way down a long hallway, lined on both sides with watercolours. Hugh was no judge of art, but they looked like competent and uninspired landscapes. All My Own Work, no doubt. Hugh made a mental note to ask Mrs Knight some questions about her art. Sometimes witnesses gave away more than they realised when talking about their obsessions. He paused to look at a large panorama of *Melbourne From Studley Park*, which happened to be hung at eye level, and noted the initials H.K. in the bottom right-hand corner.

Mrs Knight led them into a drawing room (there really was no other word for it) and gestured to a pair of deep leather armchairs. 'Would you like some tea?'

Collins was about to say yes, but his superior cut him off. 'No need for that, Mrs Knight. We'd like to know a little more about this sad event, and the days leading up to it.'

Mrs Knight put her hand on her breast. 'Yes, of course. Anything I can do to help, obviously.'

Hugh Collins's mind began to wander as Fraser went through his checklist of Interrogation And How Not To Do It. The only useful facts that Fraser managed to elicit were that the house had had only four permanent inhabitants: Mr and Mrs Knight, Claire, and Gerald, who appeared to be Mrs Knight's ne'er-do-well brother. There were a number of gardeners and servants who came and went, but none who were employed full time. The gardeners were two men in their fifties and a half-witted boy who helped out. Yes, the halfwit was under constant supervision, and no, none of the gardeners had any access to the house.

Finally Fraser held up his right hand as if on traffic duty and nodded his head. 'Thank you, Mrs Knight. That's all I need, I think. If you can give Collins here the names and addresses of the gardeners and other hired help, I'll get him to interview them. Now, this Gerald...your brother, you said? Is he home at the moment?'

Mrs Knight nodded. 'He'll be upstairs in his study. Shall I take you there?'

'No need. I'll go and surprise him.'

Mrs Knight's mouth opened and then closed, as if she wasn't quite sure she'd heard correctly. 'Second door on the right,' she managed, in an even voice. 'Please do knock, Inspector.'

'I will.' And with a clattering of shoes Fraser was off up the polished stairs.

'Well, really!' Mrs Knight pronounced in a barely audible voice. She looked at Collins, who was practising his Sympathetic Policeman expression.

'I'm sorry, Mrs Knight,' he managed. 'Inspector Fraser can be a little abrupt.'

'Never mind, I'm sure he's a Fine Officer.' The last two words were said as though they rhymed with Scum and Vermin. She sat up straight in her chair. 'Well, Sergeant, you'll be wanting those names and addresses, won't you?'

Collins leaned forward. 'Just before you do that, Mrs Knight, I was wondering... Those pictures in the hall are very good. Are they yours?'

She relaxed visibly. 'My little hobby. They're nothing special, of course. But I did study at the Slade, and it seems wrong not to use all the gifts God gave me.'

'I think you're being unduly modest, Mrs Knight. They look very fine to me. But what I wanted to know was if you have done any recent paintings of Claire?' Hugh was trying not to look at a bare patch on the wall above her chair, where a picture hook was sitting forlornly, surrounded by yet more landscapes.

Mrs Knight blushed. 'That is very observant of you, Sergeant. I took it down last night. I can't bear to look at it yet. I will, in time. When my heart heals over. If it ever does.' A tear meandered down her right cheek. She produced a lace handkerchief and wiped it away. 'Do you want to see it?'

'Yes, please. It may be important.'

Mrs Knight went upstairs and presently returned, cradling

a picture in her arms as if it were a baby. Collins stood up and accepted the picture with appropriate reverence.

'I painted this only last month. It's rather good, isn't it?' Another tear escaped and was as efficiently wiped away.

'Mrs Knight, it's a brilliant picture. And if I may make so bold, I think you should do more portraits. May I borrow this?'

'Please do! I will want it back eventually, but if—if it can help solve this mystery—then yes, you can have it.' She went to a drawer in a massive, polished wood escritoire in the corner of the room and returned with a roll of brown paper. She deftly wrapped the painting in three layers of brown paper and tied it with string in a neat double bow. 'Do look after it, please. But I'm sure you will, Sergeant.' Her eyes lifted to the top of the stairs, where voices could be perceived on the edge of hearing. She tutted. 'I really don't know what's keeping your colleague up there. It isn't as if Gerald knows anything about this. And his constitution is very weak. He shouldn't be bothered more than is necessary.'

'I'm sure the inspector won't be much longer, Mrs Knight. And I do apologise for disturbing you at such a sorrowful time.'

This drew a brisk nod, and Mrs Knight subsided into a chair. Hugh seated himself, clutching his precious parcel in one hand and his hat in the other. 'Oh!' she exclaimed. 'I'm so sorry. The names and addresses.' She strode back to the escritoire, took a sheet of paper and began to write. As she approached him with the list, the clattering on the stairs announced the second coming of Acting Detective Inspector Fraser, who swept into the drawing room.

'Thank you, Mrs Knight,' he announced regally. 'I think I've got everything I need here. I'll be in touch.'

'Oh, please do.'

It was astonishing how much concentrated loathing you could pack into three syllables, Hugh observed. If Fraser heard the implied reproach, he ignored it.

'Come on, Collins. We've got work to do.' Fraser resumed his hat, lifted it towards their hostess, and they trooped out to the car. 'What've you got there, Collins?'

'It's a painting of the deceased, sir. I thought it might be useful.'

Fraser shook his head. 'Have it your own way, Collins. Just don't waste time on it. I think we've got our man. I haven't got enough to arrest him yet, but I'll get it, never fear.'

'Um, arrest whom, sir?'

'Gerald, you idiot. Of course it's him! Who else could it be? If the coroner finds out she was pregnant, I'll make him confess.'

'Right, sir.'

As they motored back to the station, Hugh rolled his eyes. From what he had seen in Mrs Knight's portrait of her daughter, the girl might indeed have had a romantic interest in her life. He couldn't be sure yet. It was an unlikely idea, but not nearly as improbable as the idea that a girl might conceive a romantic attachment to her stay-at-home uncle. Gerald might conceivably have taken advantage of the girl, but since Mrs Knight did not appear to have the word *idiot* tattooed on her face, that was beyond the limits of normal possibilities. Until he had some facts to work with, there was no point theorising any further. Fraser would instruct him to interview the casual staff, and he would do so. You never knew what might turn up from there.

Chapter Seven

They say to mountains, 'Be ye remov'd.' They say to
the lesser floods, 'Be dry.'
Under their rods are the rocks reprov' d; they are not
afraid of that which is high.
Then do the hilltops shake to the summit, then is the
bed of the deep laid bare,
That the Sons of Mary may overcome it, pleasantly
sleeping and unaware.

—Rudyard Kipling, *The Sons of Martha*

'Miss Phryne, the Highland Gathering doesn't start till two. Where are we heading first?'

Phryne looked carefully at Dot, who was once again dressed almost entirely in shades of brown. It was cool for late summer, and Dot was taking no chances with the weather; she was adorned in woollen jumper, woollen dress, woollen scarf, and felt hat. Phryne, on the other hand, was a picture in shades of Picasso blues. Her cloche hat (aquamarine) was perched at a rakish angle; her slate blue jacket wrapped closely around her elegant figure;

and she was well prepared to outrage local sensibilities in cobalt blue trousers. Her boots were flat-heeled, thick-soled, and suitable for walking across ploughed fields were this to prove necessary. She grinned. 'Pub first, Dot. Let's take a look at this Temperance Hotel, shall we?'

'If you say so, Miss.'

Dot climbed into the passenger seat and Phryne engaged the clutch. Dot had eaten a hearty breakfast of eggs, bacon, toast and marmalade, fruit compote, and several cups of thick, sweet tea. Even Phryne had partaken somewhat, against her usual practice. She decided it must be the mountain air giving her such an appetite.

Phryne drove sedately through Hepburn and up the long hill towards Daylesford. In the light of the late morning, it looked every bit as splendid as it had the day before. Lovingly tended gardens were adorned with autumn flowers. Roses and lavender were currently predominant, though many other blooms sat in ordered beds looking eminently pleased with themselves. Standing in the centre of the road, officiously directing traffic, was Sergeant Offaly. Phryne gave him a grin and a wave and was rewarded with a scowl that might have stripped the paint off a letterbox.

'It's just off the main road, Dulcie tells me,' Phryne remarked, and peeled off a punctilious left-turn hand signal. Normally she did not bother with such matters, but this was for the sergeant's benefit. She pulled up next to the kerb and put the handbrake on. The Temperance Hotel was a two-storeyed oblong erection with a white wooden verandah running the length of both levels. Wrought-iron lacework was strongly in evidence. An impressive horse trough (three-quarters full) stood out the front next to a painted hitching-post. A painted signboard above the entrance announced that Frederick McKenzie, Esq. was licensed to sell alcoholic beverages. From within, the scent of fresh wood polish jostled with that of unwashed workman. The hotel was plainly of some antiquity: its sandstone building bespoke Gold Rush from every mortice.

With Dot following in her wake, Phryne breezed into the main bar. Polished floorboards shone in sombre splendour. There were roses in vases on mantelpieces in front of mirrors and shapely lamps. Gleaming glasses of varying size and design stood in serried ranks behind the mahogany bar, which looked strong enough to repel tanks and Visigoths. It was far lighter within than in the pubs of Melbourne, Phryne observed. Large windows let in the daylight and rendered the glowing lamps all but redundant. All that was missing were the rows of spirits behind the bar, although there were many bottles of wine. She would ask to try some at lunch.

Phryne had entered public bars before. Most were rudimentary places wherein the urban proletariat were wont to unwind after a hard day at the factory. Primeval squalor was the rule rather than the exception. The Temperance Hotel might have passed in poor light for the interior of the Windsor Hotel. She took a quick look around the bar. Three or four young men sat quietly, nursing surprisingly small glasses of beer. They were unusually quiet and restrained, and spoke only in undertones. Her eyes rested on a table, where an ancient, be-whiskered son of toil jerked a grimy thumb to his left.

'Ladies' lounge is that way, Miss.'

Phryne patted his unsavoury paw encouragingly with her gloved hand. 'Yes, dear, I'm sure it is.'

Bleared hazel eyes looked to the bar for support, but found none.

'She's a guest in town, Mr Trescowan. Can't you tell?' The voice was pitched lower than usual for a female but seemed to ooze attar of roses. The horny ancient avoided the barmaid's gaze and subsided back into the contemplation of his half-empty beer glass.

Phryne waved Dot to a table against the wall and strode up to the bar. She looked, and gaped. Surely this must be the paragon herself. The girl wore a long, dark green dress straight out of the nineteenth century, with a bodice and under-chemise that altogether failed to disguise her magnificent bosom, though it was laced up with becoming modesty. There was, needless to add, a frilly apron so resplendently white it might have glowed in the dark. Her hair was equally retrospective: unfashionably long and wrapped in two French plaits. Unbound, the girl's hair would be a golden waterfall. Her complexion was milky white; her features even, oval, and consonant; her eyes a startling dark agate; and her expression... Phryne felt, for the first time in a long while, utterly unsure. Was there anything behind the girl's eyes at all beyond a bovine complacency?

Phryne smiled at her. 'Hello, I'm Phryne Fisher. And you must be Annie?'

'I'm very pleased to meet you. Staying here long?' There was something in the voice that made you want to listen to her all day. A little bit West Country, and a little bit Scots.

'A few days. This is a beautiful town. And I've heard so much about you—and this hotel,' Phryne added hastily.

The girl's laugh was like a peal of small silver bells. 'I'm sure you have.'

Phryne looked more closely at her. The girl was laughing at herself, it seemed.

'Well, Annie, I'd like a glass of your best cider, and my companion Dot would like a lemon squash.'

'Certainly.'

The cider was on tap, Phryne noticed, nestling equably between a row of beers of varying denominations. The girl drew a long glass of foaming cider, then produced a glass bottle of lemon cordial and began to assemble a squash with practised hands. Even the girl's hands and arms were perfectly shaped and pristine. Phryne was accustomed to being the centre of male attention, but she would never be that in the Temperance Hotel so long as Annie were on the premises.

The paragon looked up at Phryne. 'That will be sixpence half-penny, please.'

Phryne handed her a shilling. 'Do keep the change, Annie. And can we get lunch here?'

The girl looked at the shilling and smiled. The smile of Gentle Annie could have illuminated a forty-acre field. And Phryne realised, with a jolt of surprise, that it was perfectly genuine. This extraordinary girl would have the world falling over itself to offer her apes, ivory, and peacocks, yet every time it happened her reaction would be that of a small girl with an unexpected birthday cake.

'Oh, yes, lunch starts at noon. Would the ladies' lounge be more convenient for you and your…companion?' Her eyebrows furrowed for a moment. They were much darker than her hair: almost Spanish-looking.

'By all means. But until then—' Phryne looked at the ancient grandfather clock in the corner of the bar, which promptly announced the hour of eleven with a series of bass tympani gongs '—we shall sit here and admire the view. I love your dress.'

Annie dimpled. 'It was my mother's. She used to wear it on duty here. I like it.'

'I expect it gets rough here at times?'

Annie shook her head. Phryne could almost feel the spines of the admiring lads vibrating in sympathy. 'No, Miss Fisher, every-one is very well-behaved here. It's only me, my sister Jessie, and my cousin Peggy. Uncle is—' there was the slightest hesitation

'—unwell. The war, you know. But Mr McAlpine comes in later on to keep an eye on things, just in case. But like I said, we rarely have any trouble.' Again the unearthly smile. 'If you're going to the Gathering later, you can see Kenneth tossing the caber. It's not really a competition, because, well, nobody else can even lift it. But it's quite a sight. And if anybody did think of causing trouble, they'll remember the caber.'

'I'll be sure not to miss that. Thank you, Annie.' Phryne turned on her heel, gave Mr Trescowan a dazzling smile, and brought the drinks to Dot's table. 'Well, Dot. We have an hour until lunch. What do you think?'

Dot looked nervously at the hunched, brooding slopes of Mount Trescowan. 'I think I'd like to have a look around before lunch, Miss.' She sipped at her drink. 'My, this is really good! I've never tasted a lemon squash like it.'

Annie sailed past their table in a rustle of skirts. 'That's because we add the local mineral water to it, Miss. It's supposed to be very good for you.'

Dot's eyes followed Annie as she collected an armful of empty glasses. There were three or four young men in the bar, and they had spoken not a word. Their eyes followed Annie as though they were on stalks. One youth in particular was staring at her with an expression of such longing in his angular, blotched face that Phryne wondered who he was. Annie smiled at them all in turn and returned to her place behind the bar.

Phryne tasted the cider. It was a little tart, but filled with apple flavour, and something else. Maybe a touch of pear? They sipped their drinks and watched. A faint smell of wood smoke wafted through the room. Presumably the kitchen was preparing for lunch.

Two more young men strolled in and joined the others in quiet contemplation. Annie greeted them by name, and their faces lit up like storm lanterns. As they watched her go about her work with quiet efficiency, Phryne was reminded of dogs watching a tennis match.

'Miss, perhaps we could have a little walk? I'd like to buy something for Hugh.'

Phryne finished her drink and followed Dot out the door. 'We'll be back at noon,' she said over her shoulder.

Outside the morning was bright, though cloudy, and filled with purpose. Housewives walked past them carrying string bags filled with groceries. Children scampered along the footpaths and were herded fitfully by their mothers. And sturdy men strode the pavement as though heading for a public meeting to complain about the drains. Phryne paused on the verge of the surprisingly steep stone gutters and admired the town hall. Like much else of the local architecture, it was built of sandstone, yet instead of the customary ochre the building was—like many others in the street—a becoming shade of light grey verging towards ecru.

Most Victorian towns boasted preposterously grandiose municipal buildings, but there was something exceedingly dapper about this one. Two storeys, each with seven Romanesque arches. The only criticism she could make of the imposing edifice was that its six plain oblong pillars were capped with Corinthian capitals. However, the entire colony of Victoria had fallen head over ears in love with acanthus leaves, so the extravagance seemed allowable. And beneath the triangular pediment above the main entrance, the words TOWN HALL were inscribed in sensible sans-serif letters. This building had been commissioned, constructed, and cherished by locals with considerable artistic sensibility. Doubtless something Greek and mathematical lurked behind its pleasing proportions.

Opposite was a building which was still under construction but bid fair to be a worthy adversary to the monolithic town hall. It was built of the same pleasing grey stone, with miniscule towers at either end and no less than eight Romanesque arches above a triple window. Two more oblong windows flanked the centrepiece. It was a brand-new cinema, constructed in a style which matched the town hall. A substantial wooden sign outside proclaimed: GRAND OPENING FRIDAY NIGHT. In smaller letters the legend *March 1st* could be discerned, in case there was any doubt about which Friday was intended. The film would be called *Benito's Treasure*. Phryne's mouth opened in surprise. No Hollywood offcuts here: the film had been made in Queenscliff. She remembered well the excitement attached thereto during her own visit to the seaside town in search of the Dead Man's Chest. It was during that adventure she had acquired Tinker, who had well repaid Phryne's trust in him and made himself useful about the house and elsewhere.

Clustered around the soon-to-be-open cinema were more shops: a most sophisticated-looking tailor offering off-the-peg and bespoke, and a couturier whose window would not have disgraced the most fashionable parts of Melbourne. To the downhill side of the cinema was a newsagent, and uphill an ice-cream parlour. It was three-quarters filled, even at this time of day and with many rival attractions.

Phryne considered the couturier again. Her only reservation about shopping there was that the favoured shade this year seemed to be variations of gold, which she eschewed in favour of silver. The milliner next door to it, on the other hand, might well repay a visit. She opened the door, which produced a tintinnabulation at the back of the shop. 'Hello, Miss,' said a young woman. 'I'm Sophie.' She waved a plump, be-ringed hand at her stock. 'What sort of hat takes your fancy?'

Phryne admired a number of creations. All were tasteful rather than opulent, and mostly darker shades, with splashes of colour.

On a stand beside the counter rested a splendid dark crimson cloche with a spray of artificial fuchsias. A miniscule card attached by a length of fine cotton announced to the browser that the hat was available for purchase at one pound and three shillings. 'Dot? What do you think?'

Her companion had not, however, followed her inside the shop. She found Dot staring through the window from the street, plainly coveting a chocolate brown hat not dissimilar to a gentleman's hat and adorned with a bunch of imitation petunias. Phryne grinned at her through the window and beckoned with her finger.

Dot entered the shop with reluctance. 'Miss Phryne, I was just looking.'

'And I am just buying, Dot. I'm having this one.' She indicated the cloche. 'I'll take this, please, Sophie, and my companion will have the brown in the window with the petunias.'

Sophie disappeared for a moment and returned with two hexagonal boxes of Prussian blue cardboard. She turned back to Phryne and the now thoroughly discomfited Dot. 'That will be two pounds and sixpence, Miss.'

'Miss Phryne, I was only window-shopping,' she whispered in an agony of embarrassment.

'Don't be silly, Dot. You wanted it, didn't you? Well, it's yours.' She turned back to Sophie and handed over two pound notes and a sixpence. 'Thank you. I love your shop.'

Sophie grinned as she played upon the keys of her cash register, which rang out its merry carillon of another sale completed. 'Thank you, Miss. Staying here long?'

'Just for the week.'

Having stowed the hatboxes in the boot of the Hispano-Suiza, Phryne walked slowly on towards the summit of the hill. Most of the stores were exactly what one would have expected to find: two-storeyed with verandahs. There were butchers and bakers (but no candlestick makers). There were banks which oozed stone-ground solidity and Victorian virtue. There was a grocer. Some of the buildings looked very much like the town hall's younger siblings: similar in architecture but not as grandiose.

Dot caught her arm. 'Look, there's a teashop! May we stop here, Miss Phryne?'

The shop was long and narrow, and womaned by a brisk, middle-aged personage with a mottled face and hair in a greying bob. She also sold chocolates, and Dot bought two packets: one for herself and one for Hugh. Dot's tea was bergamot-flavoured, and Phryne ordered coffee which turned out to be astonishingly good by Australian standards. She recollected that Italians from the Dolomites had been featured among the early settlers hereabouts.

They sat at a small wooden table and Dot sipped her tea with content.

'What do you think of the Temperance Hotel, Dot?' Phryne asked.

Dot put down her cup. 'Miss, it makes me uncomfortable. I don't know how she puts up with it.'

'The wall-to-wall Adoration of the Magi? I think I could get used to it.' Phryne leaned forward. 'What else did you notice, Dot?'

'I wonder who does all the work.'

'So do I. There is sister Jessie, who will probably serve us lunch. There was a cousin mentioned—Peggy. And you heard her refer to what seems to be a shell-shocked uncle, though he may just be a drunk. I didn't see any adult males on the strength doing anything useful. Well, we shall see.'

———

Lunch in the Temperance Hotel's ladies' lounge was indeed served by sister Jessie, who was so utterly unlike Annie that Phryne would have guessed at two different mothers and possibly three different fathers. She was tall and slight, though the muscles on her forearms looked sinewy and tough beneath her sleeves. She wore navy blue trousers, flat-heeled leather boots, and a green buttoned tunic, disdaining all fripperies of the aproned variety. Her face was pale and freckled by the sun, her eyes turquoise, and her hair brick-red, curly, and cropped short like a boy's. She exuded an air of brisk happiness with undertones of serious overwork. Phryne ordered roast chicken, with crème brulée to follow, and a half-bottle of white wine.

'And what would you like, Dot?'

Dot stared at the menu, which appeared to have a strong flavour of Foreign. She was briefly tempted by *entrecote de boeuf*, but didn't feel like risking it in case it turned out to be oven-baked overcoats. 'I'll have what you're having, Miss Phryne.'

Jessie's eyes sharpened. 'Are you Phryne Fisher? Sorry, that's a bit abrupt. I just wondered, that's all. I'm Jessie.' Her voice had become more Scots-flavoured, especially around the *w*-sound, which emerged as *hw*- from between her thin, pale lips.

Phryne inclined her chin. 'Yes, I am. Why do you ask?'

'Miss Fisher, I've heard of you.' Jessie turned to take in the three other tables with waiting guests. 'If you wouldn't mind, I would like to talk to you later on, when I'm not so busy.'

'By all means, Jessie. We're not in a hurry.'

While waiting for their lunch, Phryne admired the decor. It mirrored the main bar, though with added pictures on the pastel-painted walls. They appeared to be local vistas. Eucalypts, lavender, and rose gardens predominated. She looked harder at what she had first assumed to be prints and saw they were in fact framed watercolour paintings, clearly all executed by the same hand. One of them showed the Temperance Hotel on a rainy spring day. In the one nearest to her, the signature *Agnes Tremain* could be made out in spidery copperplate.

'They're pretty pictures, Miss Phryne,' Dot ventured.

'They are, Dot. And painted, I would guess, by Annie and Jessie's mother, or possibly an aunt.'

'My late mother.' Jessie had reappeared with a bottle and two glasses. 'This is a local wine, Miss Fisher. I hope you like it.'

'I'm sorry for your loss,' Phryne murmured. 'She was a fine artist.'

Phryne sniffed her capacious rounded glass, into which Jessie had, in the approved sommelier manner, poured a smidgeon. 'This is seriously good, Jessie. Citrus, and hints of stone fruit. Yes, please: pour away, and do not cease pouring until this half-bottle is quite exhausted.'

Seeing Jessie's eye glance upon Dot, Phryne raised an enquiring eyebrow. Dot shook her head with a smile. She had a glass of mineral water with a slice of lemon and two ice cubes floating moodily in it, and she had not the slightest desire to embroil her constitution with the fruit of the vine, however sumptuous.

When Jessie had finished pouring, Phryne held her glass up to the light and nodded. 'So many whites seem rather ashamed of themselves. This one doesn't hide its light under a bushel. This is as full-bodied a white as I have seen on these shores.'

Jessie nodded. 'I think Peggy has your chicken ready. I'll go fetch it now.'

Their chicken had, until its untimely end, plainly been raised in a health spa and waited on hand and foot by muscular attendants. The accompanying vegetables (potatoes marinated in oil and rosemary, two flavours of pumpkin, and string beans) were everything that could be wished for.

'Miss Phryne, this is wonderful.'

'It really is. Truly, we have come to the land of Canaan.'

'Yes. I saw dairy cows on the way here, and there are farms selling honey as well.'

Phryne smiled, and returned to her meal. A land of milk and honey, verily.

Their table was the last to be cleared away. As Jessie approached, Phryne gave her a winning look. The waitress paused, watching as the other guests sauntered out of the lounge. When only Phryne and Dot remained, she returned her attention to the former. 'Miss Fisher, I'm worried about my sister,' she stated without preamble.

'What in particular is concerning you, Jessie? Is it the look on the faces of the local boys, all of whom appear to have been in receipt of a large steam engine in the small of their backs?'

Jessie grinned. 'You noticed that? Well, you couldn't miss it, could you?' She drew a deep breath. 'I don't think anyone will offer her harm. There would be unfortunate consequences if they did.'

'Would this be our redoubtable caber tosser?'

'No. Kenneth is a good man. The worst he would do is drop them in a lake somewhere.' She showed her teeth. 'I, on the other hand, would skin them with a blunt knife. I love my sister dearly, but she thinks everyone is as good and kind as she is. And I don't think all of them are. I'm worried, Miss Fisher. Things have happened and I'm not convinced—well, the local polisman is not precisely...'

Jessie was clearly struggling between candour and decorum, and Phryne decided to help her out. 'Jessie, you don't have to be polite. I've met him.'

Some colour filtered into the girl's pale cheeks. 'Very well. But I would be grateful if you would keep an eye on things while you're here.'

'All right, Jessie. Now I have a question of my own. This is a big hotel. Surely you and your sister don't run it all by yourself? I know there's Peggy in the kitchen, for a start.'

'Peggy's my cousin. Her grandma is Aunty Morag McKenzie, who brought us up. Father was killed at Villers-Bretonneux, and Mother died soon after.'

'And the licensee, Frederick McKenzie, Esquire?'

Jessie looked around for eavesdroppers. Finding none, she leaned forward with a grimace. 'He was wounded in the war, but that's no excuse for being a lazy, useless drunk. I'm sorry, Miss—' her fine, almost transparent eyelashes fluttered '—but I get so angry. He should be helping and he won't. The three of us have to do everything.' She gathered up their empty plates. 'I'm sorry,' she repeated. 'But sometimes I can't hold it all in.' She blinked at Phryne, embarrassed, and drew herself up. 'That will be seven and six, Miss Fisher.'

Phryne gave her a ten-shilling note and told her to keep the change. 'One moment, Jessie.' Phryne held up her right index finger. 'You said that things have happened here. Would you care to elaborate?'

Jessie pocketed the ten shillings with a brief nod of thanks and clasped her hands together. 'I don't really know what to think. But there have been disappearances. And—' Jessie seemed about to disclose more information, but apparently thought better of it and shook her head. 'I'm sorry. I have to go.' And with that she swept out of the Ladies' Lounge.

Chapter Eight

Think, in this batter' d Caravanserai
Whose Doorways are alternate Night and Day
How Sultán after Sultán went his Pomp,
Abode his Hour or two, and went his way.

—Edward Fitzgerald, *The Rubáiyát of*
Omar Khayyám of Naishápúr

The one thing universally admitted about bagpipes, Phryne considered, is that they are unsubtle. There are some musical instruments—like lutes, recorders, and spinets—which may safely be unleashed in refined drawing rooms. They hover on the edge of polite conversation. The human ear can take them or leave them alone. By contrast, the pipes rather command attention. A score and a half of them, with as many drummers industriously pounding away two-handed at their skins, could not have been ignored by anyone in the same postal district. They were led by a fearsome-looking drum-major about eight feet six inches tall and nearly as broad across his massive shoulders. The man's black moustache quivered. His darkling eyes flashed thunderbolts. He wielded his mace in two gigantic hands as if suppressing a native rebellion, and wore his bearskin hat with such vast panache that he gave the impression of having eaten the rest of the bear for breakfast, washed down with a pibroch and soda.

The row was deafening. Next to her, Dot put her hands over her ears. This did not seem to help. 'What are they playing, Miss?'

'"Scotland the Brave", I think. It's traditional.'

Dot and Phryne were sitting on the side of the road as the procession passed down the middle of the main street. There was a sudden gust of wind, and Dot blushed scarlet beneath her felt hat, and put her hand to her mouth.

'Dot, what's wrong?'

Dot folded her hands in her lap and looked at the gutter. 'Oh, Miss. I know it's traditional, but I—'

'Inadvertently spotted a certain lack of underclothing on one or more of the pipers, despite your best efforts not to? Never mind, Dot. It is, as you say, traditional.'

They watched the wailing chorus pass on over the brow of the hill.

'And where are they going now?'

'It looks like they're ready to invade Ballarat and reduce it to servitude; but I believe they're going into the school grounds. There is very little flat ground hereabouts, Dot, and I believe the festivities will be on the school oval. Come on. It will be fun.'

By the time they reached the school oval, the pipes and drums had ceased, and Dot felt the sort of relief experienced by those who have been beaten about the head with rubber mallets when those administering the bastinado have downed tools for the afternoon. She cast a quick look at her employer, but Phryne had plainly enjoyed the music. Dot could hear fiddles in the distance, playing what sounded like country dances. Fiddles were just fine as far as she was concerned. Fiddles didn't make you feel as though your eardrums had been turned inside out and scrubbed with lye soap. And she had to admit that everything looked festive indeed. There were tents, from which came the scent of pies and roasted meats. There was enough bunting to encompass a Roman legionary camp. There was a substantial beer tent, with a hand-painted canvas sign reading THE TEMPERANCE HOTEL, LIC. F. MCKENZIE hanging from its hither tent pole. And there were stalls selling everything from boiled sweets to haggises. Dot examined one of the latter from a safe distance and shuddered. It was brown, with overtones of grey, and it lurked like a malevolent beast of prey.

'Don't fancy it, Dot? I'm told that, prepared properly, it can be quite palatable.'

Dot turned to her employer. 'If you say so, Miss.'

Phryne laughed. 'I know. It looks as if it's designed to be a battlefield projectile.'

Her eye was drawn to a wooden podium at one side of the oval. Light wooden chairs were drawn up in military-grade ranks in front of it, and the seats were filling up rapidly with tartan-clad locals. Flagpoles at either side bore the Australian flag, and the blue-and-white saltire of Scotland. 'It appears there will be speeches. Inevitable, I expect, but we don't have to listen to them. I can see a mayor, complete with gold-plated chain of office. Is he going to open proceedings, I wonder?'

But pride of place had been given to a fearsome-looking man in a tight collar and a jet-black coat, who lifted both clenched hands in the air and began like a minor prophet denouncing sin among the Tribes of Israel. His address was hearkened to with considerable respect, although it was doubtful how much of it got in among his audience, since it was uttered in what Phryne could only assume was Scots Gaelic. The appreciation was perhaps what was offered to divers or gymnasts: so many points for general style, with marks deducted for misplaced semaphore.

'Well, I'm sure that's impressing everyone here, Dot, but I feel like a drink and a sit-down. Shall we go to the beer tent? I'm sure there'll be lemon squash, and I sincerely hope there will be chairs. Tables, too, if we're lucky.'

———

Within the voluminous beer tent were all of these, and Dot and Phryne sat in relative comfort. Through the open canvas tent flap could be heard the voice of His Worship thanking the minister for his truly Highland welcome. Phryne had a glass of the local white wine she had already sampled at lunch and looked about her. Gentle Annie was serving beer to a group of awed young men from behind a trestle table, and a man limped towards them with open palms, clearly requesting an audience. Phryne beckoned, and the newcomer settled down in the third of the four chairs at their small square deal table.

'You must be Miss Fisher. My name is McKenzie. I believe you came to lunch at my hotel?'

'I did, Mr McKenzie. And may I introduce my companion, Dorothy Williams?'

His dark eyes flickered over Dot, and he nodded. 'Pleased to meet you.' His voice was unmistakably Highland Scots, and ancient sorrow was written all over it.

'The hospitality of your hotel was exceptional, Mr McKenzie. You are to be congratulated on your…nieces, I believe?'

McKenzie gave her a momentary sharp look and bowed his unshaven chin. There were patches of white in the stubble, and in the unkempt sandy hair. His face was pale, haunted, and, while it had been scrubbed to a bright sheen, the low-water mark of his ablutions could be detected below his open collar. A morose drunk in truth, as reported by the exasperated Jessie, Phryne concluded. But not a stupid one. The implied reproach in Phryne's congratulation had not gone unnoticed.

'Ach, well. I have a wound from the war, and I am not as quick on my feet as once I was. But they are good girls, both of them. Their mother was my sister, and she perished in childbed after her man was killed in battle.'

'And your wound?' Phryne prompted, wondering what the man wanted with her.

'In the same battle, at a place called Villers-Breton. It was a bad fight, and many of our men did not return. But a victory for our side over the heathen Gairmans.'

'It was. Have you lived here all your life, Mr McKenzie?'

The innkeeper shook his shaggy head. 'My grandfather was on the hell ship. The *Ticonderoga* set out from England with eight hundred Highlanders thrown off their crofts during the Clearances. A quarter of them perished on the way. It would have been many more were it not for the ship's doctor. I have forgot his name now, but he was a proper hero. Grandfather settled here, but returned to Scotland after the Crofters' Act of 1886, when the Parliament men gave us our richts.' He brooded for a moment. 'But there are still lairds in Scotland, and here there are none, so my father brought us out in the Year Four, when we were bairns.' His eyes raked over Phryne. 'You are the detective, Miss Fisher, are you not? So you will be here to find the missing women, I expect? Wives have disappeared from farms that need them.'

Phryne lifted an enquiring eyebrow. 'Indeed? I have not heard of any missing women.'

McKenzie opened both hands for a moment. 'Have you not? Well now. My mistake. I thought it must be that.'

'Just a holiday, Mr McKenzie. I am sorry to have disappointed you.' Phryne rose. 'Pleased to have met you,' she announced, sounding anything but. She did not offer her gloved hand, finding of a sudden that she had better uses for it. She swept out of the tent with Dot at her side. 'Well, that was intriguing, Dot, but unedifying,' she remarked when safely out of earshot.

'That Miss Jessie was right,' Dot concurred. 'I didn't like the way he looked at me.'

'Nor me. And I wonder what he meant about disappearing women? Is that what Jessie meant about disappearances? But in that case, why did Jessie want to talk, and then thought better of it? These are mysteries, Dot. Doubtless we shall discover for ourselves in due course. Ah! It appears we are to have Highland dancing. Just what we need after that depressing little colloquy.'

A detachment of pipers and drummers were ranged about the greensward, and the pipe-major flashed a commanding look at his troops. The skirling music broke out once more, and Dot rocked back on her heels. Phryne held firm, interested at once by the youthful dancers footing it featly in their black dancing shoes. They were filled with youthful exuberance, with many a flashing eye cast in the direction of the platoon of admirers of both sexes ranged around them. Tartan kilts appeared to be de rigueur, with numerous patterns doubtless related to the various clans in the vicinity.

One boy in particular caught Phryne's eye: a pleasant-looking lad in his late teens with a suggestion of down upon his brown chin. He was concentrating on his feet and hands, but exchanged a number of excitable glances with a vivacious girl in a green velvet jacket, a dazzling white lace shirt, and what Phryne was tolerably certain was a Black Watch kilt. The girl was a superb dancer, and her white, muscular legs kicked with more brio than the rest. Every twirl of her arms and legs exuded a primitive joyousness. And her eyes were as green as emeralds. Was this a courting couple? Watching them carefully, Phryne decided not.

But they would be close friends, comrades, and (in all probability) co-conspirators in any local high jinks.

Phryne looked sideways at Dot, who was wilting somewhat, and led her silently to a park bench. 'Dot, are you all right?' she enquired.

Dot fanned herself with her hat. 'Yes, Miss, I think so. Bagpipes are somewhat overpowering, though. And I can feel the drums through my shoes.'

They watched several vigorous dances, and the pipes wound down at last. However, the green-eyed girl then stepped forward and kicked off her shoes. She was accompanied by a single piper. She grinned at Phryne while two fearsome-looking swords were laid crossways on the grass. Dot grasped at Phryne's sleeve. 'She's not going to dance over those swords, is she, Miss Phryne?' she gasped in alarm. 'They look very sharp!'

'I believe so, Dot. But she has probably practised this so many times I expect she could manage it with her eyes closed.'

Clearly the girl thought so too. As the pipe played a slow reel, she placed her feet, one after the other, around and between the swords in a counterclockwise motion. Phryne noticed she never once looked at her feet. Dot relaxed somewhat, thinking for a long moment this was not as perilous as it might have been, but her pulse went overspeed as the tune quickened. The girl capered around the swords, placing her stockinged feet precisely. She winked twice at the beautiful boy, and her sleeves fluttered in the breeze like a challenge to combat.

When the dance finished, the girl bowed, waved to the boy, picked up her dancing shoes, and walked over to Phryne. 'Hello,' she said. 'You two look new in town.'

Phryne rose, leaving Dot to catch her breath on the seat, and extended a gloved hand. 'Phryne Fisher, and this is Miss Williams. Your sword dance was tremendously impressive.'

The girl shook Phryne's hand. 'Colleen O'Rourke.' Seeing

Phryne's eyes widen somewhat, the girl proceeded to explain. 'Yes, I'm Irish. But they let me do Scottish dancing because I'm good at it.' She tilted her head to one side. 'We moved here from Ballarat last year. They kicked me out of Irish dancing up there.'

'Why was that, Colleen?'

The girl smirked, with a flash of her round, emerald eyes. 'For using my arms.'

Phryne laughed. 'You know, I've always wondered about that. Maybe the Ancient Scrolls were missing the page telling you what to do with your arms.'

Colleen laughed, like a beakerful of Irish cream being imbibed. 'I would not be surprised. But I like Daylesford better. People in Ballarat are stuck-up.'

'There don't seem to be many Irish here,' Phryne ventured.

'No, there aren't. But I don't care. I like the Scots boys. They're good fun.' The faintest suspicion of a blush tinged Colleen's angular features, and was as speedily banished.

'I can hear a hint of Ireland in your voice, but I'm guessing your family has been in Australia a while.'

The girl nodded, as if listening to faraway laments. 'My great-grandparents came out during the Great Hunger.'

'That must have been a terrible time. I am so sorry.'

Miss O'Rourke grinned at her. 'No need to be sorry. It's much better here. We Irish can do what we like and nobody stops us.' The girl turned her head, with a flick of her tightly bound black plait. 'There's my dad. He'll be wondering where I've got meself to. Lovely to meet you, Miss Fisher.' Her narrow, charcoal eyebrows crinkled. 'Are you the detective?'

'My infamy seems to precede me everywhere.'

'You'll have plenty to keep you busy then. Loads of secrets here.' She bowed very slightly and nodded to Dot. 'Miss Williams.' And the girl was gone again in a billow of lace.

'I wonder what she meant, Dot?' Phryne mused. 'Is everybody here harbouring secrets? First Jessie, then her uncle, and now Colleen. What is going on here?'

'I don't know, Miss. Perhaps you need to talk to Jessie again?'

'I think so too, Dot.' Phryne noticed that Dot's attention had wandered.

'Miss Phryne? That looks like a travelling library over there. I wonder if I could borrow a book or two?'

Phryne smiled. 'Let's find out, Dot.'

———

The library consisted of a substantial van, with a small cabin at the front. It was parked on the edge of the oval near the entrance road, and the back was open, with a set of three folding stairs leading down to the grassy verge. Business seemed to be brisk. By the expenditure of a shilling Dot became a temporary member, and borrowed a history of the Shire of Hepburn and a detective novel. The library ladies numbered two: a sturdy young girl and a tall, formidable woman of middle years who was clearly In Charge. Her eyes surveyed the patrons constantly, seeking out malefactors and book thieves. She reproved one gormless youth who had contrived to break the binding of his returned volume. 'I'm charging you sixpence for that, Mr Forbes!' she pronounced with undertones of righteous wrath.

'I'm so sorry, Mrs Sinclair!' he squeaked. 'I just left it open on the table and I—'

'And what do you think bookmarks are for, Mr Forbes?' she boomed, sounding like a cow with its horn caught in a five-barred gate. 'Here! Take these!' She thrust a small sheaf of cardboard bookmarks into his hand and received the penitential sixpence.

Suddenly, Mrs Sinclair's eye lit upon a pale, frightened woman loitering with intent outside the ring of browsers. The library's avenging angel seemed to shrink to normal size and stepped silently across to the newcomer. They spoke in voices so soft Phryne could not pick up any of their speech. Mrs Sinclair returned to the cavernous depths of the van and brought out what appeared to be a small volume of knitting patterns. The other took it, bowed her head quickly, and fled, first tucking the book under her woollen shawl.

There was a susurrus of excitement happening out on the oval again. Phryne strode off towards it, leaving Dot to catch up in her wake. Another ring of spectators had gathered, and what looked to be a medium-sized telephone pole was being unloaded from a bullock dray. Facing up to it was a man-mountain in a loudish kilt of red and green. This must be Kenneth McAlpine, the hotel bouncer, Phryne deduced. He was young, the red beard not as full as it would clearly become in later years. He extended two fists the size of legs of pork and grasped the base of the caber. Phryne admired the movement of his muscles beneath the grimy skin. There was a collective sigh as he raised the pole and balanced it. Sweat began to pour from his face, but his bearded lips grinned. A long lane had been cleared directly in front of him, and a transverse rope had been extended across the grass. Presumably this was McAlpine's previous best. Or possibly a world record. Phryne would not have been surprised; she had seen the caber tossed before by brawny men, but never one of this magnitude.

McAlpine tottered for a moment, and his enormous bare feet pawed at the earth like a bullock about to address a red flag. And with no warning whatsoever the caber slipped sideways and fell to earth with a leaden thunk. Phryne stared in horror as one end wheeled in the air and struck one of the bystanders, who went down without a sound, and with a splash of bright vermilion blood.

Chapter Nine

I sometimes think that never blows so red
The Rose as where some buried Caesar bled;
That every Hyacinth the Garden wears
Dropt in its Lap from some once lovely Head.

—Edward Fitzgerald, *The Rubáiyát of*
Omar Khayyám of Naishápúr

The interrogation was going nowhere. Gerald Thorne had been summoned, cautioned, and sat in shapeless misery in a straight-backed deal chair. Across the table, Acting Detective Inspector Fraser was in his element. 'Come off it, Gerald—you may as well admit it. The police surgeon has confirmed that the deceased, Claire Knight, was ten weeks pregnant. There is no evidence of a paramour in her life. Who else but you could be the father of her unborn child?'

'I don't know!' Gerald wailed. 'Claire was a good girl! I never touched her!'

'Someone did!' Fraser leaned back in his comfortable arm-chair, exquisitely content with his own syllogism of guilt.

Gerald writhed, then sat up straight. His rabbity features certainly did not improve his appearance, but under Fraser's acetylene glare, something seemed to be happening. Gerald's watery eyes stared back with sudden resolution. 'Officer, I am innocent of this terrible crime. Notwithstanding that, I refuse to say another word until my lawyer is present.'

'Bit late for that, isn't it? You've already admitted to being a stay-at-home layabout who sponges off his own sister. Still, please yourself.' Fraser pushed the telephone towards him. 'You get one call and that's it.'

With the air of a drowning man clutching at a thrown lifebelt, Gerald's shaking fingers scrabbled at the spring-loaded dial. And Sergeant Hugh Collins was quietly making up his own mind that, much though it grieved him to go behind the back of his superior officer, he had better seek alternative sources of evidence. Would Detective Inspector Robinson approve? Then again, Jack had warned him that his new boss could lose a three-round bout with a revolving door, so perhaps this was all right. While listening to Gerald Thorne begging his sister to summon Mr Thackeray and that right speedily, Hugh came to the firm conclusion that Robinson would. The girls knew Claire. If Inspector Fraser chose to disdain such an evident source of information, it fell to his deputy to fill the void. The time was clearly ripe to open up a new field of enquiry, with all the special resources at his disposal. He sighed, regretting the absence of Jack Robinson more with each passing moment. Perhaps you only came to a full appreciation of the virtues of your superiors when they were replaced by machine-made numbskulls. *This is only temporary,* he told himself. Please God it was.

———

The Council of War around the kitchen table was being liberally supported with honey cake, a large pot of tea, and some Anzac biscuits. Hugh had already eaten some of both and was well into his third cup. Tinker sat up straight, watching Hugh intently. Ruth (who had provided the refreshments) took off her apron, draped it over a kitchen chair, and joined the symposium with resolute calm.

'All right,' Hugh began, folding his hands on the table and staring with intense solemnity at each of them in turn. 'I shouldn't really be doing this, but there it is. I think I need your help, and I'm asking for it now. Anything I tell you at this table goes nowhere else. You will keep your mouths firmly buttoned and you will only do what I agree you can do. Understood?'

'Understood,' they chorused. Despite their collective shock at Claire's death, they tingled with excitement at the chance to solve a real-life mystery themselves.

'All right. Now, my, er, superior officer thinks that it was Uncle Gerald who was responsible for Claire's pregnancy and death. I can't say Gerald impressed me as anything like a decent bloke, but I don't believe a word of it. I think Claire's mum would belt him with a steam-iron if he interfered with her daughter. And he is entirely dependent on her for board and lodging, so I think we can rule that out—unless...'

'Unless?' Jane prompted.

'Unless either of you can remember anything Claire said about Uncle Gerald. Did she ever mention him at all?'

'I thought I knew her well, but it seems I had no idea what was really happening. Ruth, can you remember anything? This could be really important.'

Ruth rubbed a floury hand through her hair and shook her head. 'I gathered she thought of him as part of the furniture. She didn't have any time for him, I do remember that. I asked her once who lived in her house, and she said something like, "Just Mum and Dad—and Uncle Gerald, of course, only he doesn't count really."'

'That sounds like offhand contempt, doesn't it? No suggestion of hidden secrets there?'

Jane returned his look. 'No, I really don't think so.'

'All right. And you didn't think there was anything wrong in her relations with her father?'

Ruth considered. 'She talked about her father quite normally. I don't think she felt great affection for him. He's not at home very much, she said.' Ruth's lip trembled. 'Claire thought that in his eyes she was a bit of a nuisance and nothing more.'

'Poor girl!' Hugh mused on this for a moment. 'So, a girl who's short of affection in her own home and is a loner at school. The kind of girl who might easily fall in love with some boy just because he noticed her and treated her kindly.'

'Well, yes, I think that might be possible,' Ruth agreed. 'Now you mention it, she must have been lonely. I don't think she was all that close to her mum; she was always busy with her painting, Claire said.'

'Yes. And speaking of that...' Hugh reached under the table for Claire's portrait and unwrapped the brown paper. 'Careful with this, I'll need to give it back. What do you think?'

Jane was the first to speak. 'Oh my. She has a secret admirer for certain. I never saw her look like that at school. Did you, Ruth?'

'No, never.' Ruth stared at the painting, which was modest enough at first glance. It was a garden scene, with roses in pots and lavender blooming around the seated figure. Claire was wearing a simple white tunic, and her legs were placed decorously together on the stone garden seat. Her hands were folded in her lap, and she looked straight out from the painting. The painting was executed in oils, and viewed close up the brush strokes were a jungle of swirls and daubs. Seen from a few feet back, though, the figure leaped into focus. Claire was smiling, and her features seemed to hold promise of satisfied joy. This was a girl trying not to smirk and not entirely succeeding.

'You borrowed this from Claire's mum, Mr Collins?' Jane looked at Hugh with a new respect. 'That was very clever of you. Her pupils are dilated and, inside, she is grinning her face off. I think her mum must have suspected something.'

'That's what I thought. And Mrs Knight gave me the impression that she wouldn't even have minded much. Mothers usually know if their daughter is expecting. And even though she didn't say anything about it, she must have known while she was painting the portrait. Not about the pregnancy, maybe. But certainly that she had a new interest in life. And families often cover these things up so nosy neighbours need never know.'

'I know about that,' Jane interposed. 'What happens is that the girl gets sent away to have the baby, and Mum starts wearing maternity dresses with bigger and bigger pillows inside them. The girl has the baby somewhere away out of sight and Mum brings up her grandchild as though it's her own daughter. Or son, of course.' She smiled. 'And nobody tells anybody. Not even the baby knows that their real mum is their grandma.'

'It seems a bit wrong to me.' Ruth looked a little shocked.

'I think it's got something going for it,' Hugh said. 'The important thing is that the girl isn't punished for a silly mistake. And you're quite right, Jane. It happens. The doctors know what's happening, but they don't want any kid going through life with the word *Illegitimate* stamped on their birth certificate.'

'So the doctors enter Mr Knight's name on the certificate as the father?'

'Well, yes, Ruth. It's an act of kindness.'

Ruth burst into tears. 'Nobody did that for me!' She stopped crying almost immediately in a somewhat appalled silence and blew her nose on a cambric handkerchief.

'Or me.' Jane took Ruth's right hand and held it tight. 'But it doesn't matter now, thanks to Miss Phryne.'

'It's all right. I'm fine now.' Ruth blew her nose again. 'So what should we do, Mr Collins? I want to find out what happened to Claire, and why.'

'Well, I have to interview the gardeners. What you girls should do is keep your ears open at school. You might hear something. Make friends with the snobby girls if you have to.'

'We can do better than that.' Jane sat up straight, and Ruth looked at her in silent, red-cheeked encouragement. 'Ruth and I can go to the house and say Claire lent us a book and may we have it back, please? And while we're there, we can look for clues.'

Hugh nodded thoughtfully. 'That's a good idea. Perhaps you could go tomorrow afternoon? They should be home on a Sunday.'

Jane nodded decisively. 'We'll take the tram.'

'That's settled then. Remember: stick to your story! Mrs Knight might suspect you're up to something, but don't let on. If she's intelligent enough to know what you're doing—and I suspect she might be—she'll play along.'

'What about me? What do you want me to do?' Tinker felt it was high time to break his silence.

Hugh scratched his head and looked him over. 'Look, I'm not sure, Tinker. Keep your ears open at school. You never know; you might hear something. Maybe the father of the child might be someone your friends know? It isn't likely, but longer shots have got home in police detection than that. Look out for boys acting strange.'

'You mean guilty?'

'Exactly that. Anyone who gets a girl in trouble isn't going to advertise it. And if the girl comes to harm afterwards, he's going to think he's in a whole lot of trouble.' He blinked. 'Of course, if the boy got her pregnant but had nothing to do with her death—and can prove it—then his best plan is to come forward now, before we find him and charge him.' He gave Tinker a sharp look. 'The trouble is that all too often boys keep their mouths shut when they should be speaking up.'

Tinker nodded, and blushed.

'It all sounds like Romeo and Juliet.' Ruth looked doleful again.

'It might well have been just like Romeo and Juliet.' Hugh shrugged and sighed.

Jane looked suddenly alert. 'And the Prince said that they were all to blame—and *all are punished.*'

'I remember.' Ruth looked again at the portrait of *Claire In Love*. 'We don't have a golden statue like Lord Montague promised, but we do have her painting.'

'All right, that's our plan,' Hugh concluded. 'Now I'm going to have a snooze. I was up earlier than I like this morning.'

He clumped out of the kitchen, and the three children looked at each other in turn.

'We're gonna find who did this, aren't we?' Tinker announced.

Ruth and Jane exchanged looks of resolution. 'Yes, we are. I wish Claire had told us she needed help; but this is too bad,' said Ruth. 'Whoever did this has to pay for it. It's not fair!'

Chapter Ten

There were some gilded youths that sat along the
  barber's wall.
Their eyes were dull, their heads were flat, they had
  no brains at all.

—A.B. Paterson, *The Man from Ironbark*

'Whatever d'ye think yer doing now? A terrible accident like this is no place for a lady! Get along with you!'

It had taken Sergeant Offaly no more than fifteen seconds to appear. His sergeant's stripes bristled at her. An accusing forefinger pointed directly at Phryne's sternum.

She dimpled, with maximum artifice. 'Sergeant, this is no accident,' she suggested, holding up a sliver of steel in her gloved hand. 'I found this in Mr McAlpine's neck. If you ask nicely, he will show you the puncture wound.' She indicated the shocked caber-tosser, who blinked at the sergeant and indicated a small bloom of blood on his neck.

But the sergeant was having none of it. Beads of sweat gathered on his unsightly features, which suffused with blood like an overripe tangerine.

'Be off with ye! I won't be havin' any amateur detectives on my watch, d'ye hear me now?' He shooed her away as though banishing chickens from his kitchen door, and Phryne took the unresisting McAlpine by the arm back towards the beer tent. Shocked groups of bystanders gathered in clumps, deploring the sudden calamity and speculating on what was to be done, and who was going to do it.

Meanwhile, things were happening with considerable speed on the green. An elderly man in a tweed jacket had inspected the body and pronounced life extinct. A stretcher had appeared, and the deceased had been wrapped decently in a blanket and carried off. Hats were removed, hands were clasped in reverent silence. At an imperious sign from the Gaelic-speaking clergyman, one of the pipers began to play 'Flowers of the Forest'. As the haunting lament echoed across the oval, Dot wiped away a tear. Phryne's eyes scanned back and forth in mounting frustration. Too many suspects, and virtually none of them known to her. An idiotic police sergeant who would be of no help whatever, and probably an active hindrance.

'Just sit quiet for a while, Mr McAlpine,' Phryne advised. 'You've had a bad shock, as have we all. But what I need you to know right now is that none of this was your fault. I do not believe in coincidences. Somebody deliberately sabotaged your throw.' She held out the pin. 'Since our village copper doesn't seem to be interested in this, let's have a close look at it ourselves. Do you own anything like this?'

McAlpine stared at it. 'I thought I'd been stung by a bee. But I think it's a needle from a sewing machine.' His voice was butter-soft and, though broadly antipodean, retained some of the Highland lilt of his claymore-wielding ancestors. 'No, I don't have such a thing. Any time I need any sewing done, she does it for me.' He looked at Phryne from beneath his curling eyelashes. 'She's a wonderful girl with a needle.'

'She being…' Phryne prompted.

He blushed. 'Annie! What a girl she is!'

'I see. Mr McAlpine, if I seem rude and forthright, then please believe that I have good reason for any questions I may ask you. Are you in love in Annie?'

'Mph. That I am,' he conceded.

'Does she know?'

'I don't think so.'

Phryne doubted this very much, but let it pass.

'But there it is. Everyone loves her. You can see why, can you not?'

'Yes, I really can. Now please: tell me about the deceased.'

McAlpine opened his mouth to speak, but at that moment the sergeant erupted in front of them and held out a ham-like hand. 'I'll take that, if you please, Miss. It may be nothing, but it might be Evidence.'

Phryne looked up at him and smiled winningly. 'Yes, Sergeant. Do take care of it.' She made to hand over the needle, but held up her other gloved hand in warning. 'Sergeant? Fingerprints?'

He leaned forward, his face closer to hers than was comfortable. A hot blast of boiled cabbage and potato wafted across her outraged nostrils. 'Whoever heard of fingerprints on a damned needle? Don't be daft, woman!' He grabbed the needle and turned on his heel.

As the sergeant's clumping feet receded across the lawn, Dot reached into her handbag and handed Phryne a small bottle of cologne in outraged silence. Phryne inhaled deeply.

'Thank you, Dot. Now, as I was enquiring before we were so rudely interrupted, who was the poor man?'

McAlpine laid his hand across the substantial breadth of his barrel chest and bowed his head. 'Donald Mackay. He's a farmer. Or he was. A good man! I don't know how…' He paused, silent tears running down his cheek and into his beard.

'Oh, but we do know how, Mr McAlpine. I expect somebody with a blowpipe fired this into your neck at the very instant you were going to do your party piece. They intended to kill someone and were ruthless or desperate enough not to care if your caber hit the wrong person. They fired from your left-hand side, and Mr Mackay was on your right. As I recall, he was standing by himself with nobody around him. So, this was a crime of opportunity. Now, can you tell me if the late Donald was also in love with Annie?'

'Oh, he was that. I mean to say: everybody loved her, but I believe she favoured Donald more than most. Do you think he was killed because of a jealous man?'

Phryne looked into his haunted eyes. 'I think it very possible. But unless you are the world's best actor, Mr McAlpine, I don't think the jealous lover was you. You could have stabbed yourself with the needle and pretended that your hands had slipped, but that is such a far-fetched idea that nobody would ever believe it. Except possibly Sergeant Offaly, whom I am beginning to dislike more and more.' This raised a faint smile from McAlpine, and Phryne continued. 'It will be his duty to question you at some point. He may well believe it was an accident, or he may not. With the abysmally stupid, who even knows what they think? But if he gives you any reason to suspect that he thinks you did it, then come and find me, or send word. I'm staying at the Mooltan in Hepburn Springs, but I'm here in Daylesford for the moment. And I see him come most carefully on his hour. Dot, we are leaving.'

Phryne rose as the sergeant came clumping back towards them. Once more the accusatory finger shot out like a gangrenous sausage. 'McAlpine! I want a word with you.'

Phryne and Dot departed.

'I don't think he's the one, Miss Phryne,' Dot ventured.

Phryne looked back over her shoulder. A grubby notebook

was being flourished, and the sergeant was scribbling with earnest intent. 'I don't think so either, Dot. I didn't get a good look at our corpse, but I am fairly certain our departed friend was staring at Annie in the beer tent with a lovelorn passion such as I have rarely encountered. Apparently Annie favoured him, as you heard. And this might be a jealous rival. Possibly. Do people kill off their rivals in love, except in penny novelettes?'

'They might, Miss. She's very beautiful.'

'That she is, Dot. And genuinely kind and charming. But as soon as this drama quietens down, I am going to have a serious word with Jessie. She's holding plenty back, and I want all of it, not just hints and warnings.'

Back on the green, the doctor sighed, laid the coverlet over the face of the late Donald Mackay, and stood up. He began issuing instructions to helpful bystanders. A stretcher had been produced from somewhere, and the dear departed was ferried away. Meanwhile the mayor had assumed the podium again. The locals had formed a bewildered circle around him, hoping that Someone would Take Charge, and it seemed that the mayor had assumed the role. He was orating in his best municipal voice, and it seemed that this was having the desired effect.

'—this terrible mishap. Therefore, I believe it would be best if we close this event now. Tomorrow we shall go to our respective churches and pray for the soul of this good man Donald Mackay, so unfortunately taken from us. I have spoken with all the representatives of our local churches, and they and I are of one mind here. First, we grieve, then we give thanks for Donald's life and our hopes for his soul's salvation. And thereafter... Well, now, you will all remember that the dear departed was a great man for playing the violin, and he dearly loved the country dancing. The Reverend McPherson has offered his church hall from four o'clock tomorrow. We all think it would be a worthy and fitting tribute to the life of this splendid young man if you would all come to a dance there. I hope this meets with your approval.'

There was a sigh of what seemed to be approbation. The mayor stepped down, his goldish chain clanking, and disappeared into the beer tent. After a short wait Phryne and Dot followed him in. Annie was sobbing loudly, being comforted by her sister. Phryne advanced upon the melancholic licensee and fixed him with her glittering eye. 'Mr McKenzie? I would strongly advise that you take over management of the bar, right now. I wish to speak with your nieces. Alone.'

Phryne raised her open hand in warning to Jessie, who was looking at her over Annie's shoulder. Annie burst into a fresh outbreak of tears. Phryne ignored her and approached the bar. 'Jessie? You and I are going to have a proper talk. While your uncle minds the shop.' McKenzie avoided her eye and chewed the ends of his beard for a long moment. 'Aye, well. I can do that. Do what Miss Fisher says, Jessie.'

A faint smile coloured Jessie's face. 'Very well.'

'Come along with me.'

Phryne swept out of the beer tent, with Dot and Jessie in her wake. As they crossed the green, she saw that Colleen O'Rourke had taken charge of the young men. They were gathered around her in a semicircle and she was giving them instructions.

Phryne turned to her companion. 'Watching the worthy sergeant making a complete mess of this criminal investigation is more than I can cope with right now. We're not going to find any suspects hanging around here.' She turned. 'Jessie, we are going to sit over there—' she pointed to the table and chairs where they had watched the dancing '—and you are going to tell me everything you know.'

They sat in silence for a moment, looking across the green to the beer tent. Tragedy had not, it seemed, assuaged the thirsts of the locals. Annie was clearly visible, standing by her uncle. Both were serving drinks.

'I should be there,' Jessie fretted. 'And Annie should be resting.'

Phryne glared at her. 'Annie will just have to cope, Jessie; you can't always be at her side and smoothing her way in front of her. Serving drinks is what she's good at and it will be a lot better for her if she's kept busy. She can collapse later on, if she wants to, when everything is packed up. Then you can read her bedtime stories and hold her hand and tuck her up in bed with her dolls. But right now, I need your full attention. Look at me!'

Ever sensitive to her employer's moods, Dot stood up so Phryne and she could change places. Jessie sat up, her pale, freckled face damp with tears and apprehension, and stared back into Phryne's determined countenance.

'Much better,' Phryne observed. She folded both hands in front of her on the wooden tabletop. 'I want to know what's happening around here, and I think you are the person best placed to tell me what's going on. So please do—and no holding back—before somebody else gets killed.'

Jessie looked at Phryne without speaking for a long moment. 'You don't think Donald's death was an accident, then?' she ventured at last.

'I really don't. How many times has our Highland warrior tossed that caber?'

'I can't remember. But he's never dropped it before.'

'I thought not.' Phryne leaned forward, lowering her voice. 'Our murderer came armed and ready to act, and when he saw his chance he took it, firing a needle into Kenneth's neck at the crucial moment to make him release the caber. Donald Mackay was standing by himself and there was a good chance that this would succeed. Now, I want you to give me the names of Annie's most devoted admirers. Since our sergeant seems unwilling—or unable—to take this seriously, I am taking the case on. Very presumptuous of me, no doubt. But solving mysteries is what I do, and I'm going to do it. You told me that you were afraid that not all the Admiration Brigade were as docile as they seemed, and it appears you may be right. So: names?' Phryne reached into her handbag and took out a gold fountain pen and a notebook.

Jessie closed her eyes for a moment. 'All right, I think I can do that. Poor Donald was the one she liked the most, after Pat Sullivan. Graeme Forbes goes into a swoon whenever he claps eyes on her, but never speaks to her directly. He's harmless, I'm sure of that. Anyone who keeps as many cats as he does around the house wouldn't be a killer.'

Phryne wrote quickly, then looked up in expectation. 'Next?'

'There's James Hepburn. I'm sure he loves her, but he goes red in the face and talks too much. And there's Johnnie Armstrong, though he lives a few miles away and doesn't come into town that often. He's a dark, brooding sort of man: a bit older than the others. Annie doesn't like him because he looks at her in a funny way. But anyway, he's got a wife down in Melbourne, so he's not a suitor for my sister's hand. There are the Gilded Youths who come and gawp at her in the bar, but all they do is gawp; I don't think any of them have any real designs on her.'

Phryne jotted this down. 'I see—they merely bathe in the sight of her beauty. Gilded Youths, like in "The Man from Ironbark"?'

Jessie nodded. 'I can give you their names. Robert Graham, John Hemp, and Peter Trevise. But I really don't think they had anything to do with this; they haven't the brains to plan it.'

'Does it bother you that your sister gets all the attention?'

Jessie clasped her hands in front of her: neat, strong hands marked by toil and blisters. 'Well, there's a question! All right. Yes, it does. It's annoying. But Annie's only eighteen, and I don't think she wants to marry anyone yet. She likes the attention—who wouldn't?—but she thinks she can keep the boys sweet by smiling at them and being kind. And it mostly works. But even though she's not stupid, I think she underestimates how much trouble she could get into.'

'Naive?'

'Yes. That's exactly the word. You aren't going to tell her about this, are you? She'd be horrified if she thought her admirers were killing each other.'

Phryne considered this. 'I'll leave that up to you. But I can't think of any good reason to upset her. Not yet, anyway.' Phryne closed her book, then opened it again, eyes wide. 'Wait a moment, Jessie—you said something about a Sullivan? Who's he? Is he here today?'

Jessie frowned 'Poor Patrick. He had an accident a month ago.'

'*WHAT*?' To Phryne's chagrin, she realised she had thumped the table. Jessie stared at her in astonishment. 'I'm sorry, but what happened?'

'The poor dear.' Jessie closed her eyes. 'He was a kind, gentle man.' She stopped, stuttered, and eventually blurted out her confession. 'I loved him. And he was kind to me and Annie.'

Phryne leaned across and took the girl's hand. 'How old are you, Jessie?'

A solitary droplet rolled down the girl's cheek. 'Twenty.' She burst, quite unexpectedly, into flooding tears.

Phryne took an embroidered silk handkerchief from her bag and passed it to her. Jessie blew her nose and stared at the crumpled silk.

'Keep it, Jessie. I have plenty of them and I won't miss one. You poor dear. You really are a brave, kind-hearted, and generous girl. But I need you to tell me about this accident. Did he die?'

Jessie nodded quickly and gulped. 'He fell out of the train window. He was leaning out to look at a parrot in a tree and lost his balance.' She squared her shoulders. 'That's what they said, anyway. It was the train that goes to Trentham. It's mostly used by the timber mill, but it does take passengers. Pat loved the forest. He took Annie and me there for a picnic once.'

Phryne looked into the distance. 'I think I know where the station is. I want to look at this train. All right, Jessie. Is there anything else you can think of? Nobody else who liked your sister had a fatal accident?'

This produced a weak smile. 'No, I don't think so.' Jessie raised her hand. 'Miss Fisher, about this dance tomorrow… You don't think something bad might happen, do you?'

'I sincerely hope not, Jessie. You'll be there, I suppose?'

'Oh yes. Reverend McPherson always asks us to come. He likes a dram himself, but he says young men shouldn't drink whisky. Beer and cider is good enough for them, he says. So we provide the drinks whenever there are dances in his parish hall. But tomorrow being a Sunday, we'll just have tea, coffee, and cordial, I expect.' She lowered her eyes. 'I'll keep an eye out, then?'

'Please do, Jessie. And so will we. I don't think this dance is a good idea, but I can hardly say so.' Phryne paused. 'I almost forgot. What is all this about women disappearing? Your uncle mentioned it before, and you said something about strange things happening around here yourself. Please. Tell me more.'

Jessie shook her head. 'His wife and child—our auntie and cousin—disappeared some years ago. I don't remember them all that well. He never talks about them, which seems a bit strange to me, but more recently there have been three other women who've vanished without any warning. The police have organised search parties, and we've sent men down to look in the abandoned mineshafts, but…' She shrugged.

'No bodies have been found?'

'None. It's a mystery.'

'I see. Thank you, Jessie. Take care of yourself, as well as Annie, won't you?'

Jessie rose and departed without another word. Phryne watched her go. 'Dot, that is a seriously talented girl. And she's beautiful. Have you noticed?'

'Yes, Miss. I like her. She's a good girl.'

'Well, no, Dot. Annie is the good girl everyone loves. Jessie is the Cinderella who cleans up after everybody. And she's getting well and truly exploited by that lazy melancholic of an uncle. Come on. There's nothing more we can do for the moment. I'd like to question our suspects, but the sergeant will have a fit if I do. Let's go.'

Phryne strode off in high dudgeon, with Dot following behind her as best she could.

Back at the main road, Phryne waited. 'I'm so sorry, Dot. Those shoes of yours aren't built for speed. Why not stay here and I'll bring the car?'

'I'll be all right, Miss Phryne. I'm just shocked.'

'And so am I. I don't know what we've got ourselves into here, but I intend to find out.'

More slowly now, they strode up the hill and found the Hispano-Suiza. Phryne opened the passenger-side door and Dot climbed in. They drove back to Hepburn Springs in thoughtful silence.

————

Entering the Mooltan, they encountered Dulcie near the front door.

'Did you have a pleasant day?' she enquired.

'It certainly was an exciting day,' Phryne responded. 'Pleasant? Not so much. Haven't you heard?'

'Heard what?'

'There was a bad accident. Donald Mackay has been killed by a falling caber.'

Phryne watched all the blood drain out of Dulcie's face. 'Oh no! That's awful! I didn't know him, but I had heard of him. He was Gentle Annie's sweetheart, if anyone was. And Alice! She'll still be there. I must go to her.'

'I didn't know she'd gone to the Gathering. Oh dear. Dot, you stay here and rest; I'll take Dulcie and find Alice.'

'That's very kind of you, Phryne. She went there in Dr Henderson's car, but—oh, never mind. Here he is.'

A large black car pulled up outside the guesthouse. Phryne recognised Dr Henderson as the man who had attended the body. He scrambled out of the car and held the door open for Alice. Dulcie rushed forward and helped her still-weeping lover out of the passenger seat and took her inside, oblivious to all else. The doctor mopped his brow with a large handkerchief, nodded to Phryne and Dot in brief acknowledgement, then motored off back towards Daylesford.

Phryne smiled at her companion: one of those wan, rueful smiles which emerge when all other emotions have already been spoken for. 'Dot, I think our hosts have enough on their plate without bothering about us. Let's go inside, shut the door, and read a book or something.'

'Miss, don't you want—?'

'To discuss the day's events? Well, yes, I really do, Dot. But later. When we know more. Right now, I don't feel I know nearly enough about anything to theorise. I have a splitting headache and I want to lie down.'

'So do I, Miss.'

Phryne lay on her comfortable bed, deep in thought. Tragedy had already come to Daylesford's picturesque streets. And yet they were going to have a country dance tomorrow afternoon. This, while a brave and positive step, struck Phryne as foolhardy with a probable killer on the loose. But what could she do about it? As a guest in the area she could hardly tell them to refrain. But she would go herself, with Dot, and keep a close eye on things.

Meanwhile, tomorrow being Sunday, she would drop Dot at church and do some investigation of her own. These country folks really do see life, she reflected. And death as well.

Chapter Eleven

They finger Death at their gloves' end where they
  piece and repiece the living wires.
He rears against the gates they tend: they feed him
  hungry behind their fires.
Early at dawn, ere men see clear, they stumble into
  his terrible stall,
And hale him forth like a haltered steer, and goad
  and turn him till evenfall.

—Rudyard Kipling, *The Sons of Martha*

'Dot, are you sure you don't want a lift all the way?'

'No, Miss Phryne. It's early yet, and I'd like to look around.'

Dot watched the Hispano-Suiza putter slowly back down the hill and looked again at the great clock atop the post office. Twenty to ten. Mass was at ten o'clock, and she had plenty of time. It was a still, mild, perfect day, with birds tweeting on branch and thorn, and giant elm trees presiding over the mid-morning. Over dinner last night Dulcie had spoken of the local churches. 'They're all close to the crossroads just off the main street, Dot.

We have Anglican, Catholic, Methodist, and Presbyterian, as well as one or two others. They all agreed that nobody should get the very top of the hill, though.'

Dot, who knew well that every church always wanted to get the highest ground anywhere (because of being closest to heaven), had smiled and suggested that this was a very friendly arrangement.

Dulcie had grinned and folded her arms. 'Partly—but also because the very top of the hill is a steep climb. You'll see it for yourself. So it was decided it should be a public park. It's got a tower and everything. A lot of the locals still walk to church, and you don't want your flock arriving so tired they can't sing the Lord's praises properly.'

Dot had given Dulcie a puzzled look, uncertain whether she was being gently teased. Dulcie and Alice were not, apparently, favouring any church with their Sabbath devotions, any more than Phryne was.

Now, Dot saw a few of the locals in their Sunday best, heading churchwards with pious purpose. And to her delight she saw a face she recognised. Dot quickened her pace and caught up with a demure figure in a long black skirt.

Colleen O'Rourke turned to face her. She wore a full-sleeved white blouse and black jacket, woollen stockings, laced black boots, a small golden cross on a golden chain, and a straw hat with a black band. And she was entirely beautiful. 'Miss Williams, isn't it? Look, we match!'

Dot's Sabbath attire was indeed similar, except that the band of her own hat was crimson. 'We do,' she concurred. 'There are so many churches here I was afraid I'd get lost.'

Colleen grinned at her. 'Well, if you're going my way, I can take you there.'

Colleen left the main street and cut across a leafy block towards an intimidating church. Dot stared up the frowning sides of an orange-brick church of considerable magnificence. There was a hexagonal tower on the left, and three elongated leadlight windows, the middle one uppermost—as was only proper for the Holy Trinity. Dot was a little disappointed by the lack of stained glass in the diamond-shaped leads but was willing to overlook it. This church was designed to overawe, no question about that.

As they began to climb the flight of stone stairs, all around them deep bells began to chime. All the local churches seemed to be in competition with each other, and the sound was deafening. At the top of the stairs Colleen took Dot's arm and smiled at her. 'It's all right. It's quieter inside.'

From a soberly attired verger Colleen took a pair each of hymn-books and prayer books, and a single elongated slim volume. 'For the psalms,' Colleen whispered. 'Sing along with me and you'll be fine.'

Dot entered the church and curtseyed towards the distressingly plain altar. No one said anything, but Dot became aware that people were frowning at her. The atmosphere was not exactly hostile, but general disapproval seemed to be in the air. Perhaps, Dot considered, they were merely suspicious of strangers. Colleen took Dot's arm and herded her into a hard wooden pew. Colour was rising like yeast in Dot's cheeks, and there was a sibilant whisper in the pew behind them. Colleen turned to glare at the whisperers, who subsided at once. Dot bowed her head in silent, agonised prayer and wished the floor would open beneath her. She raised her head and, standing in the pulpit, she saw not the familiar cassock and surplice of a Catholic priest about to celebrate mass, but none other than the Reverend McPherson himself, in a plain black robe and entirely innocent of dog collar.

Dot stared at Colleen, crimson with mortification. She looked at the minister then again at Colleen, an accusing eye fixed firmly on the cross at Miss O'Rourke's neck. The girl's expression was composed of equal parts mischief and defiance as her mouth shaped the words, *I thought you knew!* Dot shook her head and briefly considered the possibility of crawling on her hands and knees to the end of the pew and out of this heathen chapel. She tapped the stone floor with her foot, realising that tunnelling her way out was also a stark impossibility. Colleen reached out a slender white arm and patted Dot's hand. Her mouth now formed the words, *I'm sorry!* Dot looked at her, sighed, and resolved to brazen it out.

As the service proceeded, Dot found herself relaxing some-what. The minister welcomed them all, deplored the recent tragedy, exhorted the faithful to be Strong In the Fear of the Lord, and to welcome the newcomer among them. This with a stern look straight at Colleen O'Rourke, who had the grace to blush and bow her head. The liturgy was oddly familiar, even though it struck Dot as vaguely blasphemous, not being in proper Latin. Dot was able to join in one of the hymns, which she recognised as the Anglican 'Old Hundredth', and was startled to hear a glorious, soaring soprano voice beside her. Clearly Colleen's talents did not end with ethnic dancing. Singing in Dot's home church of St Ignatius was a delicate affair, with a choir of boys and a few adults in the stalls carrying tune and harmony, and the congregation decorously following. Here, the congregation bawled out the hymns and psalms as if they were carrying bullocks under each arm and calling the stragglers home across the Sands of Dee. One of the psalms was in a strange tongue which Dot supposed had to be Gaelic, and Colleen sang her way through the impossible words, pointing with her forefinger at each marked syllable.

When it came time for the sacrament, Dot sat frozen on her seat, lips closed like a bank vault and an expression of silent mutiny on her face. Nothing on earth or above it was going to persuade her to partake in a Protestant communion, or whatever they called it.

Colleen leaned over and whispered in her ear, 'It's all right, I won't go up either. I'm just visiting. The minister doesn't mind. I told him I'm still making up my mind.'

'And are you?'

'Not really. But the boys here are very sweet. And I love the metrical psalms.'

Dot pursed her lips and fumed in silent patience.

When the service had wound to its conclusion, Dot staggered out into the brilliant sunshine of the porch. The minister shook the hand of all the men, and sketched a perfunctory bow to all the ladies. When it was Dot's turn, the Reverend McPherson gave her a deeper nod. 'Miss Williams? I fear that Miss O'Rourke has been leading you astray.' His eye fastened upon the cross at Dot's neck. Beside her, Colleen flushed scarlet and looked at the floor. 'She is high-spirited, but a good girl nonetheless and a fine one for the singing.'

He turned back to Dot, who looked at him in sudden curiosity. He was under forty, with round spectacles and thinning, sandy hair. 'Miss Williams, we are many, but we are one in Christ hereabouts. I am sorry that you have missed Father O'Reilly's mass. Will you accept instead the hand of friendship from a Protestant?'

Dot extended her gloved hand. Even through the fabric it was as if she had been slapped with a sea wind from the Hebrides, yet a warm glow spread through her body. 'Thank you, Father— Reverend,' she managed. 'I will indeed.'

Colleen led her back down the hill. 'Miss Williams, I am so sorry,' she said. 'Please forgive me.'

Dot stopped and put both hands on her hips. 'I thought you were a Catholic!'

'I am! But I like the minister. He's such a kind man.' Colleen walked around to stand in front of Dot. 'It isn't just the boys! Miss Williams—'

'Oh, for heaven's sake, Colleen, call me Dot, please!'

Colleen opened her palms outwards and lowered her voice. Her customary expression of gleeful mischief had evaporated, and she gave Dot a searching glance from under her long, curling eyelashes. 'Dot, we remember a lot of things in my house. We remember the *Gorta Mór*—the Great Hunger. We remember the Protestant Ascendancy; the Penal Laws; the murders; the gentry with no pity; and all the endless, stupid bloodshed and cruelty. And here it's all so different. This is how we should live. I'm a good Catholic and I go to a Presbyterian church and nobody wants to kill me for it, least of all Father O'Reilly. I think he knows what I'm doing. And he knows I'll be back. We must love each other! And we're doing it here.'

To Dot's surprise Colleen was weeping now. Dot took the girl in her arms and felt the wiry strength in her shoulders. Colleen hugged her and gasped. 'All right. I won't say any more.' She disentangled herself and looked at Dot sidelong. 'Are we friends?'

Dot smiled. 'Colleen, we are. And I'm sorry. I've been proud and lacking in charity. The minister is right. You really are a good girl.'

'Would you care to come to my house? Mum will have tea and scones ready.'

'I'd like that, but Miss Fisher is going to pick me up at noon.'

Colleen craned her eyes towards the clock tower. 'It's a quarter to now. All right. Some other time.'

Dot reached out her hand and touched Colleen's wrist. 'Before you go home, there's something I'd like to ask you.'

Colleen leaned against a garden fence and inhaled the scent of a late summer rose. 'Ask away.'

'Do you have any ideas about what happened yesterday?'

Colleen O'Rourke folded her arms and glared. 'That was no accident! Kenneth McAlpine would not drop the caber. Someone distracted him and on purpose—wasn't there a needle or something?—but I don't know who it was. Is your Miss Fisher going to find out?'

Dot nodded. 'She will.'

'Good. Anything more?'

'I'm wondering if it's a jealous lover.'

'Maybe. But if you and Miss Fisher think it's one of Annie's admirers that won't help you much. Half the Shire wants to marry her. Good luck!'

Colleen turned off to the right, and Dot watched the girl marching along as if she owned the place. If half the Shire's men wanted to marry Gentle Annie, it was equally likely that the other half wanted Colleen O'Rourke. Dot could see why, and for a fleeting moment wished that she herself were as glamorous as Colleen, before dismissing the thought at once as being utterly unworthy, especially for a Sunday.

———

The Captain met Phryne in the vestibule of the spa. It was red-brick, long, low, and exuding comfort from every cornice. Herbal scents filled the atmosphere, and Phryne inhaled deeply. 'We use many different scents,' he expounded. 'We discovered that lavender is very good for asthma and others are sovereign for different ailments.' Phryne looked steadily at him. He wore the same navy blue suit as he had worn during their dinner two nights ago. His face was steady, grave, but good-humoured. He showed her everything: the massage cubicles; the little bathrooms with their bathtubs; the big, heated pool in the centre.

'Would you care for a bath and massage yourself?' he concluded.

She undressed in one of the cubicles and had a sumptuous bath, scented with lavender. The water was unlike anything she had ever encountered: warm and spritzig to the touch. She could feel the mineral salts gently scouring her skin and smoothing away the tension in her limbs. She arose, threw her wrap around herself and was conducted by one of the masseuses into another alcove.

'Hello,' said a pretty girl in a white dressing-gown. 'I'm Sheila. Just lie down on the bed, Miss, and I'll do the rest.'

Phryne lay on her front in silence while strong hands kneaded her back, shoulders, arms, and legs. This would be the standard massage for the soldiers, she assumed: personal without being indecorous. Both Sheila's hands began to drum on her back in a jazzy rhythm. Phryne considered that being treated as a percussion instrument was a little over the odds, but Sheila should be encouraged to talk.

'Tell me about the Captain,' Phryne urged.

The drum solo ceased for a moment. 'He's very kind, Miss. Self-contained. But he means well.'

And that appeared to be it from Sheila, who finished the massage in silence. Phryne stood up.

'Thank you. And now I think I would like a swim.' Sounds of splashing could be discerned, and somebody began to sing 'Someone To Watch Over Me'. One or two other voices joined in. Phryne doffed her wrap in one movement and walked out of the cubicle.

'Miss, the pool's full of soldiers! You can't go in there...'

But it was too late. The singing stopped dead as eight young men, entirely without clothing, stared at the naked goddess who entered the water and began to swim towards them. Then one of the men began to sing 'My Blue Heaven'. Some averted their gaze.

Others did not and goggled at her. She waved and swam in a curve around them. Nobody so much as moved. Phryne nodded to herself. She swam for around three minutes, then stood up in the pool, her porcelain breasts bobbing in the water in front of them.

'So where does a girl go for a smoke around here?' she enquired.

One of the men pointed. 'There's a courtyard next to the tea house, Miss.'

Phryne inclined her head, swam back towards the cubicles, and dressed carefully. She found the courtyard and lit a gasper. There were several men there smoking at their ease. They nodded politely. One by one, they introduced themselves. There was a Jonno, a Bert, two Daves (Big Dave and Tiny Dave—who was, inevitably, the taller of the pair), a Stevo, a Billy, and a Kevvy. Some worked the still for the Captain's tonic—at which Phryne raised her eyebrows, for the Captain had said nothing of his tonic during dinner—some were masseurs, and one, a slim, elegant man called Gareth, appeared to be the dance instructor. All appeared well-content with their lot and praised the Captain highly. In Australian, this was expressed as 'a good bastard.'

Suddenly there was a tremendous sound of an engine. It seemed to be in pain and roared like a hippopotamus with toothache. An ancient, dirty white truck had pulled up, and Phryne watched, fascinated, as an enormous man climbed out of the cabin. Wooden barrels, presumably filled with mineral water, were stacked in a tidy row along the back of the tea house. The giant leaned over, picked up one under each arm, and carried them to the truck's tray. They must have weighed a hundred pounds each, but he seemed not even to notice the weight. Sitting in the cabin, and glaring through the window, was a thin-faced, cold-eyed man. He did not deign to assist but wound down the window. 'Come on! Get on with it, ya big idiot!' Then he wound the window up again and stared forward at nothing.

As the huge man returned for the next pair, Phryne looked him over. Six and a half feet tall, and several axe handles across his shoulders. He was not so much fat as exceedingly well-armoured. In the Middle Ages, he might have been used as a battering ram. But his strangely unlined face was mild and gentle, and his brown eyes were kind and filled with simple wonderment, as if looking at everything for the first time. Sheila came out to stand beside Phryne and lit a cigarette herself. The man looked adoringly at both women for a long moment, smiled, and hoisted two more barrels.

'That's Vern,' said Gareth. 'Quite a specimen, isn't he?'

Soon the tray was full. The man secured his load with thick rope to the back of the cabin and climbed aboard. The protesting motor roared back into life, and the truck slowly chugged back up the hill.

'What do those men want with the barrels?' Phryne asked.

Gareth blew a smoke ring. 'They're taking them to the bottling plant. Vern's brother Sid—he's the moody one in the truck—is in charge. You have to feel sorry for Vern, being cooped up out there with only his brother for company. He's a lovely fellow; simple but harmless. I did hear something about them offering him a room at the pub. He'll be happier there. He likes looking at girls, you know, though he never does anything untoward.'

'I see.' Phryne put out her cigarette. 'Well, thank you.'

It was all very interesting at the spa, but it was time for Phryne to return to Daylesford and pick up Dot.

————

She found her companion standing forlornly in the middle of the roundabout at the very top of the hill, looking like the Little Mermaid on her rock in Copenhagen harbour. As a girl, Phryne had pronounced that fairy tale the rottenest she had ever read and had in consequence never visited the place. But she had once met the Danish ambassador in London—a genial fellow with the sort of white moustache that made you think of baleen whales and plankton—and registered her strong disapproval of Hans Christian Andersen. His Excellency had made Promethean gestures and confided: 'Yes, Hans was a serious worry, you know. That morbid interest in young girls—it would never be allowed now. But what would you? My people like to think of ourselves as Vikings, but we have a sentimental streak a mile wide. And so...'

And so, indeed. That awful statue certainly brought the tourists in. But not Phryne. She waved at her companion, and Dot's anxious face blossomed into a floral tribute of gratitude and relief. Phryne leaned over and opened the passenger door. Dot clambered in, adjusted her hat, and assumed her standard Driving with Miss Phryne pose: hands clasped together in her lap, knees pressed together, inner voice reciting Latin prayers for Those in Peril on the Sea.

'Dot, lunch at the Mooltan isn't till one, but I've been to the spa, and there's a pleasant-looking tea house on the premises. Shall we try it out?'

Dot nodded, and Phryne put the car into gear and went forth, parking on the side of the road next to the spa building. The tea house was of the same brick, single-storeyed, and with a cosy, welcoming feel to it. Phryne ordered a pot of tea for Dot, coffee for herself, and a brace of biscuits just for the look of the thing. She noted that Sabbatarianism appeared to be extinct in Hepburn Springs, though it was undoubtedly alive and well in Daylesford, since every shop and pub she had passed was shut fast according to the ordinances of the State of Victoria. There were only two or three other patrons present, and their drinks arrived with commendable promptitude.

'Well, Dot, I have had an intriguing morning, but tell me about yours first.'

Dot paused in delivery of cup to lip and exclaimed, 'That Colleen O'Rourke took me to the wrong church!'

Phryne put down her coffee cup. 'Really? Tell me all.'

Dot poured out her morning's embarrassments, and Phryne patted her hand encouragingly. 'Never mind, Dot. You have done very well, and probably better than if you'd gone to Father O'Reilly's church. It is confusing with the four of them, one on each corner of the same crossroads. So, it seems that the Reverend McPherson is a kind and good man, and far more tolerant than you would expect of a Presbyterian. I may have to revise my Views on the Church of Scotland. And Colleen O'Rourke interests me more and more.'

'Miss Phryne, all along we've been wondering about Annie's suitors, and you think that Donald Mackay might have been killed by a jealous lover—but what if it's Colleen rather than Annie?'

'I'm wondering that too, Dot. And yet...Colleen likes boys, obviously. But there is something very hearty and clean-living about the girl that makes me think it unlikely. She seems more like the kind of girl that a boy would want to go off on expeditions of mischief with. I can readily imagine all the boys wanting her company, but as an object of romantic affection? I doubt it.'

'I'm not so sure, Miss.' Dot nibbled at a Scotch Finger in thoughtful reverie. 'I think the noisy, self-confident boys would think of her like that. But what if it's a shy boy? For a really shy young man, Colleen might be his dream come true.'

Phryne inclined her chin approvingly. 'Dot, that really is a good point. Well done!' She leaned forward in her chair, and her eyes flicked restlessly around the room. The other patrons got up and left with a rustle of newsprint. The black-and-white clad waitress accepted payment, dispensed coins in change, and disappeared into the kitchen, and they had, for the moment, the tearooms to themselves. 'I really didn't take to Mr McKenzie, Dot. Did you?'

Dot poured herself another cup of strong tea and loaded it with milk and sugar. 'No, Miss. He's a bit gloomy, and it isn't fair on those girls having to do so much when he just sits around all day.'

'I wonder about his missing wife and child,' Phryne mused. 'I'd like to find out more about this.'

'Maybe that's why Mr McKenzie is a drunk. He drinks to forget his missing wife?'

'We don't know how she went missing, Dot. He might have pushed her down a mineshaft; there are plenty of them around here. But Jessie says they've been searched. And of course there was another death: Patrick Sullivan. Jessie told me he used to take her and Annie for picnics. And Jessie confessed that she loved him.'

'I remember.' Dot dropped her silver teaspoon and gaped at Phryne. 'Miss? I've just had a dreadful thought.'

'Do tell, Dot.'

'Miss, there's a horrible song called "Cruel Sister".' Phryne looked enquiringly at her. 'It's awful, Miss. The young man courts both sisters, but he loves the younger one best. And the older girl kills her sister, and she becomes a harp and—well, it's complicated, Miss.'

'Let me guess: the harp plays all by itself at the wedding, and tells the story of how she was murdered?'

'Yes, Miss. I heard it once at a church social. Only here—if you're right—instead of killing her sister, she kills off the lovers. Did Jessie say how Mr Sullivan died?'

'He fell out of a train window, apparently. I'm going to see that train tomorrow and check the carriages. We may have two murders now.' Phryne took in the general air of comfort, ease, and friendliness of the tea house and wondered how to reconcile these admirable communities with the mysteries that were infesting the locale. 'We have a possible murder on a railway which managed not to be noticed. We have a deliberate murder right in front of our eyes, and an unknown number of suspects. We don't know why it was done, but we think it might be a jealous lover, though we don't know for sure who is the adored object. It might be Annie, or it could be Colleen—or maybe it's nothing to do with either of them and it was a sordid murder for gain. Meanwhile, we can't go around asking questions too openly because we've got a half-witted local copper who resents my intrusion into the local community. Short of being chained by the wrist in an abandoned mineshaft with water rising about my knees, I can't see how this could be any harder. And let's not forget that we also have an unknown number of women quietly disappearing.'

'Miss Phryne, you don't have to solve all the world's problems.'

Phryne's eyes flashed lightning for a moment. 'Dot, they killed that poor man right in front of us!' Seeing her beloved companion's face pale, she relented. 'I'm sorry, Dot,' she went on, lowering her voice again, 'but that was too much. I'm not going to let him—or her—get away with it.'

She took out her notebook and began to write in silence. The waitress returned and began to issue heavy hints about Closing Time: sweeping floors, putting tables on chairs, removing salt and pepper shakers, and so on. Phryne ignored both the heavy hints and Dot's embarrassment. Only when she had finished writing did Phryne rise to her feet and sweep out with Dot in her wake.

When they were both seated in the car, Phryne handed the book, open, to Dot. 'Have a read of this after lunch, Dot. Tell me if you think I've missed anything, and *don't* let this book out of your sight. Meanwhile, I have a book of my own to read.' She held aloft a thick, blackavised hardback. 'I'm hoping it might dispel the fogs hereabouts somewhat.' Dot noted the title *Bleak House* in goldish lettering on the cover.

Dot stowed the notebook in her reticule. It was but a momentary journey back to the Mooltan, and the hallway clock was striking one as they entered. Alice seemed quite recovered from yesterday's trauma, and Dulcie was her usual imperturbable self. Her brother was elsewhere, it seemed.

Lunch was a splendid roast lamb with vegetables: local potatoes, pumpkin, sweet potato and sweet peas, with apple pie and fresh cream to follow.

At the meal's conclusion, Phryne laid down her spoon in her bowl as Dulcie arrived to clear the dishes. 'That was wonderful, Dulcie. Well done to you and Alice!'

'Do you have plans for the afternoon, Phryne?' Dulcie asked. 'I'm not sure if you heard, but there's to be a dance this afternoon at the Presbyterian church hall to celebrate the life of poor Donald Mackay.'

Phryne nodded. 'We did hear, and we intend to go.'

'Then would you take Alice along? She loves dancing, and I don't care for it.'

'Certainly.'

Alice, loitering by the kitchen door, glowed and coloured.

'Can you be ready at four?' Phryne asked. 'I'm going to retire to my room and see if Mr Dickens can help me out.'

It was not long, however, before Phryne laid down the chronicles of Jarndyce vs Jarndyce and slipped into a daydream in which beautiful girls appeared and disappeared in London fog. Someone was laughing maniacally, but could not be seen. Phryne woke herself up, drank from a glass of water, and slipped into a dreamless doze.

———

Dot, meanwhile, closed her own bedroom door and sat down at the room's small desk. She opened Phryne's notebook, flipped past a number of prior entries, and began to read at the page headed *Mysteries of Daylesford.*

- *Mysterious disappearances of women, including Mrs McKenzie.*
- *Possible murder of Patrick Sullivan, falling out of a train window. Check train to see if this is credible. Was he pushed? Too late to check passenger lists now, and too dangerous to make enquiries in case we put murderer on guard.*
- *Almost certain murder of Donald Mackay.*

Theories:

- *Murder for gain? Find out if Sullivan and Mackay owned significant property. Who stands to gain by their deaths?*
- *Crime of passion? Mysterious deaths of two of Annie's admirers. Did they also pay court to Colleen? Find someone safe to ask! And did either girl ever Take Matters Further than mere flirtation? How on earth can we find out???*

If crime of passion, the suspects are:

- *James Hepburn. Known to be very fond of Annie. Colleen also?*
- *Graeme Forbes. Ditto*
- *Johnnie Armstrong. Less likely because married, but not impossible.*

- *The Gilded Youths. Probably not.*
- *Jessie. Either over-protecting her sister from undue admiration, or else brooding resentment of Annie getting all the attention. Possible!*

Opportunity? Jessie definitely at scene of crime. Others? Who even knows? Sgt Offaly does, but not letting on. Must find answers!

Dot put down the notebook and sighed. Who could be trusted to provide information without risk? At the present moment, probably only Reverend McPherson. Perhaps there would be opportunity at the dance to talk to him. With that thought, Dot laid herself on her bed and passed into an uneasy slumber.

Chapter Twelve

'It is competent,' said Mr Barnacle, 'to any member of the—
Public,' mentioning that obscure body with reluctance, as
his natural enemy, 'to memorialise the Circumlocution
Department. Such formalities as are required to be observed
in so doing, may be known on application to the proper
branch of that department.'

—Charles Dickens, *Bleak House*

'Where to, ladies?' As the tram rattled along Balaclava Road, the moustachioed conductor hefted his leather bag and opened it in front of Ruth and Jane like the gaping maw of a dubious sea monster.

'Two to Cotham Road, please.' Ruth handed over a shilling, and two crisp tickets appeared in the man's grimy hand and were duly clipped.

The tram rattled onwards. Presently they reached Hawthorn Road, and the driver opened the door, armed with a long crowbar. He thrust the end of it into a gap in the tramlines with a practiced twist, then removed it and climbed back into his cabin. As the tram responded and groaned around the corner, the lights flickered; there was a metallic cracking noise and an acrid tang in the air.

'Smell that ozone. Isn't it awful?' Ruth patted her throat and took out her handkerchief.

'I suspect it's ionised nitrogen and oxygen.' Jane could not help herself. 'But—' she added hastily '—I expect there's ozone there as well. After all, a lone oxygen atom is bound to team up with a molecule every now and again when subjected to strong electrical discharge.'

Ruth nodded and smiled, as she generally did when Jane was attempting to explain science to her. The important point—that Jane was correcting herself in order to spare Ruth's feelings—did not escape her. 'You're so clever, Jane.'

They watched the stately elegance of Caulfield Park go by. Picnics were happening there, with spread tablecloths, wicker baskets, and cooked meats. Children ran about chasing dogs, and were chased by them in turn while adults looked on with amused indulgence.

Jane stood up and stretched, braving the reproving eye of the conductor. 'I wish they could do something about these blasted wooden seats!' she complained.

Ruth, who was somewhat more padded than Jane, merely nodded.

The tram groaned arthritically up the long hill to Dandenong Road. The tram driver once more wielded his crowbar, and they lurched around into Glenferrie Road. At the terminus, they clambered down onto the road.

'Wait,' Jane suggested. 'I want to check the timetable.' She peered at the glass-covered cardboard oblong screwed into a lamppost. 'The next tram home is at one o'clock. Including our walk to and from, we've got forty minutes or so. That should be enough.'

They turned right into Barkers Road and found the house without difficulty.

'It does look very grand,' Ruth remarked, gazing at the high hedges and elaborately manicured front garden. 'But it doesn't seem as though anyone's at home. Should we look around first?'

Jane considered the suggestion then said, 'I think we'd better knock first. We can always look at the exterior later. And if there's nobody home, I think we can look around the grounds. But we need to know which window was Claire's.'

They knocked, not without the odd tremor. The house felt oppressive and brooding, and it was a considerable relief when Mrs Knight opened the door. 'Hello, young ladies. How may I help you?'

Claire's mother was dressed in Sunday Best: a severe long black dress with full sleeves and a buttoned jacket, despite the warm weather. Clearly she had been to church. Claire had told Ruth that her family were Baptists, and her parents had moved to the neighbourhood so that their future sons could attend Carey Grammar School. Alas, of sons they had none, nor any children now that Claire had gone.

Jane was ready with her story. 'Hello, Mrs Knight. We're very sorry to trouble you at this terrible time, but we're Jane and Ruth, friends of Claire's from school. I lent her my maths book and I really need it back, if that's all right. It will be in her room.'

Mrs Knight gave them a long, inquisitorial look. 'All right. I'll take you to her room.'

She led the way up the gloomy mahogany staircase and opened the last door at the end of the passage. 'Take all the time you need,' she offered, while contriving to suggest that a short stay would be altogether more agreeable than a long one. She closed the door on them. The girls exchanged an embarrassed glance and divided the room between them.

Alas: Claire was either the tidiest schoolgirl in the history of the world, or else the room had already been tidied by the bereaved mother. Neither wardrobe, desk drawer, nor under the bed produced the slightest clue.

Jane opened the window and stared out over the garden. Claire's room faced onto the front of the house at the left-hand end of the building. She looked down to the garden bed and uttered a tiny gasp. 'Ruth,' she whispered. 'Look straight down.'

Ruth joined her at the window and did so. 'I can see two square indentations in the dirt about a foot from the outer wall. Is that what you wanted me to see?'

Jane nodded. 'The indentations wouldn't be visible from the garden because of the azaleas and the hedge border, but there's been a ladder there. Several times, I think. And it's right under Claire's window.'

'Could anyone climb in through the window?'

'An adult couldn't. But a boy might, if he was slim and agile.'

Ruth's lips formed an O of conspiratorial secrecy. 'You're right. So that's how she met her lover. And there's something else there too.'

'What is it?'

'I don't know. But it's metal, with two holes in it. Should we fetch it?'

Jane nodded. 'We really should. I can't see it properly, but it might be a clue.'

'That's good. Now we know how it was done, all we need to discover is who.'

'Who indeed?'

There was nothing more they could do for the present. They trooped back downstairs, thanked the wraith-like Mrs Knight— who did not even ask about the mythical textbook and barely acknowledged them—and made a quick detour among the azaleas, where Jane picked up the object they had seen from above.

They both stared at it: two small, flat pieces of metal bound together with what looked like strips of mica pinned between them, and two holes bored into it. They looked at each other and shrugged, and Jane stowed it away in her tunic pocket. They took the tram home in thoughtful silence.

———

Back in St Kilda, Ruth and Jane sat down to a late lunch: a cold collation of roast lamb and salad. Tinker and Hugh browsed meanwhile on a selection of fruit, nuts, and mince pies provided by Mrs Butler. While they ate, the girls provided a bulletin on their discoveries, and Jane produced the mysterious object. 'Does this mean anything to you?' she enquired, looking at Hugh Collins.

He frowned. 'Dunno. Something electrical, maybe? Tinker, what's up?'

Tinker was staring at the object. 'Yair, it's a capacitor. For a crystal set.'

'And this means something to you?'

'Yair.' Tinker nodded. 'I'm making one at school.' He did not mention that he was also making one at home.

'So it might have belonged to one of your school friends?' Hugh suggested.

'Could be, though I dunno how many other schools are usin' capacitors. But it looks exactly like the one our electronics teacher showed us.'

There was a long pause while the company took this in. Finally Hugh spoke. 'Improbable as it might seem, our mysterious boyfriend might well be in your class, Tinker.'

'Yair. Could be. 'Course, it might be an electrician who dropped it.'

Hugh nodded. 'Yes, it could. But I doubt it. We seem to have a lover who visited by ladder, and somehow I don't think it's the electrician.' Hugh reached for a small and extremely red apple. 'As I recall, the upper storey is a long way up. And you say the ladder marks were very close to the wall?'

Jane took a mince pie and inhaled the scent of cinnamon, nutmeg, and cloves. 'Yes,' she confirmed, taking a bite out of the pie. It was exquisite, and she directed a grateful smile at Ruth, who had baked them the previous night. 'Which tells us two things. The first is that it's unlikely to have been anyone old. It's a good twenty feet almost straight up. And you'd need a good head for heights.'

Tinker felt it was time to make a contribution. He laid down the orange he had been excavating. 'And second, it was someone who knew where to find a ladder. I s'pose they'd use a ladder belonging to the house?'

Jane nodded with emphasis and finished the mince pie.

'I reckon so, Tinker.' Hugh leaned back in his chair, finally replete. 'You wouldn't want to be walking along Barkers Road with a ladder under your arm.'

'Could it have been one of the gardeners?' Ruth interposed. 'They'd know where the ladders were kept.'

'It could, Ruth,' Hugh conceded. 'I'm supposed to interview the gardeners tomorrow. If one of them looks young and fit, and a likely sort, then maybe. I was told otherwise, but I'm not taking anybody's word for that. I'll find out tomorrow if we have a suspect.' He looked at the girls. 'I think you should go back to Kew after school on Tuesday and talk to Mrs Knight again. Tell her everything; she's aware that Acting Detective Inspector Fraser is focused on her brother and I'm sure she'd be eager to see other avenues explored. Ask for permission to search Claire's room properly for a clue to the identity of her boyfriend. Letters, perhaps. Would Claire be the sort of girl to keep a diary?'

Jane snorted. 'Hardly! She wanted to be a doctor, or a scientist.'

Hugh's glance passed to Ruth, who was looking sheepish. He raised an eyebrow and Ruth hung her head. 'I kept a diary until recently. We all kept diaries. Even you had one.'

Jane blushed. 'Yes, I did. You're right. But I stopped because it was silly.'

'And I stopped when I realised my life was boring. Now I just write recipes in mine.'

'All right.' Hugh surveyed the girls' discomfiture, aware of the transitory nature of youthful crazes. 'So she might have kept one. She did have a secret admirer, and she doesn't seem to have confided in anyone at school. I think she'd have to tell somebody, and a diary seems probable, doesn't it?'

'It might be in code,' Jane suggested.

'If it is, then we can probably break it. As for you, Tinker… Boys who've managed to, er, get their way with girls tend to boast about it. He won't be boasting now, but there might be a flicker of gossip somewhere. Find out if any of your school friends live in Kew. It's highly likely that our missing boy lives near her. Agreed?'

'Agreed.'

And with that, the meeting broke up. The girls returned to their room and read books (Ruth: *Cooking the Australian Way*; Jane: *An Approach to Physiology*). Hugh returned to his guest room and imagined himself telling Jack Robinson how he had cracked a case despite the best endeavours of Acting Detective Inspector Fraser. Tinker went out to his shed and locked the door behind him. A plan was forming…

Later that afternoon, Tinker returned to the house proper and knocked on the door to Mr Butler's room.

The door opened a little way and a balding, friendly, wrinkled face appeared. 'Yes, Tinker? May I be of assistance?'

Tinker looked at him nervously. 'Mr B, have you got a soldering iron?'

Mr Butler's greying eyebrows raised themselves by half an inch. 'Yes, of course. But tell me: what do you need it for?'

'Makin' something.' Tinker avoided Mr Butler's intelligent, questioning eyes.

'I'm sure you are. But what, exactly?'

Tinker reached into his pocket, produced a grubby sheet of paper, and handed it over. Mr Butler examined it carefully. 'Ah, I see. A circuit diagram for, let me see—a crystal set?'

Tinker looked up expectantly, suddenly enlivened. 'Do you know about this stuff?'

'Indeed I do, Tinker. When I had the honour to serve in the war, I was for a time a radio operator and I am very familiar with electronic circuits. Would you like a hand?'

Tinker thought about this. 'I want to do it meself, if that's all right. I've got all the parts from school, 'cos the teacher let me have 'em, but I'm not sure about soldering irons. I've never used one before. It sounds dangerous.'

Mr Butler inclined his substantial chin in affirmation. 'Soldering irons are indeed a source of considerable peril. I would be happy to instruct you in the use of the instrument. Oh, and Tinker?' He looked again at the somewhat smeared circuit diagram. 'You've got three resistors here. I think you might find that two will be sufficient for your purposes.'

'Thanks, Mr B.' Tinker's mouth split in a broad grin. 'After dinner?'

'After dinner it is. As soon as I have helped Mrs B with the dishes.'

Chapter Thirteen

They do not preach that their God will rouse them a
little before the nuts work loose.
They do not preach that His Pity allows them to
drop their job when they damn-well choose.
As in the thronged and the lighted ways, so in the
dark and the desert they stand,
Wary and watchful all their days that their
brethren's ways may be long in the land.

—Rudyard Kipling, *The Sons of Martha*

'Are you sure you don't want to dance, Dot?'

Phryne had parked the Hispano-Suiza outside the formidable fortress that was the Presbyterian church. She had not seen it before, but now understood Dot's discomfiture earlier in the day. While none of the churches had bagged the summit of the hill, this one was well-placed to repel schism and Border raiding parties alike. The sound of violins tuning up could be heard, apparently from around the back of the orange-brick edifice. A narrow stairway had been lined with coloured balloons. Alice had already ascended the stairs, looking, Phryne considered, like a church mouse fleeing the attentions of the vestry cat. Dot turned to her employer and shook her head with finality. She had had her toes trodden on too often by clumsy boys. 'No, thank you, Miss Phryne. I'll help in the kitchen and keep an eye out.'

Phryne nodded. 'A good idea, Dot. I'll watch the hall.'

'Do you think anything bad is likely to happen?'

'A sensible criminal wouldn't risk it. But...'

'You don't think they're sensible?'

'No, Dot. I don't think so. Never mind.' She grinned. 'Let's have some fun, anyway.'

They mounted the steps and entered the church hall. It was spotlessly clean, with dazzling white paint and plaster throughout, and clean, polished stone underfoot. At one end, the kitchen opened onto a broad serving table. Trays of sandwiches were already in evidence, as well as a punchbowl substantial enough to bath a medium-sized dog or Miniature horse. Clean glasses awaited to be filled with what looked like fruit cup. On the Sabbath it would be non-alcoholic, but Phryne's cognac-laden hip flask would be available to remedy this oversight. At the other end of the room was a picture of a heavily bearded King George V doing a commendable impression of the Wrath of the Lord, flanked by the Australian flag and the cross of St Andrew.

On either side of the hall a great many chairs had been arrayed, and guests were already seated. While you could not say that there was a firm policy of separation between the sexes, there did appear to be an informal rule thereto. The boys were on the right-hand side, the girls upon the left, and at the back of the hall several rows of tables and chairs had been set out for the elders and the terpsichorean-challenged. There was desultory traffic to and from the drinks table, but without haste or conviction. In one corner was a low platform, on which the band members were tuning their instruments. The oldest—a slight, aggressively bearded character in a checked shirt, bush hat, black boots, and faded blue gorblimey trousers—carried, of all things, a large banjo with every apparent intention of playing it. Peeking unobtrusively from his trouser pocket was a small flourish of penny whistles of differing sizes. He gave Phryne a flirtatious wink, and proceeded to strum the opening bars of 'See the Conquering Hero Comes' from Handel's *Judas Maccabaeus*. Phryne grinned at his visage and promised herself that this man might well repay closer inspection—if she got the chance, which on current trends seemed unlikely in the extreme.

Phryne dismissed the remainder of the band after the most cursory of glances. These might be labelled Nervous Girl on Fiddle (in the height of Connemara fashion circa 1860), Shy Boy on Double Bass, and Gormless Uncle on Percussion and Auxiliary Fiddle. Phryne looked with more intent through the kitchen hatch and was unsurprised to see the Tremain sisters moving laden trays about and tending the stove. 'All right, Dot. Go and say hello to Annie and Jessie and keep a weather eye out.'

'Yes, Miss.'

Dot hied herself kitchenwards and Phryne surveyed the room. Someone, or more likely many people, had gone to considerable trouble to hang paper lanterns in all the colours of the rainbow around the room. Small electric lights were hidden inside them and the effect was festive. By night it would approach the description magical, with a little extra faith and goodwill. She wondered if the dance would get that far. Tomorrow was Monday morning, and cows would need milking before dawn.

More locals of all ages were arriving, some still in their Sunday best and others in appropriate dancing gear: swirly dresses and white blouses for the girls, and loose shirts and trousers for the boys, and waistcoats for pretty much everyone. Most of the menfolk had taken the safe option of black and white, although Kenneth McAlpine had come in his dress kilt of red and dark green, with a frilly shirt which matched his vast and intimidating muscles in the way that Corinthian capitals look good on a box-girder bridge. But many of the women had gone all out for colour. Crimson skirts and waistcoats seemed popular, as did emerald. A rule of thumb seemed to be that the young were there to dress up and impress each other, and the older guests were there to be the humble backdrop. Phryne recollected that in most places the formal dance was the socially approved venue for matchmaking. She smiled inwardly; she had never had much time for this theory.

Before the dancing began in earnest, Phryne decided to use the opportunity to cross-examine the male youth of Daylesford and surrounding districts. She made her way across the room, blithely ignoring the standing waves of disapproval emanating from pretty much every female over the age of thirty.

As she established herself in their midst, a good quarter of the young men were frankly terrified of this paragon of fashionable womanhood in patterned silk, another quarter were optimistically lascivious, but not notably downcast when their advances were politely rebuffed, and the rest were frankly flattered by her glamorous attentions.

'Hello,' she said to one frank admirer. 'I'm Phryne Fisher.' She gave him her gloved hand, and the youth bent over it and allowed his lips to brush the fabric. He was medium-sized, freckled, and of a decidedly sunny demeanour. His trousers, white shirt, and waistcoat were well-mended, but definitely second-hand. 'I'm James Hepburn.' The voice was deep, but uncertain of itself, as if it were a bass trombone not all of whose lower notes had as yet been thoroughly explored. His hair was dark and curly, and his eyes soft agates.

'And what do you do, James?'

'Me? I work on Dad's farm. But what I love best is cricket. Do you like cricket, Miss Fisher?'

Like all women, Phryne was fully prepared to be bored senseless by Men Explaining Things if there happened to be a good reason for it. As it happened, Phryne loved cricket, and probably knew more about it than Mr Hepburn. But she would probably learn more about her interlocutor if she pretended wide-eyed ignorance.

'I'm not sure,' she temporised. 'What do you like about it?'

The boy's face glowed like a lighthouse. 'I love that it's never over, even if all seems lost. And it's a battle of wits between bat and ball, so utterly unlike football. We play that here, of course, but I—' his hands briefly indicated his limbs '—I'm not very coordinated. But I bowl leg spin. And googlies.'

This boy might indeed be a suitor for Annie's hand, and indeed other parts of her, but she would for the present have to take second place to the mysteries of bat and ball. 'I've only just learned how to bowl it.'

Phryne turned, for a blond young man handed James an orange from the fruit bowl with an air of faint mockery. It was received with, 'Thanks, Graeme. Now, this is the leg break.' He flipped the orange so it spun viciously. 'Here's the topspinner.' Another whirl of orange peel. 'And this is the googly.' Phryne noted that he spun the googly mostly with his little finger. There were other ways of making the ball spin in the opposite direction, but this was one acceptable method.

'I see,' Phryne murmured, resting her hand on his arm. 'That looks very clever.'

The honest, sunburned face looked up at her. 'Thanks, Miss Fisher. There's another thing called the flipper, which Clarrie Grimmett bowls. I think it goes like this.' The orange began its trajectory between thumb and forefinger, but swerved wildly out of his reach, heading straight towards the abundant cleavage of a young girl, whose mouth opened wide enough to swallow the orange, flipper and all. Out of nowhere, a hand plucked the ball out of mid-air and restored it to the fruit bowl. The tall, saturnine man attached to the hand gave the girl a formal bow, made a gesture of head-slapping towards Mr Hepburn, and stalked off.

Phryne turned back to the discomfited youth. 'Who was that man, James?'

'Johnnie Armstrong. He's always ticking me off in the field. He says I don't concentrate.'

'I see. And does he bowl flippers too?'

The young man's face looked a little downcast. 'He can, and should. It's those long fingers of his. Such an advantage, and I don't have them. But he prefers to bowl left-arm fast. He likes hitting batsmen.'

'Well, I mustn't keep you.'

The youth gave Phryne a puzzled look, and his face brightened. 'Oh, I see. Yes, of course. Delighted to meet you, Miss Fisher.' He bowed and departed, presumably pursued by a bear.

'And you, young man. What do you bowl?' Phryne turned to the donor of the orange, who seemed vaguely familiar. He laughed with tolerant scepticism.

'I'm Graeme Forbes. I bowl left-arm orthodox and bat a bit. I only gave him the orange because otherwise he'd have upset the whole table rummaging for it. He's a bit clumsy, but a splendid chap. I say, I love your dress, Miss Fisher. Is it Erté?'

'Not quite, but a splendid guess, Mr Forbes. Are you interested in fashion?' She looked this young man over carefully. By sheer chance her three main suspects had all introduced themselves, more or less. This one was a bit on the plump side, with wavy blond hair and gentle blue eyes.

'Not really,' he conceded. 'But I've been reading up on it.

Because of girls, you know? See, the problem with us boys is that most of us live on farms, and no one wants to hear you talk about farming. I mean, we already know all about it, and it's a bit dull, to be honest. And lots of girls aren't interested in cricket. You aren't, are you, Miss Fisher?'

Phryne gave him a shrewd look. 'Well, yes, Mr Forbes, I am. I once saw Lionel Tennyson bat with one hand against McDonald and Gregory in the Headingley Test. You don't get cricketers like him anymore. But that aside, I do like to listen to people talk. I learn such a lot about them that way.'

This, if it went home at all, was allowed to pass harmlessly through to the wicketkeeper. He nodded. 'Indeed? Well, that's wonderful to hear. But most girls don't care for it, so I thought I'd learn about fashion, because girls like to talk about dresses and suchlike.'

'Any particular girl you have in mind?'

The man blushed beneath his freckled suntan. 'Well, yes. But she's working in the kitchen tonight. It's all right. She's a splendid girl. I don't really hope, you know. I think she's too far above the likes of me. But she's very sweet, and I admire her greatly.' Suddenly embarrassed, he straightened his back. 'I'm so sorry, Miss Fisher. I talk too much. But I am delighted to meet you.' He clicked his boots together, bowed, and retreated.

Phryne sat herself down with a large mug of fruit cup, laced it unobtrusively with cognac and watched as the girls and boys paired off with decorous invitations. No girl refused a proffered hand, and in their place Phryne would not have either. The band began to play in earnest, and the youth of Daylesford disported themselves on the dance floor. The evening's entertainment had a decidedly Irish flavour. The Waves of Tory, the Pride of Erin, and the Walls of Limerick were three which remained in Phryne's memory. Each was briefly announced, and everyone seemed to know what to do immediately. Her suspects? James Hepburn was dancing ably and cleverly, despite his mishap with the orange. A faintly mocking Johnnie Armstrong danced as if he were a trifle bored by it all, but he never missed a step. Graeme Forbes was on occasion caught out of position, zigging when he should have been zagging and vice versa, but each time a dextrous female hand would drag him back into position. Phryne observed the girls intently as they did so. While Mr Forbes was clearly known to be awkward on the dance floor, it appeared he was not only tolerated but possibly loved. The rolling of eyeballs at his repeated missteps was kept to an all but imperceptible level. All three men danced with Colleen O'Rourke and not one gave any sign of brooding menace or proprietorship. And, finally, she watched Kenneth McAlpine, who danced like a battleship surrounded by pinnaces, clumping his massive feet down only after a lightning inspection to ensure that no one's feet were likely to be trapped underneath his mighty tread.

The boys, taken en masse, were handsome enough, and none seemed notably ill at ease or exuded the unmistakable perfume of Warning! Danger! *Pericoloso!* to be expected from at least one member of a medium-sized crowd. Alice, Phryne noticed, had accepted the hand of a grave young man who offered his to her. Phryne could not recall seeing him around before. He was better dressed than the other boys. He wore a dark amethyst silk waistcoat, his shirt was a dazzling white, his trousers clearly tailored, and his small feet encased in black patent leather. Alice and her favoured boy grinned at each other and danced expertly. This was a new development, and Phryne did not know how to interpret it. Meanwhile, sets were turned, willows stripped, arches formed, and dimpling girls flirted soundlessly with admiring boys—and none was more admired than Colleen O'Rourke, dressed in her Highland Dancing costume and trailing a scarf of dark blue and green from her shoulder.

Phryne sipped her drink and considered. Colleen was careful to change partners after every dance. Nobody seemed to mind this, and Phryne commended the girl's judgement. And the band, she realised, were seriously good at what they did. The banjo gave place betimes to the penny whistles (different ones for whichever key the rest were occupying), the violins seesawed with vigour and delicacy, the round hand drum was chastised with what looked like a porridge stirrer, and from time to time a pair of what she could swear were mutton bones clashed together. The effect ought to have been macabre enough (summoning to mind visions of dancing skeletons), but the good-humoured swing of the music somehow rendered this acceptable.

'May I sit next to you, Miss Fisher?'

Phryne looked up at a looming figure. That really was the *mot juste*. Some men lean, but this one was a natural-born loomer. He was well over six feet tall, somewhat portly, with a middle-aged mid-section which strained at his off-white waistcoat like a spring flood at a levee. The weak chin—inexpertly shaved—was inadequately disguised by a ridiculous pantomime villain moustache, and a tidal wave of eau de cologne failed to mask what Phryne's sensitive palate recognised as industrial-grade gin. Dry party or not, the man was as plastered as a Giotto fresco.

She smiled a dazzling smile. 'Well, possibly, Mr No We Really Haven't Been Introduced. But then you would be occupying space which I require for other purposes. At any moment, my companion will return to this chair, and I do not wish her to find it so abundantly tenanted.'

Bleary eyes rolled around in their sockets as feeble neurons collided with each other. Try as he might, the interloper could find nothing to his liking in any of the three sentences he had just taken on board. He attempted a gallant bow, which caused something within his superstructure to go *ping*, followed by *snap*. He all but overbalanced into Phryne's lap then retreated, muttering incoherent apologies.

Phryne looked around and caught the eye of Reverend McPherson, whose normally severe expression so far unbent itself as to give her a radiant smile. Phryne smiled back. Doubtless the minister was grimly pleased at seeing what Phryne could only conceive was one of his Problem Flock being given public chastisement.

Eventually the bandleader gave his banjo a mighty flourish and announced A Little Break for Refreshments, Ladies and Gentlemen. Colleen O'Rourke flounced straight towards him and gave him an enthusiastic embrace and a kiss on the cheek. Phryne's eyes flicked around the room but caught no one giving her anything vaguely resembling a look of smouldering jealousy. Phryne was beginning to feel that the local lads regarded Colleen more in the role of a force of nature, like a thunderstorm or a flash flood, rather than an object of romance. There was coming and going hither and yon. Phryne, having sat out the dancing, had already eaten her fill of dainty sandwiches and decided to invite herself into the kitchen.

No one stopped her. Jessie looked up at her with floury hands and grinned. 'Hello, Miss Fisher. Having a good time, I hope?'

Phryne nodded, watching a heavily aproned Annie as she opened the oven door. A warm gust of spicy fruit wafted through the kitchen. 'That's the last of the pies, Jessie.' Annie lifted the large oven tray without apparent effort and placed it on a wooden chopping board.

'That's fine, Annie. You can take a rest—and get changed.'

Annie looked up hopefully.

'You know you want to dance and have some fun. So do it! There's a whole second half still to come.'

Annie moved forward, fell into Jessie's arms, and kissed her cheek. 'You're so kind to me, Jessie. Thank you.'

Over her sister's shoulder, Jessie seemed to be staring into the middle distance. Phryne motioned to Dot, and they slipped out the back door. It was late afternoon, but a broad beam of sunlight was blazing across the backyard. 'Well, Dot? Did you see anything untoward?'

'No, Miss. Nobody came into the kitchen at all. One or two of the boys opened the door looking for Annie, but Jessie scared them off and they went away.'

'Thank you, Dot. Well, I've been watching all our other suspects. Alice is dancing with a young man who seems a cut above all the other locals. He's danced with some other girls, but he goes straight back to her every time. What's going on there I can't imagine. As far the others, I can't see anyone actually pining for Miss O'Rourke, and I haven't seen any malicious looks directed at anyone. Dot, has all the food been put out? There isn't anything else?'

'The last of the pies are going out now, Miss Phryne.'

Phryne lit a cigarette and watched through the open back door as Jessie womanhandled the plates of pies onto the serving area separating the kitchen from the hall. She couldn't see any point in Jessie trying to poison the food, even if she were the culprit. The method was far too random, since there was no way of knowing which pie would finish up inside which young man. No, Jessie was looking less and less likely as a suspect; if you could trust atmosphere, Jessie and Annie were the best of friends.

'Dot, there's nothing more to be got out of kitchen-minding. Why not come and sit with me in the second half? I would welcome your company, and it might preserve me from unwelcome attention.'

Dot nodded. 'Miss Phryne, I think we'll find out more now that Annie's going to join the dancing.'

'I agree, Dot. And I would like to talk to the minister. Of all the locals I can possibly confide in, he seems to be the Man Most Likely.' Having said which, she mused in silence. In a mystery novel that would probably make him the villain. 'Well, we shall see.'

———

If the appearance of Colleen O'Rourke had enlivened proceedings in the first half, this was merely in the nature of a curtain-raiser. Annie Tremain had undergone a dazzling transformation with the aid of the ladies' room, and now appeared resplendent in a black velvet gown. The contrast with her milk-white complexion was striking enough, but her bodice, normally so demure and tight-laced, allowed onlookers a small glimpse of hidden pleasures in her neckline, which was adorned by a small amethyst pendant suspended just, and only just, above the creamy curve of her not-quite-completely-covered bosom. Her hair was unbound, enthusiastically brushed, and swung at her waist like an enchantress's girdle. The band struck up, a new dance was announced, and Gentle Annie offered her hand to Graeme Forbes moments before she was bowled over in the rush of breathless young manhood.

Dot watched the dancers while Phryne examined the onlookers. Some of the Obviously Married had now joined in, and so more chairs had been cleared to accommodate them. These latter appeared engrossed in one another, and if wandering eyes occasionally strayed over the beauteous girls as they passed, no one was going to take cognisance thereof. Phryne was looking for evidence of murderous intent from the onlookers but saw only the enraptured and the oblivious. One old man sat in the corner, sipping tea and reading the *Daylesford Advocate*. Her importuner appeared to have departed the premises, possibly with words of strenuous encouragement from The Management.

She turned her attention to the dancing. The daylight outside was fading, and the glowing paper lanterns bathed the hall in a kaleidoscope of colour. Phryne noted that Annie, like Colleen, changed partners after every dance. Phryne awarded herself some more surreptitious refreshment from her flask and sat back to watch Annie. The girl was perfectly aware of the effect she was making. Her eyes danced, exulting in the moment. She knew how gorgeous she was and loved every moment of it. Yet where was the harm in that? Phryne looked at each of the other girls' faces to see if any were looking daggers at her but could discern not so much as a nail file of envy. Colleen and Annie were the undisputed queens of the ball, and nobody seemed to mind.

For the last dance, and amid overdone groans from the panting youths, Colleen O'Rourke extended her arm to Annie, who smiled, dimpled, and nodded. Colleen took the male role to Annie's left, and the two girls flung themselves into a vigorous dance in pairs, then fours, then eights. Youths and maidens twirled around each other, and the band roused itself for one final flourish. During one moment of stasis, Colleen O'Rourke leaned over to another couple and gave James Hepburn an impudent kiss on the cheek. Hepburn's partner (a thin-faced girl with freckles) looked momentarily scandalised but appeared to accept this. As the dance quickened, she swept Hepburn into her arms for a moment. Then she stood stock-still and stared as James Hepburn slithered downwards to the floor and lay there in an untidy heap.

Everyone except Colleen O'Rourke gasped and gaped. The music wound down slowly, as if the air had leaked out of a giant balloon. The band members stared as well. Colleen, meanwhile, kneeled and put her hand to the side of Hepburn's neck. She shook her head, raked the gawpers with an expression of scorn and dismissal, and erupted through the crowd.

Phryne watched, fascinated. Miss O'Rourke re-emerged from

the press of bodies, dragging Dr Henderson by the arm. She led him to the recumbent figure and stood facing the mob with both hands on her defiant hips. Presently the doctor shook his head, took out his handkerchief and placed it reverently on the face of the dear departed. Colleen O'Rourke stamped off in search of... Phryne could not imagine what. The thin-faced girl stood where she was, both hands pressed to her cheeks, frozen to the spot. No one was screaming. And no one seemed to know how to react.

'Miss? What are we going to do about this?' Dot whispered.

'Nothing, Dot. I'm watching to see what the locals do. Keep an eye on Annie and her admirers for me, will you? I can't look at everything at once.'

Shocked whispers began to break out across the room. The minister strode into the centre of the hall, stood right next to the fallen body, and raised his hand. The murmurs subsided. The minister did not even raise his voice.

'Ladies and gentlemen, until we know what has happened, I will have to insist that nobody leaves the hall. The washrooms are out the back, for any that need it. I have sent for the polis, and they will have questions for you. I repeat: until we know more, nobody should leave.'

All eyes turned to the exit. There stood Sergeant Offaly, in uniform. He smiled.

Chapter Fourteen

To these from birth is Belief forbidden; from these
till death is Relief afar.
They are concerned with matters hidden, under the
earthline their altars are
The secret fountains to follow up, waters withdrawn
to restore to the mouth,
And gather the floods as in a cup, and pour them
again at a city's drouth.

—Rudyard Kipling, *The Sons of Martha*

'Miss Fisher? I'm Detective Inspector Brian Kelly. But most people call me Mick, so you may as well too.'

The manse office had been converted, with the Reverend McPherson's consent, into an impromptu interview room. Phryne held out her gloved hand and received a manly, muscular hand-shake. Both subsided into sturdy, plain wooden chairs opposite each other across a plain, somewhat chipped wooden table. Phryne looked with interest at Kelly. He was a colossus, built to endure when towers crumbled, cities fell, and civilisations came and went. His shoulders strained at the boundaries of his coat. These were the shoulders of a man who carried home strayed oxen and chastised their misdeeds. His face was crowned with a clipped furze of dark auburn hair, and an absurd ginger moustache lurked beneath a craggy nose like a small turnip. Taken as a whole, his features reminded the viewer of a cliff face of weathered rock left out in the desert sun. Both hands were clenched on the wooden table. They had unquestionably Seen Life, probably after closing time at the pub or in the apprehension of innumerable malefactors. There were lumps in the knuckles. Even the lumps had lumps of their own. Ancient scars presumably remembered the impact of departing teeth.

But the eyes! They were greenish-blue, and blinked slowly, and took in absolutely everything with a calm impassivity which spoke of a rough-and-tumble life's lessons well learned. Once you blocked out his vast self-assurance, you came to see him as an inquisitive crow, or possibly a magpie, with white shirt cuffs contrasting with his black waistcoat, jacket, trousers, and necktie. Whatever Hibernian lilt might still lurk in Kelly's vocal cords had been heavily overlaid with a standard Australian bush drawl.

'Pleased to meet you, Mick,' Phryne ventured.

He inclined his granite jaw and gave her a small smile. 'To save time and fuss, I may as well tell you that your fame precedes you. And while I'm not gonna play Dumb Cop to your Aristocratic Detective, I need a result here and I'd be a fool if I didn't use whatever help you can give me.' He blinked, and put his massive head on one side, looking now like a kookaburra eyeing off an unattended sausage at a barbecue. 'Sergeant Offaly tells me you're staying up at the Springs?'

'I am. At the Mooltan guesthouse.'

'That's where you'll be if I want to find you? Good-o. So tell me about the death of Donald Mackay.'

'At the Highland Gathering yesterday, Kenneth McAlpine was tossing the caber when he was stung by what he thought was a bee. As a result, the caber slipped out of his hand, fell to earth, and bounced up into the head of Donald Mackay, who was standing pretty much by himself to the right. I found a sewing machine needle which had been fired into McAlpine's neck, probably by a blowpipe. Unfortunately, there were a lot of people standing around and, frankly, it could have been any of them.'

'And where is this needle now?'

'Your sergeant has it. He took it away from me.' Phryne and the inspector exchanged a glance which suggested an unspoken observation that Sergeant Offaly's talents would be taxed to the limit by remembering his own name and address, or the number of digits on his extremities.

'I see. And it's too late to question the bystanders. I have some notes from the sergeant about his subsequent enquiries, but they were less than informative. A pity. Now, Miss Fisher, where were you when James Hepburn met with his misadventure tonight?'

'Please, call me Phryne.' She was beginning to warm to the inspector. 'I was sitting on a chair watching the dancers, and everything else. And regrettably I did not manage to see anything suspicious.'

'But you were looking for trouble, were you?'

'I was. I have a theory, which you may or may not wish to hear, and I do not think either of these two mishaps were an accident. I don't believe in coincidences as a rule.'

'Neither do I.' The inspector sat hunched forward in his chair and stared at the low plaster ceiling for a moment. 'All right, Phryne. What's your theory?'

Phryne leaned forward and lowered her voice. 'Mick, as you may be aware, we have two extraordinarily beautiful girls hereabouts. And, fantastic as this may seem, I am beginning to suspect that somebody—a jealous lover, presumably—is systematically eliminating rivals in love.'

Kelly blinked several times and shook his head. He inhaled, briefly, the aromatic scent of Jicky and sighed. 'Well, it's a possibility, I suppose. Both young men were suitors for one or both of these girls, were they?'

'Both Hepburn and Mackay were known to be great admirers of the Temperance Hotel barmaid, Annie Tremain.'

'The girl with the long blonde hair?'

'And other attributes which are rather too notable to be ignored.'

'Yes, she's very well-developed, is she not? And the other girl?'

'Colleen O'Rourke is also very popular with the boys. She's a Highland dancer.'

The inspector's hard eyes softened. 'Indeed she is.' After a pause, he asked, 'What brings you to Daylesford, by the way?'

'Just a holiday, or so I had believed until yesterday. We seem to have too many mysteries around here.'

Mick Kelly gave a short, fox-like bark of amusement. 'Welcome to the wonderful world of policing, Miss Fisher.'

They sat in silence for a moment, then the inspector sighed again. 'Well, Phryne, I'll be staying at the Station Hotel if you chance upon anything you think I should know. If I want to speak to you again, I'll ask at the Mooltan. Send in Colleen, will you?'

Phryne rose, left the interview room and gestured to Colleen, who was waiting outside, to enter. As the door was closing behind the imperious Miss O'Rourke, she heard the latter say, 'Hello, Uncle Brian!'

Phryne grinned to herself.

Re-entering the hall, she saw that Sergeant Offaly was occupying the main doorway, which left very little room for anyone else. While cerebral detection was utterly beyond his imagination, the role of sheepdog with errant flock was one he felt he could comfortably manage, and he was doing so with relentless patience. The only other exit had been locked fast, and the still night air only entered the hall after the sergeant had frisked it thoroughly. The gathering was suitably chastened. The customary After the Party is Over feeling of general letdown was amplified a hundred-fold. Everyone was sitting down, either on chairs or on the floor, heedless of their party finery, and clearly wishful to go home at the earliest opportunity. Conversation was whispered, and sporadic.

She spotted Dot sitting on a chair in the corner of the hall. Standing over her was the minister, dispensing tea and biscuits. Dot looked up at Phryne and gave her employer a weary I'm-All-Right-Miss look.

'Miss Fisher? I believe you may wish to converse with me?'

Reverend McPherson had an unmistakable Highland accent overlaid with what was, if not Glasgow, somewhere within the County of Lanark. A hand reached out and Phryne took it gingerly in her glove, feeling the same thrill of what was probably Protestant Enthusiasm that Dot had reported to her.

'I have another small office,' the minister continued, 'if you and your companion would like to accompany me there.'

'That is an excellent idea. Dot?'

Dot drank the remainder of her tea then rose, and the minister led the way to a small office with seating for three around a wooden table. There was a single bare electric bulb hanging from a long cord, and no other light. The minister waited until they had seated themselves, then himself assumed a chair.

'Miss Fisher, your companion has confided in me to a degree, and suggested that you may wish for further information from a reliable source. I would be happy to assist you.'

Phryne gave him a forty-watt smile. 'Reverend McPherson, Miss Williams was indeed prescient. I have been given to understand that my repute, or possibly infamy, precedes me.' This brought a faint smile from the minister. 'I have far too many mysteries here and not nearly enough information to go on. Or, rather, I have a great deal of what might well turn out to be misinformation.'

The minister scratched his chin. 'I see. And you regard me as a reliable source of uncompromised information? Very well. I hope that you can assist the polis with their investigations. Events here are taking a calamitous turn.'

Phryne marshalled her thoughts. Where even to begin? Since Inspector Kelly was continuing enquiries in one case, she decided she should use the opportunity to investigate the other more thoroughly. 'Aside from our unfortunate deaths, it seems that women have been disappearing in mysterious circumstances. Can you tell me anything about that?'

The Minister regarded her steadily. 'I can. Three women from this town have disappeared from their homes without trace in the last year from farms between here and Sailors Falls. I have no idea where they are now, and neither has anyone else. However…' He reached into his coat pocket and produced a small pair of half-moon spectacles, which he perched on his ears. 'Have you made the acquaintance of the licensee of the Temperance Hotel?'

'I have indeed met Mr McKenzie,' Phryne confirmed. 'Please go on.'

'McKenzie does not frequent my kirk very often, but I have reached an opinion as to his character. His wife is one of the three missing women. Janet McKenzie was a good woman, but there was too little spark about her. I doubt that theirs was a happy home.' The minister's eyes were boring into her. 'But if he were to be suspected of doing away with her, then where is his motive for the other two women? He was never a ladies' man—not even in his own secret thoughts, I would guess. And their bairn Robert also went missing at the same time as Janet.'

'Could they have run away?'

'It's possible. But that doesn't explain the other disappearances. If we have an abductor of women among us, Janet McKenzie may have been one of his victims, with the bairn an ancillary consequence.'

'What can you tell me about the other two women?'

'Not from my flock, so I cannot say.'

'What about the Tremain girls?'

The minister shook his head. 'Those two young women work too hard, while their uncle does little except drink and brood. I don't know them well. I do think him capable of Human Weakness, yet I doubt he has the willpower to do active harm to anyone.'

'And the other women?'

The minister opened his hands in a gesture of tolerant resignation. 'We simply do not know. They may be victims of foul play. Or they may have run off somewhere. I really cannot give you any more information than that.'

If the minister knew any more than this, he wasn't letting on. Phryne decided she may as well return to the main mystery. 'All right. Now we have at least two murders—'

'Are you certain of that, Miss Fisher? Poor Mr Hepburn may have merely had a seizure of some kind. Dr Henderson has formed no opinion as yet. And the mishap at the Gathering may have been an accident.'

Phryne and Dot both stirred in their uncomfortable seats. Caution was all very well, but it seemed that the minister was taking it to extremes. Phryne put her head on one side and gave him a look of highly charged scepticism. 'I doubt it very much, Reverend. I am assuming murder until I am shown otherwise.

Did either of these poor lads own property worth committing murder for?'

McPherson shook his head. 'Both have living fathers and elder brothers. I doubt they had more than a few pounds between them. I cannot see a murder for gain in either case.'

'And what if it were murder to gain the love of a beautiful girl?'

The minister shook his head, smiled, and looked at the low ceiling. 'Really, Miss Fisher! Do young men kill their rivals in love anywhere but in storybooks? I hardly think so.'

Dot didn't think it likely either, but she watched her employer lean forward with animation. 'Well, I admit it's unlikely; but the one thing our victims had in common was that they both paid court to Annie Tremain. Improbable as it seems, I can't think of any other motive right now.'

'I do wish that girl would marry.' Now the minister was shaking his head in frustration. 'I know she's young, but she's demoralising the regiment. Half the young men in this town spend their lives gawping at her instead of getting on with their work.'

'What is your opinion of her?'

'She is a good girl. Even though she works in a public house, there has never been a breath of scandal about her.' He paused, allowing this to sink in. Phryne had been wondering about that. Would the minister even know if there had been? Probably he would. 'She is kind and good-hearted and thinks well of everyone,' he went on. 'This is a perilous delusion. The world is filled with snares for the godly and ungodly alike.'

'Do either of the girls come to your church?'

'Not very often. As I have remarked already, McKenzie works them too hard. And, though I hesitate to say it, the presence of Miss Annie in church is a sore distraction to the young men of my flock. The girls were raised Anglican, but their father was killed in the war, and the mother died of grief thereafter.'

'And what of Colleen O'Rourke?'

The minister broke into an unexpected broad grin. 'Miss O'Rourke is certainly high-spirited, Miss Fisher. But she is a fine lassie.' He paused to look at Dot, who blushed and cast her eyes down. 'She takes charge of things. As soon as that poor boy fell to the floor, she dragged Dr Henderson away from his wife and brought him to the boy within seconds. Did you see that now? And when it became apparent that the boy was dead, she asked if she could borrow my telephone.'

'So she's the one who called Inspector Kelly? I heard her call him Uncle Brian.'

'The Kellys and the O'Rourkes form what you might call a powerful clan hereabouts. They're Catholics, of course, but they are good people, though a little rough around the edges. She is a very level-headed young woman. She likes the lads fine, but does not allow liberties.'

Phryne felt she could not allow this to pass. 'Really? I saw her kiss one of the boys.'

'Girlish high spirits. It was not a sinful kiss.'

'And she hugged and kissed the bandleader.'

To her astonishment, the minister burst out laughing: a rich, rolling torrent of mirth. 'Kevin O'Rourke is her father, Miss Fisher. The band members are all relatives of hers.'

Phryne laughed with him. 'I see. Now, do you think it possible that anyone might conceive a forbidden passion for her?'

'I doubt it. I really do. She isn't that sort of girl.'

'And Annie Tremain is. You're probably right, Reverend. And yet...' Phryne eyed him steadily. 'There's no denying that she kissed James Hepburn, and a few seconds later he dropped dead. It's a coincidence that might point somewhere.'

'I suppose so, Miss Fisher, but—' He was interrupted by a strident knock on the door. 'Come in,' he called.

The door opened and Dr Henderson bustled into the room. 'Reverend, I've just been talking to the Inspector and—' He stopped suddenly as he took in the presence of Dot and Phryne. 'I'm sorry. Shall I come back later?'

'By no means.' McPherson rose, and shut the door behind the doctor. 'If you have news for me, Miss Fisher and Miss Williams may be told also. Miss Fisher is a private investigator.'

Henderson's brown eyes flickered, then returned to the minister. 'Well, I have been reluctant to form any definite theories, but I have reason to suspect an overdose of atropine.'

The minister frowned. 'Deadly nightshade? How was it administered, do you think?'

Henderson shook his head. 'I cannot imagine. The man was dancing, and suddenly toppled over. But...' The man kept looking at the two women as if hoping they might disappear through the floorboards.

Phryne decided to help him out. 'But a fatal dosage might not be immediate in its effects. It would interfere with the nervous system, and cause erratic movements, dizziness, and disorientation. However, the man was dancing and it might not have been noticed until far too late.'

The doctor's mouth opened and shut repeatedly, like a goldfish taking breadcrumbs on board. 'Why, er, yes, Miss Fisher. I am surprised you know that.' He drew himself upright. 'The coroner will have to sit on him, I'm afraid.'

'That sounds exquisitely uncomfortable.' Phryne rose. 'Reverend, thank you very much for your time. You've been most helpful.'

She and Dot left the room, closing the door behind them. The low voices continued, but Phryne did not eavesdrop. There seemed no point.

———

With a weary sigh of satisfaction, Tinker inserted the final screw into his pinewood cabinet. Two black Bakelite knobs protruded from the front. He switched them on and played with them. After a while, far-off voices mingled with static. He grinned to himself with considerable satisfaction. Now to put the rest of his plan in motion.

Chapter Fifteen

And we, that now make merry in the Room
They left, and Summer dresses in new Bloom,
Ourselves must we beneath the Couch of Earth
Descend, ourselves to make a couch—for whom?

—Edward Fitzgerald, *The Rubáiyát of*
Omar Khayyám of Naishápúr

The hall had emptied somewhat. Having brought Alice to the dance, Phryne felt responsible for getting her home again, but Alice was not there. Neither was Dr Henderson, last seen in the minister's office. The body had also disappeared. From the main office, the sound of Mick Kelly's gruff interrogative voice could be heard. Sergeant Offaly still stood impassively, beaming with a general sense of Horatius at the Bridge. As Phryne paused in the middle of the hall, the office door opened, and Phryne watched Graeme Forbes wander towards the sergeant, who did not move. Forbes looked tired, shocked, and resigned in equal measure. His waistcoat was unbuttoned, his white shirt stained with perspiration, and he gave the imperturbable sergeant a most pitiful look.

'Sergeant? The inspector says I can go now. Please?'

Phryne wondered for a moment if Offaly was going to ask for the secret password, but he finally relented, unbending sufficiently to allow Forbes's egress. Then he resumed his blank-eyed stare and folded his arms behind his back.

Dot put a tentative hand on Phryne's sleeve. 'Miss? It's getting late. Can we go too?'

Phryne led her companion to the side of the hall and sat down, indicating that Dot should join her. She did so, with some reluctance, and Phryne put her rouged lips close to Dot's ear. 'I want to observe these people, Dot. We'll never get a better chance to watch them with their defences down.'

'As you say, Miss.'

What Dot mostly looked at was Annie Tremain with her face buried in the vast and companionable chest of Kenneth McAlpine. With infinite patience, the tosser of cabers lifted the diagonal hem of his plaid from his shoulder and gradually inched it over Annie's head. Whimpers were emerging therefrom, and it was clear that there were indeed tears before bedtime. As there might well be. When Annie's golden waterfall of hair was completely covered, the whimpering died away. His mild eyes locked with Dot's for a moment. He looked to be resigned to his fate, but did not appear to be in any great discomfort. Seated a little away from the pair was Jessie, looking both concerned and more than a little martyred.

Phryne's eyes were flicking around the hall. Nearly everyone looked shocked and out of countenance. The band had been interviewed already and had disappeared along with Colleen. Of her main persons of interest, only Johnnie Armstrong was still there. He looked, as usual, bored, but in control of himself. He sat on his chair with his hands folded, looking at the ceiling and virtually immobile. But Phryne looked away from him to something which caught her eye. Seated along the opposite wall was a woman in early middle age, dressed in a faded black crepe gown and wielding a fan in her thin hands. The woman's face looked sunken, like a failed soufflé. Her pale, steady eyes and the determined set of her narrow jaw told a different tale. Phryne had seen her earlier and had found nothing remarkable there. Now she wore, against the late summer night, a knitted scarf in bands of red, green, white, and purple. The same colour scheme, in sober fact, as the scarf Phryne and Dot had noted at Misery Farm near Sailors Falls. She tucked it closer around her neck and stared in mute defiance around the hall. Phryne's thumbs pricked. Somehow this apparition struck her as important, though she could not fathom it as yet.

The mystery deepened when the inspector's door opened again and Mrs Sinclair the librarian emerged. Rather than heading for freedom, she walked straight up to the woman with the scarf and sat next to her. They spoke in low voices well beyond hearing, but Phryne watched their hands and faces. She detected enquiry, cross-examination, questions, answers, and a general air of resolution. The two women left together. The sergeant opened his mouth to protest when the formidable librarian impaled him with a look of scorn and disgust. The two women passed unhindered into the great outdoors.

The procession in and out of the office became more abbreviated and cursory. Men and women came and went, and gave away nothing but shock, bewilderment, and a general sense of quiet despair—excepting, again, the magnificently bored Armstrong, who flicked his fingers down his jacket front and stalked away.

Phryne turned to Dot, who was by now well advanced in weariness. 'All right, Dot, we've seen enough, I think. Time to go.'

As they passed by the massive figure of Kenneth McAlpine, still with his voluptuous cargo of Gentle Annie, his eyes met

Phryne's. She smiled at him, then sailed past the sergeant into the cool night.

Dot fell fast asleep in the passenger seat of the Hispano-Suiza, and Phryne drove slowly. The night was deep around them, and the streetlights few. She drove sedately along the high road with the motor barely turning over. By contrast, her mind was racing. Was her theory of jealous love even tenable? Who could possibly be stupid enough to imagine they could murder their way to a girl's heart? There had to be more to this. Who had a motive? If the series of tragedies had really been designed to drive Annie into somebody's arms, then the clear winner was McAlpine. Could he have spiked himself with the needle and faked the mishap?

He could have. It was absolutely possible. It was in sober fact the most likely explanation of the death of Donald Mackay. The blowpipe idea was a lot less easy to believe in. Who better would know how to throw a caber directly at his rival? Against this she had only the gentle giant's reputation for placid calm, plus her observation of his face when holding Annie's head to his herculean chest. Yet that look was a serious point against the theory. Phryne had been manhandled herself by a great many ardent suitors. She knew what men were like with a beautiful woman in their arms. If McAlpine were truly a murderer, then surely his demeanour would have betrayed something. Barely concealed lust would have been evident. Even a hint of possessiveness would be enough to harden Phryne's suspicions. But Phryne had seen nothing beyond good-natured resignation at being used as a shoulder to cry on.

She shook her head in frustration, parked the car, and conducted her somnolent companion up the stairs. Dot stumbled into her room and shut the door. Phryne stormed silently into her own room and flung herself onto her bed. After five minutes' quiet fuming, she opened the door to the balcony, lit a gasper, and stared out into the darkness, willing it to yield up its secrets.

What on earth was going on with Alice and her unexpected boyfriend? The unwelcome excitements of the evening had driven this strange development into the background. Now, in the stilly night, she saw them again. Preoccupied as she had been, she had barely noticed Alice's dress when she had climbed into the car that afternoon. She had worn a dark blue waistcoat, a matching long skirt, and a frilly white blouse. Her hair had been brushed with extra care. She had wanted to make a serious impression, and had done so. And what of the beautiful young man, dressed far more expensively than anyone else? Alice had clung to him for at least four dances. Had she danced with anyone else? Phryne could not remember her doing so. Had he? Yes, he had. Several girls offered him their arms, and he had accepted all of them. Once. There was something about this young man which quietly screamed incomer. No one hailed him as a friend nor even an acquaintance. Indeed, several of the young men had looked daggers at him, if not scimitars.

Who was he? Had he and Alice been dancing the last dance? Yes, they had. And had they slipped away afterwards? Phryne supposed so. Dr Henderson had driven Alice to and from the Highland Gathering the day before, but he would not have been in any position to drive Alice anywhere tonight—not with a dead body on his hands. The mysterious young man had doubtless spirited her away. Phryne grimaced. Girls like Alice and Annie never seemed short of helpful hands to hold them above the storm-tossed waves, did they? Annie had Jessie. Alice had Dulcie, Dr Henderson, and now this youth as well. Phryne had never seen the attraction of leaning on someone else's shoulder—after all, she had two of her own—and she found it trying in others. Whatever would these women do if they found themselves alone, tied up in a cellar and threatened with macabre mayhem? As a woman to whom this sort of thing had happened frequently,

Phryne wondered what it would be like to look to somebody else for rescue.

After due consideration, she concluded that it would not do. She had almost invariably rescued herself from her own predicaments. Jack Robinson had occasionally assisted, and this had been most welcome. But setting out with a firm intention of self-reliance was always best. She pondered anew the problem of Jessie. On her note of aide-mémoire she had set out a possible case against Jessie Tremain. If she really were jealous of the attention Annie attracted, she would not have sent her sister out to dance while she cleaned up the kitchen. This was a possible martyr complex in action, but it seemed less and less likely now. Jessie had asked for Phryne's help. Yes, sometimes criminals did that, but only in detective novels. Sometimes a good girl was just a good girl.

Phryne lit another cigarette and thought about Colleen O'Rourke instead. Now there was a girl with the right stuff in her. Phryne could not quite let go of the idea that the putative jealous lovers might be pinning their hopes on Colleen, but she was obliged to consider it unlikely. Nevertheless, Phryne had warmed to the girl more than she had expected, recognising a kindred spirit. Had she herself been born into a prosperous rural Irish family, she might well have turned into Colleen O'Rourke. The girl took charge. Wilful, headstrong, decisive, very sure of herself, and (according to Dot's account of her ecclesiastical prank) able to admit herself in the wrong on occasion. Phryne could find plenty to like, and nothing to dislike, about this girl. She was fortunate indeed to find herself in a community which tolerated her exuberance. All too often high-spirited girls got the life crushed out of them by their elders. With that reflection, Phryne put out her cigarette and retired to her bed.

———

The next morning, Dot was still worn out from the excitements of the weekend, so Phryne let her return to bed after breakfast. Phryne herself dressed in a dark blue skirt, with a loose white blouse and an open jacket of dark green, then drove the car to Daylesford station. There she discovered that the train to Bullarto was not departing until eight thirty, so she admired the view for a while. The railway station was just off the main street at the top of a gentle rise and presented a most attractive prospect. The station was the usual single-storey red-brick arrangement, nestling beneath a fine stand of elms. A black-painted steam engine coughed asthmatically to itself, emitting clouds of steam and impatience. Three wooden carriages were yoked behind it, and several passengers had already embarked. Phryne went to the ticket office and bought a platform ticket (one penny) from the taciturn station guard. Stepping into one of the carriages, she placed both hands against the window and jerked it open. Then she stared out the window, before exiting the carriage again, conscious of admiring glances as she did so. It was pleasing, in a way, to know she could still turn heads.

She turned back to the ticket office and smiled her most winning smile. 'Excuse me, but can you tell me if all the carriages on this line are just like those ones?' She pointed her gloved hand at the Bullarto train, which was gathering itself for noisy action.

The station guard stared at her as if she had asked him about the nocturnal habits of beetroot. He was aged, weather-beaten and balding, and reckoned he'd heard it all until today. 'Yair, missus. The carriages are all the same. What sort were youse after?'

'I was wondering about the windows. Are they all the same size?'

She received another long, slow stare. The beetroot had

perhaps now grown beards and whiskers. 'Yair, they are. What size would youse like 'em to be?'

'Just as they are. Thank you.'

She left the thoroughly bewildered station guard and returned to her car. It was time for another talk with Inspector Mick Kelly. But first, back to the Mooltan guesthouse, where she found Alice sitting companionably with Dulcie in the sitting room. Whatever secrets Alice might be incubating on her own part, there was no doubt about the love between the two women. Dulcie's broad, callused paw enclosed Alice's pale, slender, unmarked hand. They were reading from the same book, while Dulcie's left hand turned the pages. Both were dressed simply in white cotton housedresses, and Alice's free arm was wrapped around Dulcie's substantial waist.

Phryne waved to them both. Dulcie looked up and grinned. 'Dot's in her room, Phryne. Can I get you anything?'

'No, thanks. We're going into town. Can I get you anything?'

'We're pretty right, thanks.'

Alice looked up from the book and gave Phryne a look of utter peace, tranquillity, and adoration. Yes, she was harbouring a secret, and Phryne meant to discover it. But there was nothing there to plant any suspicion that Alice might be a suspect in the murders.

Dot appeared on the stairway dressed in her beige ensemble, with her straw hat tied around her chin. 'Miss Phryne, are you going back to Daylesford? I need some more wool.'

Dulcie grinned at her. 'There's a good mercer's shop near the town hall, Dot.'

'Thanks, Dulcie.'

Phryne fired up the massive engine, while Dot climbed into the passenger seat and shut the door. 'They do look very happy together, don't they, Miss?'

Phryne engaged the clutch. 'Yes, they do.'

The massive car climbed the hill out of Hepburn Springs, while Phryne admired the scented morning air. It was a warmish day. In Melbourne it would be hot and stifling, but the mountain air, scented with lavender and roses, was intoxicating.

'Miss Phryne, I'd like to look around Daylesford for a while. Can you meet me for lunch somewhere?'

'Let's have lunch at the Temperance Hotel, Dot. I'd like another look around there. I'm still groping for answers, and maybe something there will ring a bell. Shall we say twelve thirty?'

'Yes, Miss.'

———

Phryne deposited Dot outside the town hall then sat in the driver's seat of the Hispano-Suiza and lit a gasper, considering her position. Things had been happening with such terrible speed that she had been much more of a passive bystander than was her wont. Now for some detecting on her own part, she decided. But where to begin? Phryne considered her options. Too many places to go; too many people to see. Why not begin at Hepburn Springs and proceed towards Daylesford? Drop in to shops and make conversation. One thing the people of the spa country did not exhibit to any great extent was taciturnity. Walk around, talk to people, and hope for some cross-bearings.

She drove back to Hepburn Springs and walked into a baker's shop. Mrs Jenkins' Pies were advertised prominently there, and Mrs Jenkins herself, if this was the woman behind the counter, seemed an amiable and, most importantly, chatty person. Another housewifely woman bought three loaves of bread and they exchanged a good deal of news.

'Sorry, Mrs Jones, but I'm all out of pies this morning. I've just sold them all to Paddy the publican!'

This seemed to be cause for significant glances betwixt them, and Phryne's ears pricked up. She examined instead a tray of loaves on a high table, intending not to miss a word. She noted also a box of shortbread biscuits and resolved to buy some.

'Well, I can't say I'm surprised, Mrs Jenkins,' Mrs Jones responded. 'That Captain Spencer's a good man, but it's cruel hard on those poor soldiers. Some of them live at the pub, of course, and the Captain doesn't think they should eat meat. And so...'

'Yes. I didn't ask Paddy why he wanted them, but I think we can guess. Nobody will tell the Captain. We don't want to hurt his feelings, but those poor men will be all the better for my pies, I'm sure.' The baker leaned closer and added in a low voice. 'And there's other news there too, I hear. Vern's going to live at the pub as well!'

'He'll be better off there.' Mrs Jones was now nodding emphatically. 'We all know he likes looking at the young women, but there's no harm in him. Gentle as they come, he is. And there's no reason he should have to live at the bottling plant, is there?'

'I really don't like that Sid. He's awful. Anything else today, Mrs Jones?'

'No, thank you.' And out walked Mrs Jones with her string bag filled with aromatic bread.

Phryne looked up to see Mrs Jenkins looking her over. Her bright blue eyes flickered over Phryne's hands—looking for wedding bands, doubtless—and she leaned forward on her spotless counter.

'Can I help you this morning, Miss?'

'I believe I'd like some of this shortbread, please. It smells wonderful. Maybe a pound?'

Mrs Jenkins wrapped them up in a brown-paper bag which she perched in the gleaming bowl of her scales. The black needle hovered directly over the mark reading 1 lb, and she nodded. To

Phryne's enquiring glance she smiled. 'Long practice, Miss. That will be ninepence. I believe you're staying at the Mooltan?'

'Yes. It's very pleasant there.' Phryne handed over a shilling and received a shiny threepence from a work-callused and capable hand.

'I'm sure of it. And I don't care what anyone says about Dulcie and Alice. They're fine women, and so happy with each other.'

'Indeed they are. I'm sorry to have missed your pies, Mrs Jenkins. They're quite famous.'

Mrs Jenkins preened a little. 'Well, I take a lot of trouble over them. But—well, you probably overheard us talking. Have you met the Captain? He runs the spa, you know.'

'Yes, I've met him. He's a good man. Perhaps I might find some of your pies at this hotel of Paddy the Publican?'

'The Station.' Mrs Jenkins put her head on one side and gave Phryne a curious look. 'Miss, you might find it a bit rough. If you're after a hotel for lunch, the Temperance might suit you?'

'Thanks for the tip, Mrs Jenkins.' Phryne left the shop, clutching her bag of biscuits, and walked back to the car. She wondered why she had asked about the hotelier. But then, anything of absorbing interest to the locals would be worth looking into. As she was pulling out into the main street of Hepburn Springs she all but ran over Dulcie's brother Aubrey. He was obviously distrait and gaped at Phryne as she applied the brake and ground the car to a halt.

'Miss Fisher? Please! A terrible thing has happened. Helena's gone missing!'

Phryne opened the passenger door. 'Come with me, Aubrey. I'll take you to the Mooltan and you can tell me all about it.'

———

The house was a ramshackle weatherboard affair in the back streets of Abbotsford. It was early in the afternoon, and Hugh Collins knocked on the door, noting that the plywood had been kicked in on some previous occasion. As it creaked open, Hugh noted that the lock was now only there for the look of the thing. He was met by a round-faced youth with an enormous grin plastered over his clean-shaven features.

'Hello!' The high-pitched voice emerged from the most astonishingly misshapen teeth Hugh had ever seen.

Hugh consulted his notes. 'Are you Alfred Greenwood, sir?'

The boy snickered. 'No. I'm Bill.' He stood in the doorway, radiating innocent helpfulness and a complete disinclination to let the police into the house.

After another quick look at his notebook, Hugh made a suggestion. 'You wouldn't be William Squire, would you, sir?'

The boy snickered again, like a horse who has just brushed off its jockey against a passing tree branch. A decisive thumb jabbed against the boy's chest. 'That's me!'

Hugh Collins had had mongolism described to him, but had never been confronted by it in the course of his duties before. He tried to remember what he had been told about these folk. Sunny disposition, eagerness to please, and studied literal-mindedness came into it, he recalled. 'May I come in, Bill?'

'Sure!' Bill turned his back and ambled down the long corridor. It was the standard inner-city single-storey affair, with several bedrooms to the left, and the corridor culminating in a communal living room, opening onto what was clearly a kitchen. Presumably there was a bathroom and toilet somewhere further in the hinterland. Seated around a table in the living room were two other men, playing cards. Next to the deck was a small pile of pennies. Three mounds of pennies occupied the space in front of the chairs. A large golden labrador was seated on the grubby linoleum, looking optimistically at the table. Bill Squire sat down at the table, picked up his cards, and placed them face down again on the table.

'Al? We got a visitor. He's a cop!'

The other card players surveyed Hugh without enthusiasm. They were clearly Blokes with a capital B. They wore eau-de-Nil trousers with braces, checked shirts, and horrible old boots. They smoked. In the very centre of the table, a large, slightly broken glass ashtray was filled with the remnants of several hundred roll-your-own smokes and enough fallen ash for a medium-sized bushfire. Two pairs of eyes raked over Hugh then returned to their cards. The elder of the Blokes put a card on the table, face down. Bill dealt him another card and replaced the pack on the tabletop. 'Whaddaya want, Steve?'

The younger man folded his cards. 'I'm sittin'.'

'Me too,' put in Bill.

Hugh turned to the elder. 'Sorry to butt in on your game, sir, but are you Alfred Greenwood?'

The man put down his cards again. 'I might be. Who're you when yer at home?'

'Detective Sergeant Collins, sir. I'm just making some routine enquiries about—'

The grizzled gardener cut him off. 'Bill, get 'im a chair, will ya? D'you play poker? Youse can take over from Bluey, if ya like.'

'And Bluey would be?'

'The dog.'

Bluey looked up with a sudden hope that food might be forthcoming. Even though it wasn't, he waddled over to Hugh Collins and rubbed his ample flanks against Hugh's trouser leg.

'Sir, are you telling me that the dog plays cards?'

The unshaven mouth split into a grin. 'Yair but 'e's no good at it. 'E keeps drawing to inside straights.'

Hugh scratched the dog's cheeks and neck and allowed his trousers to be massaged and assailed by an enthusiastic tail. Bill, meanwhile, had reappeared with a kitchen chair and placed it at the table. Mr Greenwood looked Hugh over once more and gestured to the chair. 'Siddown, sport.'

Hugh did so.

Greenwood turned over his cards. 'I got two pair, kings and tens. What've youse blokes got?'

The younger bloke, Steve (presumably Stephen Horner), threw his cards in. 'Pair o' nines.'

Bill was cradling his cards with an air of exuberant triumph. He turned them face up. 'I got three queens!' Bill reached out a chubby hand and swept the pennies into his pile.

'Well done, mate.' Al Greenwood watched Hugh gaping at Bill's hand. Queen of clubs, eight of spades, two of spades, four of clubs, and two of diamonds. 'It's all right, son. That hand's on a ryebuck and a straight wire. We play twos wild.' His deep brown eyes narrowed. 'Well, copper? You in or not?'

Hugh's brain went into overdrive for a moment. As long as he didn't drink on duty, there was no actual directive about playing cards. It was all part of his investigation, and he may as well do it in comfort. He reached into his pocket and disinterred seven pennies, three halfpennies, and a threepenny bit. These blokes would probably clean him out in half an hour, but he'd be saving on tram fares. And he would get a better impression of his witnesses playing cards than interrogating them according to the manual.

'Yep. I'm in.'

It took only twenty-five minutes for Hugh's stake to be engulfed into the other piles of coins, including the time it took Bill to boil the kettle and make a pot of foul-smelling tea which might have been used to tan hiking boots. Hugh would normally have accepted tea from householders, but this looked to be best left alone. His fellows took it with milk and a great deal of sugar, and drank it with what appeared to be pleasure. Hugh wondered if Al and Steve were letting Bill win, but this did not appear to be the case. Hugh's Waterloo moment was when he had managed to acquire a full house, which was unsympathetically swept aside by Al's diamond flush. As he watched his stake engulfed by a mud-stained fist, Hugh reflected that losing to the witnesses was far better than winning.

Al fixed him with a glittering eye. 'All right, sport. What can we do fer ya?'

Hugh cleared his throat. 'You three gentlemen are gardeners, I believe?'

This produced an inclination of an unshaven jaw, which might have passed as a nod.

'And you are regularly employed by Mrs Knight in Barkers Road?'

Two nods and a grin.

'And are you aware that there has been a recent death in the family?'

Two nods and a heart-rending look of pain from Bill.

'Yair, mate, we are. 'Cos it was in the paper.' Hugh had not known this and wondered who had spilled the beans. Not Mrs Knight. Probably his over-eager superior. 'And it said that the Police Were Confident of an Early Arrest.' Al was watching Hugh's face with considerable care, and he wondered how much of his bewilderment was showing.

'Well, Mr Greenwood, we're always confident. But we'd like to know if you noticed anything unusual of late at the house?'

'Well, maybe,' Al conceded. 'Not that we were ever in the house. Mrs Knight brought us a tea trolley once when we were putting in a long shift, but we weren't invited in. 'Cos why would we be?'

'But you may have seen the deceased in the garden?' Hugh prompted.

'Yair, we did. Cat that got the cream, that one.'

'I see. Did this newspaper report say anything about the deceased's condition?'

There was a grin this time. 'You mean was she up the spout? Yair.'

'Had you formed any impressions as to who might have been responsible?' This was on the face of it an absurd question, but you never knew your luck.

'It wasn't any of us.' A gap-toothed smile invited Hugh to consider the possibility that any of them might have been a teenage girl's sweetheart. 'Did youse blokes find the prints of the ladder under her window?'

'Yes, we did,' Hugh responded. 'And you never mentioned this to anyone?'

'No, we didn't, on account of it bein' none of our bloody business. We do the garden. That's what we're paid for, and that's what we do. Tell ya what, though, it'd have to be a fit young bloke. It's a decent climb up to 'er room, and the prints were close to the wall.'

'That's what we thought, too.' Hugh looked at Bill, whose moon face was clouded with anxiety.

He gave vent to an agonised yelp, and Bluey obediently raised himself off the lino and put his head in Bill's lap. 'What's happened? Is something wrong with the pretty girl?'

Al leaned forward over the table, with both gnarled fists closed together. 'Bill, that pretty girl at the house has gone away. That's all it is. She's gone away, mate; but she's happy.'

Bill considered this. 'Has she gone somewhere nice?'

'Yair, mate. She gets to play with dogs and cats and unicorns all day. Play yer cards right an' you'll get to go there too.'

'Oh.' Bill's hands were out of sight under the table, but going by the thwacking of Bluey's tail it appeared that Aid and Comfort was being administered.

Al eyeballed Hugh anew. 'That's pretty much all we can tell ya, sport,' he concluded.

'I see.' Hugh was on his feet in an instant. 'Thank you for your time, gentlemen.'

Hugh saw himself out, escorted at a distance by Al. He turned at the door. 'You do realise that the front door doesn't lock, don't you?'

Al grunted. ''S'orright, though. We got a dog. Burglars are scared of Bluey.'

'Why is that, sir?'

'On account of gettin' slobbered on a lot. Nuthin' worse than an overenthusiastic dog when yer tryin' to rob a house.'

'Right. Thanks.'

As Hugh walked through the mean streets of Abbotsford towards Victoria Park station, he realized that the best thing about his morning's work was that he had found all three gardeners in Al's house. He had informed his superior officer that he would interview all three suspects, and that it would take all afternoon. He would not have considered taking the rest of the day off had Jack Robinson been on the case, but the temptation to go straight home and put up his substantial feet was too much for him. He considered that while he had learned nothing of consequence, the gardeners could be safely scratched from the list of suspects. Which was, at the present moment, a very short list. Hugh could not imagine what had possessed his superior to blurt out everything to the daily press. Surely Claire's pregnancy was something to be sprung on a suspect without warning in mid-interrogation? But there it was. The acting detective inspector was already convinced that the culprit was Uncle Gerald and saw no need to hedge his bets. Not for the first time, Hugh found himself longing for the calm and reassuring presence of Jack Robinson. And it was time to tell the girls to go and see Mrs Knight and confess all.

Chapter Sixteen

Myself when young did eagerly frequent
Doctor and Saint, and heard great Argument
About it and about: but evermore
Came out by the same Door as I went in.

—Edward Fitzgerald, *The Rubáiyát of*
Omar Khayyám of Naishápúr

Having been let out next to the town hall, Dot alighted with difficulty onto the steep cobblestone gutter. Stepping carefully in her sensible flat shoes, she mounted the footpath and made her way into the mercer's shop. Bolts of cotton and linen towered over her. Boxes and cases of costume jewellery adorned the path towards the counter, behind which a series of wooden trays held a bewildering array of coloured wools. Perched upon great wicker cabinets were lampshades of every shape and colour. Stacked in trays were coloured beads of amber, coral, amethyst, and beryl. There were needles and cotton thread, silks and satins, leaded glass, dried flower pictures and arrangements, tatting, crochet hooks, tassels, ribbons, and laces. A pleasant middle-aged woman in a long, green cotton dress and long, unbound greying hair presently appeared, and smiled at Dot.

'Good morning, Miss. How may I help you?'

'I want some wool, please.'

A beatific smile illumined the rounded face. 'What are you making, dear?'

'I was thinking of knitting a scarf for the winter.'

'Do you have a pattern in mind?'

'Just thin stripes, I think.'

'All right. Suffragette colours are popular hereabouts?'

There was a definite frisson in the atmosphere now. Dot stared at the saleslady, trying to remember what these were.

'Green for creativity, purple for passion, and white for purity,' the woman prompted.

'They do a very good red here, if you want it?'

The voice—deep and rough-edged, as though it emerged from an internal combustion engine—came from behind her. Dot turned to see another woman, though Dot could have sworn she and the saleslady had been alone in the shop. She was tall and angular, with her iron-grey hair cut short as though by a combine harvester. It was the haircut of a woman who had heard about hairstyling and didn't want anything to do with it. She was dressed in grey dungarees and a blue checked shirt, and from under an old straw hat a pair of grey-blue eyes raked critically over Dot.

'Oh, right. Thank you.' For a long moment Dot felt as though she was acting a part in a play where she had forgotten to bring her script. She looked again at the woman behind the counter. 'I think I'd like autumn colours, actually. Brown and yellow, with some light orange?'

Six large balls of wool were duly laid on the counter by a plump, unlined hand. Dot admired the orange, which was a perilous colour to match with anything else. This was light, and held a tinge of ochre which would blend beautifully with the yellows and browns. Meanwhile a large brown-paper bag was laid on the counter with a significant look, and the newcomer hefted it onto her shoulder and headed for the door.

'Anything else I can help you with, Miss?'

Dot had only intended to buy wool, but found herself fifteen minutes later with a quantity of costume jewellery and a beautiful calico bag embroidered with a black cat *couchant* on the front. As she was opening the shop door, she turned to the saleslady. 'Um, may I ask who was that other lady in the shop just now?'

A guarded look filmed over the woman's pleasant features. 'That's Miss McKenzie. She lives over in Musk.'

Since that was plainly all the information on offer, Dot nodded. 'Thank you.'

———

Back at the Mooltan, Aubrey poured out his tale. He had woken as usual at the Station Hotel and had walked to the spa for his day's therapy. Some of the blokes got a lift in a truck, but he preferred to walk, for the exercise, and the Captain agreed that this was good for him. At the spa he had found the staff all in a dither, and Helena nowhere to be seen. She had, as far as anyone knew, slept in her quarters at the spa last night as usual, but when she had not showed up for work a search had been made. There was no sign of her anywhere.

Dulcie gave her brother some valerian in a glass, and he sipped it carefully, eyes darting to and fro all the while. Dulcie and Alice sat on either side of him on the sofa in a protective phalanx. All three pairs of eyes were fixed on Phryne in patently optimistic hope.

'Please tell me about Helena,' Phryne began. 'Who is she?'

Aubrey's face blushed scarlet. 'She's my fiancée. She works at the spa as a masseuse. Her mother lives in Daylesford and she's been ringing every few hours.'

'And how old is Helena?'

'Seventeen. But she's very grown-up.'

Phryne nodded, and rose. 'You two look after Aubrey and see no harm comes to him. I'll go to the spa to talk to the Captain.'

'Please do, Phryne.' Dulcie took her brother's hand and stroked it. 'I know you're only here on holiday, but if you could help, we'd really appreciate it.'

In no good temper, Phryne strode along the road to the spa. Another mystery! Just what she needed. Captain Spencer was standing outside. 'Phryne? To what do we owe the pleasure this time?' He was beautifully dressed for a Monday morning, but his face looked haggard.

'Herbert, this is probably none of my business, but I'd like to see Helena's room at once, if that is at all convenient.'

The tension in his face eased a little. 'So you've heard? I rather hoped you would. In fact, I was waiting out here hoping you might pass by. This unexplained absence is so unlike Helena, I fear…mischief.'

'All right. Let's have a look.'

Helena's room was small, neat, and relatively spartan. There was little to indicate human habitation other than the single wardrobe, a rough wooden desk and chair, and an unmade bed. Captain Spencer stood next to Phryne, as if willing the room to yield up its secrets.

'We're on the upper floor here. Could she have got out the window?' Phryne asked.

'I doubt it.' The Captain tested the window. It was locked from the inside. 'No. But she might have got up early.'

'Do you know if any of her clothes are missing?'

The Captain looked nonplussed. 'Well, I don't take much notice of the girls' wardrobes—' he began.

Phryne cut him short. 'Then please go and get one of the other girls who would know!'

He hurried off obediently, and Phryne examined the room. There were no signs of a struggle. The disordered bed looked as though the occupant had flung back the covers, got out of bed, and vanished into thin air.

Spencer returned with a slight young woman, who introduced herself as Mary. She rummaged through the wardrobe, looked under the bed, then looked at Phryne in quiet alarm.

'I can't be sure, Miss Fisher, but as far as I can see, nothing is missing—except the nightgown she was wearing last night. She keeps her handbag in the bottom of the wardrobe, and it's still there. She's not the sort to run off, and she would never have left it behind.'

'Have you seen her this morning?'

'No, Miss Fisher. But she's normally first up, so I wouldn't expect to.'

'I see.' Phryne turned to the Captain. 'All right. I'll look for her. You'd better put her handbag in the safe. No, wait. Let me see it before you do.'

With a dubious glance at Phryne, Mary retrieved it and handed it over. The contents were singularly lacking in clues. Three handkerchiefs, a plain leather purse containing nine shillings and fourpence, some basic toiletries, and that was all. Of incriminating letters or summonses to meet a mysterious stranger at midnight by the old oak tree wearing only her nightgown, there were none.

'I'm sorry,' Phryne declared, handing the bag back to the girl. 'I'm a little pushed for time today, but I'll do my best for her.'

Phryne returned to the Hispano-Suiza and drove to Daylesford in a silently flaming temper. As if she didn't have enough on her plate already! She went straight into the Station Hotel and ordered a whisky sour. The Station was somewhat less decorous than the Temperance. The main bar was more like main bars elsewhere: dirty carpet, half-filled ashtrays, and a smell of cheap beer. Mick Kelly had ensconced his formidable frame in a corner snug, a large beaker of what appeared to be lemon squash parked on the table next to his right hand. As she approached, he gave her a nod of greeting and gestured to her to take a seat. Phryne received Looks of Disapproval from one or two customers and ignored them.

'Well, Mick,' she said without preamble, 'I'm afraid I have some bad news for you. One of the girls at the spa has gone missing.'

'Yes, I've heard. Captain Spencer came to the station first thing this morning. Any other damage at your end, apart from the missing girl?'

'I've uncovered another murder, I fear—and all of them known to be admirers of Annie Tremain.'

A massive forefinger rubbed across the ginger moustache. 'A third? When? Who was it?'

'A month ago, a Patrick Sullivan is alleged to have fallen out of a train window while leaning out to admire the scenery. The trouble is, Mick, I have inspected the train and its carriages and it isn't possible. The windows aren't low enough, or wide enough.'

'So yer telling me he was pushed?'

'I'm afraid so, though I have no evidence. The story really was a bit thin. Perhaps the coroner sat on him?'

'I expect so. But, then, it wouldn't have seemed suspicious in itself, because it was the first of our murders and no one was looking for trouble.' The inspector shook his massive head and made a noise like a bear with its foot in a trap. 'It really is suspicious that all three of our corpses seem to have been suitors for the same girl, and I agree with you that this can't be a coincidence.

But all the same…killing off rivals in love? I can't see it, Phryne. You gotta admit it's improbable.'

Phryne tasted her whisky sour. It wasn't bad at all, despite the pub's unpromising decor. 'Mick, I have to agree with you. But I had a long talk with the Reverend McPherson last night, and he tells me that this couldn't have been done for financial gain. None of the deceased had anything worth inheriting. So rivals in love it must be. Though presumably our villain is round the twist—only a madman would think this would work. But what if he really is mad?'

'He'd have to be.' The inspector took a big slurp out of his lemon squash. 'So, who are our suspects?'

'We're running out of them. Of the people who might have some sort of realistic romantic motive, we only have three left alive: Kenneth McAlpine, Graeme Forbes, and Johnnie Armstrong. McAlpine seems to have been the big winner so far, at least in terms of getting Annie into his arms.'

'He's the caber tosser? Yes, I saw those two. What's your impression of him, though?'

'I really don't believe it, Mick. The only thing against him is that the needle in his neck was a highly speculative murder, if it was that. That caber could have gone anywhere. It was sheer bad luck that Donald Mackay was in the way.'

'So you're thinking he could have stabbed himself with it and then pretended to be distracted? It's possible. It is a point against him. Trouble is—' Inspector Kelly spread his arms in frustration '—I've known him since he was a youngster. He's a good worker, barely drinks, keeps a ginger tomcat at home, and is famous throughout the district for being kind and equable. He's one of them blokes who's always gettin' more out of life than he expects. Blokes like that don't do crime, in my experience.'

Phryne finished her whisky sour. The lingering after-burn was a pleasant counterpoint to her squalid surroundings. 'I have to agree with you. At the dance yesterday I took the opportunity to watch all our suspects, and I really don't think it's him.'

Kelly nodded. 'Okay, how about Forbes?'

'Graeme Forbes,' Phryne mused. 'He is one of the surviving admirers of Miss Tremain, it's true, but to be honest he'd have to be a superb actor. He's awkward, clumsy on the dance floor, and as far as I can see everyone likes him. I don't think it's him either.'

Again Kelly nodded. 'Doesn't sound like our bloke, does he?'

'No. And then there is Johnnie Armstrong, reputed to have a wife back in Melbourne. Now *he* is a possibility. He's very self-possessed. Opaque would be the word I'd use of him. Most of the locals hereabouts are—well, nice. And completely transparent. Armstrong gave a wonderful impression of a man who was bored out of his mind when he was waiting to talk to you. I think he at least is a man capable of deep-laid plots. And it really does call for someone capable of deep planning: we have three murders, and three entirely different murder methods. Here is someone who doesn't want to repeat himself. Or, possibly, someone who views murder as a fine art, like de Quincey of horrible memory.'

The inspector gave a grunt, like a steam engine knocking against a carriage. 'Armstrong…yair, I think that young man's got a few secrets. And he could be mad. If it is jealous love, we need someone who's so far off his trolley he's in the middle of next week. But I'm still not happy with this theory. And now we've got a missing girl at the Springs. Could that be related?'

Kelly shook his head and signalled to the barman. 'Another squash for me thanks, Paddy,' he called. 'One more thing,' he added, turning back to Phryne and lowering his voice again. 'Another woman has gone missing. Her husband reported it this morning.'

Phryne looked hard at the inspector. 'Now that really is interesting. Can you tell me her name?'

Kelly blinked at her. 'Don't see why not.' He rummaged in his pocket for his notebook and glanced at it. 'Mrs Frances Pollock, of 169 Main Road, Sailors Falls. Do you think it might be relevant?'

Phryne wrote the woman's name and address down in her own notebook and smiled brightly. 'Thanks for seeing me, Mick. If I find anything out, I'll let you know as soon as possible.'

'You do that, Phryne.'

As she rose, she saw his eyes cloud over. The inspector was cogitating. As well he might.

———

Phryne returned to her car and drove slowly up the hill. The cinema grand opening was still a few days away, but she noted fresh bunting stretched across the facade of the newly built edifice. If it had occurred to anybody to suggest they delay, or cancel, their municipal celebrations, then the proposal had been dismissed in favour of Full Steam Ahead and To Hell with Misfortune. Phryne applauded the local community's determined resilience, but she was seriously concerned about it. This meant she had little time to wrap up the case of the murdered suitors. Though surely the murderer would not strike again? The prospect was sheer nonsense, she told herself. There was no reason to fear the worst just because it was another local gala. And yet... Two local celebrations had been held on the weekend, and both had resulted in deaths. If she had learned anything about criminal investigation, it was to trust her instincts when her thumbs pricked. They were pricking now as though entwined in a rosebush.

She manoeuvred the Hispano-Suiza around the roundabout at the top of the hill and selected second gear. As she cruised gently down the hill, she stared out at the incipient lake. There was a good deal of wooden scaffolding erected around a smallish pool of fresh water. Presumably it would take time for the lake to fill, especially in late summer when there was little rain. The landscaping seemed to have been cleverly done. It would be a beautiful park when it was completed.

On reaching the open road, Phryne slipped the car into third gear, but in contrast with her usual habits kept her speed moderate. She wanted to keep a sharp lookout, which was incompatible with her customary seventy-miles-per-hour rampages through the landscape. But nothing out of the ordinary struck her eye until she reached Sailors Falls and pulled up on the other side of the road from number 169. Her pointed chin made a nod of recognition. The farmhouse was the same one she and Dot had noted on their way into town.

The house looked more desolate than ever. A tethered horse munched at a corner of grass in mournful contemplation. There was a general air of neglect, as if the whole business of keeping house had become all too much. A man in dungarees and a straw hat sat by himself on the verandah, staring at nothing. And where the multi-coloured scarf had been hanging, there was now but a few coloured threads of wool.

Phryne turned the car around and drove slowly back towards Daylesford. In one of her accumulated mysteries, at least, light had begun to dawn.

———

It took surprisingly little time to track down the mobile library. An enquiry at the town hall elicited the information that Mrs Sinclair had taken the van to the improbably named hamlet of Musk—wherein, on arrival, she found no musk to speak of, but prosperous-looking fields, a number of farms, and a pleasingly well-stocked general store, outside which the library van was parked. Three locals were rummaging within, engrossed in railway editions of popular books. H.G. Wells seemed to be popular. Phryne wrapped her silk scarf around her neck and prepared to face the dragon in her lair.

Mrs Sinclair stared coldly at this glamorous young woman in her shocking pants suit and silken fripperies. She saw the world through the stern spectacles of thrift, self-improvement, and Education for Women, and was not inclined to be helpful.

'You're Miss Fisher, aren't you? I saw you in Daylesford. What brings you to Musk?'

Phryne smiled winningly at her. 'Just a little jaunt of my own. I could hardly believe in a village called Musk without seeing it for myself. It looks splendid.'

This did not go over big. 'I see. And can I help you with a book? As you are a visitor, I will have to charge you a shilling's membership.'

Phryne reached into her purse and produced a ten-shilling note. 'Please accept this as a donation. You are doing wonderful work here, I am certain.'

The glacial atmosphere melted somewhat, to be replaced by a sort of guarded truce. 'I'll have to give you a receipt, Miss Fisher. Please wait.'

A tin cashbox was disinterred from under the counter, and Mrs Sinclair took her time writing out a slip reading *Received With Thanks From the Hon. Miss Phryne Fisher, the Sum of Ten Shillings*. She lifted the blue carbon paper underneath the page to verify that the impression had taken and tucked the ten-shilling note in the tin's nether recesses. Then she nodded, tore off the receipt, and handed it to Phryne, who stowed it in her purse.

'And what sort of book would you be wanting, then, Miss Fisher?'

'I was wondering if you had any knitting patterns?'

Mrs Sinclair moved, almost imperceptibly, so that her sub-stantial undercarriage was blocking Phryne's view of the Returns trolley. 'I'm terribly sorry, Miss Fisher, but they're all out on loan at the moment.'

Phryne inclined her head. 'Such a pity. Never mind. Sorry to have troubled you.'

With a debonair wave, Phryne leaped lightly back into the car and retraced her route back to Daylesford.

On a whim, she decided to call in at the police station. Sergeant Offaly was looming behind the counter. He did not look at all pleased to see Miss Fisher.

'Ah, Sergeant! And how are you on this pleasant day?'

It was indeed a pleasant day, with light winds, butterflies, warm temperatures, and a general sense of bonhomie. Sergeant Offaly seemed disinclined to share it. A deep crimson coloured his pasty features. 'Well? What do you want?'

Phryne looked around the anteroom. 'I was wondering if there were any photographs of Missing Persons, Sergeant. You have had a few of those of late, have you not?'

The sergeant harrumphed. 'They're on the wall there, if you think it's any of your business.'

'Oh, but I do.' Phryne examined the photographs. Six women and one youth. There was Janet McKenzie, who did indeed look tired and joyless. A separate photo was labelled Master Robert McKenzie. He looked pale, and haunted. The two most recent were labelled Mrs Frances Pollock, of Sailors Falls, and Miss Helena Ogilvie, of Hepburn Springs. Both pictures were brand-new and obviously only placed there this morning. Ignoring the obvious fidgets of the sergeant, she studied Helena's face carefully. A headstrong girl, she decided. Not overly bright, but determined. It was a kind face, as well as an undeniably pretty one. One look at

Frances Pollock was enough to confirm Phryne's theory. This was the sunken-cheeked woman who had attended the dance wearing the brightly coloured scarf—and who had last been seen in the company of none other than Mrs Sinclair the librarian. Phryne smiled to herself. With so many mysteries piling up around her, it appeared one had been elucidated.

———

Tinker had not been idle on Monday. His sudden outbreak of inquisitiveness had drawn several looks of doubt and puzzlement, but as he took the tram home to 221B The Esplanade, he felt quietly triumphant. He would find out who lived in Kew and he would set his plans in motion. Electronics was Tinker's favourite class, and a fellow enthusiast could be drawn in by his latest project. He was building a crystal set, and an invitation to test it out might well prove an irresistible bait. The problem was that the trap could only be sprung once. So the girls would have to do their part before he could do his.

When he got home, Ruth and Jane were sitting around the kitchen table, eating scones and jam. With them was Hugh Collins, who had shamelessly taken the rest of the day off rather than listen to the grotesque rantings of his superior officer.

'How was school, Tink?' Hugh enquired, smearing a large dollop of strawberry jam over his scone.

'All right, Mr Collins.'

Hugh took a sip of his tea and set down the mug. 'That's good. Tinker, I was waiting until you got here so I didn't have to tell everything twice.'

Ruth and Jane looked up expectantly.

'Today I interviewed the gardeners. There's nothing doing with them. They're two dinkum Aussie blokes and one mongoloid kid. I found them all playing cards, which is how I was able to come home early.' Hugh outlined his card session, which brought smiles from everybody. 'So as you see, they knew about the ladder, but they didn't think it was any of their business. And it wasn't, either. I don't believe for a moment they had anything to do with it.'

'Is your inspector still convinced it was Uncle Gerald?' Jane asked.

Hugh Collins grimaced. 'Yes. We had to let him go, though. The inspector hasn't got anything to make an arrest warrant out of. I'm hoping we can solve the case together, the four of us, before Fraser has another crack at him. Jane, Ruth, I'd like you to go see Mrs Knight again tomorrow after school, like we discussed, and search her room for a diary.'

'Maybe there'll be a secret compartment somewhere?' Tinker had grown up as an enthusiast for Sexton Blake and other sensationalist crime novels in which secret compartments figured strongly.

Hugh gave Tinker an indulgent glance and refrained from mockery. 'There may well be. Though she might have taken a more conventional approach. Under her bed? A little niche at the back of a bookcase? Inside her wardrobe?'

'Behind the back of the wardrobe,' Jane suggested.

'Look everywhere. If there is a diary, it will be in her bedroom, I think we can be sure of that.'

'Orright.' Tinker looked around the table. 'And if the diary helps us to identify her secret admirer, I think I can get him to confess.'

Hugh looked at Tinker with eyebrows raised. 'Go on.'

Tinker explained his plan.

Hugh nodded. 'Yes, I think that will work. All right. Everyone know what you have to do?'

Three young faces stared back at him, glowing with incandescent pride. All possessed by a single thought. They were imagining telling Miss Phryne how they had solved a real-life mystery all by themselves.

Chapter Seventeen

Well the river bank makes a mighty good road
Dead trees will show you the way
Left foot, peg foot, travelin' on
Follow the drinkin' gourd
For the old man is waiting to carry you to freedom
Follow the drinkin' gourd
Well the river ends, between two hills
Follow the drinkin' gourd
There's another river on the other side
Follow the drinkin' gourd
For the old man is waiting to carry you to freedom
Follow the drinkin' gourd.

—Song from the Underground Railroad

Over a splendid lunch (roast beef, vegetables, and apricot pie with cream) Dot expounded the details of her visit to the mercer's shop. Phryne listened attentively and closed her eyes for a moment. 'A Miss McKenzie, you say? Surely this can't have been the runaway *Mrs* McKenzie?'

'I don't think so, Miss. She didn't look like the sort of woman who runs away.'

'You mean rather than run away she'd be saying it with rolling pins and frying pans?'

'Yes, Miss. She isn't scared of anybody, I'd guess.'

'Least of all our mousy melancholic of a publican. The name must be a coincidence. Show me what you bought, Dot.'

Phryne was prepared to smile indulgently, but her eyes widened as the purchases were displayed. 'But like I always say, I don't believe in coincidences. Look here, Dot.' Phryne's elegant finger pointed to the bottom corner of the bag's reverse. The initials J.M. had been embroidered in purple cotton. 'Dot, I'm beginning to see light on one of our mysteries. This may be just a wild guess, but I wouldn't be surprised if J.M. stands for Janet McKenzie.'

'Mr McKenzie's lost wife?'

'I believe so. And you were told that suffragette colours and red were popular around here?'

'Yes. They were talking as though there was a plot of some sort going on, but they weren't sure if I was part of it or not.'

'Indeed. Well, this afternoon we're going to straighten this out, and possibly learn something useful. Now, on the subject of disappearing women, I should tell you that Aubrey's fiancée Helena has vanished. I almost ran over Aubrey earlier, and he told me all about it.' Phryne outlined her investigations, while Dot sat quite still with her hands folded. 'I have one or two ideas about this, but I'm not sure yet. I think Helena is alive but being held against her will. But who is responsible? Well, this afternoon we will find out whether she is one of the many disappearing women in these parts, or whether her case is quite different.'

Phryne paused, as Jessie brought in the bill. Today she was wearing a plain light blue dress with a voluminous frilled apron.

She gave Phryne a look of unaccustomed shyness. 'Miss Fisher, on Mondays we close early and some of us like to play cards in the evening. Do you by any chance play bridge?'

'Contract or auction?' A look of mystification crossed over Jessie's face, and Phryne realised that the contract version—which had taken the fashionable world by storm of late—had doubtless not made it to these parts as yet. 'It doesn't matter, Jessie. I'd be delighted. Who's in?'

'I partner Uncle, so you can have Annie. Unless Miss Williams...?' Seeing Dot's look of alarm, Jessie did not press the point. As far as Dot was concerned cards were the Devil's Picture-Book, a view she had had dinned into her ears by her parish priest and had never quite abandoned.

'That would be lovely,' Phryne broke in smoothly. 'What time?'

'A tick after seven.' Jessie's face split into a happy grin. 'This is very kind of you, Miss Fisher. We all like to play, but we need a fourth person. We usually ask Dr Henderson, but he's attending a birth and probably won't be able to make it.'

Jessie was about to depart, but Phryne stopped her. 'Just one question, Jessie. It's probably very rude of me, but I was wondering who raised you after your mother passed away.'

Jessie's eyes widened in surprise. 'I can't think why you'd want to know that. It was Aunty Morag McKenzie. She doesn't live in Daylesford, so we don't see her much these days. Some people said...' Jessie drew in a deep breath. 'Some people said she was a witch in a gingerbread cottage, but the Minister told them not to be so silly. All I know is that she was very kind to us. But she doesn't like town life and doesn't come into town often.'

'So she lives somewhere close by?' Phryne prompted.

'Yes—in Musk. We haven't been back since we came to work here four years ago.' Jessie seemed about to ask what in thunderation Phryne was getting at, but thought better of it—perhaps reluctant to put a potential bridge partner offside—and disappeared back into the kitchen.

As Phryne led the way back to the car, Dot asked, 'Are you sure you want to play cards, Miss?'

Phryne fired up the motor and engaged the clutch. 'Yes, Dot. There's still something niggling at me about this hotel. You can learn a lot about people by playing cards with them.'

———

To Dot's surprise, the Hispano-Suiza headed up a different hill from that she was expecting. 'Where are we going now, Miss?'

'To Musk, Dot. Keep a close eye out for a multi-coloured scarf.'

'Oh.' Dot was mystified but forbore to question her imperious employer. Doubtless she would find out in due course. In the meantime, she adjusted her Freda Storm Veil and did her best to admire the rolling meadows.

Before long they reached Musk, and Phryne slowed the car down. She turned right down the first road and went for a couple of miles, before executing a difficult three-point turn. Then it was back to the main highway, and another try at the next turnoff. It took nearly an hour before Dot pointed excitedly. They were far off the beaten track now. The farm looked like so many others they had passed, but hanging from one of the two fence posts was a knitted woollen scarf in purple, white, green, and blue. Phryne stopped the car.

'Dot, I think we should walk from here. Will your shoes be all right?'

Dot surveyed the brown, beaten earth, dotted with tussocks of yellow forage. Two horses looked at them briefly and resumed their diurnal munching. Ahead, on the verandah of a stone farmhouse, sat a woman accompanied by two enormous black dogs.

She was lean, angular, and looked as though she had been carved out of mandrake roots. Across her knees was a large double-barrelled shotgun. The dogs looked up as they approached, but did not utter a sound. The woman stared at them without speaking.

'Is that the woman you saw in the shop, Dot?' Phryne whispered.

'Yes, Miss. I'm sure.'

Phryne stopped about ten yards in front of the verandah and smiled her most winning smile. 'Mrs McKenzie, I believe? My name is Phryne Fisher, and this is my companion Dorothy Williams.'

If Phryne was expecting a welcoming smile in return, it failed to materialise. 'Yair, I've heard of you,' the woman commented. And that appeared to be that for the moment.

Phryne continued to broadcast Goodwill to All Womenkind at sixty watts until a sequel of sorts was reluctantly produced.

'All right. Whaddaya want?'

'I followed the scarves. And would I be right in thinking you are Annie and Jessie's Aunty Morag?'

'I might be. But them girls dunno nuthin' 'bout scarves.'

'No, I wouldn't think they do. But they're both good girls. I'm trying to give them some assistance.' Phryne raised her voice a fraction. 'And you're not helping.'

Both dogs growled at her. The old woman leaned down and patted them back into quiescence. 'They're all right,' she confided. 'They only bite men.' Hard blue eyes bored into her. 'That's right, Miss Fisher. I'm not helpin' because I dunno what you want. I did ask, and you're not answering me.'

Phryne laughed. 'That's perfectly true, Mrs McKenzie.'

'*Miss* McKenzie.' The first syllable was loaded with more sibilants than a basketful of cobras. Phryne pondered the insistence on Miss. Wasn't she someone's mother or grandmother? Very well, then. Miss it was to be.

'Miss McKenzie,' Phryne continued, 'I know the secret of the scarves and I think it's a wonderful idea. But...'

Aunty Morag gripped the shotgun tightly. 'What would you know about domestic slavery, Miss Titled Lady? Tell me that!' she rasped. The acid scorn in her voice could have dissolved the Hispano-Suiza's engine block.

Phryne glared back. 'You'd be amazed, Miss McKenzie. I wasn't always rich and titled. I grew up in the malodorous back streets of Richmond and Collingwood, scavenging for fruit and vegetables at the end of market day while my idiot father drank away our money—what there was of it. I know all about poverty, and I'm not in favour of it.'

The dogs looked to their mistress for orders, and she stretched out her hand again. It was a battered hand, with years of manual labour carved into it, but she caressed the dogs with surprising gentleness. 'Fair enough, Miss Fisher. All right. Who've you come to see? Anyone who's here ain't goin' back, you know.'

'Quite. What I do want to know, more than anything else, is have you got Helena Ogilvie from Hepburn Springs?'

'Who's she when she's at home?'

'She works at the spa for Captain Herbert. She's about seventeen—'

Aunty Morag laughed. It was like an armful of twigs being broken in half. 'There's no one here under thirty-five, Miss Fisher.' Her eyes raked Phryne's elegant clothes again. 'You're not gonna give me any peace until I show ya round, are ya?'

'Possibly not, but I'm inclined to believe you. Also, though this is not directly germane to my investigations, I would be intrigued to know if you also have Mrs Frances Pollock of Sailors Falls.'

'Ain't sayin.'

Phryne was beginning to lose what patience she had left. 'Miss McKenzie, the moment I am satisfied, you will never hear from me again. In addition, I will give you ten pounds to help carry on your work, and I will keep your secret organisation a secret. Last night, I was at the dance in Daylesford, and Mrs Pollock turned up wearing the scarf with the red band that signals I Need Help. It was the same scarf I saw hanging outside her dismal little farm last Friday when I drove into town for the first time. She went off with Mrs Sinclair the librarian and she was reported missing today, presumably by her husband. I have no interest in returning her to the House of Horrors. I might even be able to help get any belongings she needs.'

'Such as?'

'Her false teeth. Would I be right to assume her husband has hidden them from her?'

'Ha! Drunken bastard took 'em away as punishment. That was the last straw. These poor bloomin' women think if they keep on sufferin' in silence then their man might love 'em again. Ptui!'

'And they never do,' Phryne agreed. 'I have a plan, Miss McKenzie. I will arrange to have her husband removed from the premises, then I will take Mrs Pollock to her house and we can get anything she needs.'

'How're ya gonna do that?'

Phryne smiled. 'Trade secrets. Look, I'll go back to town now. As soon as the house is empty and ready, I'll take her there. I don't know how long it will take me, but I'll come back when it's organised. Deal?'

The old woman nodded. 'Deal. And good luck.'

As they walked back across the paddock to the road, Phryne turned to Dot. 'Well, wasn't she nice?'

'Not really, Miss. But she looks like she means business.'

'She does. And I believe her. It really is a splendid idea, though.

Someone lets it be known, on the QT, that any woman who can't stand it any longer and wants rescuing can go to the portable library and get the knitting books. Because who pays attention to knitting patterns? She knits the scarf with the red band that says *Help!* and hangs it on the front fence. Presumably some preliminary contact is made. And the women are told to keep an eye out for another scarf like this one with the blue stripe—' Phryne paused at the front gate and gestured to it '—because that's where your help is. And, as we saw last night, a woman from the organisation will carry you off to freedom.'

'It's a bit complicated, isn't it?'

'Well, yes, Dot, it is. But running away from home isn't a decision you take lightly. The time you spend knitting the scarf is your time for reflection. If you finish it, Aunty Morag knows you really mean it, and you're not wasting her time.' Phryne leaned on the gatepost and began to sing softly. '*When the sun comes back, and the first quail calls, Follow the drinkin' gourd, For the old man is waiting just to carry you to freedom, Follow the drinkin' gourd.* That, Dot, was a slaves' song. It gave instructions to slaves escaping from the American South—or, more correctly, from the slave states—as to how to get over Jordan and to freedom.'

'I've always wondered about the River Jordan in those Negro songs. Didn't they know that the Jordan is in Palestine?'

'I think it was the Missouri River they were talking about. North of that were the free states. And—' she turned to face Dot '—the Underground Railroad that helped the slaves to reach freedom was run by a woman. Her name was Harriet Tubman. I suspect our Aunty Morag is a woman of that sort. Now, let's go and see if we can get Mrs Pollock's house emptied of bullies, shall we?'

'As you say, Miss.'

'But while we may have solved the mystery of the disappearing wives, we're still in the dark on the matter of Helena Ogilvie.'

They drove in silence, until they were nearing the town.

Dot turned to Phryne. 'Miss, I wonder about this tonic Captain Spencer's been giving his patients.'

'What about it, Dot?'

'Miss, what about the licensing laws? You said it had alcohol.'

'I never even thought about that, Dot. But you're right. Some of the men I met at the spa said they worked the still. Which makes it sound rather like strong drink.'

'No, Miss, I suppose you wouldn't. But it's serious. He could go to prison for breaking the law, couldn't he?'

'What are you suggesting, Dot?'

'Miss, what if Helena threatened to tell on him, so he kidnapped her?'

'He certainly would have a strong motive in that case. I wonder? Can one smile, and smile, and yet be a villain? If so, why would he have dragged me into this?'

'Well, Miss, maybe he likes Aubrey and hopes to put the blame on someone else, and he's hoping you will help him do it.'

'I suppose it had to happen one day—the villain calls in the detective, hoping to outwit her. But there is another problem: the only policeman around here is Sergeant Offaly. Can you see Helena wanting to tell him anything at all? And what would be her motive for incriminating the Captain?'

'Money?'

'It's possible. We will have to bear your theory in mind, Dot.'

Phryne felt a shiver down her lower back. She had been sorely tempted by the Captain. Rule One of Detection: never get romantically involved with suspects.

———

Their luck was in. Mr Pollock of Sailors Falls, it transpired, was a well-known habitué of the Station Hotel. So was the man whose help she would require.

'Yair, Pollock's just over there,' said Inspector Kelly, pointing his cauliflower nose towards a lean, morose individual drinking by himself at the other end of the bar. He wore a long, drooping black moustache that looked like a caterpillar making a break for freedom. His clothes were dirty, his face unwashed and unshaven, and he was one of nature's mutterers. The other patrons in the bar studiously avoided him. 'I know the bastard. Offaly has done him twice for drunk driving, and I've been to his bloody awful farm looking for sly grog. He had a still and we pinched him for that, too. I remember him because he's got Wife-beater written all over his ugly face. I hate bastards like that.'

'Funny you should mention that, Mick. As it happens, I want you to do me a small favour.'

Phryne and the inspector conversed in lowered voices for a minute or so, and Dot could not hear the substance of their talk.

Finally, Mick Kelly rose to his feet and sauntered off down the bar. 'So, George. How're ya goin'? Still in the sly-grog trade?'

Pollock turned his skinny head and glared. 'Does it bloody look like it?'

'No. And how's the missus?'

'Gone.'

'I don't blame 'er. Livin' with you must be a real treat.' Kelly had been inching closer all the time and was now looming right over Pollock's bar stool. 'Yair, go on,' he encouraged in a smooth undertone. 'You know you want to. Go on, George. Have a swing. You get a free one. I won't belt ya. Not this time. And you owe me one or two, don'tcha?'

Neurons appeared to be colliding inside Pollock's brain, but he made no move as yet.

Kelly brought his face down next to Pollock's. 'You're a free man, George. Youse can have any woman you want now, 'cos she ain't comin' back. That's if yer capable, o' course,' he added, raising his voice a little. 'When was the last time you got it up, George?'

There was a stifled giggle from one of the other patrons. Suddenly Pollock's fist shot out, and was seized and pinioned by a massive claw. 'You're hurtin' me!' Pollock squealed.

'Yair, 'cos you're resistin' arrest. I'm takin' youse in for assault on a police officer, George. Youse can cool down in the cells. You'll like it there. And if you're really good, Sergeant Offaly might read you a bedtime story. Come on.'

With calm, unhurried movements, Kelly attached his other fist to the collar of Pollock's villainous black overcoat and propelled him towards the door. The prisoner appealed to the denizens of the bar. 'You all heard! He provoked me!'

Pollock was destined to experience a disappointing audience. There was a general movement of glasses to mouths, and no support of any kind. As Kelly opened the bar door with the toe of his boot, one of the drinkers finally made a contribution. 'Didn't hear a thing.'

Dot was looking at this display of formation blokedom with wide eyes. The only really strident Aussie blokes she had met before were Bert and Cec. These men might have been their immediate family, and she began to realise that perhaps the two wharfies were not so unusual after all.

Phryne, meanwhile, nodded and beamed at the company. 'Thank you for your assistance, gentlemen.'

There was a general inclination of heads. The man nearest to Phryne gave her the ghost of a wink. 'Mick's a decent bloke, for a copper. And that one's a bad bastard.' A pointed jaw was jerked towards the exit with maximum derision. He looked into Phryne's face with a mixture of disdain and embarrassment. 'We don't like wife-beaters either.' There was another mute expression of masculine solidarity from the company, followed by a general raising of glasses.

'Good for you,' Phryne enthused. 'Come on, Dot.'

———

An hour later, Phryne and Dot helped Mrs Pollock into the back seat of the Hispano-Suiza. She looked pale, thin, and beaten down, but little sproutings of defiance and rebellion seemed to be erupting quietly from her demeanour. 'This is very kind of you,' she mouthed.

'Mrs Pollock, it's all right,' Phryne assured her. 'You don't have to say another word. I know where you live and we'll get all your things. He'll never touch you again.'

Embarrassed and grateful, the runaway wrapped a shawl around her bony shoulders and stared out the window at the countryside. Phryne did not hurry. The experience of riding in a limousine might be therapeutic, she considered.

As they drove through the streets of Daylesford, Dot was watching, as discreetly as she could, in the rear-vision mirror. Mrs Pollock hunched her shoulders and pulled her straw hat down over her face, doing her best to be invisible. As they passed the Station Hotel, Dot saw her shudder. As soon as the car reached the town limits she sat upright, composed and determined.

Phryne pulled off the road outside the doom-laden farm and stopped the motor. 'Take all the time you want. We've got all afternoon. He's behind bars at the police station. Do you have a key?'

Mrs Pollock shook her head and squared her bony shoulders. As she led them up the dusty path towards the front door, the black-and-white cat stalked towards her, mewing a litany of complaints. She stopped, kneeled down, and began to caress the cat's head. Soothing, cooing noises emerged from her mouth, and the cat rubbed itself frantically against her thin legs. Phryne and Dot addressed themselves to the front door and shook it. 'I'll break it down if I have to, Dot. But it might not be necessary.' Phryne reached into her handbag and produced her set of lock picks. Thirty seconds later the lock clicked open, and Phryne stepped inside.

Some houses exude an atmosphere of welcoming. This wasn't one of them. The prevailing atmosphere was of Doom, with undercurrents of dread and frustration. There was surprisingly little furniture. Perhaps it had all been pawned, or sold. As they paced through the drear interior, Dot's nose wrinkled in disgust.

Phryne turned to her. 'We have to find her teeth, Dot. Search the kitchen. You might find them in his tobacco jar, if he has one.'

As it happened, it took until Phryne searched the repellent outhouse to discover the missing dentures stowed behind the lavatory bowl. As she picked them up in a handkerchief a large spider gave her a look of concentrated malevolence. She returned to the house to find Mrs Pollock standing in the middle of the kitchen with a large bag on the floor next to her. The black-and-white cat was perched precariously on top of the bag, determined not to let her protector leave without her bodyguard.

'Mrs Pollock, I've found them, but you wouldn't want to know where they were. I'd like to boil them for twenty minutes, but the fire's out. If you don't mind the taste of fancy grog I think we can expedite the process.'

Mrs Pollock eyed the grimy dentures, sighed, and nodded. Phryne produced her hip flask, strode into the indescribable wash-house, and rinsed the dentures with thirty-year-old Armagnac. More spiders glared at her, but she ignored them. Dusty sunlight oozed between the cracks in the walls. She produced another handkerchief, wrapped up the teeth, and returned to the kitchen to find Mrs Pollock sweeping the floor. The broom was fighting a losing battle.

'Here they are, and please keep the handkerchief. And look: you don't have to sweep this dump ever again. The only thing that would successfully redecorate this house is three minutes' worth of flamethrower. I have to say I'm very tempted.'

Mrs Pollock turned her back, inserted her dentures, and burst into tears. Dot put her arms around her and waited until the tempest had subsided.

'Let's go, Frances,' Phryne suggested. 'And good riddance to bad rubbish.'

Mrs Pollock sniffed, nodded, and picked up the bag. 'Come on, Mr Whiskers. You're coming home with me.'

The triumphal procession (Miss Fisher at the front, Mr Whiskers bringing up the rear) made its way to the car. The door had been slammed shut. Mrs Pollock thought that she had never heard a sound of such satisfying finality.

Chapter Eighteen

Raise ye the stone or cleave the wood to make a path
  more fair or flat;
Lo, it is black already with the blood some Son of
  Martha spilled for that!
Not as a ladder from earth to Heaven, not as a
  witness to any creed,
But simple service simply given to his own kind in
  their common need.

—Rudyard Kipling, *The Sons of Martha*

Inspector Kelly was not having a good afternoon, though his day had begun with infinite promise and had continued through a pleasant lunchtime. He had sent Offaly out to Be Visible and do good, and promptly annexed his desk. Leaning back in the comfortable wooden chair, he had amused himself listening to Mr Pollock his prisoner carrying on like a pork chop. To all his complaints and entreaties Kelly had turned a deaf ear, save only to supply him with a plate of sandwiches. When the dreary litany of complaints and general whining had wound its way to a stop,

Kelly confided that he would be happy to turn Pollock adrift at some not-too-distant time in the future. Phryne had asked for two hours, but why stop at that? He decided, as a matter of public policy, to extend Pollock's hours of incarceration to four. Nothing like prison bars to bring a new sense of social responsibility to domestic abusers.

All that had been rather fun in its own way, but he had decided to get some compass bearings on this Armstrong bloke. If they really were looking for a jealous suitor, he seemed to be the only possible. Finding the date of the ill-fated train trip of Patrick Sullivan had been simple enough because it was in the coroner's report, which was only one phone call away. And here he was, at the man's house, and having anything but a good time. Yes, the suspect had been at both the Highland Gathering and the dance. His motive was anybody's guess, but a man so sure of himself might well imagine himself a suitable husband for Annie Tremain, if one ignored the fact that he was allegedly wedded already. But what of the train journey? Where had he been on the second of February?

The man had both hands in his insolent pockets, and lounged against the post of his front verandah. The house was a modest weatherboard bungalow, neither well-kept nor the reverse, on the edge of town. He was dressed for manual labour of some sort in dungarees, a singlet, and heavy boots, but he had flatly declined to discuss the nature of his work. Now Johnnie Armstrong stared down his long nose at the inspector and smirked.

'I was in Melbourne that day,' he volunteered, and proceeded to roll himself a cigarette.

'Can you prove that?'

'Yair, prob'ly.'

Now the smugness was unmistakable. Kelly could feel the conceit rising in the insolent young man like yeast in a bowl of dough. He bit down on his annoyance and dropped his voice. 'Well, would you care to tell me where you were, and who you were with?'

'Yair, the missus.'

'And what is her name?'

'Susan Armstrong.'

'And can you give me an address at which she might be found?' Mick Kelly had fallen into his customary habit, when faced with dumb insolence, of treating his witness as one of the Hard of Thinking brigade. Spell everything out as though they had the intelligence of a concussed beetle. That way they might lose their rag, but he wouldn't. Ever.

'Waterford Street, East Richmond. Number fourteen.'

'And did anybody else happen to see you on that day, apart from the missus?'

Armstrong folded his arms and smiled. The smile had all the warmth of a polar midnight. 'Yair, they did.'

Kelly waited, and made a silent mime of encouragement.

'Reverend McThomais. He's her brother.'

'I see. Well, thank you for your time, Mr Armstrong.'

'Don't mention it.'

As Inspector Kelly stumped back to his battered old Ford, he decided that Armstrong's alibi could wait for the present. And Miss Fisher still owed him one, if not more.

———

On the way back to the Mooltan, having deposited Frances Pollock and possessions into the care of Morag McKenzie, Dot was still curious. 'Miss Phryne, what's the connection with the mercer's shop? I don't understand that bit.'

Phryne swerved suddenly to avoid a large dog intent on sinking its teeth into the Hispano-Suiza's front bumper bar. 'Simple. The runaway women supply craft objects for the shop and help earn their keep that way. You said that Aunty Morag brought in a big brown-paper bag with her—that will be the latest consignment of knitted and embroidered stuff. What she took away was raw materials for more. Your new calico bag was embroidered by Janet McKenzie, whom we did not see. I'm guessing she and the other runaways are on the premises, but Miss McKenzie is not letting us into any more secrets than she can help.'

'And you're sure you believe her about Helena?'

'Yes, Dot, I do. She has no reason to lie, and every reason to speed me on my way. The last thing she wants is a visit from the cops.'

Dot subsided, feeling that a little more gratitude from Aunty Morag would have been only proper. As it was, the latter had accepted Phryne's proffered two five-pound notes in her ancient claw and grunted the briefest of thankyous.

The comforting bluestone solidity of the Mooltan hove into view, and Phryne stopped the car outside. 'I'm resting up until dinner,' she declared. 'We might as well dine at the Temperance again, if we're playing cards there. If I fall asleep, come and get me at a quarter to six, will you?'

'Yes, Miss.'

Dot found it hard to sleep during the day, preferring healthful early nights to obtain her necessary recuperation. Phryne had heard of early nights but considered them hideously overrated. She strode upstairs and stripped off her street clothes. As she lay on her bed in her blue silk pyjamas, she found it hard to relax. Only one of her mysteries was solved. Who was Alice's Young Man of Mystery? While decidedly less urgent a question than the others, it nonetheless niggled at Phryne. And, more significantly, where was Helena? It was still possible that Captain Spencer was holding her hostage somewhere. She found the Captain very attractive, but he might still be capable of drastic measures to protect his beloved spa. Dot's theory was a very attractive one. Good old Dot! She had learned much about detective work during her time with Phryne. Tomorrow Phryne would return to the spa and renew her acquaintance with the worthy Captain.

As for the murders, she was still in the dark. Mick Kelly was right to doubt the theory of murder to eliminate rivals in love. It was scarcely credible. Most of the young men about town were guileless youths, and the worthy caber tosser the most guileless of the lot. Only Johnnie Armstrong looked even possible as a candidate. She had disliked the man on sight, finding him arrogant, over-sure of himself, and disdainful of his fellow creatures. She must have another talk with the inspector. She owed him a substantial favour now—but if she were able to nab his murderer for him, that splendid copper would count himself in her debt. She smiled to herself. Phryne wondered why she was so certain that the murderer would strike again at the cinema opening. Surely not? And yet the murderer had struck three times already. The two murders Phryne had been witness to were both done in the open. Lots of witnesses, but also innumerable suspects. This argued a cool, calculating brain and immense self-control. She supposed Mick Kelly was patiently sifting through what evidence was available at this late date in order to work out the possibilities. One thing was certain. The suspect must have been present at the Highland Gathering, the dance, and the train ride. Good luck with that, she mused, and promptly fell asleep.

———

When Dot's nervous knock sounded on her door Phryne was already dressed in a dark green trouser suit and substantial boots.

Phryne had concluded that Daylesford's cobbled bluestone walkways were too pointy for more delicate footwear. Dot was dressed in beige and brown, with beige overtones. One day, Phryne swore, she would persuade Dot to try on some brighter colours. They were waved on their way by Dulcie, who was carrying a substantial laundry basket on her hip with no apparent effort.

As they made their sedate way towards Daylesford, Phryne half turned to Dot. 'I need you to keep an eye on our three hosts, Dot. Since you're not playing, you'll notice more than me.'

'Are you still thinking Jessie might be our murderer?'

'I don't think that anymore, Dot. These murders are a complete mystery, I'm sorry to say, though I intend to solve them. No, there's something else niggling away at me. My subconscious is tapping me on the shoulder and saying, *Excuse me?* So keep an eye out.'

'I will, Miss. What's wrong?' For Phryne had clasped both hands on the steering wheel and groaned.

'Dot, I am an idiot! Actually, what I want you to do is this. Apparently, they're closing at seven tonight, but serving an early dinner. And that means washing-up for someone. I want you to help out.'

'All right, Miss. May I ask why?'

Phryne turned to face her companion, her face set and hard. 'Dot, if there is a Cinderella in this pub, it isn't Jessie—it's the mysterious cousin Peggy. The girl who slaves over a hot stove and never gets to see anyone. She'll be doing the cleaning up while the two barmaids get to play cards. While I'm finding out if they enjoy bridge or just play it to keep Uncle Drunkard happy, I want you to determine if she's a possible suspect.'

Dot thought about this. What if she really were the eternal outcast, and had gone mad and started killing boys out of sheer resentment? It wasn't likely, but neither were any of the other possible explanations. 'That's a good idea, Miss. I'll let you know.'

They were met in the main bar by Annie, dressed in a simple long skirt, blouse and apron in light blue and white. There were no other patrons. 'Hello, Miss Fisher,' she said, her face opening up like a summer rose. 'If you're here for dinner, there's only lamb chops, I'm afraid. It looks like everyone else is staying home tonight.'

'Lamb chops for two would be lovely, Annie. And I believe you're to be my partner tonight?'

Annie's smile could have kick-started a tractor. 'Really? Jessie said you were playing tonight and I thought she was joking. I'll look forward to that. We play in the dining room, so you won't have to move.' With that, Annie wafted back behind the bar, in case of late patrons wishing to drink in her extraordinary beauty.

Phryne and Dot ate a pleasant meal with steamed vegetables and gooseberry pie, served by Jessie wearing dark blue trousers and a check shirt. When it was all cleared away, Phryne said casually, 'Jessie, Dot doesn't play cards, so she'd like to help with the washing-up, if that's all right.'

Jessie looked at Phryne quizzically. 'If you're sure, Miss Fisher. Peggy could do with the company. She doesn't play either.' She gestured to Dot, who rose and followed, taking the salt and pepper shakers with her.

Jessie led the way through some narrow corridors into a cream-painted kitchen. A pleasant-looking young woman in a huge apron and a mob cap was bent over a kitchen sink filled with suds and saucepans. 'Peggy, this is Dot. She's going to help you out tonight.'

A freckled, pointed face turned towards them. 'Sweet! Hello, Dot. There's a spare apron over there on the hook. Can you scrub down the table for me?'

———

Mr McKenzie opened a side door and sat himself at the table after removing his hat with a courtly bow. 'It is very kind of you to indulge the girls in this way, Miss Fisher,' he said in his throaty voice. 'Annie and Jessie love their cards, and the doctor is indisposed the nicht. You are to partner Annie, I believe?'

Phryne had stood up, thus allowing her host to seat himself. She looked him over. The man had scrubbed up rather well this evening. He wore a dark suit with waistcoat, and there was even a necktie around his shiny, scrubbed neck. A fob-watch chain disappeared into the left-hand pocket of the jacket. All that was missing was a black hat and moustache for him to have looked the complete riverboat gambler. There was one nick on his cheek, showing where he and his razor had been renewing their acquaintance, though the horrible beard was still very much in evidence. Annie wafted in and sat herself opposite Phryne with a look of innocent excitement. McKenzie drew out a newish pack of cards from his other pocket. Then Jessie returned from the kitchen, carrying a bottle of dark beer and four glasses. These she placed on the white linen tablecloth before she disappeared through another door, emerging a moment later with a blank sheet of paper and a large pencil. 'Who wants to score?' she enquired, with a look around the table.

'May I?'

Jessie gave Annie a look of sisterly affection and handed over the page and pencil.

Annie wrote, in large capitals, the words *ANNIE/PHRYNE* and *UNCLE/JESSIE* next to each other. A thick vertical line was drawn down the middle of the paper, and two horizontal lines.

'High card for dealer,' Jessie announced and cut the pack. Jessie won with the king of diamonds and dealt the cards swiftly. She fiddled with her hand for a short moment, then folded it up and laid it down on the tablecloth. 'Pass,' she announced, and stared at the ceiling.

Annie gave her cards a solid workout and announced One Club.

McKenzie passed, and Phryne, looking at the dismal collection in front of her, announced, 'One diamond.'

'Two clubs,' Annie responded, a crease of puzzlement adorning her lovely brow.

There were no more bids. Jessie gave Phryne a sidelong look and laid the four of spades on the table. Since Phryne's only high card was the ace of spades, she laid that over the four. She collected the cards and led her solitary diamond, which Annie took with the ace and returned a small diamond, which Phryne was able to ruff with the three of clubs. Annie took the rest of the tricks except for the king of trumps, which McKenzie claimed.

'Six clubs made,' Annie announced, and wrote thirty-six above the line, and fifty below it. Her brow clouded again. 'I hope you don't mind me asking, Miss Fisher, but what made you bid diamonds when you only had the one?'

Phryne lightly slapped her forehead. 'I'm so sorry. I forgot we were playing auction, not contract. In contract bridge one club is a bid announcing a very strong hand. As your partner, I'd need to tell you something about my own hand. So one diamond just means that my hand was very weak.'

'So it turned out all right then. I did have a strong hand anyway. And you led the singleton because you wanted a return ruff?'

'Indeed yes, Annie. And you gave it to me. Well done.'

They played many more hands. There could be no doubt about the fact that her three companions were enjoying themselves immensely. The battle swayed to and fro, with Phryne and Annie ahead with a comfortable margin, until a crisis was reached. McKenzie was playing in six diamonds, having beaten off a spirited auction from Annie, who clearly had a whale of a spade suit and intended to bid it until the cows came home and tucked themselves into bed. McKenzie had the spade ace, which he was obliged to play at trick one, since Annie had opened with the king. He then ran the rest of his tricks from his hand until he ruffed a club in dummy, which was holding three small hearts and the three of trumps. Phryne had discarded everything else and was grimly hanging on to the heart king, jack, and four, plus an unimportant club. *This time,* Phryne vowed to herself, *you are going down, Mr McKenzie. Yes, you have, I believe, the ace and the queen, and probably also the five, plus a trump. But you have two heart losers. No slam for you, my inebriate friend.*

McKenzie stared at dummy, and then at Annie, and closed his eyes for a long moment. Then he selected the five of hearts and laid it on the table. Annie stared at it as though it were a red-back spider, and with a small sigh laid the nine on it. And McKenzie reached into his own hand and played not the ace or queen, but the eight. He then closed his eyes again, leaned back in his chair, and gave Phryne a sidelong grin.

Phryne's frown deepened. *Let's see. If I play the king or the jack, he wins the last two hearts. But if I duck as well, Annie's probably only got spades, which gives him a ruff and discard. Well, the endplay is certain. Annie might have something other than spades, but I doubt it.* Phryne played the four of hearts and looked expectantly at her partner, who shook her head, collected the trick, and laid down the queen of spades. McKenzie tossed the queen of hearts onto the table, took the trick with dummy's last trump, and laid down the ace of hearts and the final trump from his own hand.

Jessie clapped her hands. 'Oh, well played, Uncle! That was brilliantly done!'

McKenzie beamed at her. 'Well, well, that was unfortunate,

Miss Fisher,' he commiserated with maximum magnanimity. 'It just came to me in a moment. Jessie? Another bottle, please?'

They played for another half-hour, but Mr McKenzie's bolt was clearly shot, and he began to play erratically, and drink freely. Twice he failed to follow suit, but was immediately corrected by Jessie, who replaced the cards in his hand and called for a more proper response. He then opened a third bottle, but Annie laid her hand on his arm. 'Uncle? We shouldn't take up any more of Miss Fisher's time. The score's pretty much even, so that's a good place to leave it.'

McKenzie was instantly contrite, and rose unsteadily to his feet, like a schooner tacking in a high wind. 'My thanks to you, Miss Fisher. You played splendidly. I and my nieces thank you for your indulgence.'

Jessie, meanwhile, disappeared down the corridor, returning with Dot, who appeared to have spent a more convivial evening than might have been expected.

'Thank you all for your hospitality,' Phryne said, nodding to each in turn. 'Dot? It's time we were on our way.'

———

The street was dark, save for a single streetlight. Bright stars blazed down out of a cloudless sky, and in the west Orion was leaning towards Ballarat. They drove home in silence and parked the car outside the Mooltan. Night creatures fussed in the treetops and whickered to themselves. 'Dot, before we go inside, tell all. Is the mystery Cinderella a likely suspect?'

Dot grimaced. 'I'm sorry, Miss, but she has no motive at all. I liked Peggy a lot, and she's perfectly happy. The only thing is that she doesn't feel she belongs here.'

Phryne considered this. 'We're really looking for someone

with a considerable stake in the local community, aren't we? But are you really telling me she's happy just to cook and wash up?'

'For the moment, Miss. But I heard all about her young man. He's finishing his apprenticeship as a motor mechanic in Melbourne, and his boss says he'll take him on full-time soon.'

'And when that happens, Cousin Peggy goes off to Melbourne to get married and live happily ever after?'

'I'm afraid so, Miss Phryne. She talked a lot about it.'

'Drat! Another dead end. So, what's she like, anyway?'

Dot considered this. Fragments of Peggy's conversation drifted back to her. 'Another good girl, Miss—but she's got a sharp tongue on her. The things she said about Mr McKenzie! She's only working at the Temperance to earn some money towards their house in Melbourne. And she said—what did she say? Oh yes. "Dot, I'm only here to help out Jessie and Annie. We've known each other since we were little kids, and they're both saints. If they want to keep on working for that drunken Gawd-help-us that's their affair. If it were up to me, I'd throw the old man into Jubilee Lake." And she said a few other things about him, too.'

In the pallid light of the front door lamp, Phryne saw Dot colour.

'Do go on, Dot. This is fascinating.'

'She said that McKenzie was exploiting the girls rotten, and something oughta be done about it.'

'Oh.' Phryne had hoped for something more lurid than that, but there was nothing to be made of any possible Wrongness in the relationship between uncle and nieces. Having spent two hours in their company, she felt certain she was in a position to rule that out. The girls were totally at ease in the company of their Gawd-help-us and treated him with far more kindness and sympathy than he merited.

'So how did you get on with the card game, Miss? I don't think I've ever seen you play bridge before.'

'It was surprisingly pleasant. I learned how to play the game in Fashionable London before I got completely fed up with it all.'

'London, or bridge?'

Phryne grinned. 'Both. But it was the perfect opportunity to see the Tremain girls and their uncle out of uniform, as it were. And there's nothing peculiar about their relationship, Dot. It was a man and his two nieces, playing cards. Everyone at their ease and nothing weird underneath it. I think they genuinely like the man. I can't see it myself, but there it is.' She smiled. 'One thing I can tell you: they play an excellent game, all three of them. They'd give the London ladies who bored me stiff a good run for their money. Oh, and speaking of money, absolutely none changed hands. They were just playing for points, and pencil-marks on a piece of paper. So if we were thinking about gambling habits, that's out, too. Golly, but this is a tough case, Dot.'

'What's on tomorrow, Miss?'

'Back to the spa for me, to look for Helena Ogilvie; you can have the morning off. If I don't see my way clear by tomorrow night, I may go ahead with my plan.'

Accustomed as she was to her employer, Dot's ears pricked up. 'A plan? Is it going to be dangerous, Miss?'

'A little bit, Dot. And that's why I want to be sure I can trust the Captain first.'

'Does this mean you think you know where Helena is?'

'Well, yes, Dot—I have an idea, nothing more. And a plan to go with the idea, yes: I have one of those, too. Look, I know you haven't met him, but the Captain really is a fine man. The work he's doing with the shell-shock patients is wonderful. I like him a lot. But he's exactly the sort of man who could make some serious trouble for anyone who got in his way, and I want to be able to clear him before I go any further.' Phryne patted Dot's arm. 'Dot, that idea of yours was a really good one, and it may even be the key to Helena's disappearance. I just hope not.'

'How are you going to find out if it's true?'

'By looking. Dot, for the moment I'm washing my hands of Daylesford. It's a wonderful place filled with charming people, but I don't know enough about them. The real villain is probably laughing himself sick at my expense, and I intend to get my own back on him. Assuming it is a him, which I think it must be now. But Hepburn Springs? It's such a small community that I should be able to crack the case quickly. Tomorrow I'll find Helena, one way or another.'

'Bravo, Miss.' Dot froze. 'Miss—look!'

Away on the very edge of the lamplight, a large chocolate-brown wombat was striding purposefully through the undergrowth. Phryne admired the sturdy muscles beneath the dark fur, short stubby legs bowling happily through any and every obstacle. Then there was a rustle in the grass, and it had gone.

'It's beautiful,' Dot exclaimed.

'I agree, Dot. Tomorrow, I shall emulate that wombat's excellent example. When all else fails, stomp through everything until you get what you want. Come on, let's go to bed. We've had a big day.'

Chapter Nineteen

And the Sons of Mary smile and are bless' d, they
  know the Angels are on their side.
They know in them is the Grace confess' d, and for
  them are the Mercies multiplied.
They sit at the feet, they hear the Word, they see how
  truly the Promise runs.
They have cast their burden upon the Lord, and the
  Lord He lays it on Martha's Sons!

—Rudyard Kipling, *The Sons of Martha*

Dot rose early on Tuesday morning and went for a soothing walk. It was set fair to be a warm day, and there was no wind to speak of. She listened to a vociferous kookaburra exulting about something, presumably related to the morning bill of fare. She stared at the turning in the road which led to the spa and wondered if they were ready for Miss Fisher's full state visit. She wandered through the forest pathways for a while, admiring the sunlight glinting through the verdant tree branches, and marvelling at how different things were hereabouts. Back in

Melbourne, she knew, summer's end was a time for vegetation's panting survivors to keep a low profile until the coming of the autumn rains. It was as if there were veins of water running all through these hills. In fact, she realised, this was precisely the case.

Well before eight a.m., she set her course for home; her stomach was rumbling. Dulcie and Alice's breakfasts were of the traditional English variety: eggs, bacon, sausages, toast, jam, and pots of fragrant tea. She wished Miss Phryne would share the breakfast table with her, but her employer either partook of a French roll with coffee, or else eschewed the meal entirely. Until lunchtime she subsisted mostly upon coffee and cigarettes. As Dot walked up the brick pathway to the front door she could smell both, but especially the strong black espresso favoured by Miss Phryne. Dot was still regarding this foreign intrusion into the traditional breakfast table with suspicion.

Dulcie had just finished laying a small table for one. The intoxicating scent of viands fried, steamed, boiled, and toasted went to her head like wine. 'Hello, Dulcie. Is that for Miss Fisher or for me?'

Dulcie wrapped her morning robe tighter around her bosom and smiled. 'It's for you, Dot. Phryne's already left on her travels. She said she'd be back later on and that you should have a relaxing morning.'

'Oh. Thanks, Dulcie.' There being nothing else for it, Dot sat down at her spotless white tablecloth and prepared, however reluctantly, to sit back, relax, and enjoy a hearty breakfast.

Presently a thought occurred to her. As Dulcie returned to clear away Dot's empty plate—which had been occupied by two poached eggs, three Cumberland sausages, three strips of bacon, a dollop of steamed mushrooms, and something which after some doubtful reconnaissance Dot identified as spinach leaves—Dot looked questioningly at her. 'Dulcie? Is Aubrey still here?' Dulcie gave Dot an odd look but smiled easily.

'Yes, he's here in one of the spare rooms. I'm keeping a close eye on him. Why do you ask?'

'I just wondered.' Dot stared fixedly at the teapot. 'We might find Helena soon, and I thought he'd want to be here when it happens.'

'If it happens.' Dulcie's mouth set in a line. 'Does Phryne see light in our quest, do you know?'

Dot looked her straight in the eye. 'I'm hoping so, Dulcie.'

'So do I, Dot. Anything else you'd like?'

Dot shook her head. 'No, thanks. I'm full up. It was wonderful, though.'

Dulcie inclined a gracious head and Dot nibbled moodily at a piece of toast and strawberry jam. Miss Phryne had solved the mystery of the other disappearing women, at least. Perhaps this was a good omen for the immediate future.

Dot rose, walked into the parlour, and found Tamsin the cat playing with a ball of wool. Dot was about to confiscate it, but instead she paused to watch as the little paws reduced a skein of blue wool into a confused jumble. Only when Tamsin had finished playing did Dot bend down, gather up the wool, and begin to restore it to its former state.

———

Phryne had, unbeknownst to Dot, also gone for a fast thinking walk not long after first light. These murder cases were driving her to the edge of distraction. She stopped in the middle of a pleasant glade above a gently murmuring pool and listened to the morning chorus. She breathed easier. There was something magical about this part of the world. A rough bench was set in a tiny lookout so passers-by could enjoy the view in comfort. Phryne sat, emptied her mind of everything but the gentle tinkle of running water, and enjoyed a long moment of perfect peace. She felt her pulse slow down. A tiny wagtail hopped onto the ground in front of her and shifted its miniature head this way and that. Even the birds here were unafraid of humans. 'Hello, little friend,' she murmured. 'Can you help me out?'

The bird hopped away and spread its wings, having suddenly recalled a previous appointment. Phryne watched the sunlight flash on its blue tail with pure delight. *All right,* she admonished herself. *Here you are, by yourself, with nothing to distract you. We have a bold, cunning, highly intelligent, and utterly ruthless murderer in our midst. He kills in the middle of crowds where there are suspects galore and betrays nothing to mark him out. None of this points to a jealous lover, does it? What on earth is his motive? Come on. You can do this. You have an unbroken record of criminal detection. No rural Tiberius is going to outwit you. Don't think. Clear your mind, recall everything you have seen in Daylesford, and make no assumptions. There has been far too much furious action, and too many distractions. Motive, method, opportunity. Find someone who fits all three, and you have him.*

Phryne lit a cigarette and inhaled once. Then she sat quite still, with eyes closed. Her cigarette slowly went out. She didn't notice it. Because it had all come to her in a blinding flash of insight. She knew now beyond doubt who it was, and why. The criminal genius had left nothing to incriminate him. And he would try again, on Friday night, at the cinema opening. There was nothing for it but to catch him in the act. And she intended to do just that.

———

Twenty minutes later she was bathing in the spa again, striking out across the narrow pool, naked and self-assured. She had no visible audience until Sheila made an appearance and waved at her. 'You're all right, Miss Fisher,' Sheila called. 'The Captain says you're to have the run of the place.' She laid two large white fluffy towels on a deckchair within easy reach.

Phryne admired Sheila's nurse's uniform (plain white, comfortable, and minus all the annoying extras hospital nurses have to endure) and grinned. *I bet he has. He's hoping for a substantial cheque from me. But we will see.* She dived under the surface of the gloriously effervescent pool and luxuriated in her freedom from clothes of any sort. She had bathed naked many times before, and in more romantic circumstances. A complacent smile settled on her mouth. After another few laps of the pool she emerged, dried herself off, and wrapped the second towel around herself. She heard low male voices outside and retreated into the ladies' dressing room, wherein her clothes were bestowed. As she got dressed, she heard the gentle splosh of bodies entering the water. Fully clad (another trouser suit: cream, with blue trimmings) she walked alongside the pool and waved at the patients, who greeted her with a combination of admiration and shyness.

She opened the door that led out the back to Smokers' Corner. It was already well-tenanted. Four of the blokes from her previous visit were gathered. She thought she recalled the names of some of them. The Daves seemed very much in evidence; anyone as tall as Tiny Dave (six feet five or so) was not hard to remember. 'Hello, Dave,' Phryne addressed the tallest of them. 'Got a light for a girl?'

Tiny Dave produced a brass lighter, leaned down, and ignited the end of Phryne's cocktail Sobranie. 'Did yer have a good swim this morning, Miss?'

'Indeed I did.' Phryne inhaled, wondering how many faces had been pressed to the big glass windows while she had been doing her Nereid impersonation. Well, they were welcome to look if they wanted to. 'Dave, I was wondering about the Captain's special tonic. Can you tell me more about it?'

Looking around the ring of faces, there appeared to be some concentrated ratiocination happening. Finally, a collective decision was reached. 'There's a placard over there if yer interested, Miss.'

Phryne strolled towards the back of the tea house and noticed a large tin placard nailed to the brick wall. She read the following: *Pharmaceutical tonic, Hepburn Spa. This product carries the approval of the Chief Medical Officer of the State of Victoria.* Big Dave watched her and spoke out of the corner of his thin mouth.

'Yair, Miss. It's all above board. I run the still. It's a beauty. Want to try some?'

He was a wiry, middle-aged man with a face scored with lines and cheerful brown eyes. He held out a small medicine bottle and poured out a measure into a teaspoon. Phryne accepted the spoon and tasted. Very like green chartreuse, she thought, and far stronger than the herbal wine the Captain had given her the other night. Clearly Big Dave was not above keeping a sample with him at all times, for medicinal purposes, obviously.

The man looked conspiratorial. 'Jeez, the old biddies love this stuff. 'Specially the Methodists. They're s'posed to be dry, but nerve tonic doesn't count.' He held out the bottle for her to read. SPENCER'S NERVE TONIC. TAKE ONE TEASPOON AS REQUIRED.

Phryne smiled. 'Yes, I can see that they would. Thank you.' She surveyed the company. 'Well, gentlemen, have a splendid day.'

She waved her hand in dismissal and walked back to the Mooltan, where she found Dot engrossed in the *Daylesford Advocate* in the yard, surrounded by wildflowers, lavender, and a murmuration of bees. Phryne filled in the details of what she had seen this morning, and explained. 'Dot, it looks like it can't be the Captain, because he has no motive. So we're not going to waste any time rescuing Helena. I'm pretty sure I know where she is, and we're going to spring her tonight.'

As Phryne expounded her plan, she wondered briefly whether or not to share with Dot her illumination about the murder suspect. She decided against it. Dot had learned a lot about keeping her thoughts to herself, but Phryne felt she could not risk any premature disclosure. But she did write a brief account of her reasoning and the name of the murderer in her notebook, which she stowed away in her handbag. Just in case.

———

It was Tuesday afternoon after school, and the two girls looked at each other in pent-up excitement. 'Well, here we are again, Jane.'

Ruth admired her adoptive sister's neat appearance. School uniforms did nothing much for female beauty. They were not supposed to. Show me the most beautiful girl, the designers might have said, and I will transform her into a nondescript sack of wet spaghetti. But Jane looked like she meant business. Her cropped hair—after its mauling from the phantom pigtail-snipper of Queenscliff—was beginning to grow out again. What Jane looked like was a private investigator, just like Miss Phryne. Ruth was nervous and wondered if Jane was as well. If so, she gave no sign of it.

The great front door opened slowly, and Mrs Knight, pale as a ghost, eyed the two girls on her front door step. 'Yes?' she enquired, frowning slightly.

They had rehearsed this many times on the tram to Kew, having been counselled by Hugh Collins that full disclosure was the only way. The one thing they hadn't decided upon was who was going to tell it. Ruth had assumed that Jane was going to, but Jane was showing signs of irresolution, so Ruth wasted no more time.

'Mrs Knight, I fear we were less than frank with you last time we were here. We said that we had just come to retrieve a textbook, but what we were really looking for was a clue to Claire's death. The policeman in charge, he thinks Claire's uncle did it, but we think he's got the wrong end of the stick—and so does Sergeant Collins, who is staying in our house. He asked us to investigate, because he thought we'd have more chance of finding things out. And we don't want to bother you, but we think the solution to this mystery is in Claire's room. Will you allow us to have a proper search? I think she probably kept a diary, hidden away somewhere. And if we can find it, we can either bring the culprit to justice, or else—well, maybe it was just an accident after all. We're so sorry to intrude, but surely it's better to know the truth.' Ruth ground to a halt.

Mrs Knight looked down at the pair of them. The merest flicker of a smile lit her features. 'Girls, I guessed what you were up to. I've searched her room already, but by all means have another try. Take all the time you need. I'll be in the parlour. Let me know if you find anything.'

The bereaved mother led them to the foot of the staircase, and they ran up the stairs two at a time. At the top, they exchanged a look. 'Which room was it?' Ruth whispered.

'This one.' Jane opened the door, the girls slipped through it, and Jane shut it again behind her. 'All right, Ruth, let's use the Pinkerton method, dividing the room into small squares. And don't forget to look outside the window. It might be hidden under the eaves.'

They scoured the room, looking under the bed; in the cupboard; in, under, and on top of the wardrobe. They opened her school diary and looked right through it. On the back page, Ruth pointed in mounting excitement. 'Jane, this has to be a clue! Look.'

'*I love my love with an e, for my heart is reciprocal,*' Jane read, and frowned. 'Does this mean that the boy's name begins with an E? Edward? Ernest? And what does reciprocal mean?'

'It means her love was returned. But...I wonder.'

However, they searched for another twenty minutes or so and found nothing of substance. Claire's books were all in Dewey Decimal order: a poignant reminder of how methodical she had been. In the fiction section, there were a few historical romances. She seemed to have liked, of all people, Sir Walter Scott, since her copy of *Ivanhoe* was well-thumbed and briskly annotated. Closer inspection revealed some very tart comments in pencil. It appeared Scott's romantic imagination had disappointed her. *A very ordinary depiction of love at bottom,* she had inscribed in her neat handwriting. *All he does is put Rebecca in mortal danger. No wonder her father takes them away to Spain and safety. England was a bad place to be a Jew!*

'She was hard to please,' Ruth commented. She had loved *Ivanhoe* herself when younger, though she had not read it since.

They exchanged a look of helplessness. 'Do we give up?' Ruth asked.

'Miss Phryne wouldn't,' Jane objected. 'I still think there's a diary here. We have to find it.'

'It's very well hidden.'

'It is. But we'll find it.'

In the end, they did find it. Between the wardrobe and the wall, one of the floorboards seemed slightly out of whack with the others. Since the entire house was otherwise as close to perfection as possible, this seemed significant. With difficulty, Jane prised the loose board out. Inside was a small, flat box with a combination lock on it.

'Jane, can you pick locks?'

'No. But we may not need to.' Jane tried a few combinations, but the four wheels refused to click open. She laid the box on the bed. 'Ruth, can you give me her diary again?'

Ruth handed over the school diary and Jane flipped the pages until she found what she wanted. 'Claire wrote here *I love my love with an e…*' Jane flicked the wheels to the numbers 2718. But the box resolutely refused to yield up its secrets. 'Blast. I thought I'd solved it. Two-seven-one-eight are the first four digits of the number *e*. It's an irrational number, like pi.'

'Oh.' Higher mathematics were a matter of complete bewilderment to Ruth. 'Did she ever talk about this *e* thing to you?'

'Oh yes. We had some good conversations about it. The number *e* is the foundation of calculus. And logarithms. Oh, wait. She did say her love was reciprocal…'

Her fingers moved quickly, and the lock sprang open. 'I thought so! The first four digits of one over *e* are three-six-seven-eight. And now we have the diary.'

With Ruth looking assiduously over her shoulder, Jane flicked through the pages. 'Oh.'

After five minutes or so of breathless reading, Jane handed it to Ruth. 'Keep reading if you want to. I've seen enough.'

'So her lover's name begins with T. Unless it's another misdirection.'

'I doubt it. We need to tell Mr Hugh. And Tinker.'

'Are we going to give this to Mrs Knight?' It was Ruth's first encounter with erotic prose, and she was very reluctant to hand it over.

Jane gave her a severe look. 'I'll give you five more minutes with it, and then we give it to her.'

'Won't she be horrified?'

Jane thought about this. 'Not as much as you might think. I guess she will be pleased that her daughter was greatly loved and appreciated. It's something to put against her untimely death.'

'Poor Claire. It really was a bit Romeo and Juliet, wasn't it?'
Ruth was still flicking through the pages as slowly as she dared.

Jane bit her lip in frustration. 'It shouldn't have been like that!'
she protested. 'Lots of young girls get pregnant. It didn't have to
end like this. I have no patience with pointless tragedy.' There
was a tense silence while Ruth read to the last page. 'All right,
what's the last entry?'

Ruth handed it over in silence, tears furrowing down her cheeks.

Jane read as follows:

*Today I am going to break the news to T. He promised we'd be
together, and we will be. Mum will be mad at us, but I think she'll let
us marry. And Father does what Mum tells him to. I'm sixteen and
T is seventeen. That's old enough. And while I'm nursing the baby,
I'll finish school. I'm going to be a doctor no matter what. Nothing is
going to stop me. And we'll be together. It won't be easy. We can't start
a family living at home. Maybe we'll have to live apart for a while. But
T will finish school this year. He's clever. And when he's working next
year we can be a proper family. I love him so much. Does he love me
enough? I hope so. When he holds me in his strong arms I can see the
love in his eyes. Marry me! Love me. Kiss me. Hold me!!!*

'Oh, Jane!' Ruth put her hand to her chest. 'So what happened,
do you think?'

'I expect she broke the news and he ran a mile.'

'Did he kill her, though? Surely not!'

'We don't know, Ruth. It might have been an accident. Come
on. We need to talk to Mrs Knight.'

———

Downstairs, the bereaved mother leafed through the pages
in frozen silence then handed the book back to Jane. 'It's as I
expected,' she said. 'You are clever girls. How did you find it?'

Jane described the missing board and the combination lock. 'You must give this to the police. Give it to the sergeant, please. I suppose that inspector will have to see it in due course—' for a moment, Mrs Knight looked daggers at the relentlessly polished floorboards '—but I would much rather he didn't.'

'He needn't,' Jane interposed. 'If we can find this boy and persuade him to confess, I don't think we need tell the inspector anything. If he's stupid enough to think that your brother is... what he thinks he is...then he isn't entitled to any consideration. And I don't think he should be allowed to gawp at your daughter's private diary. Let him eat cake!'

This time Mrs Knight allowed herself a proper smile. 'You are good girls, both of you. All right. I'll keep this for a few days. But you must tell your sergeant about it. And—good luck. Would you like some tea before you go?'

The girls exchanged a lightning glance; both had noted the imminent arrival of tears on that stern visage.

'No thanks, Mrs Knight,' said Ruth. 'We need to go home now. Don't worry—we'll find him!'

Chapter Twenty

Ah, my Belovéd, fill the Cup that clears
Today of past Regrets and future Fears:
Tomorrow!—Why, Tomorrow I may be
Myself with Yesterday's Sev'n thousand Years.

—Edward Fitzgerald, *The Rubáiyát of*
Omar Khayyám of Naishápúr

Phryne returned to the Mooltan for an afternoon rest, which she spent lying on her bed with a gin and tonic, reading a light detective story. It was Dorothy L. Sayers' *Whose Body?* and it was a splendid read. How simple life was in that fictional world! She read through to the end, having picked the wrong villain on page five and the correct villain on page sixty-nine. She laid down the book and smiled. Miss Sayers had done splendidly, and Phryne would read anything further she chose to release to the world; but real life was so much more complex. She wondered whether or not she should see the inspector again, but decided against it. Mick Kelly was a good copper, no question about it, but he didn't want theories; he wanted results. Phryne was reasonably certain that she would be able to give him what he had asked for. Her guess at the intended target was probably right, but if she stayed unobtrusively close to the villain it would not greatly matter if she had picked the wrong victim. She finished her drink and shook her head in utter loathing and revulsion. Which would not do. She needed to treat the murderer as a worthy foe, which he undoubtedly was. Aside from one single oversight, he had committed three all-but-perfect murders. Save the loathing for afterwards.

Meanwhile, there was tonight to think about. She ran through her plan in her head and could find no fault with it. She was all but certain that Helena was alive and being tolerably well-treated, apart from being held in durance reasonably vile. Should she have investigated earlier? This was always a thorny issue. But she would only get one chance at this or the kidnapper might take fright, with incalculable consequences. She decided to take Dulcie and Dot with her. They would need three pursuers, preferably spread out around a tight perimeter so as to preclude all possibility of escape. She decided against taking Aubrey. Dulcie had told Aubrey to stay put at the Mooltan until called for. Feeling as ready as she ever would be, Phryne drifted into a light and dreamless sleep.

At six o'clock there was a knock on her door. 'Miss Phryne? It's dinnertime.'

'I'll be down in a few minutes, Dot.' When she arrived in the dining room, Alice was laying out a simple dinner of ham and cheese sandwiches, along with slices from a fresh apricot-and-pear pie and Italian coffee. Dulcie emerged from the kitchen, and the four of them sat down to eat, at Phryne's invitation. No one asked any questions, which pleased Phryne greatly. Only when the meal was over did Dulcie look up expectantly.

'Dulcie,' Phryne announced, 'you, Dot, and I are going on an expedition tonight.'

Dulcie put down her coffee cup. 'Where are we going?'

Phryne outlined her plan. 'Comfortable clothes and boots, black if you have them. We will require secrecy. And I will bring my flashlight. Country nights are so surprisingly dark.'

'Is Aubrey going with you?' Alice asked.

Phryne shook her head. 'Men get overexcited in rescues—and other delicate moments. We will manage.'

'Be careful,' said Alice in a melting voice, gazing at Dulcie, who clasped her hand for a moment and stroked her hair.

'Alice,' Phryne continued, 'I need you to ring Helena's mother around eight and ask her to meet us here. I hope to be able to return her daughter to her, but you never know. If it's a washout, I'll come back and tell you it's off. But I really don't think I'll need to do so.'

Alice glowed, happy to be given some responsibility without actual danger.

'All right, everybody know what we're doing? Good. Now, let's get changed.'

———

When they met downstairs a short while later, Dot had attired herself in a long, dark brown woollen dress with matching jumper. Phryne wore black trousers, shirt, and jacket, with her best walking boots. Boots were good in a scuffle, and the road, she remembered, was broken and stony.

The light had drained out of the sky as they set off up the road. It smelled eerily of mineral springs and wattle, and the nocturnal creatures were out and about their customary errands, and making a decent racket over them. A koala grunted, and an offended night-bird swooped off through the trees. Looking at her companions, Phryne belatedly realised that Dot's disguise was, if anything, better than her own. Surprisingly, Dulcie was dressed in emerald green trousers and jacket, which, as soon as they moved out of range of the outside light, simply vanished into the Stygian darkness.

When they neared the bottling plant, Phryne beckoned to Dot to close up behind her. Her companion slipped on a stone and would have fallen over had Phryne not gripped her arm tightly. Dulcie's measured footsteps paced the road without a slip. She was doubtless more accustomed to unmade roads. By unspoken consent they stopped in a huddle. Ahead of them, buildings loomed up in the dusk. A little light was spilling out of one of them.

'All right.' Phryne grinned at them. 'Over the top!'

Dulcie smiled. Dot gritted her teeth and looked stoic. Phryne switched off the torch. Her jacket pocket contained her gun, and a spare box of ammunition in case Vern needed more suppression than six bullets could provide.

The plant was nothing more than three large galvanised-iron sheds. Phryne waved the others back and crept up to a lighted window in one of them. She peered in to look. Vern was filling bottles from a keg by the light of a kerosene lamp, quietly and slowly, with concentrated efficiency. Sid sat lounging in a wicker chair, watching him. There was no one else there. Phryne tiptoed back to Dot and Dulcie. 'Try the other two.' They slipped away and Phryne went back to the window to keep watch there.

Dulcie approached the second shed and pulled the door open with agonising slowness, wary of creaking hinges. 'Hello?' she said in a low voice. 'Anyone there?'

There was no answer. She did not dare step inside in case she tripped over something.

'Dulcie,' said Dot next to her ear, 'the other one's locked from the inside.'

Dulcie followed Dot back to the third shed, which stood a

little apart from the others. She knocked gently. 'Helena? It's me, Dulcie. We're going home now. Come on.'

There was a sound of a rusty bar being pulled back. The door opened. In the faint light, there was Helena, still in her white nurse's dress. Her feet were bare. 'Dulcie?' said the girl. 'Thank God for that! But he took my shoes. I'll have to walk barefoot. Not that I care!'

The three women hastened soundlessly into the night.

Back at Shed One, Phryne heard Sid speak, but she could not catch the words. Vern's reply, however, was loud and emphatic.

'No! Mum said not to play with girls! And I won't!'

A vast realisation flooded Phryne's brain. She'd been right about the place, but all wrong about the villain.

Now Sid raised his voice. 'Vern, I got ya the girl so youse could stay here with me! Mum told me to look after ya. Youse don't need to go live at the pub!'

At that moment, bright moonlight appeared above the hill. Sid chanced to look out another window, and what he saw there caused him to leap up from his chair. He ran out the door and yelled, 'You come back, ya little slut! You live here now!'

'No!' said Vern. 'Don't hurt her, Sid!'

Phryne moved quickly around the shed, drew out her pistol, and pointed it directly at Sid's head. 'Stop right where you are, Sid. Hands in the air!'

Sid gaped at her, froze, and put up his hands.

Phryne turned to Vern, who had followed his brother through the door. 'Hello, Vern,' she said. 'I'm Phryne Fisher. Why don't you drive the girls home while I deal with Sid?'

Vern blinked at her. The yellow light spilling out of the open door showed a slim, black-coated figure holding a gun to his brother. He nodded. 'Thank you, Miss. I'll do that.'

Dulcie, Dot, and Helena climbed onto the tray of the ancient truck. Vern got into the cabin and opened the window to address the girls. 'Got to wait here for the lady,' he explained, and sat immobile. His three passengers watched in admiration as Phryne advanced on Sid.

'I'm not going to shoot you right now—' Phryne steadied her hand so the gun was pointing between Sid's eyes '—because we don't want any trouble for the Captain. But you're going into the shed where you locked up Helena, and I'm going to lock you in. Or you can receive, at no extra charge, several more holes in your worthless body. Of course, if you have violated Helena, then I'm going to shoot you anyway. I've nothing else to do with my evening, you horrible creature.'

'Nah, I haven't touched her. I got her for Vern. He likes lookin' at girls.'

'And you don't, of course. Well then, in you go.'

Sid marched obediently into the third shed. There was no light inside, and Phryne did not offer him any. There was a separate lock on the outside, and she shot the bolt home with a loud snick. 'Have fun!' she exclaimed, and joined Vern in the cabin. He started the engine, and the truck galumphed its way down the hill towards Hepburn Springs.

'Where are we going, Miss?'

'The Mooltan. We want our supper. Would you like some too?'

'Yes, Miss. But Sid says I eat too much.'

'Never mind Sid. But your mum would be proud of you, Vern.'

He thought about this. 'Can I have apple pie, Miss?'

'As it happens, Vern, you may. There's half a pie left. And you can have it all.'

The truck groaned to a halt out the front of the Mooltan. The front door was open, and Alice stood beside a frazzled-looking woman in a brown overcoat. The newcomer gazed at the truck, and her face glowed with relief. Helena leaped down and embraced her. 'I'm back, Mum!' Tears ran down her mother's cheeks, and she wrapped both arms around her daughter, and did not let go for a long moment.

Alice stared at Phryne and Dulcie in unabashed hero-worship. And behind her, Phryne saw Aubrey standing in the doorway. Phryne gave Aubrey full marks for allowing Mum to have first go at the Welcome Home.

Soon after, Phryne surveyed the dining room with satisfaction. Everyone was talking excitedly except for Vern, who sat at the table with a napkin tucked into his grimy shirt front, methodically working his way through three-fifths of an apple pie, with extra cream. She let them talk themselves into a lull, then tapped a teaspoon on the side of her coffee cup.

'I think we need to take note of local sensibilities tomorrow, Helena. You, your mother, and Dulcie should go and visit Sergeant Offaly and explain that you and Aubrey had experienced a bridal argument, and as a result you came to stay here at the Mooltan, giving strict instructions that no one was to know where you were. Does that suit?'

Phryne looked the girl over. Helena was very pretty, with short hair cut in a bob. The nurse's uniform suited her well. There was a sweetness in her manner, but Phryne detected a whim of iron beneath it.

The girl took Aubrey's hand in hers and held it tight. Then she fixed a penetrating blue gaze on her mother's face and nodded.

'Yes, Mum. That's what we'll tell him. Because we don't want the village gossips talking about me and what goings-on there might have been up at the bottling plant, do we?'

Her mother (a thin, mousy woman with faded hair) stared at Helena. 'A bridal argument?' she said hesitantly.

'Yes, Mum. Because Aubrey and I are getting married next summer.'

The maternal face turned to Aubrey. His face was set, his jaw was square, and he looked like a man who had been offered two separate lifelines: his beloved's rescue, and the chance to secure parental permission at pistol-point. He had no intention whatever of letting go of either of them.

'Yes, we are,' he stated with finality.

'And Vern will stay at the pub in future,' Phryne added, to head off any more dispute. Vern gazed adoringly at her for a moment, and bent his head to the last of the pie. 'Sid didn't want to have to pay for Vern's keep at the pub, you see, so he kidnapped Helena so Vern could look at her instead of the women he would meet at the pub. A mad scheme, you may say, and you would be right. But Sid is not a nice person.'

'Mean as a dunny rat,' Dulcie pronounced.

'Miss Phryne, are you going to let Sid out?' enquired Dot.

'No. He can find his own way out. Or someone will rescue him, in due course. And he won't say anything. He can't. Not without getting arrested for kidnapping. I think he will be a new man when he is released.'

'A penitent sinner?' Helena's mother looked sceptical.

'I doubt it. But being locked up overnight in his own prison isn't going to be pleasant. He's a small, mean bully. He won't recover from this.'

'I'll keep an eye on him, Miss,' Vern offered. 'What he did was bad. Mum wouldn't've liked it. I'm not gonna listen to him anymore.'

Phryne inclined her head. 'You stick to it, Vern.'

———

The celebrations went on late into the night, by rural standards. It was around ten when the party broke up. Vern had been dispatched earlier to the Station Hotel, where presumably he would be settling in and looking at all the girls he wanted to, within reason. Alice finished the washing-up and retired to bed with a loving kiss from Dulcie, who seemed to want to talk. Phryne was happy to oblige. After the excitements of the evening she felt relief, but also curiosity.

'Cup of tea, Phryne?'

'Something a trifle stronger, I think.'

Dulcie grinned and produced a bottle of cognac. She poured two glasses and handed one to Phryne.

'To Aubrey and Helena.'

The glasses chinked together satisfactorily, and Dulcie sat down in her armchair. Tamsin immediately leaped from the floor and curled up in her lap.

Phryne sipped at the fiery liquid gold and sighed with contentment. 'Dulcie, I really must remember that about emerald green. I couldn't see you at all. I have much to learn about concealment, it appears.'

'Everyone thinks that black is the best disguise for night-time, but it really isn't. Black doesn't occur in nature, except in burnt trees.' Dulcie set down her glass. 'What was it put you on to the bottling plant?'

Phryne shook her head. 'There was nowhere else around here that was sufficiently secluded. Everywhere else has busy, enquiring eyes and people coming and going all the time. I got the right place, and more or less the right motive. But I thought it was Vern—even though everyone has been telling me ever since I got here that Vern is utterly harmless. It was only tonight that I realised it was the appalling Sid, who is a complete waste of space and beyond doubt one of the most revolting specimens I have ever met. And I've met a few.'

Dulcie stroked the cat in her lap without speaking for a while.

Phryne admired the gentleness of her hands. This was a woman well-accustomed to manual labour, but her caresses were as light as thistledown. 'Phryne, I have heard a rumour that one of our local secrets is a secret no longer. May I ask what you are intending to do about it?'

'Would this be related to knitting?' Phryne enquired, looking artlessly at Dulcie, who gave a single, emphatic nod. 'Why, nothing at all. I don't know anything about knitting. Do you?'

Dulcie grinned. 'A little. We country people like to keep a few secrets.'

'I think that is very wise. But there is one secret I would like you to divulge, if you have a mind to. It won't go any further.'

Dulcie eased herself back in her chair and gave Phryne a look of suspicion. 'Oh yes?'

'I truly hope that it isn't relevant to—to the other matter I am investigating. Really I do. And I certainly won't be sharing it with Inspector Kelly or—God forbid—Sergeant Offaly.'

'But what if you felt you had to?'

Phryne's mind was racing now, but it was as if the wheels were slipping in a pool of mud. To gain time, she sipped again from the cognac glass. 'If it turned out to be relevant to my murder investigation, then I might have to. But I'm hoping like hell it has nothing whatever to do with it.'

'And if it turned out not to be germane to your investigation? What would you do then?' Dulcie's eyes were still boring into her, and it felt most uncomfortable. Not too dissimilar, she felt, from looking down the wrong end of a gun. Dulcie would be a formidable enemy, she realised. She never raised her voice, but she would act without hesitation if she felt she needed to.

'If it turned out to have nothing to do with these murders, then I would consider that the police—or anybody else, for that matter—should keep their noses right out of it, on the grounds that it was none of their flaming business.'

This seemed to have hit the spot, for the tension in Dulcie's slight body relaxed visibly. 'All right, Phryne, ask away. I think I already know what it is you want to know.'

'Do you now? All right. You know how eager Alice was to go to the dance. Do you know whom she met there?'

Dulcie rolled her eyes and laughed softly. 'Well of course I do, Phryne! And I think it's very sweet of them. They aren't lovers, you know.'

'No?'

Now Dulcie was completely at ease. 'No, not by a country mile. But they like each other. A lot. His name is Robert Fitzgerald. He comes of Good Family back in Melbourne. Money to burn, I gather. He's an ex-school friend of Alice's.'

'Oh I see.' Phryne leaned forward in her chair. 'And would I be right in suggesting that Robert, while not entirely immune to Alice's obvious beauty, actually prefers the company of men?'

Dulcie nodded. 'Got it in one, Phryne. He was sent to live in the country after a scandal at school. All hushed up, of course, because that's what the rich do. Alice knew. Of course she did. And because she prefers the company of women, it gave them something in common. So now he lives...elsewhere...and he comes in to see her every now and again. And we look after him and shield him from the world's harsh judgements.'

'In the same way that you shield the knitting fraternity?'

This produced a grim smile. 'Oh yes. Not quite the same, but close enough.'

'Dulcie, I may add that I thought he was utterly charming. We didn't exchange a word, but I noticed him with the other girls. His manner was everything it should have been: polite, courtly, and playing no favourites. Apart from Alice.'

'That's him. Beau of the ball wherever he goes. Terribly shy, but he hides it well.'

'I can believe it.' Phryne finished her drink and stood up. 'All right, Dulcie. I just wanted to know if he might be a suspect for our murders. I thought not; and now I know he isn't. This is going absolutely nowhere. Not even Dot needs to know. And I'm happy to leave it there.'

Dulcie rose also, and Tamsin got up and stretched with maximum ostentation. 'And your murder cases?' she asked.

'Enquiries Are Continuing.'

Chapter Twenty-One

Up from Earth's Centre, through the Seventh Gate
I rose, and on the Throne of Saturn sate,
And many Knots unravel'd by the Road;
But not the Knot of Human Death and Fate.

—Edward Fitzgerald, *The Rubáiyát of*
Omar Khayyám of Naishápúr

Tinker was having a good day. By the end of morning break he had, by dint of some discreet questioning, managed to find two suspects at Lonsdale Technical School. He had wantonly started a dispute by pretending to be full of himself about his fine house on The Esplanade. From his school friends who knew him, this produced surprise and a certain level of disappointment. However, by fuelling the flames with outrageous bragging he had managed to elicit the home suburbs of a wide cross-section of his fellows. His main suspects were Tim, who lived in East Hawthorn; and Tom, who lived in Kew. During a spectacularly dull mathematics lesson, he considered them. Tim was in most of his classes. He had bragged of this and that to do with girls and his success therewith, but the details, when he was pressed, were regrettably vague. Tinker crossed Tim off his list, diagnosing immature boasting. If ever there was a lad who told and didn't kiss, Tim was surely it. Which left Tom, who was in the other classes for everything except woodwork and electronics. He thought hard about Tom. He was a quiet boy: good-looking, but reserved. Just the sort of young man that a girl like Claire might easily fall for.

At the same time, how likely was it that Claire's mystery boyfriend went to his school? he asked himself. Would she not rather have set her heart on a boy from Scotch, or Carey, or even Grammar? Lonsdale Technical School was, considering the rampant snobbery of the middle classes, a highly improbable—and possibly even discreditable—place of schooling. But the more Tinker thought about it, the less unlikely it seemed. Consider the evidence. Claire was pretty much a social outcast, shunned and humiliated by the Fashionable Ones at her school. She would not even get an introduction to the high-status rich boys her fellow students would set their hearts on. Over breakfast, Sergeant Collins had laid considerable emphasis on this.

'I don't imagine a girl like Claire would ever get invited to the sort of parties the snobby girls go to, Tinker. Ruth and Jane have told us how the in-crowd at her school had no time for her. And even supposing one of those rich young blokes fancied Claire, they'd get hooted down by their sisters. And there was the capacity-thing the girls found beneath her window. They don't go for anything related to the trades at those posh schools. That does point more towards someone at your school, doesn't it?'

Indeed it did, and so Tinker had put on the mask, and provoked a response. And here was Tom, who started with a T and lived in Kew.

By the time lunch hour arrived, Tinker was ready with his plan.

He would watch Tom and see if he was sitting by himself; if Tom really was the mystery lover whose girlfriend had just been found dead, the rowdy horseplay of his fellows would not be for him. If he was alone, Tinker would go and share his lunch with him.

———

There were three impromptu cricket matches underway in the asphalt schoolyard that lunchtime, but Tom was not among those present. Tinker could not see any point in cricket, being over-filled with hearty good humour and uncouth shouts of "Owzat!' He retired towards the back of the school grounds, where overhanging trees provided a measure of shade for a rough-hewn park bench. And there was Thomas, in his school uniform, sitting in a brown study and staring disconsolately at his tinplate lunchbox. His face was pale (where it wasn't sunburned), his mouth was shut tight, and he looked as though he had just been told that he had six months to live.

'Can a bloke join ya?'

Tom looked at him, sighed, and made room.

Tinker sat down and drew out his own lunchbox. 'What'd they give ya today, mate?'

Tom sighed again and opened the box.

Tinker inspected the contents. 'Jeez, mate, ya don't wanna touch that stuff. It'd kill a brown dog.'

Tom's sandwiches were of white bread cut diagonally. Between the slices, a suspicious-looking greyish substance oozed menacingly. 'It's fish paste, apparently,' Tom confessed. 'Want some?'

Tinker sniffed one corner and shook his head. 'Bet it tastes like library paste.'

Tom's mouth creased in what might have been a laugh. 'I wouldn't be surprised. I have made it absolutely clear that I loathe

the stuff, and Mum gives it to me at least twice a week. What've you got, Tink?'

At that moment, Tinker realised that they were no longer alone. A small tabby cat was rubbing its scrawny body around his ankles. He looked at his companion. 'Mate, if you give yours to the cat, ya can have some o' mine. I always make me own, and I reckon me eyes are bigger'n me stomach.' He showed the contents of his own tin.

Tom looked with palpable interest. 'What've you got there? It looks like cheese, honey, and roast beef.'

'Yep. Tom, you should make yer own lunch. That way ya'd get what ya wanted. Three halves each, and the cat gets the library paste?'

Tom nodded. 'Deal.'

Tom wolfed down his three halves, while the cat, delighted at having found such an excellent provider, ate the fish paste sandwiches bread, butter, and all, then promptly disappeared under the fence.

'Poor little feller,' Tom said.

'Yair. But he's good at foraging. 'E'll be right, I reckon. Hey, Tom, we've got electronics this arvo. You know how we're makin' crystal sets?'

Tom looked sidelong at Tinker. 'Yes?'

Tinker allowed himself a smile of quiet pride. 'I've made one already. Want to see it? It works. I've tried it out and all.'

Some animation crept into Tom's haggard features. 'Yair, I'd like that.'

'Come home with me this arvo after school and you can see it.'

'Won't your parents mind?'

Tinker laughed. 'No, they won't, 'cos they're a long way away. I live with a lady and a couple of girls she's adopted. And the butler and housekeeper, o' course.'

Tom stared at Tinker with his mouth so wide open he seemed to be in danger of catching flies. No doubt he was on the verge of saying that he had scarcely pictured Tinker as possessing such grandeur as the presence of both a butler and a housekeeper. As if realising just in time that this would be extremely rude, he closed his mouth with a snap. 'And the lady?'

'She's away—and she wouldn't mind anyway. All right, I'll see yer after school, mate.'

Tom nodded. 'Sure. And thanks for the lunch.'

———

The afternoon passed pleasantly enough. Tinker helped out the gormless Tim with his electrical circuits and wondered briefly why so many of his classmates seemed to take going to school for granted. Afterwards, he met Tom at the school gate. Tom looked nervous; his shoulders twitched, and he passed his school satchel from hand to hand as if uncertain what to do with it. Tinker felt a small glow of satisfaction. The suspect was now in the desired condition.

'Where to, Tinker?' Tom enquired.

'Tram to St Kilda, of course.'

Tom coloured. 'Oh, right. You said you lived on The Esplanade. Yair.'

As the tram barrelled down St Kilda Road, the shouts and flurries of uniformed scholars drowned out any possibility of in-depth communication. Tinker noted that Tom's uneasiness was increasing. His necktie was askew, and his nostrils were twitching. Doubtless he was finding the scent of unwashed proletariat overwhelming. Tinker himself was at ease with it. Anything was better than the everlasting reek of stale fish which had marked his own childhood. All around them youths were laughing and talking nonsense of the usual sort. Tinker was watching Tom and listening with only half an ear. When the tram reached Kerferd Road the carriage began to empty, and Tom hunched down in one of the seats. Tinker was about to open the conversation by asking about Tom's home life, but he was forestalled by Tom, who turned to look at him with apprehension.

'Tinker? You said you lived with a lady. Is it Miss Fisher the lady detective?'

'Where'd you get that idea, mate?'

'One of the blokes in class told me.'

Tinker nodded slowly. 'Yair. That's right. She adopted me as well as the girls.'

At the word 'girls', Tom's shoulders shook, and his hands clasped into fists. This looked like naked fear now. 'What girls?' he asked.

'Ruth and Jane. They go to PLC.'

Tom now stared straight ahead, closely inspecting the wooden back of the seat in front of him. The suspect was now trying not to react. *He knows I'm on to him and doesn't want to give himself away*, Tinker surmised. *But he's still playing along. That's fine. The fish is hooked. Now we give him more line.*

The tram ground into the terminus, and the boys disembarked. The bay was a pale blue in the afternoon light. The beach was ochre yellow, and the afternoon bathers were out in force. Tom looked at the prospect with dry lips.

'D'you swim there much, Tinker? It must be great being next to the sea.'

'No, mate. I'm from Queenscliff. I grew up by the sea. It's just there. Maybe one day. The girls like swimming, but.'

Again the twitch of the shoulders.

They strolled in silence until number 221B stood before them. Mr Butler was outside, watering the garden with a large galvanised-iron bucket. He inclined his head with solemn gravitas. 'Afternoon, Tinker. Young sir.'

'Mr B, this is my friend Tom from school. I'm gonna show 'im my crystal set.'

Mr Butler ignored Tom's obvious embarrassment. 'And would you be requiring any refreshment?'

'Later on, maybe.' Tinker turned to Tom and indicated the way forward. Tom slunk into the portico. The door was open. 'Come on through, Tom. I live out the back.'

They passed through the house. Tinker led the way, but was vaguely aware that Tom was looking around at the high ceilings, the paintings on the walls, and the general air of unimaginable luxury. Ember the cat rubbed her face around Tinker's ankles, and he paused, bending down to stroke the little cat's features. 'Sorry, Ember. Tucker comes later, mate. You know that by now.' Ember gave Tinker another nuzzle, on the grounds that possibly this time it might be different, but stiffened as a fusillade of barking erupted at the back of the house, then disappeared with alacrity. Tinker opened the back door and Molly stood up on both hind paws and pushed Tinker hard in the chest. *You're home! You're HOME! And I'm here! I'm HERE!!!* Her tail whacked Tom hard in the stomach and he staggered. 'It's okay, mate. She's friendly,' Tinker assured him. 'It's fine. Come on.'

Tinker led the way into the shed and switched on the light. Molly accompanied them, tail thumping against Tinker's leg, apparently barked out for the present.

'This is my place,' Tinker confided, suddenly shy. If Tom was surprised at the contrast between the opulent townhouse and this spartan accommodation, he gave no sign of it, merely taking in the narrow iron bed, the single chest of drawers, the iron hook on the back of the shed door, and the single window looking out onto the back garden. On a small desk in the corner was the crystal set. Tinker leaned forward and turned the knob. There was a faint hum as the innards came to life. Tinker fiddled with the other knob until conversation appeared to be happening somewhere. It was like listening to someone talking at the bottom of a full bathtub, but words could definitely be heard in there somewhere. Tinker frowned and twiddled the knobs again. Tinny music began to emerge, as if at the end of a long tunnel.

'There you go, mate. Have a play with it.'

Tom carefully approached the crystal set as though it were one of the fiercer animals and twiddled one of the knobs. With a good deal of coaxing, he managed to restore the music. The boys exchanged a glance. 'Tinker, that's really clever. How did you manage it?'

Tinker gave a faint grin. 'Mr Butler helped me a bit. But it's just cabinet-making, a circuit drawing, some parts, and a soldering iron. It's not hard.'

'How does it work?'

Tinker sat down on his bed and indicated the wooden chair. 'Take a seat, Tom,' he suggested. Then, as the boy sat, he went on, 'Look, mate, I'm happy to explain it all some time, but that isn't actually why I asked you here.'

Leaden silence descended on the room like a cloud of doom. Even Molly crouched down on the concrete floor and looked up at Tinker for instructions. Without a word, Tinker took the capacitor from his pocket and handed it to Tom, who stared at it as though it were a poisonous reptile.

Finally, Tom broke the silence. 'Yair. I did wonder what had happened to it.'

'You dropped it under Claire's window, didn't you, Tom?'

Whatever colour Tom's face had held now vanished. He looked as pale as a calico sheet and hung his head. 'Yair.'

'And here's the bit I haven't told you: I was the one who found her body down at the docks. So if you're wondering what business this is of mine, well, now you know. I think you oughta tell me all about it.'

Tom shook his head in naked horror. 'I didn't kill her! She fell and hit her head!'

'No, Tom. Go back a bit. I know how youse two use to meet—I mean with the ladder and everythin'. And I know she was, well, expecting a baby. *Your* baby. What I want you to explain is how she came to be down at the docks.'

Molly's head was now stretched out on the cool floor. Whatever her human was doing sounded important. Even more important than playing with his dog. She could wait this out.

Tom put his head in his hands and moaned. 'Oh, no! Going there was my idea, because she said she had something important to tell me, and we didn't want to be seen together yet. So I suggested we meet under the clocks at Flinders Street.'

'When was this?'

'We said ten o'clock, when there wouldn't be anyone about.'

'Ten at night?'

'Yair. And we started walking. And...'

'And?' Tinker's voice was soft, endlessly patient, and prompting. 'What happened next?'

'So we started walking. All down Flinders Street. At first she was just talking about how we'd be together forever—how we'd get married and all that.'

'What did you think, Tom?'

'I was scared.'

'Yair. Reckon you would be. Go on.'

'And then, when we were standing on the dock, she told me.'

'That she was expecting?'

Tom nodded, now struck mute.

'Tom, yer can't stop there. Keep goin'. Ya gotta tell me. Cos I found her, mate, and I need to know how she finished up floatin' in the water.' Tinker turned off the tinny music. 'Come on, Tom. Tell me.'

Tom's fists bunched over his eyes and he let out a long groan of pain. 'And she said, "Will you marry me, Tom?"'

'And?'

'And I said no!' Tom's voice was now a dismal howl. Molly lifted herself up and rested her head in Tom's lap. Automatically, he began to stroke Molly's ears and neck, and Molly's tail began to thump against his trouser leg.

'D'ya wish ya'd said yes now?'

'Yes. I liked her. A *lot*. But it was all too much at the time.' Tears were streaming down his face.

'All right. So what happened next?'

'I never touched her, I swear. She was yelling at me, and pacing around, and she—she lost her footing.' His voice sank into a whisper. 'And she tumbled down the steps, and hit her head on one of them. Then she fell into the water.'

'Did ya leave her there?'

'No! I ran down the steps and grabbed her. But she wasn't breathing. I checked her pulse and there was nothing there. She was already dead.'

'How long did you stand there holdin' her?'

'A few minutes. I've done that first-aid course. I tried to get her breathing again but nothing worked!' He shook his head, a picture of desolation. 'Nothing worked.'

'And then?'

'I let her slip back into the water. It was so stupid. I don't know why I did it. I should've owned up. But I was so scared.'

'Not surprisin'. All right.' Tinker stood. 'Tom, there's somethin' else I didn't tell yer: the cop who's leading the investigation thinks it was her uncle who killed her.'

'Why would he think that? That's crazy! Oh.' Tom's face turned cherry red. 'No, surely he couldn't think that, could he?'

'He does, mate, because 'e's not very bright. You have to talk to the cops, so the uncle doesn't get charged.'

Tom hunched his shoulders and shivered. 'Yair. I suppose I'll have to.'

'Want to know somethin'? The smart cop on the case lives here. And I want ya to talk to 'im as soon as possible.' More tears flooded down Tom's cheeks.

'Sergeant Collins is a beaut bloke. Tell 'im what ya told me and you'll feel better.'

'All right. But I'd better call home first. Mum'll be worried about where I am. Is there a telephone?'

'Yair, there is. But I'm gonna call the sergeant first. If yer lucky, you might get home for tea.'

———

Summoned by Tinker, Hugh Collins was home in fifteen minutes.

He sat on the bed in Tinker's shed and listened as Tom retold the story. He said nothing until Tom finally ran down, then he turned to Tinker. 'Is this the same story he told you?'

'Yair.' Tinker was about to add that he believed every word, but stopped himself in time.

Hugh gave Tom a long, steady look.

'Thomas, this is very bad. But it might not be as bad as you think. I am not making any promises. I will need a sworn statement down at the station, and your parents need to be there. Do they know about this?'

The look of terror on the suspect's face was more eloquent than words.

'So what you do is this. Ring your parents now. Do they have a car?'

Tom nodded.

'Tell them to meet you at City South police station, and that you've got something important to tell them. Then you make your statement, in their presence, and I'll take it from there. Understood?'

Tom rose unsteadily to his feet and nodded again.

As he left the shed, Hugh Collins clapped Tinker on the shoulder. 'Well done, mate,' he whispered. 'I'm proud of you.'

———

Next morning dawned bright and full of promise. Morag McKenzie, having made herself a cup of tea and a piece of toast, sat in her chair on her front verandah with her dogs and sighed contentedly. Currently she had only two runaway wives on her hands: her niece-in-law Janet and Mrs Pollock. Her other refugees had gone away, very properly regarding her house and land as a purely temporary expedient. What they all wanted, more than anything else, was time and space. Given these things, and a feeling of safety and security they had probably never known in their whole lives, women were perfectly capable of making sensible arrangements for their own futures. There would be relatives who could be persuaded to take in folk in distress who could work and earn their keep. And this was what had happened. There had been some difficulty with Mrs Walker, who had shown every inclination to outstay her welcome and had, moreover, all the survival skills of a dandelion in a snowstorm. Some stern words of encouragement had produced her elder brother Michael, who took her away with him—to what fate none could foresee. But Morag, who had very little time for men in any form, judged that this one was a good deal better than most and would look after her.

Janet was different. She was a wonder in the kitchen, and cleaned house and managed things with quiet, calm efficiency. She earned her keep without fuss several times over. As far as Miss McKenzie was concerned, she could stay as long as she wanted to. That drunk mongrel of a husband wasn't fit to polish her shoes. If he ever turned up to reclaim his wife and son, there would be harsh words, and harsher consequences.

Suddenly the dogs looked up. There was a man wandering towards her with his brain clearly at half-mast. He appeared unarmed, but he had opened her gate without leave—and committed the unpardonable solecism of Failing to Shut It Behind Him—and now trekked along her pathway straight towards her.

He stopped about ten yards from her verandah. She remained sitting where she was, with a hand on the neck of one of her dogs. 'Where's my wife?' he demanded, swaying somewhat in the light breeze. 'Her name's Frances Pollock and she belongs at home. Where is she?'

'No one of that name here, mister.'

He glared at her. 'I don't believe ya. I'm gonna look for meself.'

She stood up and grasped her shotgun in her skinny arms. 'No you ain't, son. You're goin' home right now. Get off my land.'

The dogs also rose and growled. It was a sound that echoed in the hindbrain and spoke of primitive, cave-dwelling bipeds and the fear of giant, razor-toothed predators. But Pollock was too angry to pay any attention. 'You wouldn't shoot me. Ya wouldn't dare!'

'Suit yerself,' she answered in a hardened monotone. She raised the gun to her shoulder and aimed it right at his head. As he made a move to advance on her, she called out 'Wait!', lowered the barrel, and shot him on the lower leg. As he collapsed to the dry, scrubby dirt, she walked forward, leaned over him, and smiled. 'Lucky you didn't ride that poor underfed horse o' yours or I'da shot you in the head, son. Can't go hurtin' dumb animals just 'cos their master's a witless drongo.' The two dogs stood up, preparing if necessary to administer further chastisement, and showed their teeth.

Now that the immediate shock had worn off, the impact of a well-filled cartridge full of shot had begun to make itself felt. Agonised moans and oaths filled the air, and she grinned again. 'All right, son. I'll bring out me truck and you can get in the back. Yer not going in the cabin. I'm takin' youse into town and we'll get ya fixed up. And remember—' she leaned over the recumbent figure '—I've still got another shot. And if youse don't behave I'm gonna blow your head right orf.'

Pollock, the eternal proponent of the Helplessness of Woman, looked into her dark, grim eyes and found himself believing otherwise.

Chapter Twenty-Two

One Moment in Annihilation's Waste,
One Moment, of the Well of Life to taste—
The Stars are setting and the Caravan
Starts for the Dawn of Nothing—Oh, make haste!

—Edward Fitzgerald, *The Rubáiyát of
Omar Khayyám of Naishápúr*

Phryne awoke refreshed and content. Her bed was just right, she decided. Not too hard and not too soft. Goldilocks would have loved it. The bewitching scent of coffee wafted up the stairway, but Phryne decided it could wait. She doffed her silk pyjamas and assumed a cream ensemble of blouse, jacket, and skirt, with patent leather shoes instead of boots. She was expecting neither alarums nor excursions today. She lit a quiet cigarette and held silent colloquy through the open window with a kookaburra, which chirruped hopefully at her in plain search of something edible. 'Sorry, little friend,' she told her companion. 'Unless you like tobacco or gin, I haven't a thing to offer.'

The kookaburra considered this statement, then flew away

into the trees. Phryne considered her morning. If she was right, and she was fairly certain she was, then she had two clear days to relax and finally have that holiday she'd been intending. On the other hand, there was nothing to stop her dropping by the police station to pass the time of day. It had given Phryne some satisfaction to see Inspector Kelly elbow the local flatfoot out of his desk and send him out to menial duties around town. Sergeant Offaly had not endeared himself to anyone, it seemed. Had there been a local popularity contest, he would not have been in the running for a podium finish.

Phryne paused at the breakfast table long enough to drink a cup of espresso, wave to Alice—who was more radiant than ever in a pale blue dress and crocheted shawl of purest white—and admire Dot's quietly modest demeanour at the breakfast table.

'Miss, what are we doing today?' the latter enquired.

'Dot, I am hoping for a day of quietude and peace. I would, in fact, be more than happy to experience a day of unparalleled tedium, if such a thing were indeed possible in these heavenly surroundings. Anything you would like to do, please let me know and I shall accommodate you.'

Dot thought this over. 'Actually, Miss Phryne, I think the same. It's been all go ever since we got here, hasn't it?'

Phryne inclined her head.

'So I'd like to sit in the garden and read a book. Some knitting, maybe?'

'That sounds like a truly splendid plan, Dot. I'm going to run into town to see the good inspector and find out if there's any news, though I'm not expecting any. I'll be back for a lunch. A quiet afternoon in the garden sounds wonderful.' She hesitated. 'Perhaps later on I'll go to see the Captain again—possibly for dinner.'

Dot coloured somewhat, which did not match well with her brown-on-beige ensemble. She could guess at her employer's intentions now that Captain Spencer was cleared of all suspicion, and this came under the general heading of Things She Did Not Think About. So much for unparalleled tedium! But that was Miss Phryne's way, and Dot accepted it in the same way she accepted the existence of thunderstorms and earthquakes.

'Very good, Miss.'

Phryne cranked up the Hispano-Suiza and proceeded into Daylesford. It was a glorious morning with a hint of humidity in the air, but it was delightfully cool and sunny, with fluffy white clouds wafting across the sky with not a care in the world. Phryne hummed to herself and parked the car near the police station. Where she opened her mouth into a small, ruby-lipped O of surprise. For things were happening at the customarily sleepy cop shop. There was a male voice, loud in lamentation and protestations of injustice. Other low voices could be heard within. One was definitely Inspector Kelly's Aussie drawl. There was also Sergeant Offaly's Irish blarney, calling for calm and silence. And there was a third which seemed vaguely familiar: low, rasping, and quietly belligerent.

Phryne spotted an open window and slipped quietly beneath it. She had not had any opportunity to eavesdrop on any private conversations on this trip, and the chance was far too succulent to miss. Nor was she disappointed.

The first voice she identified was Sergeant Offaly. 'All right, you, settle yourself down now! This is a decent police station, not the public bar at the Station Hotel! Don't you be carryin' on like a two-bob watch, Pollock. Just you answer the inspector's questions and let's be havin' none of your lip. Understand?'

There was a vague muttering from someone—presumably Pollock—then Mick Kelly called the meeting to order. 'Suppose you start at the beginning, Pollock. What were you doing on Miss McKenzie's property?'

Phryne gasped, and all but gave herself away. Fortunately, any sound of surprise from her was drowned out by the loud voice of Mr Pollock, who spoke in tones of rancorous grievance.

'I found out where my missus was hiding so I went to fetch her back. And that bitch bloody well shot me! Why aren't you charging her?'

'All things in their proper time, Pollock.' This was Kelly again. 'So why did you think your wife was on Miss McKenzie's property?'

There was a snarl, as if Pollock had a foot caught in a rabbit trap. 'Bloke at the pub told me.'

'I see. And you always believe what the blokes at the pub say, don'tcha?'

'Well, sometimes.'

'Well, sometimes. Now you listen to me, Pollock. Your missus is gone, and I doubt she's comin' back. She isn't at Miss McKenzie's property. Even if she had been, she wouldn't be there now, would she? So on the basis of a wild rumour you heard down the pub, you went off trespassing on someone else's land, and they saw you off. That right?'

'With a bloody shotgun! She shot me in the foot!'

'Lucky for you it wasn't yer big mouth. All right, Sergeant, put this bloke in a cell and go and get Dr Henderson. Tell 'im I want 'im here in fifteen minutes.'

'What? You can't lock me up! You should be lockin' 'er up, not me!'

'The charges will be trespass, public nuisance, assault, uttering threats in a public place, and anything else we can think of. Pollock, I'd like you to think of this as protective custody. It's for your own good, son. You're causin' me trouble, and I don't like trouble. When I see trouble, I spread it around. Go on! Off you go.'

There was a certain amount of percussion thereafter, and what was presumably the cell door slamming shut. Then a jingle of keys, and Phryne hid around the back of the wooden building as Sergeant Offaly erupted out the front door. Low voices resumed a discussion of something or other. Moving with infinite stealth, Phryne resumed her position under the open window. A new voice entered the fray, rasping something, though the actual text was unclear. The inspector interrupted.

'Look, Miss McKenzie, I'm not makin' meself clear, am I? Let's just rewind the clock a bit. You were sittin' out on the verandah with your dogs having a quiet, pleasant morning, and you just happened to have your gun with you 'cos you were gonna shoot some cockies who'd bin strippin' yer fruit trees. Suddenly, this man you've never seen before comes barrelling up your drive with a look of murderous intent. So you, a poor frightened woman all alone in the world, asked 'im his business and 'e kept on comin' at yer. And you dropped the gun—quite accidentally—and as it fell it discharged one barrel and hit the man in the shins and feet.' There was a significant pause. 'Is that what happened, Miss McKenzie?'

'Yeah,' came the low, belligerent rasp Phryne recollected. 'Yeah. I was very frightened and I dropped the gun an' it went off. By accident.'

Phryne stifled a giggle.

'All right, youse can go home as soon as you've written that up in the spare room over there and signed it in my presence. Deal?'

'Deal.'

A door closed, and silence resumed. Phryne counted to a silent sixty seconds and entered the room with her most winning smile. Mick Kelly offered a grin of his own, with interest.

'Well, Phryne, I trust you found that very educational?'

Phryne tried to effect a look of innocence.

'You were very quiet, but a couple of twigs cracked under yer feet and at one point you giggled.'

'I'm so sorry, Mick. Yes, it was very educational indeed. I came to let you know about the missing girl from Hepburn. I found her last night.'

He nodded, massive and self-assured, behind his desk. 'Yair, I heard all about it from Offaly. A very neat job. Congratulations are definitely in order. If yer gonna tell a pack of lies, make it a good story that's got a fair chance of bein' believed. Oh, and by the way, I went to get Sid meself early this mornin'. Know what 'e told me?'

Phryne sat in the chair opposite and made herself comfortable. 'Mick, I'm agog to hear.'

'Apparently 'e locked 'imself in that shed by mistake. Would ya believe it?'

Phryne considered this. 'Possibly.'

Mick regarded the slim woman before him with paternal benevolence. 'News travels fast in the country, Phryne. I've interviewed the girl, her mother, and that Aubrey bloke. I'm told it was all a Bridal Misunderstanding and she's been at the Mooltan with you all along? And you'll be pleased to know we've also nicked Sid for receivin' stolen goods. We found a nice little collection at the bottlin' plant. Offaly's gonna throw the book at the little bastard fer that, and 'e's welcome. So, you got a good result there, Phryne. Any progress on our murders?'

Phryne leaned back in her chair and sighed. 'Mick, I'm not entirely sure, but I do have a suspect and a theory. I'm planning to test it on Friday night. You'd do well to be there.'

'At the cinema opening? Look, I'm under pressure to go back to Ballarat. I've only got till the weekend. You reckon you're onto someone? Mind tellin' me who?'

Phryne considered in silence for some time. 'Mick, I'd rather not. I think you've got an excellent deadpan and I don't think you'd give yourself away, but my intended method of capture is…a bit unorthodox, and I think it's better if you don't know.'

'I've got some other news for you. The suspect Armstrong? I went to see 'im and it gave me no pleasure. He's a wide boy all right. I don't trust 'im at all. But 'e's got an alibi. I haven't checked it out, but apparently he's vouched for not only by his wife, but her brother, who is a minister. Besides, I doubt he loves anybody but his own good self.'

Phryne nodded. 'All right, Mick. Thanks for telling me.'

'By the way, Sergeant Offaly did some very handy spadework and came up with a passenger list for that train you were askin' about.' He passed over a sheet of foolscap paper. 'Is your suspect on it?'

Phryne scanned the page quickly. 'Yes. And that's good, because the same person did all three murders and absolutely had to be on that train. Thanks, Mick.'

'You reckon 'e'll try again?'

'Yes, I do. This murderer specialises in killing in the middle of a crowd, and it's a different method every time. I may add that this is a criminal of extraordinary cunning, and is moreover quite, quite mad and horribly dangerous.'

'Very well. We'll play it your way, Phryne.'

She rose and shook hands with him, feeling through her glove the grip of a man of immense strength trying desperately not to crush her bones. She left the station in high spirits and drove back to the Mooltan much pleased.

Inducing the gallant Captain Spencer to produce a dinner invitation had been simplicity itself. She had merely presented herself at the spa, admired the view and the limpid water of the pool, and showed no inclination to disappear. The Captain—who was too well-bred to ask if he had been a suspect in Helena's disappearance, but also too intelligent not to realise that this had been a possibility floating, inevitably, in the middle distance— asked if Miss Fisher would care to join him at dinner tonight? Miss Fisher would indeed, and had dressed herself in a glittering blue dress, pearl necklace, and matching cloche hat. Dot had assisted her into this costume with her lips pursed, and forbore any comment beyond the standard compliments.

Phryne looked across the immaculate table and sighed. The Captain was immaculate in white tie and waistcoat, black jacket and trousers. His starched shirt front crackled with what she hoped was barely suppressed passion. The table itself was dressed in a spotless cloth, adorned with a superabundance of red roses in a dark blue glazed pottery vase. The dishes (still, alas, militantly vegetarian) were, if possible, even more splendid than last time. There was a French tart—a *quiche*, no less—with cheese, tomato, some unobtrusive vegetables, a dash of red onion, fennel, and mushroom, encased in golden pastry which melted into buttery oblivion on the tongue. There were peppers stuffed with wild rice, garlic, and pickled walnuts. The wines were superb. On the surface, dinner appeared to be going splendidly.

Beneath the glamour of the golden candlelight, however, things were not going so well. The Captain was talking too much. He repeated himself and expounded once more the verities of his regimen for his patients, with subordinate clauses and adverbial fortifications. As Violette came and went, Phryne saw eyeballs being expressively rolled, with Gallic overtones. As one of Phryne's plates was deftly slipped from under her gaze, Madame whispered out of the corner of her mouth. '*Madame, je regrete, mais M'sieur est sans vie.*'

'*On verra,*' Phryne had responded. The Captain, preoccupied with his own expositions, had not noticed the exchange.

Ices, meringues, and liqueurs came and went, and still Captain

Spencer expounded. A momentary apprehension assailed her that she must be losing her touch, but she batted the thought aside. If Violette—who clearly adored him—had not succeeded, then this was a seduction comparable with attempting the ascent of Mont Blanc in your underwear with a slow-combustion stove attached to each ankle. What the occasion demanded was a distraction.

With dinner all but over, Phryne heard the tinkling of a piano beneath them. The Captain's face lit up. 'Ah! That will be the evening singalong. Have I mentioned our music therapy for the patients?'

Phryne rose. 'Indeed you have, Captain. And I fancy some music therapy of my own. Shall we dance?'

'Oh my.' Confusion spread like spilt soup across his honest, manly features. 'Why, I cannot remember when last I danced.'

'Do not, in that case, leave it any longer.' She held out her white arms to him across the table, and he rose with her and took her hand.

Ragged singing broke out below them. Since the Captain seemed disposed to remain at arm's length, Phryne took no more than four bars (in 4/4 time) to enfold his body in hers. She manoeuvred him around the room, and by some deft foot-work managed not to be trodden on. Then, blessedly, the piano changed to triple time.

'Just follow me, and do what I do,' she breathed into his ear. It was somewhat like waltzing with a shop mannequin, but the Captain did his best. It seemed that in some long-forgotten past age the Captain had been introduced to the waltz and managed a passable one-two-three around the room. Clasped around him, Phryne steered him away from the table and inhaled the scent of his neck. She detected brisk aftershave, frequent washing, rose-scented soap, and an undercurrent of erotic hunger. There was more singing beneath them, and the Captain sighed in what might have been content.

The next chorus was in 4/4 time again, and Phryne felt it was time to pause. The Captain was all but sleepwalking now, with his head resting on her shoulder. With aching slowness, she pulled back just enough so that the somnolent head rested against her left breast. She felt his lips enclose her nipple through the fabric and arched her back with a swooning murmuration. His right hand curled around her back, and with gentle strength he pressed his body against hers. The Captain was lifeless no longer.

With his left hand, he lifted her head towards his, and kissed her lips with infinite gentleness. Feeling that this was indeed the proverbial tide in the affairs of men, she returned his kiss with interest. 'My dear! My darling girl!' he breathed.

She stood upright. Her tongue explored his mouth and found it eminently palatable.

'Beautiful man, be mine this night,' she whispered.

Herbert Spencer took a pace back, lifted her left hand to his mouth, and kissed it. 'Oh yes!' His voice was all but soundless. 'I am yours!'

As he led her towards his bedroom, they passed Violette in the passage. She was smirking, and raised her right hand to her lips, kissed it, and inclined her head in satisfaction. Herbert Spencer might indeed be Phryne's tonight, but he would be Violette's before long.

Phryne's lips shaped the words, '*Bon appetit, Madame!*' and followed Captain Spencer to the end of his self-imposed celibacy.

Chapter Twenty-Three

Ah! Fill the Cup:—what boots it to repeat
How Time is slipping underneath our Feet:
Unborn Tomorrow and dead Yesterday,
Why fret about them if Today be sweet!

—Edward Fitzgerald, *The Rubáiyát of*
Omar Khayyám of Naishápúr

Phryne awoke in the grey light of dawn, gently drew back the covers, and examined herself. All ten of her toes were curling upwards uncontrollably, and she smiled with infinite complacency. The Captain had indeed given of his best the previous evening. Who would have guessed it? She thought it unlikely he had enjoyed a woman's embraces for a very long time. A girl always knows. Yet such ardent attention to detail! Her body had been caressed, nibbled, ravished, fulfilled, and enchanted. She stretched like a cat, and stroked his naked flank. She would have liked to arise, but her right arm was still held captive over her lover's shoulder. He cradled her hand like a holy relic. Had he been a cat, he would be purring. Phryne took a deep breath, inhaled the intoxicating scent of satisfied passion, and gently eased her hand out of his grip. Instead of rising, however, she settled her back and buttocks against his, and luxuriated in the warmth of his body. Without in any way meaning to, she fell asleep again, while the tree branches outside the window whispered lullabies and endearments.

Sometime later she awoke again to find Herbert Spencer, discreetly attired in a crimson dressing-gown, leaning over her with evident solicitude. In one hand he held a cup of espresso, which he placed on the bedside table.

She smiled at him. 'Why, thank you. That is most thoughtful of you.'

'Dear Phryne, the gratitude is all mine.' He sat on the bed and caressed her cheek. 'I do not know how to thank you.'

Phryne reached for the cup and sipped. 'You have made a splendid start, dear man. What time is it?'

He consulted his wristwatch, during which process the front of his gown gaped a little, revealing an all but hairless chest. 'It's past nine.'

'Time I was up and doing, then.' She sipped the coffee, put down the cup, and kissed his hand.

He kissed hers back. 'Must you go?' he pleaded, and immediately a shadow crossed his face. 'No, I do apologise. Please, forget I said that. I must not be greedy.'

'Come here!' Phryne reached out, grabbed him around the neck with both hands, and hauled him down onto the bed beside her. They shared a lingering kiss, following which Phryne put one finger on his lips. 'My dear man, I have many things to say to you. First and foremost, thank you very much for your hospitality. That was indeed a night to remember.'

Another cloud seemed to pass across his honest face. 'I'm so sorry. I talked far too much, and I—'

Once more, Phryne's finger closed his lips. 'And you're going to do it again, unless I stop you. It was sheer nerves. You are a very nervous man. Did you not know that? Some of the treatments you give your patients might be better applied to your good self. Herbert, you don't have to be a brave little soldier anymore. Yes, I am going home to Melbourne soon, but you need not be alone. There is someone here who loves you devotedly. Are you seriously telling me you haven't noticed?'

He kissed her again, impulsively and with considerable passion. 'What are you saying? Surely you don't mean Violette?'

'Yes, I do mean Violette. How much longer are you going to torment her?'

He sat up straight and clapped both hands to his head. 'Phryne, I cannot possibly take advantage of Violette. She is a sacred trust! I cannot even consider such a thing. It would be a violation!' He blinked, as though lightly struck in the face with a rubber mallet. 'Am I talking too much again?'

She kissed him again. 'Of course you are. Don't you think that such a violation is what she most fervently wishes? Not that it would be anything of the sort. Treat her as you treated me last night and she will be thrilled beyond words.'

'Are you sure?' Now his hands were theatrically clenching and grasping, as if looking for missing house keys.

'Yes. Perfectly sure. We have an understanding, Violette and I. She needed me to overcome your many-scrupled chastity. In return, I am handing you over to her. And if that seems unfair to you, all I can say is that this is an imperfect world, and we make the best justice we can with what we have. Deal?'

He shook violently, like a ship which has struck a passing lighthouse, and blinked a number of times. 'Deal. Yes, of course. She is a wonderful woman, and I am not—'

'Don't you dare, Captain. I know what you were about to say

and it doesn't become you. Of course you're worthy of her, you addle-brained nincompoop. Stop maundering and accept your fate. You won't regret this. Oh, and another thing...'

'Yes?'

'In my handbag is a cheque for a hundred pounds for your sanatorium, for the wounded soldiers you are tending. If that makes you feel like a gigolo, then—'

'*À la bonheure?*' Now he was grinning.

'*À la bonheure.* Now you're getting the idea.' She rose, and stretched, allowing his hands to caress her body. 'Sorry, Captain. I really must dash.'

He bowed. 'But of course. There is a bathroom next door, on your right.'

'And I believe my clothes are on the floor. Thank you. I will attempt to say goodbye before I leave the area, but you never know in my line of work. It has been wonderful. Thank you!'

The Captain withdrew, and Phryne grinned to herself. She laid the signed cheque on the bedside table and put her coffee cup on top of it. One more snarled thread unscrambled, and two more healed hearts in prospect. Things were looking up.

———

Phryne's arrival back at the Mooltan was greeted in contrasting fashion. Dulcie was her customary offhand self. It seemed that nothing surprised her, and if her paying guest wished to spend the night out on the tiles with the neighbours that was no concern of hers. Dot was, as ever on such occasions, resigned, long-suffering, and necessarily mute. Alice, resplendent in a flowing dress of dark green, was radiant, solicitous, and happy. 'I do worry about the Captain,' she said, effusively fluttering around Phryne at the coffee table like a mother duck with a refractory duckling. 'He always seems to be harbouring a secret sorrow.'

Since there was no polite alternative, Phryne decided upon frankness. 'Alice, I think that Captain Spencer will be experiencing a new lease of life in the near future.'

Alice glowed like a hurricane lamp. 'I am so pleased! Do you think that Violette. . .' She left the sentence hanging in the air, like a house brick under the influence of anti-gravity.

'I think that Violette will also be far happier than she has been until now.'

Alice inclined her head. For a moment it looked as though Phryne was about to receive a rain of enthusiastic kisses, but she was reprieved at the last minute. From the kitchen, Dulcie's voice called out in warning. 'Alice? The toast's burning, and I'm all over flour.'

With a rustle of skirts Alice vanished, and Phryne devoted herself to another cup of espresso.

————

The remainder of Wednesday, all of Thursday, and most of Friday passed with delectable calm and recuperative comfort. After the tumults of the past five days it was wonderful to be able to sit back and relax. Dot finished her knitted scarf, and displayed it proudly. Phryne admired it, and Dot stowed it away in her valise against the oncoming of winter. The first signs of autumn were upon them now. The mornings were fresh and cool, and the deciduous trees had begun to turn yellow and ochre. There was nothing to do, and Phryne enjoyed it all immensely. She heard nothing from the spa, but convinced herself that she could feel a wave of gratified pleasure wafting around the corner from the red-brick building. She felt she could rely on Violette to take advantage of the situation. Alice reported that Vern had settled in at the Station Hotel and was exhibiting every sign of being happy. The barmaids at the Station had reported that Vern did indeed visibly admire them, but his little halo of I'm Being a Good Dog had showed no signs of slipping. Sid was apparently lurking in solitary at the bottling plant, and not a word had escaped his lips that anyone was able to discern. And Aubrey and Helena had visited the Mooltan twice, so closely entwined that it seemed they had already become twin souls in a single body. Phryne did not speculate. Such thoughts were better left uncanvassed.

———

Friday evening approached, and at Phryne's insistence both she and Dot were wearing their new hats, with matching ensembles: Phryne in a maroon and crimson trouser suit, and Dot in her inevitable brown and beige. After an early dinner, they climbed into the Hispano-Suiza and motored along the well-trodden path to the cinema. The queue was long and colourful, and Dot looked askance at her employer. 'Miss, are we going to wait in the line?'

Phryne grinned. 'No, Dot. I think we should be fashionably late. After all, we know how the film starts, don't we?'

'Yes, Miss. It's very strange to be seeing a film we saw them making.'

'Indeed it is, Dot. I fancy the ice-cream parlour next door. What do you say?'

'Yes, Miss.'

Inside the mock-Victorian ice-cream parlour, Phryne ordered a sorbet for herself and a chocolate ice-cream for her companion. Dot had no idea what Phryne was planning. Phryne had decided to keep it that way. Dot had no want of discretion, but she lacked the necessary sangfroid for the occasion. Explanations could come afterwards. Two tables away, Phryne saw Colleen O'Rourke holding court among a collection of boys, all of whom hung on her every word. The girl looked completely at ease, and was smartly dressed in a shortish skirt and blouse in contrasting blues. Phryne did her best not to listen in, and exchanged a look with Dot. They made the smallest of small talk in the intervals between shouts of laughter from the boys and Colleen, until the mass exodus began. They noticed the untidy-looking figure of Graeme Forbes hanging back from the other boys. He waited until last, gave Phryne a quizzical look, and walked outside. 'Not yet, Dot,' Phryne whispered, and followed the boy a good ten seconds later. As they stepped onto the footpath, Phryne whispered to her companion, 'Dot, I may need to move around. Whatever you do, please don't draw attention to me. It's important!'

Dot nodded and closed her mouth tight, suspicion that her employer was Up to Something hardening towards certainty. The cinema queue had almost evaporated, and from the interior beyond the huge doors it appeared the newsreel had already begun. 'Two shillings, Miss,' said a uniformed girl behind the counter. She looked as excited as the patrons. The girl was remarkably pretty in a conventional way, with blonde hair, blue eyes, and a small neat figure only partly disguised by her black, short-sleeved dress. Phryne handed her two florins and received her tickets.

They showed the tickets to an upright youth at the door, who gestured for them to pass inside.

'Are the seats numbered?' Dot enquired of him.

'Not tonight, Miss. Sit anywhere you like. We're only going to be two-thirds full.'

Within the darkened auditorium a flickering newsreel showed a bouncing kangaroo, whose antics seemed to produce ironic cheers. Phryne found a pair of seats near the door and motioned to Dot to join her there.

The newsreel wandered from marsupials to Sydney Harbour, where the bridge was still under construction, but the curving span was showing signs of looking pontifical. White letters across the bottom proclaimed the hope that the bridge would be open by 1931. 'Fat chance!' Phryne whispered.

In due time the scene changed to London, where a fiercely bearded King-Emperor was wrestling with a horse. The horse was temporarily getting the better of it, urged on by an obviously cheering crowd. The camera then zoomed in on the heir to the throne, a gormless-looking youth in a dark coat. He was smiling as if accepting the plaudits of the crowd.

'What do you think, Dot?' Phryne whispered. 'He's supposed to be very handsome.'

'Looks like a bit of dill, Miss.'

'Good for you, Dot. I don't like him either. Prince Bertie would be a far better king, but I don't suppose we'll get him.'

Inevitably, a large flock of sheep then took centre stage from the royal family, and a series of mind-numbing statistics about wool were triumphantly announced. Dot's attention wavered, and she noticed that Phryne was looking around her in the gloom. Dot sighed. She had her orders, and would obey them. She hoped Miss Phryne wasn't going to do anything dangerous.

Finally, the newsreel wound down, and an unseen piece of machinery began to play some vigorous jazz music. There seemed to be some movement in the audience in front of them. Dot kept her eyes firmly ahead, but became aware that Phryne was watching carefully. The flickering screen now showed the familiar beach of Queenscliff, and enormous white letters proclaimed *Benito's Treasure*. And there was Lily, standing on the beach in her white dress! In her excitement, Dot was only vaguely aware that Phryne had left her side.

Phryne, meanwhile, had found her quarry, who had moved to a seat next to Graeme Forbes, the young man clearly identifiable by his protruding ears. A stealthy hand was holding something, and there was no time to lose. She moved in front of the crouched figure and sat down in his lap, grabbing his left hand around the wrist. 'Not so fast! I'll take that, Mr McKenzie, unless you'd rather I broke your arm first.' The man gasped, struggled for a moment, and received Phryne's right elbow onto his nose. 'Play nice for me, you murdering louse, or I'll hurt you even more.'

'Shh!' came an outraged whisper from behind.

Phryne removed the syringe from his fingers and stowed it in her handbag. 'All right then,' she hissed. 'Tell me, purely for my own curiosity, why you murdered those innocent youths. Was it all about Annie?'

'Beautiful Annie,' the man breathed in her ear. 'I wanted her pure and unstained. I just wanted to bask in the light of her perfect beauty. There was nothing improper in that.'

Phryne tightened her grip on his wrist. 'All you wanted was to be kept in drink and idleness while the girls did all the work, and you were prepared to kill off Annie's suitors to keep her under your roof. Because once she was married your business would lose its chief attraction, wouldn't it? You loathsome little reptile!'

There was a sigh from the body jammed into the velvet cushion, and suddenly all the fight went out of the man. He subsided back into the chair, and Phryne removed herself from on top of him. 'You're coming along with me. Now.'

'May I not stay and see the end of the fillum?'

'Of course not! What do you think this is?' Phryne dragged him out of his chair and frogmarched him towards the exit.

Outraged whispers followed them, as did the giant figure of

Inspector Kelly. They emerged from the darkness into the light of the high street and blinked for a moment. It was all the respite McKenzie needed. He plunged his hand into his pocket, removed something, and thrust it into his mouth.

'I won't be hanged,' he stated. 'Cyanide in a capsule. It will take a wee minute to work, but there's no stopping it now.' He grinned at them: the proud grin of a man with nothing more to lose. He blinked at Kelly, who clapped handcuffs over his wrists. 'How did you know it was myself? Three perfect murders! Who else can say as much?'

Kelly grunted. 'If anyone thinks I'm going to stick my hand or anything else down your throat just to stop you dyin' here and now, they can forget it. I might catch something and it won't work anyway. Go on, Phryne. I'm listening.'

'It was when we were playing cards.' Phryne was watching the murderer carefully, but no symptoms had manifested themselves as yet. 'A pleasant evening of bridge with the two girls. They all play well. But McKenzie here was altogether too good. In one hand, he pulled off a brilliant endplay which could never have been imagined by the drunken fool we all took him to be. Then, fearing he had given himself away, he proceeded to get drunk in earnest and started playing badly—so badly I should have realised at once. A man who could dream up that brilliant coup was nothing like what he seemed. And since I was looking for a criminal mastermind, and nobody else fit the bill, then I had him. Isn't that right, McKenzie?'

The man grinned feebly at her. 'What an artist dies in me,' he murmured. Foam dribbled from his lips, and he fell onto the footpath like a sack of flour. His face suddenly contorted. 'It's not supposed to hurt!' he screamed. 'That's not fair!' The body writhed in agony for a second or two, then lay still. The face was a frightful rictus of infinite pain. Phryne felt that, contrary to the man's last words, this was eminently fair.

Mick Kelly put a hand to the body's neck, and nodded. He then proceeded to rifle through the corpse's pockets, and grunted. His ham-like hand produced a sealed envelope, addressed to The Hon. Miss Phryne Fisher. 'It's for you. But I'm going to read over your shoulder.'

Phryne nodded, and slid her fingernail along the edge of the envelope. Inside were two foolscap pages, handwritten in an educated copperplate. And this is what she read:

My dear Miss Fisher,

It has indeed been a pleasure to match my intellect against that of the most famous sleuth in Melbourne. If you are reading this, you will have triumphed. I will find some solace in knowing that I gave you an excellent run for your money.

The world owed me, Miss Fisher. I was born poor. My parents hated me. Until I was twenty I had barely survived. Then I became a most accomplished sponger: just inoffensive enough to be tolerated, and never too importunate. But the war gave me my real chance, and I took it. I contrived, by the use of strategic malingering, not to be fed into the furnace which devoured so many. Unfortunately, I was wounded, though by no means as badly as I persuaded the world I was. And after? Then it was truly time for the world to pay me back for the privations I had endured.

I laughed at you when you thought Annie's suitors were killing each other off. It was what I wanted you, and the world, to believe. So long as it was only our good town sergeant I had to fool, I was in clover and could lay my plans at leisure. Then you turned up, out of the blue. Was I going to stop, simply because the famed Miss Fisher was here? No.

I matched my wits against yours and won. I killed those two boys right under your aristocratic nose.

You know about the boy I threw out a train window? Everyone said it was an accident. The truth was that a pretty girl waved at the train, and everyone turned to look at her. And I seized that stupid oaf and tipped him out on the opposite side. There were seven witnesses, and I fooled them all. I killed Mackay by McAlpine's caber, and I put atropine in Hepburn's drink. (Though why people leave their drinks unattended is more than I can tell.) I intend to kill that idiot Forbes tonight with an injection of strychnine. I expect I will get away with it, too. Murder in private is child's play, quite unworthy of my talents. But murder under the noses of the multitude is a challenge worthy of a master.

Why did I do all this? You must have stumbled upon my secret, if you have at length beaten me. If I can't have Annie, then nobody else shall either—especially not that muscle-bound fool McAlpine. Of late, I have begun to think Annie now prefers him above all others. I have a special fate already in store for him. If I perish, so also shall he, in a shower of ordure. It is no more than he deserves. Why should he have so much? Youth, good looks, immense strength, a winning disposition...I had nothing but my wits. It is fitting he should die, under circumstances of ultimate humiliation.

I have long pondered how I might talk Annie into yielding her wonderful body to me. I deserve no less! But while I still believe I might have sweet-talked her into it, Jessie would never allow it. I devised several means of doing away with Jessie, but the sad truth is that I need her too.

And I made elaborate plans to avail myself of the defence of insanity should I be captured and exposed. I have made a considerable study of mental impairment and had a workable scheme wherein I could be held, at a fair level of personal comfort, in perpetuity. It is not difficult to deceive doctors; they always want to think the best of their patients. You and I know better, of course.

But at the last minute I have rebelled. I do not care to live on, even in relative comfort, while Annie will inevitably go to another. For inevitable it is. Pitiless youth has little sympathy for age.

You may wonder why I did not kill her, and thus preserve her beauty unstained in memory? The thought did occur to me, many times. But Jessie watches her sister day and night with inexorable patience and vigilance. I do not fear you, Miss Fisher, but I fear Jessie exceedingly. Perhaps I should have killed her after all.

I should never have succumbed to the vanity of that magnificent endplay during our bridge night. But such a chance comes seldom, and it was too tempting to refuse. However, as the evening wore on I felt that I might have aroused your suspicions. If you are reading this, then that was my only mistake. I now depart, unconquered. The hangman shall not have me. You I salute, for you have conquered. But I have had my innings and revenged myself upon the young and beautiful who did nothing whatever to earn it. And none of the dead shall possess that superb body which I longed for daily and could not have. But I did gain her love. No one and nothing can take that away from me now.

Yours sincerely,
F.S. McKenzie

There was a sudden clamour of voices. Phryne whirled around. The first people she caught sight of were Kenneth McAlpine and Annie Tremain, who had followed them out of the cinema.

'Annie!' Phryne shouted. 'Do *not* let Kenneth out of your sight, and do not allow him to go home until I return. Understood?'

Annie dimpled, and held both her hands tight around his mighty fist. 'I won't.' She looked both shocked and happy.

Phryne looked around. 'Dot? Where are you?' Then she ground her teeth and turned to the inspector. 'Damn! I told her not to move. Ah—Colleen!'

Colleen O'Rourke had also slipped out and looked up at Phryne with a face of alert enquiry. 'What do you need, Miss Fisher?'

'Colleen, please go back inside, find Dot, and sit with her. She is not to follow me. I will come back for her.'

'All right, Miss. I can do that.' With that, the admirable girl disappeared once more into the maw of the cinema. She turned back to find Mick Kelly giving instructions to a tall, dark-avised man she did not recognise.

'Go and fetch Dr Henderson—or any other doctor you can find. And deal with this, will you?' He turned to another bystander. 'Put a cover over him, especially the face.' Finally, he turned to face Phryne. 'Where are we going now?'

She addressed the man beside Annie. 'Kenneth, what is your address?'

'I live on the main road, Miss,' the giant answered. 'Number four thirty-six, halfway to Sailors Falls.'

'All right. Now stay right here and do not go anywhere. Annie? You understand?'

Annie gripped hold of Kenneth's sleeve and held it tight. 'No, Miss Fisher, I don't. But we'll do as you ask.'

'Thank you. Inspector?' Phryne said. 'You're coming with me.

And nobody else is to approach anywhere near Mr McAlpine's home. Is that clear?'

By now a reasonable crowd had assembled on the footpath and in the twilit street. She raked them all with a look, and a general sense of obedience seemed to be catching. Phryne nodded, and took Mick Kelly by the arm. 'Come on. We'll go in my car and with any luck we won't get ourselves blown up.'

Chapter Twenty-Four

The Grape that can with Logic absolute
The Two-and-Seventy jarring sects confute:
The subtle Alchemist that in a trice
Life's leaden Metal into Gold transmute.

—Edward Fitzgerald, *The Rubáiyát of*
Omar Khayyám of Naishápúr

The Hispano-Suiza tore around the main street and down the hill. If Inspector Kelly was outraged by such flagrant disregard for speed limits, he gave no sign of it. Within minutes they had pulled up outside a small, prosperous-looking farm. It was no more than four acres, but the grass was well-tended, the house newly painted, and the horse in the back paddock looked abundantly fed and glossy. Phryne switched the motor off and gave her companion a smile. 'I'm sorry, Mick. I only wanted to get here before anybody else did. And preferably while there's still some twilight to see by. Now, I think we're looking at a booby-trap. What do you think?'

'Yeah. I reckon. So what, if anything, is your plan, Phryne?'

She grimaced. 'Well, normally we'd send for the army, wouldn't we? Except that I have no idea where the nearest base might be, nor if they've got any bomb disposal experts even if we went there. Bombs aren't as prevalent as they used to be. And so...'

He grunted, ill at ease. 'And so you're intending to go in, find it, and disarm it. Is that your bright idea?'

'Unless you have an alternative plan to suggest, Mick?'

'Yeah, I do. Have I mentioned I did some bomb disposal during the war?'

Phryne patted his arm encouragingly. 'So does this mean you're volunteering?'

'If I tell you to stay in the car, you're not gonna take orders from me, are ya?'

'I might, Mick. But don't you think it's safer to have some backup?'

'All right. If we're gonna do something utterly stupid, then let's do it together. What we'll do is this. One room at a time, slowly and carefully. And if you see anythin' you don't like the look of, then you get the hell outta there and come and tell me about it.'

'Right-o.'

They alighted from the car and examined the front gate. It did not appear to be attached to anything except the wire fence. They proceeded through it, closed it behind them, and approached the front verandah. There was a ginger cat asleep on it. He looked up for a moment, then went straight back to sleep. Phryne bent down and examined the ground beneath the wooden floor. 'Mick, I really can't see anything here. And he wouldn't booby-trap the front entrance, would he?'

''E bloody might, Phryne. Did this bloke strike you as having any sense of discrimination?'

'No, there is that. So, do we try the front door?'

'Yep. But first...' Mick Kelly had seen something leaning

against the side of a wooden shed. Waving Phryne into immobility, he returned with a large sheet of well-polished sheet iron. 'Dunno what this was, but I'm goin' in behind it. Youse comin'?'

The iron sheet did not offer much in the way of hand-holds, but there were some dints in it which might accommodate hands sufficiently desperate. Crouched behind their makeshift shield, they climbed onto the wooden verandah and pushed against the front door. Nothing happened. Mick grinned at her.

'I think it's locked, Mick,' she suggested. 'I like this as a battering ram, but I think we've missed the point somewhere.'

'Yeah. What did that useless bludger say? Something about a shower of shit?'

Phryne considered. 'The letter is in my handbag. But he definitely said something about humiliation. And a shower of ordure.'

'Bastard wouldn't booby-trap the horse, would 'e?'

'I don't think any horse I've ever met would appreciate that. All McKenzie would've got from any such attempt was a serious kicking.' Phryne closed her eyes for a moment then opened them with sudden apprehension. 'Oh no! Maybe he meant it literally?'

'The outhouse?'

They exchanged a glance of wild surmise. 'All right, Mick. What's the betting it's that? All right, let's consider the possibilities. First: the door. When you open the door, take the battering ram. You may need it. Second: the toilet roll might be attached to something unpleasant. Third (and I think this most likely): the seat.'

Kelly thought about this. 'A bastard like that's probably had women telling him to put the toilet seat down all 'is life. Yep. That's suspect number one. I think it might be a grenade. There's still all sorts of ordnance left behind from the war.' He grinned at her. 'I hope it's not a nine-inch shell.'

'So do I, Mick. What do you want me to do?'

'If it's a grenade, I'll need to throw it out across the paddock. You any good with horses?'

'All right. I'll get Dobbin out of harm's way.'

Phryne went and introduced herself to the horse. It was a good seventeen hands at the shoulder and glared at her, tossing its head up and down. *I do not know you, puny human!* seemed to be the rejoinder of the day. Phryne spotted a clump of toothsome clover, still green despite the lateness of the season, and offered it in her outstretched left hand. Out of the corner of her eye she could see the inspector crouched behind his makeshift bomb shelter and fought down a sense of panic. This admirable man was too good to be wasted. Equally, it wasn't easy to see what else either of them could have done. The overwhelming probability was that something here was a death-trap, and Kenneth McAlpine had done nothing whatever to merit being blown up in his own home.

The horse accepted the offering with sombre gravitas while Phryne's other hand caressed the mighty neck. Phryne reached up and grasped a handful of mane behind the horse's ear. The horse shook its head.

'Please, Dobbin. We need to get away from here. It's for your own good.'

The horse swished its tail, clearly thinking this over. *All right, human. If you say so.*

Phryne led the horse slowly and carefully across the field, wishing it was wearing a halter. Horses were a lot more tractable when led by the cheekstrap. She began to sing to him.

> 'Twinkle, twinkle, little horse
> Do we love you?
> Yes, of course.
> High above your field you stand
> Never lived a horse so grand.'

The horse seemingly approved of this and nuzzled her impa-
tiently. *More music, human!*

Obediently, she sang 'Baa Baa, Black Sheep' in French.

'Phryne!' came a bellowing voice from the outhouse. 'Comin',
ready or not!'

Phryne dragged the horse around behind the back of the
house. A shattering explosion rent the summer evening. Dobbin
kicked out and narrowly missed Phryne's leg. And she heard a
loud thump as something, presumably the ginger cat, ran under
the house. 'Hush, now, my dear!' she cooed. *'Soyez tranquille, mon
enfant!* It's all right!' The horse was trembling all over now. She
caressed the head and neck, murmuring endearments. In due
course, she became aware that Mick had joined her.

'I see you coped, Mick. Well done you.'

'You all right, Phryne?'

'Well, I nearly got the kicking of a lifetime, but otherwise I'm
fine.'

'It's getting dark, and we'd better be heading back to town to
tell our caber-tossing giant that it's all clear.'

'You sure about that? There might be more surprises in store
in the house.'

'Oh, that is a point, of course. Wait here.' Kelly took the horse
and led it away. Presently, he returned. 'I think it's all right, but
I'll have a better look tomorrow. Are you sure you're all right,
Phryne?'

'I think so.' This appeared to be the case, but a strong arm
like a bridge support held out was very pleasing to lean upon.
Just for once. The adrenalin backwash was leaving her feeling
unaccustomedly drained.

It was all but dark when they reached the car on the roadside.
'You're not gonna let me drive, are ya?'

'What do you think, Mick?'

'Fine. Just bloody well take it easy this time.'

Phryne drove with unaccustomed sobriety back to the cin-ema, where she sat inertly in the driver's seat, vaguely aware of Mick Kelly barking orders at everyone. She dimly registered that McAlpine had been instructed to stay at the Temperance Hotel and saw Annie's face bloom in the lamplight like a child being offered an ice-cream. Her hand reached out and took his arm.

Dot joined her in the passenger seat and leaned over with maximum solicitude. 'Miss Phryne, the inspector thinks you should go home now, and I agree with him.'

Phryne grinned weakly. 'Do you know, Dot? I think I agree with him, too.'

———

Saturday dawned cool and cloudy. Phryne could hear sounds of breakfast downstairs. Memories of yesterday's tumultu-ous evening drifted across her memory. She must have slept almost around the clock. She wondered why this should be. Admittedly, being almost blown up by a grenade was a shock even by her own exacting standards. But lying in bed at her rel-ative ease, there was something still nagging away at her. The murders were now solved, and another two had been narrowly averted. Mick Kelly had quietly confiscated the syringe she had taken from the deceased. No doubt it would turn out to have been strychnine, or similar. But while the mystery was solved, she could not escape the feeling that there was yet more to be discovered.

The charming scene of domestic harmony over the bridge table was now overlaid with a patina of horror she could not shake. Did uncles really lust after blood relatives? And how well he had covered it up! The girls suspected that he was a lazy malingerer, but their enjoyment of their card evenings had been perfectly genuine. But what a maelstrom that horrible man had been holding in! Phryne resolved, then and there, that she would keep this secret from Annie. And Jessie, too. Why on earth should their few pleasant recollections of the man be thus polluted? To what end? Nevertheless, she resolved to revisit the Temperance Hotel. Now that the licensee was dead, what would happen to the place? Was there a will? Jessie would be searching for it, she was certain. She would go there this very day and see whatever there was to be seen.

———

Dot took very little persuasion to have lunch at the Temperance. It was roast lamb with mint sauce and vegetables, washed down with a fine local red wine, followed by apricot pie with fresh cream. They were served by Gentle Annie. If Annie had looked any happier, she would have been glowing like a radium clock. And Phryne noticed McAlpine's giant frame serving behind the bar. Any encouragement for this Caledonian caber tosser to replace the utterly unworthy previous incumbent was clearly going to be redundant. She grinned across the table to Dot, and raised her glass.

'Miss Fisher?'

Phryne looked up to see Jessie standing in front of her wearing an expression of open puzzlement.

'Yes, Jessie, what is it?'

The girl stood on one foot, and then the other, as if unable to make an appropriate choice. 'I was going through the office desk, looking at all the paperwork… I found the will, by the way. He's left the place to us, which is such a relief.'

'Congratulations! But it's no more than you deserve.'

'Well, yes, I suppose so. I've seen the accounts and we're not doing too badly. But right at the bottom of the desk I found this.' She handed over a reddish-brown disc with a hole in it, and a loop of grubby string tied through the hole. 'It's probably nothing important, but I wondered why it was there.'

Phryne read the following: *Strangeways N 101467*, and a deep frown settled over her features. 'Jessie, I'd like to keep this, if I may. Suddenly, I have a call to make.'

Outside, Phryne cranked the Hispano-Suiza into raucous life and set off down the road to Musk. The last piece of the puzzle had fallen into place. And yes, the late criminal had indeed been a thoroughly vile piece of work.

———

Aunty Morag McKenzie was not happy to see her and did not scruple to say so. 'Whaddaya want now, Miss?'

Phryne looked at the dogs. They looked at her and made vaguely threatening noises in their throats. At least the shotgun did not appear to be among those present.

'Just a quick word with Janet McKenzie.'

'And what if she don't want to talk to youse?'

Phryne smiled, and adjusted her cloche cap at a jaunty angle. 'I think she will. Miss McKenzie, believe it or not, I am actually trying to help. An unfortunate situation has arisen, and in order that it does not get out of control, I think a certain amount of confabulation would be in order.' She gave her most seraphic smile. 'Ever since I arrived here in the spa country I have been surrounded by secrets, Miss McKenzie! Great secrets, small secrets, middle-sized secrets, secrets with carnival masks and false moustaches, and secrets with long, trailing tree roots leading back into the past—some of them heading right back to the war.'

Watching intently, Phryne saw that this had finally produced a reaction. Aunty Morag's black eyes blazed for a moment then narrowed. 'And what if some o' these secrets want to stay hidden? Eh?'

Phryne smiled, and rested her right hand on the verandah rail. 'I'm thinking about one secret in particular that is longing to stay hidden. It is a secret clamouring as no other secret has ever clamoured to be buried at a crossroads on a stormy midnight with not even owls to bear witness to its sepulture. Miss McKenzie, have you always known that the recently deceased was not who he purported to be?'

There was a long, dragging silence while Aunty Morag caressed the heads of the dogs. 'It's best ya don't talk to 'er. I'll do the talkin', Miss Detective Fisher. 'Course I knew. Ya think I'm daft? I'd know me own nephew even after five years of war. He looked similar, granted. Same height, same weight, more or less, and same long face. Only not really, and I reckon that's why 'e grew that bloody awful beard—so's no one'd notice the little differences. 'E was a lazy drongo with nowhere to go, and 'e found out our Fred stood to inherit the pub because Tremain 'ad already died. I expect after the real Fred was killed in action somewhere the bastard covered it up, stole Fred's dog tag, and persuaded the authorities that 'e was Frederick McKenzie. That's if 'e didn't kill the poor bastard. But I don't think so. An' 'e looks me in the eye and says 'e's Frederick McKenzie, home from the war. And if I'd called 'im a liar, the pub woulda gone to some other drongo. So I looked 'im in the eye back and said 'e'd hafta take it up with his missus.'

'And Janet accepted him in good faith?'

Aunty Morag gave a harsh bark. Both dogs barked back, and she stroked their flanks and watched them wag their tails and relax. 'She wanted to believe it. The alternative was losin' the pub to a comparative stranger. And at first the drongo put 'is back into the business and it all worked out.'

'Until the question of conjugal rights came up?'

Aunty Morag rubbed a grimy finger on her cheek and grimaced. 'Yeah. Conjugals. They're an absolute bugger, conjugals. There's bloody nowhere to hide when it's a question o' conjugals. So after that she knew all right. While she's wonderin' what to do about it, she finds out she's bin knocked up. And once she'd given birth to young Robert she was committed, totally.' Aunty Morag rose menacingly from her chair and glared at Phryne, hands on hips in the full Sugar Bowl. 'There's still time to get me gun, y'know. What are ya gonna do about all this?'

Phryne folded her arms and glared back. 'What I am going to do is persuade Janet McKenzie to go back to the pub, as soon as possible, and search the joint from top to bottom, removing every last scrap of evidence that the person everyone knew as Frederick McKenzie was actually called Strangeways.' Phryne handed over the dog tag. 'Here. My little gesture of good faith. I can't do it, Miss McKenzie. I have no *locus standi* in this matter, and neither have you. But Janet McKenzie does. She is the relict of the licensee and she has every right to strip the place of incriminating evidence. I urge her to do so.'

Aunty Morag considered this and rubbed the beak of her nose with the back of her hand. She stared at the disc in settled gloom. 'Yair, yer right. Where'd ya get this?'

'Jessie gave it to me. That was a big clue, of course. It might have belonged to a deceased friend of his, but I thought not. There was something bothering me about him all along. His Highland accent came and went, you know. And since I already knew he was a murderer, I wondered if his whole life had been one vast fraud.'

'Well, ya got that right. I knew the bastard was a bastard. I 'ad no idea about the murders. Jeez.' She shook her head in vexation.

'Miss McKenzie, he was a criminal genius the like of which you have probably never encountered before. Neither have I, so don't blame yourself. Please, there's no time to waste. If I've worked this out, there's always the chance someone else might have too.'

'Yair, you wanna watch that Mick Kelly. There's no flies on 'im. All right, I'm on it. And I want youse to stay away from the pub until tomorrer. Janet's gonna be a busy woman today.' She looked up at the sky. 'D'ya know if she'll be allowed to be the new licensee, bein' a woman and all?'

'I'm not sure. But I suspect there might soon be a newcomer to the family who will be allowed. Keep an eye out for wedding bells, Miss McKenzie.'

The old woman glared up at her, her features dark with suspicion and alarm. 'Who's getting' married?'

'I think Annie might be going to marry Kenneth McAlpine. If they do want a man to be the licensee, I expect he'll be acceptable to the authorities.'

An angry snort escaped from Aunty Morag's nostrils. 'Kenneth who? Ya don't mean the caber-tossing giant, do ya?'

'Indeed I do. Know him at all?'

'Yair, we've met. I s'pose if the girl really must marry, she could do a lot worse. All right. You better scarper, Miss Fisher. I'll explain matters and we'll deal with it.' She glared once more at Phryne, like a bull about to charge a red flag. 'Yer a very clever sheila, y'know that?'

———

On Sunday morning, Phryne awoke from a restful sleep. She threw open the doors to the balcony and looked out over the peaceable valley. It was a golden morning. Birds sang and twittered in the sweet-smelling wattles. She yawned, stretched, and pondered the bizarre adventures of the last eight days. She sighed with pure pleasure and watched two kookaburras in a nearby gum tree disputing ownership of some tasty morsel they had unearthed. It appeared that a truce was eventually attained involving Division of the Spoils, and each retired to a different branch to be alone with whatever it was.

There was a tentative knock at the door. 'Miss Phryne? We've got visitors.'

'Dot, it's only eight-thirty. Who comes calling at this unearthly hour?'

'It's Miss McKenzie, and Annie and Jessie, and—I think you'd better come down.'

'All right, Dot. Give me ten minutes.'

Phryne rummaged in her wardrobe, looking for clean clothes. She had been intending to stay only a week and her supply of fresh clothes had run dry. She found a black trouser suit which did not appear notably second-hand and struggled into it. Blast country people and their early rising! She assumed her new crimson cloche hat and went downstairs.

Seated around the breakfast table were Dot, Annie, Jessie, the threatening figure of Miss McKenzie, and a thin, faded woman Phryne did not recognise. A full English breakfast had been laid out on the buffet. It smelled so appetising Phryne decided to break with custom and partake of a light breakfast; she helped herself to bacon, eggs, a piece of toast and marmalade, and a cup of espresso from the steaming pot. She then assumed an empty chair at the head of table and smiled at the assembled women, noting that both Annie and Jessie seemed to be glowing with health and a general sense of vitamin-enhanced optimism.

'I was going to ask to what do I owe the pleasure, but I suspect I already know most of it,' she began. 'Annie, you look notably radiant this morning?'

Annie dimpled. She was wearing a white dress with a blue shirt, decorously buttoned, and her relentlessly brushed golden hair flowed over it like the plains of heaven. 'Mr McAlpine has proposed,' she admitted, with what she imagined was becoming coyness.

'And have you accepted?' Phryne nibbled at her toast.

'I have. But I asked him to wait until next year, and he said he didn't mind a bit. I'm in no hurry, and neither is he.'

'Congratulations, Annie. If I am any judge of men, he will make you a devoted husband.' She turned to Annie's gently glowing sister. 'And you, Jessie? You look as though you have news also?'

'Mr Forbes proposed to me last night.'

Phryne dropped her coffee spoon, which fell to the floor with a resounding tinkle. 'Good gracious! And have you also accepted?' Jessie was wearing her customary shirt and trousers, but there was a relaxed comfort about her slight figure that Phryne had never seen before. 'I said I'd think about it. It's all a bit sudden. I mean, I thought he wanted Annie, but—' she coloured a deep crimson '—he seems to have been more interested in me all along. Or so he says. But he's very shy. I will need to be more sure of him.'

'Bloody oath you will.' Aunty Morag McKenzie drained her tea mug. 'Girls, I'm saying nothin' against Kenneth McAlpine. He's a grown man and knows 'is own mind. Graeme Forbes is still wet behind the ears. Let's see if 'e grows some character first.'

Phryne turned her gaze to the stranger. 'You're very quiet,' she suggested. 'May I assume that you are Mrs Janet McKenzie?'

The woman gave a decisive nod. 'I am. And you must be Miss Phryne Fisher. I have heard a great deal about you.'

Chapter Twenty-Five

And this I know: whether the one True Light
Kindle to Love, or wrath-consume me quite,
One glimpse of it within the Tavern caught
Better than in the Temple lost outright.

—Edward Fitzgerald, *The Rubáiyát of*
Omar Khayyám of Naishápúr

Aunty Morag raked the circle of faces with a stern look, clearly feeling that it was time she took charge. 'Look, anything that gets said here goes nowhere else. Got that?'

There was a chorus of nods.

'Miss Fisher, the reason we're trespassin' on your hospitality is because you can't bloody sneeze anywhere near Daylesford without half-a-dozen nosy neighbours offerin' youse a hanky and home-brewed cough remedies. An' if yer wonderin' 'bout Dulcie and Alice, they've gone out for the morning, leavin' me in charge. That all right with you?'

The table, trembling in a few cases, concurred.

'Now, here's the deal today: we've left McAlpine in charge of the Temperance. It don't open on Sunday anyway, so there ain't much fer the bloke to do 'cept look pleasantly threatenin'. An' I think youse'd agree 'e's pretty bloody good at that. I've had a visit from Inspector Kelly an' 'e sends you 'is best regards.' Aunty Morag paused, and pondered, with the little finger of her left hand exploring the interior of her ear. 'Oh yair, 'e also told me to tell ya 'e's bin right through McAlpine's house and there's nuthin' wrong. The horse and the cat are fine, and some brother of his is lookin' after the place.'

'I am very glad to hear it. So it's safe for McAlpine to return.'

'Yair. I wouldna put it past that bastard to've had more little surprises in store, but apparently the hand grenade was 'is best shot. Did it go off?'

'It did, and my teeth are still reverberating from the aftershock. Mick Kelly is a singularly fearless man.'

'Yair, well, 'e didn't want to put your life at risk, did he? But 'e's gone off home to Ballarat. An' I think ya know why, don'tcha?'

'Yes, I think I do.' Phryne looked again at this terrifying old woman and wondered vaguely why she wasn't leading regiments into battle. 'Because his murder case is now solved, and he doesn't want to feel obliged to notice anything that might not add up.'

'Yep. Now, I'm gonna hand over to Janet to tell her story.'

Phryne looked the woman over. Her print dress was old and had been skilfully mended a number of times. She might have been forty, though she looked older. Her hair was cut short, but had been subjected to some moderately skilled hairdressing, and her natural curl was held in place by a phalanx of hairpins. Her eyes were pale blue, and looked ancient, but her wrinkled hands looked strong and capable.

She looked the two girls over with regretful fondness. 'Annie, Jessie, I barely know what to say. Please believe me that I had no idea that that—' she shuddered '—*creature* was not my husband until it was, well, too late for second thoughts. When he came home from the war, bearded and injured, I think I suspected something was wrong.' She folded her hands on the table and bent her head, as if listening to voices from the distant past. 'But he knew so much! He recounted our courtship with a hundred details. He even knew certain things about me that—that only a husband should know. I fear that my lost love spoke very much out of turn to his false friend.'

Annie reached out her spotless white arm and took Janet McKenzie's hand in hers. Mrs McKenzie resumed, with a grateful look at Annie. 'Girls, the pub is still yours. Your late father Luke owned it, and it should go to you. Under Luke's will it went to my husband, however. The will of the man purporting to be my husband, however, is recent. It was signed and witnessed only last year, and I don't think it can be contested, unless we expose him as a fraud. He was a monster, but he could have done so much worse. He could have left the hotel to anyone, but I think he liked you girls and was grateful in his own way for all the work you did there.'

With a supreme effort of self-control Phryne sat frozen in her chair and gave no betraying sign of discomfort. But Aunty Morag's eyes were boring into her, and the fierce chin jerked downwards. Phryne realised that Miss McKenzie had already guessed the deceased's terrible secret.

'So what we are planning to do is to let things take their course,' Janet went on. 'The deceased may go to his grave as my husband and his will shall stand, despite him being a multiple murderer. If we let it come out that he was an impostor, we'll never hear the end of it. We'd have to go back to Luke's will, and that leads to a dead end because Frederick never made a will, poor man. I begged him to before he went to the war, but it appears he didn't. I've searched everywhere and I can't find it.' Tears rolled down her cheeks. Annie squeezed her hand again. Jessie offered a white handkerchief and Janet McKenzie blew her nose with considerable force.

'I don't know about that,' Phryne offered. 'He may have made a will and Mr Strangeways found it and destroyed it. He was already in possession of the pub, and nobody would question his tenure.'

Jessie looked at Phryne in surprise. 'Was that his name? Oh, of course. That little disc I found. Is that what made you realise he wasn't who he said he was?'

Phryne nodded, and chose her words with care, aware of Aunty Morag's black eyes still bearing down upon her like a battery of field guns. 'Yes, it was. I don't even know why he kept it. But I couldn't get my head around the fact that he would be happy to wipe out Annie's suitors wholesale. It didn't make sense to me. But his motive, since he was an impostor, was clear enough.' She made her body relax and smiled her most winning smile. 'He didn't want Annie getting married, because she'd probably leave the pub and that would be bad for business. He was a wicked man, but I think he was mentally ill. Completely bonkers, in fact, though he hid it well. You may think it's a stupid reason to commit murders, and you'd be right. But he wasn't in his right mind. The war did things to people's sanity.'

'Was he ever in the war at all?' Jessie demanded, leaning her clenched fists against the tabletop.

'Well, yes, Jessie, I think he must have been. How else could he have got to know your real uncle? And while it seems your uncle was indiscreet in his reminiscences of home, war breaks down a lot of barriers. This story has happened before. There was a famous case in France in the sixteenth century featuring a man called Martin Guerre. An impostor came home from the wars and supplanted the dead Martin Guerre in his own home.

So yes, the only way this story makes any sense is if Strangeways and your uncle were mates in the war.'

'And how did you realise he was the murderer?' Jessie persisted.

'Remember our card night? That endplay he engineered to get home in six diamonds was brilliant—far too clever for the harmless drunk we all thought him. And I don't think I ever saw him really drunk. I think that was all pretence.'

Annie's clear white brow furrowed. 'I wondered about that too. He never drank a lot, Jessie, but he acted drunk.'

'Yes, he did.' Janet McKenzie took a deep breath and leaned back in her chair. 'And I was completely fooled by that. I wondered the same thing, because he never seemed to drink that much. He didn't mistreat me. I think he even loved me at first. But when that seemed to die away I had nothing to keep me there. I noticed he liked the girls, and they seemed to like him. But I couldn't bear sharing my bed with him a moment longer. Once he had got what he wanted, he stopped even pretending to care for me. So Aunty Morag took me and Robert in. Robert's eight now,' she added with quiet pride.

'Like you took us in when Dad was killed in the war.' Annie looked upon her fearsome aunt with a fond indulgence Phryne was barely able to credit. The girl turned back to Mrs McKenzie. 'Now that the impostor is dead, could we invite you back to the pub? It is your proper home. It really should be yours.'

Mrs McKenzie gave Jessie a nervous look. 'That's very kind of you, Annie. But are you sure? Jessie? What do you think?'

Jessie looked her aunt straight in the eye. 'Mrs McKenzie, please do come home.'

'Well, I suppose you could do with another hand. But only if you're sure? Maybe on three months' trial, to see if we suit?'

Aunty Morag gave a sharp nod. 'Good idea. You don't know how this is gonna work out, do ya? And what about you, Annie? You gonna stay on at the pub after you get married?'

Annie folded her hands in front of her and nodded. 'Yes. For as long as I can. It's our pub. Yours, Jessie's, and Mrs Mac's and mine. We've worked hard for it. I don't want to abandon it. And Mr McAlpine—Kenneth—says he's happy to sell his farm to his brother after we get married.'

Dot had not said a word, but she was watching everyone's faces carefully, and noticed that a beatific smile had spread across Janet McKenzie's face. It was not a face accustomed to smiles, and some of the necessary muscles seemed to be creaking with underuse, but she lifted her head and gave a gentle laugh. 'Mrs Mac! You girls used to call me that when you were children. All right. Three months, yes? And it's all right to bring young Robert?'

'Of course!' Jessie and Annie exclaimed in a dead heat.

'All right, that's settled then. I'll go and pick up your things and bring them to the pub this arvo, Janet.' Aunty Morag rose, and inclined her chin towards Phryne. 'Glad to meet you, Miss Fisher. I c'n see why you're a famous detective. You know how ter keep yer trap shut, too. Most young wimmin can't do it, fer some reason.' She dipped her head towards Dot. 'You're good at it, too, Miss. Keep it up!'

The company listened to the roar of Aunty Morag's truck exploding into life and grinned at each other. 'She's a wonderful woman,' Mrs Mac observed. 'She brought the girls up when their mother died, and their father went off to war. I had a difficult confinement—the poor little mite was stillborn, you know—and I was struggling to look after them myself, when one day that truck came roaring up to the pub and she took the kids away with her.'

'What was it like, living with her?' Dot wanted to know.

'She was a bit hard on us.' Jessie's eyes were unfocused, thinking over her childhood. 'But she kept us safe, fed, and well looked after. One day Annie and I got lost in the forest. We were only seven and nine, and we were terrified, because last century there were three children got lost not far from her house and they were never found until long afterwards.'

'Dead, I assume?' Phryne had not heard this story.

'I'm afraid so. And we both knew we'd been silly and we thought we were going to die, too. It got dark, and I thought I knew the way home and it turned out I didn't. It was a cold, wet night with no stars to steer by. So I put my arms around Annie and we sat under a tree, waiting for morning.'

'What happened then?' Dot prompted.

'She found us,' answered Annie. 'It must have been past midnight. She had a kero lantern, and I think she must have scoured the woods up and down, like Rat looking for Mole in *The Wind in the Willows*, until she found us. I can still remember seeing a ghostly light through the trees and I thought it was the Banksia Men coming to take us away.'

'I hope you weren't punished too much.' Dot was finding this tale harrowing.

Jessie laughed gently. 'No. She said we'd already punished ourselves. She put us both to bed and we slept until lunchtime.'

'So when did she send you back to the pub?' Phryne asked.

Mrs Mac sighed. 'People in town were being so tiresome about it. They said the girls were being held captive by a wicked witch in a gingerbread cottage. Until the minister put them all in their place, that is. He was quite forthright about it. But they still talked, and Aunty Morag said they'd better go home to us.'

'I can imagine. We've met the minister; he is a man of forceful character. So Aunty Morag sent them to you?'

'I was fourteen, and Jessie was sixteen,' answered Annie. 'And we started helping around the pub and learning the business. It was fun.'

'After school, I hope?'

'Oh yes. Aunty Morag sent us to school. We got teased about

her, but I didn't care.' Jessie flicked her head defiantly, as if confining schoolyard gossip to the rubbish bin.

'I did.' Annie looked sorrowful. 'But Jessie and I talked it over and we decided we'd been enough of a burden to Aunty Morag. And Mrs Mac said yes please.'

Mrs Mac looked doleful. 'I knew by then that my so-called husband was nothing of the kind. And even though I had a child of my own, I realised I was lonely. I thought the girls would brighten the place up. And you certainly did, my dears. Until I wanted to get away because I couldn't bear that man anymore.'

'Thanks, Mrs Mac. Look, I shall intrude no further.' Phryne looked around the table. 'Oh, by the way, were the scarves your idea?'

This produced some blank looks right around the table. If this had been Aunty Morag's idea—which she strongly suspected—then the secret had not been passed on as yet. Although if the girls' marriages turned out badly, Phryne was certain that Scarves and Knitting would be introduced into their lives. She smiled brightly. 'I appear to have been chosen by Aunty Morag to drive you back to town.'

'We can walk. No need to trouble yourself.' Mrs Mac was suddenly on her dignity again: hands folded, shoulders hunched, and face reminiscent of a barbed-wire entrenchment.

'Well, yes, you can, Mrs Mac, but you needn't. Because we're going home. It's been wonderful here, and I wouldn't have missed it for worlds, but I have urgent business back in town. Before that, however, I would very much like to take you three back to the Temperance. Dot?'

'Yes, Miss?'

'I want you to go and get my good blue overcoat and the matching hat. I'll just leave a note for our hosts, so Dulcie and Alice don't think we've slipped town without paying.'

Dot gasped, and then understanding dawned. 'As you say, Miss.'

———

Mrs Mac almost proved obdurate. Three times Phryne expostulated before she finally relented. She sat in the front seat, and the three young women squashed in at the back. As Phryne drove up the hill into Daylesford, the churches were emptying their flock, with everyone in their Sunday best and doubtless refreshed by invigorating hymns and sermons. Phryne had timed her run to perfection. She drew up outside the Presbyterian church and stopped the car, leaving the motor just ticking over. As the admiring crowd gathered around the car, Janet McKenzie, resplendent in her new dark blue ensemble, lifted her head and acknowledged the crowd. Which began to applaud. No one knew who began it, but suddenly the entire congregation joined in.

Reverend McPherson strode around to the passenger side. 'Janet McKenzie, as I live. In the name of the Lord, I bid you welcome.'

Mrs Mac attempted to rise in her seat, and tottered. The minister made a decisive gesture of demurral. 'No, do not trouble! I hope to see you here next Sunday?'

'Indeed you will, Reverend.' She opened her mouth to say more, but could not.

Phryne intervened. 'Minister, it has been a pleasure to know you. We are going home to Melbourne today, but I hope to return before too long to this wonderful town.'

The minister inclined his head with the gravity of an alderman laying a foundation stone. 'Miss Fisher, may the Lord make His face to shine upon you, and Miss Williams also. And you too, Annie and Jessie.'

Phryne waved a gloved hand at the congregation and engaged first gear. The applause broke out anew as they trundled along the road back towards the Temperance Hotel.

As soon as the car had stopped, Annie climbed out and assisted Mrs Mac out of the passenger seat. At once Mrs Mac made her way around the front of the car and looked Phryne in the eye. 'That was a kind deed, Miss Fisher. Thank you.'

Phryne descended to the footpath and received a loving embrace from Annie. It was like being kissed by a goddess: inevitable, pleasing, and somehow not as perilous as it perhaps ought to have been. 'Do come back soon,' the girl enthused. 'And thank you so much!'

'It was my pleasure. I'm happy to have been of service. Good luck to all of you. I think you will find life more enjoyable hereafter.'

'Goodbye.' Dot waved from the back seat, feeling a little left out, and trying not to resent it. Just as Phryne was about to depart, Annie put both hands on the back door and gave Dot a kiss.

'Safe journey, Dot.'

And somehow Dot's world seemed to be filled with orange blossom as well.

———

When they got back to the Mooltan, Dulcie and Alice had returned. Phryne settled up while Dot packed their luggage, and she and Dot received more unexpected embraces from them both as they made their goodbyes, as well as an affectionate embrace from Tamsin the cat, who rubbed herself against Phryne's cheek as if hoping for more valerian. Dulcie and Alice waved them off, arm in arm and looking radiantly happy.

As they passed through Daylesford, Phryne looked at her companion with fondness and concern in equal proportions. 'Dot, what's wrong?'

Dot did look a bit stricken, and Phryne slowed down.

'I didn't say goodbye to Colleen.'

'Neither we did. But, then, it's been an eventful week, hasn't it? Oh!'

Phryne pulled over just below the brow of the hill. Standing by herself on the roadside was a slender girl in her plain black Sunday best. Her hand was out, thumb upright, as if hitching a lift.

Phryne called out to her. 'Where to, Colleen?'

'To the end of the rainbow? No, I'm just fine where I am. But I heard you were leaving, so I thought I'd wait for you. Dot, here's my address.'

Dot received a folded piece of paper, and sat, a trifle bewildered. Colleen O'Rourke climbed onto the running board and leaned her head forward. Dot kissed the girl's perfect cheek with what she hoped was maximum decorum.

'Please write, Dot, and tell me all your news.' Colleen looked across at Phryne. 'Miss Fisher? I just wanted to say you are the most astonishing person I have ever met. Thank you for sorting everything out.'

'My pleasure, Colleen.' Phryne admired the girl anew. 'Please tell me you're not getting married any time soon?'

The girl grinned, showing her immaculate white teeth. 'Not a chance! Safe trip!'

As they drove off, Dot turned her head back to see Colleen O'Rourke still waving, until the Hispano-Suiza rounded the bend and she was lost to sight.

———

Acting Detective Inspector Fraser sat in the commissioner's anteroom with his legs stretched out in front of him, admiring his faultless grey suit and handmade black shoes. He had put in his report on the accidental death of Claire Knight, and it seemed to have wound its way up to the Big Boss. Admittedly he had had to rewrite his report from the beginning, after that whipper-snapper Collins had produced the Guilty Party, but it had all come out all right. After his barely subordinate assistant had made forceful representations, he had agreed that there was, in truth, No Further Action to be taken. The boy had behaved reprehensibly, but there really was no evidence to suggest that his account of the deceased girl's demise was anything other than the truth, the whole truth, and nothing but the truth. It was unfortunate also that there was nothing to suggest that the layabout uncle was guilty of anything. That was, however, just a misunderstanding and had been cleared up. Perhaps he would have the word 'acting' removed from his title now. Plain old 'detective inspector' would be far more suitable. Doubtless that was why he had been summoned to the August Presence.

'The commissioner will see you now, Mr Fraser.'

He looked up. Bending over him was the boss's private secretary: a severe woman with iron-grey hair pulled back into a ferocious bun. The woman was smirking at him, and he vaguely wondered why. He rose, gave her a condescending nod, and opened the door.

'Take a seat, Fraser.'

He did so, crossing his legs. Upon receipt of an Antarctic stare, he uncrossed them again.

'Well, I have some news for you. After your egregious performance in solving the Knight case, I'm giving you a new job.'

Fraser brightened. He had no idea what the word 'egregious' meant, but it certainly sounded impressive.

The commissioner gazed at him and smiled. There was not the slightest vestige of warmth in his smile, nor in anything else about him. His balding head gleamed with perspiration, and he mopped his brow.

'As of tomorrow morning, you will report to the Racing Task Force. You'll be replacing Detective Inspector Robinson, who will be returning to his previous duties.'

'Thank you, sir.' Fraser hesitated, drew in a couple of deep breaths, and stuttered.

The commissioner glared at him. 'What's the matter, man? You look like you've swallowed a bucket of week-old prawns! What's on your mind?'

Taking his courage in both hands, Fraser swallowed. 'And my promotion, sir?'

For an instant, it seemed that the commissioner was about to undergo spontaneous combustion. His face turned pillar-box scarlet. Veins throbbed on his temples, and both shoulders hunched forward, like a beast of prey coiling itself to strike.

'Sir, are you feeling quite well?'

'God give me strength!' As abruptly as the volcano had threatened to erupt, the crisis passed. The commissioner produced a white handkerchief and mopped his face. 'I'm quite well, thank you. Better than you, anyway.' He pressed the telephone button before him. 'Margot? Show Detective Sergeant Fraser out, will you?'

Chapter Twenty-Six

And when Thyself with shining Foot shall pass
Among the Guests star-scatter' d on the Grass,
And in thy joyous Errand reach the Spot
Where I made one—turn down an empty Glass.

—Edward Fitzgerald, *The Rubáiyát of*
Omar Khayyám of Naishápúr

'Good to be home, Dot?'

'Yes, Miss Phryne.' Dot looked at the familiar walls of 221B The Esplanade and sighed with relief. It would take her some time to recover fully from the revelation that her mistress had come far too close to being blown up by a hand grenade; and the winding road home at seventy miles an hour had not improved her nerves, even with the assistance of the Freda Storm Veil for Frightened Passengers. Dot considered that the eponymous Freda had not imagined Miss Fisher's driving when devising it.

While Dot unpacked the car, Ruth and Jane came running out to meet them.

'Miss Phryne!' they chorused.

Phryne admired them both in their house smocks: Ruth with her long, brown plaits, and Jane with her bob now beginning to grow out. Soon Jane would have to make up her mind whether to abbreviate further, or else attempt the long, slow journey back to long-haired splendour. Phryne suspected that the former course would prevail. They embraced her, and she felt a degree of pent-up excitement in their youthful bodies.

'Hello, girls. Have you had a good week?'

'We've had an exciting week!' The girls exchanged glances and nudged each other. 'Tinker helped, too. We solved a mystery!'

'Really? What sort of mystery?'

'We'll tell you when we're inside,' answered Ruth. She took Phryne's arm and led her towards the front door. 'It was actually terrible. It was a case Mr Hugh was investigating, only it was a girl at our school and—'

Phryne placed her gloved forefinger in the air next to Ruth's eager face. 'Not another word until I've got inside, changed my clothes, and settled in, Ruth. Then you can tell me everything. But, please, start at the beginning.'

'Then go through to the end, and then stop,' Ruth quoted. The *Alice* books were part of her favourite bedtime reading. She liked Alice because she was the sort of girl who did not allow adults to push her around and tell her what to think. Ruth imagined that Phryne had been somewhat like Alice Liddell as a child, and she would not have been far wrong.

Phryne and Dot got changed into comfortable house clothes and were served refreshments by Mr Butler (lemonade for Dot and the girls, gin and tonic for Phryne) and seated comfortably around the kitchen table. Phryne looked around her adoptive family and raised her glass. 'All right, girls. Now for your tale, and don't rush it.'

The story took a good deal of telling, and Phryne made them

go back over a couple of points. When all was expounded, Phryne looked at them with a swelling sense of pride.

'You have done remarkably well, girls. I am sorry for poor Claire. That really is awful. But it's all happened so many times before.'

Ruth's eyes glistened, while Jane was ruminating in her head on the mysteries of birth control, and what a boon it would be for the young and foolish. She guessed it was not a topic for public canvassing, even in front of Miss Fisher, who presumably knew all about it, and kept her peace.

'Oh, and by the way, where is Tinker?'

'Mr Hugh took him out fishing,' Ruth volunteered. 'But they'll be home for dinner.'

'I see. Poor Hugh! And whatever happened to Jack, I wonder? Hugh's new boss sounds like a prize idiot.'

Jane considered this. 'We don't really know, because we haven't met him. But Mr Hugh got very frustrated by him, which was why he asked us to help out. You aren't cross?'

Phryne shook her head. 'No, not at all. He didn't put you in harm's way, from the sound of it. And it was very clever of you to work it out. What was that key for the lock?'

Only too delighted to explain all over again about reciprocals and the number *e*, Jane proceeded to do so. Ruth watched her sister carefully, and when she was certain that she could not be seen doing so, rolled her eyes theatrically. As she did, she became aware that Mr Butler was standing beside Miss Phryne holding out a silver salver, on which rested a scented envelope. Phryne looked at the address on the back, smiled, and tucked it into her purse.

'Who's it from, Miss? An admirer?' Ruth suddenly put her hand over her mouth and looked at her in horror, unable to believe what she had just said.

'In a way, Ruth. I'll read it later.'

Jane nudged her sister, who had gone from magenta to mid-beetroot. 'And did you have a pleasant week in the country, Miss Phryne?' Jane enquired.

Phryne and Dot exchanged glances. Dot stared at the ceiling, wondering how much, if anything, ought to be shared with the younger persons. Phryne thought about it for a moment and decided to wait. 'Well, I think you could say it was eventful, Jane, to say the least. But I think that when Hugh and Tinker return, we should have a welcome home party, and over dinner we will tell you all about our adventures. Agreed?'

'Yes, please. That would be lovely.'

Ruth spent the rest of the afternoon in the kitchen with Mrs Butler, preparing a suitable summer feast. Jane retired to her room to read Glaister on poisons. Dot retired to her room to knit, and Phryne ran herself a luxuriant bath in her green malachite bath-tub. She was already finding Melbourne considerably hotter and more sultry than usual, having accustomed herself to Daylesford's more alpine climate. And she realised that she had not got to see *Benito's Treasure*. Another time, perhaps. Having undressed, she paused for a minute, inhaling the scent of Floris and bath salts. She reached into her purse, removed the letter from its envelope, and smiled. Enclosed was a single sheet of perfumed notepaper, on which was written: *Mme: Mille remerciements! Violette*. Enclosed in the envelope were twelve crimson rose petals. She stepped into the bath, felt the luxurious water embrace her body, and wished Violette every happiness and more.

———

Six o'clock brought Tinker and Hugh, with a small string of flat-heads harvested from the bay. Phryne looked carefully at the boy. She had only been a short time away, but Tinker seemed to have grown. He no longer avoided Phryne's glance. 'Well, Tinker. The girls have been telling me about your detective work,' she said.

Tinker looked her straight in the eye. 'It was really tough,' he admitted. 'I like Tom. I still do, even though he messed it all up with that poor girl. I'm glad I brought the truth to light, though.'

'Why is that, Tinker?' Phryne was finding this new, reflective Tinker something of a revelation.

The boy leaned forward in his chair and clasped his hands together. He was dressed in shorts and a plain grey shirt, both of which had seen better days, probably a very long time ago. Though he had discarded most of his Queenscliff past, these were his fishing clothes and he would wear them until they no longer fit or fell off him where he stood. They were in some peril of dissolution already. 'Is it hard to solve cases when you know the person, and care about them?'

'All the time, Tink.'

He nodded. 'But if I hadn't found out what happened, he'd never be happy again.'

'And will he be happy now?'

Tinker looked enquiringly at Hugh, who was also in the plainest of plain clothes.

Hugh nodded. 'Pretty much. There's not going to be any charges laid, I think. The problem is my new boss. He'd love to charge somebody with something. I think I convinced him there was no point, but I really don't know.'

'What has happened to Jack? Do you know anything?'

Hugh gave her a cautious look. 'Miss Phryne, I didn't know you'd be home today, so I asked him to dinner. Better he tells you himself.'

'Hugh, that's wonderful! And—'

Hugh shook his head, showing moderate levels of embarrassment. 'Oh, no, Miss. I'm going home later tonight. It wouldn't be right now that Dot is back home. And the renovations at my place are all done.'

'I was wondering. All right, Hugh. If you feel that way.'

'I'm not in a hurry, but I think Dot might feel—'

'I think you can count on that, Hugh.'

Tinker made to slip out of the room, clearly catching something in the atmosphere of Discretion Now Required, but Phryne waved him back. 'Tinker, you're an adult now. You've proven yourself. But I was wondering, Hugh. Have you and Dot...'

'Chosen a date? We think so. I can afford to support her now I'm a sergeant. But she wants to go on working for you, at least for a while. Is that what you want?'

'Well, yes, Hugh, it is. And I don't feel like looking too far ahead. Let's leave it there, shall we?'

The doorbell rang, and the stately, measured tread of Mr Butler could be heard proceeding down the passage like Black Rod at the opening of the House of Lords. A murmur of voices ensued, followed by the entry of Inspector Robinson in person. He looked jaunty. He swept off his hat, handed it to Mr Butler, and entered the parlour with a spring in his step.

'Jack! How splendid to see you. We've all missed you. Please, sit down. Mr B, a glass of beer for the inspector.'

'Miss Fisher. Collins. Tinker.' Jack Robinson seated himself and beamed.

'I gather you have news, Jack. You certainly look like the cat who not only got the cream, but an entire salmon from the sideboard.'

Mr Butler rematerialised with a glass of the foaming restorative, and Robinson sipped at it with satisfaction. 'I'm not sure how much I'm allowed to tell you, but I was seconded to a special task force to look into...a certain industry.'

Phryne laughed. 'Oh, Jack, you don't have to be so secretive. Is this about Barry the Shark?'

'Well.' He looked at her with his head on one side. 'Let's assume that a certain notorious SP bookmaker had become A Matter of Concern to both the public and the Commissioner of Police. And let us also assume, purely for the sake of argument, that investigations of breaches of the law had a habit of being frustrated by special interests acting not altogether in the public interest. And it is possible that Exceptional Measures might have been deemed necessary to get to grips with the matter.' He gave her another sidelong look. 'I'm not sure if even that is sufficiently discreet, but—'

'But Barry the Shark is a notorious crook with half the government in his pocket; and your boss is one honest man trying, and failing, to get the little swine put away.'

'Well, that is certainly—'

'A good deal less discreet.' Phryne leaned forward in her chair. 'Jack, that isn't good. Bad things happen to people who tread on Barry's feet. They get trodden on right back. Surely you're not telling me you've nailed him?'

Robinson shook his head with regret. 'I wish I had. Look, we know what he does, we know where he hangs out and conducts his business, but we can't touch him. My boss is a good man. He feels he can't just let all this carry on unchecked. I've interviewed the people I needed to, and not one of them is saying a word.' He grimaced. 'Because none of them wants to finish up face down in the Yarra any more than I do. But I gave it a decent go. I've got a few things on him, which I gave to my boss and nobody else.'

'So you did the best you could, yes? What's new?'

Jack turned to Collins and grinned. 'Meanwhile, Collins here has had to put up with...' He paused. 'With a man who has considerably more faith in his own abilities than I or anyone else does.'

'You mean he couldn't find his own backside with an atlas?'

'Well, Miss Fisher, that's one way of putting it. But as a result of this individual's stellar skills in policing, the commissioner has decided to give him my place on the task force, and I'm back at City South. So, Collins, I'm sorry to say that you've got me as your boss again.'

'Believe me, sir, I couldn't be happier,' Hugh interposed.

'And the idiot boy who's been giving Hugh a hard time is now on the task force and sets fair to finish up face down in the Yarra?'

Jack Robinson's shoulders trembled in what might have been suppressed mirth. 'Actually, I don't think he's in much danger. If any of the Shark's hard men come up against him, they'll laugh their socks off and ignore him. He's safe enough.'

'Forgive me, Jack, but how does someone that thick ever get promoted even to sergeant?'

Hugh Collins, who was wondering the same thing, looked at his superior with anticipation.

Tinker was watching and listening, glowing inside at being regarded as one of the grown-ups. It was an odd feeling, but one he liked.

Jack Robinson frowned, drank another instalment of his beer, and put the glass on the table. 'He's very well connected. He has, shall we say, influential relatives.' He pondered this. 'But so has a certain lady who was seriously offended by his unique approach to policing.'

'This wouldn't be Mrs Knight, by any chance, would it, sir?' Hugh enquired.

Robinson allowed himself a smirk. 'Yes it would. She and the commissioner play bridge together at the same club. I am given to understand that information changed hands.'

Phryne's brows knitted together. 'Mrs Knight? Is this the bereaved mother?'

Jack nodded. 'I don't know, because I wasn't there, but apparently Fraser's professional conduct could do with some polish. So there we have it. Patronage only gets you so far.'

'Well, that's all good news. Jack, I have a tale to tell you over dinner which may well make your knotted and combinéd locks to part like quills upon the fretful porpentine, but that can wait. Mr B?'

Materialising once more in the manner of butlers everywhere, the faithful servitor raised an enquiring eyebrow.

'Two bottles of the Widow, I think. And glasses for everyone. This calls for a celebration.'

'Yes, Miss Phryne.'

Ruth emerged from the kitchen in a vast, floury apron. 'Dinner's all but ready. We have roast chicken, cold salmon, steamed vegetables, three salads, and ices to follow.'

Mr Butler returned with a bottle of Veuve Clicquot in one hand and a silver tray in the other, with seven glasses perched upon it. Somehow the tray remained perfectly level, and the glasses barely clinked against each other.

'Ruth, call your sister. Dot?'

'Coming, Miss.' Dot emerged from her room, in a light brown dress and a beige scarf. She looked at the champagne bottle with doubt in her face. 'Miss, what are we celebrating?'

'Our homecoming, Dot. And Jack's as well, from troubled waters. And the successful conclusion of all our mysteries.'

The members of the household gathered, and each accepted a glass of champagne. Phryne raised her own. 'The detectives!'

The glasses chinked together. 'The detectives!'

'And confusion to our enemies!'

'Hear, hear!'

AUTHOR'S NOTE

The spa country in the Shire of Hepburn is to this day every bit as wonderful as I have portrayed it here. I have, however, taken a number of liberties with history for narrative purposes. The Daylesford Highland Gathering is held annually in November. It was never held in late summer; nor was it held during the 1920s, so far as we know. Its first recorded appearance was in 1952. Nor are there any records of anything called the Temperance Hotel. Nevertheless, the debate between outright Prohibition and Open Slather was fierce and prolonged, and proponents of the former were only narrowly defeated in the Western Australian referendum of 1950. We do know that some hotels and licensed premises did choose the very antipodean compromise described in the form of the Temperance. Other compromises between the two camps resulted in the distressing phenomenon known as the six o'clock swill, wherein workers who left their places of employment at five p.m. flocked to their nearest watering hole in competition to see how much beer they could manage to order and consume before the bar staff called Last Drinks. This was not a good thing, and we don't do it any more, for good and sufficient reasons.

Contract bridge as it is now played was invented—or at least popularised—by Harold Vanderbilt during a cruise to Havana in 1925. It is very unlikely, though, that it would have spread to rural Victoria by 1929, and since auction bridge (the earlier form) is roughly the same game except for its bidding conventions, I have my characters playing the easier form. While even at its highest levels bridge is not as difficult as chess, it is nevertheless a highly cerebral game, and reveals more of the players' character. Bridge players might note that Vanderbilt originally proposed the One Club opening bid for all strong hands. Under the tyranny of Ely Culbertson, such frivolities were not tolerated, but the modern game has resurrected Vanderbilt's innovation, which I believe to be a very fine one.

I have been less than kind to the Victoria Police in this book, also for reasons of narrative. As my readers will be aware, police officers who appear in my books are generally intelligent, dedicated, hard-working, and utterly admirable—as are the vast majority of their real-life counterparts. But in this, my sixty-fifth book, I felt it was time to show the Other Side of policing, as (regrettably) it sometimes occurs. The serving officers of my acquaintance will, I am certain, recognise the type of bone-headed ignoramus portrayed herein from their own careers, and will I hope accept my assurance that I hold them, and their doughty comrades, in the highest regard.

Kerry Greenwood

BIBLIOGRAPHY

Bertrand, Ina and Gael Elliott, *A Hard Day's Work: Growing Spuds Around Trentham*, Trentham Historical Society, Trentham, Vic., 2009.

Crawford, Richard, *Men, Women and Bridge*, Sterling, New York, 1978. Culbertson Ely, *Contract Bridge*, Penguin, New York, 1949.

Darwin, Norm, *Gold'n Spa: History of the Hepburn Shire*, H@nd Publishing, Ballarat, Vic., 2005.

Kyneton Guardian, History of Kyneton, Kyneton, Vic., 1935.

Menadue, John E., *The Story of the Three Lost Children*, Daylesford & District Historical Society, Daylesford, Vic., 1967.

Osborne, Murrell, *Timber, Spuds and Spa: A Descriptive History and Lineside Guide of the Railways in the Daylesford District, 1880–1978*, Australian Railway Historical Society Victorian Division, Daylesford, Vic., 1993.

Patterson, R. D., *A Most Commodious Up-Country Hall: A Brief History of the Daylesford Town Hall*, Shire of Daylesford and Glenlyon, Daylesford, Vic., 1985.

Victorian Railways Advertising Division, *Where to Go in Victoria*, Victorian Railways, Melbourne, 1927.

Wishart, Edward, Maura Wishart, and Derrick Stone, *Spa Country: Victoria's Mineral Springs*, Victorian Government, Department of Sustainability and Environment, Melbourne, 2010.

ACKNOWLEDGMENTS

My thanks to the indefatigable Heather Mutimer from the Daylesford & District Historical Society, Mari Eleanor, Amanda Butcher, Julie Waugh, Canon Judith Hall, Brian Kelly, Paul Kelly, Mick Miller, David Greagg (without whom etc.), Annette Barlow, and all the wonderful team at Allen & Unwin, and the people of Daylesford and Hepburn Springs.

ABOUT THE AUTHOR

Kerry Greenwood is the author of more than fifty novels, a book of short stories, and six nonfiction works and the editor of two collections of crime writing. Her beloved Phryne Fisher series has become a successful series, *Miss Fisher's Murder Mysteries*, which has aired in more than one hundred countries and is available on PBS and Netflix in the U.S. A feature film titled *Miss Fisher and the Crypt of Tears* was released in 2020. She is also the author of the contemporary crime series featuring Corinna Chapman, baker and reluctant investigator. The most recent Corinna Chapman novel was *The Spotted Dog*. In addition, Kerry is the author of several books for young adults and the Delphic Women series. When not writing, Kerry has been an advocate in magistrates' courts for the Legal Aid Commission and, in the 2020 Australia Day Honours, was awarded the Medal of the Order of Australia (OAM) for services to literature. She is not married, has no children, is the co-warden of a Found Cats' Home, and lives with an accredited wizard. In her spare time, she stares blankly out the window.